PLANESHIFTER KNIGHT

The Blademage Saga

Volume 4

Chris Hollaway

*To my family, for putting up with me while I was
tearing this story out of my brain*

To fans of 'The Blademage Saga' , for not giving up on me

To Kevon, for allowing me to tell his story.

CHAPTER 1

"That's a relief," Kevon laughed, still shaken from the ride.

"I don't know about the others, but Brightwing doesn't seem to have an issue with unicorn," Rhysabeth-Dane giggled, scratching her griffin under its beak, to his apparent delight. "The Griffinsworn never mentioned akembi, their little winged horses, being hunted as prey, either. I was fairly sure unicorn would be no different."

"We'll set up camp on the southeast corner of the island this time, to maintain a reasonable separation. I'd rather be too cautious than not enough." Kevon peered at the cluster of unicorn across the glade, moving in a fashion that read somewhere between 'reserved' and 'wary'. "Let the others know, and have my sword brought ashore, if you would. I'll make my way from here on foot."

The tiny Rider nodded, and resumed ruffling and smoothing the feathers on her steed's neck. "We'll do that. Then we'll come back here and eat some apples, won't we?"

Brightwing squawked in affirmation. Rhysabeth-Dane ducked under a lifted wing and hopped up into the combat saddle, easing into the stirrups and checking the tether on the crossbow that hung from one of the saddle rings. She pulled on the cinch straps, tucked the leather flap back down over them, and gave a shrill whistle. The griffin crouched, and sprang into the air.

I never would have thought... Kevon watched the Rider's ascent, marveling at her practiced ease. Her left hand grasped the strap inset into the saddle's low pommel, her right trailing

1

behind her for balance as she leaned forward into the climb, rocking with the griffin's motion as they dwindled from sight. *A timid Dwarven librarian, now an accomplished Griffin Rider. Guess we've all become things we'd never expected.*

He thought about Ashera, and the other Griffinsworn, the fierce inhabitants of the Highplain that had helped them the last few weeks. Kylgren-Wode moved to the forefront of his thoughts. The Dwarven Ambassador had been anything but soft as he stood shoulder to shoulder with the elite Stoneguard troops against the chimaera and other dangers of the savage highlands they had braved.

Kevon grinned at his memories of Carlo, who Kevon had thought nothing more than a Merchant's bodyguard when they met. In reality, he was a Blademaster and now commander of the armed forces of their home nation, when it suited him. Bertus was just a boy when Kevon had rescued him from servitude in Eastport. Then there was Mirsa, the Mage who was raising the child Kevon's slain friend Waine had fathered with her. *Heroes, they called us,* Kevon thought, fighting back tears as Waine's last moments forced themselves into his awareness, as they all too often did. *Would we have made those same choices, if we knew what we were facing? I could have run away, when that bear killed the Warrior in the woods outside of Laston. I could have buried that sword with him. Maybe I should have.*

"*Alanna,*" Kevon whispered her name as he thought it, the reason that often made all of the extra trouble worth it. He remembered back to the first time they'd met. *Things were much different then. Two kids that didn't know much of anything. Sometimes I still wonder if we...* Thoughts of their chaotic reunion after years of separation, and the tumultuous relationship that they still maintained started both his heart and head pounding. *Out of rhythm. Out of synch. Just like...*

Kevon smiled as he noticed the unicorn spreading back out and resuming their grazing. He turned toward the center of the island, and began walking.

◆ ◆ ◆

"As chief military advisor to Alacrit, prince of Kærtis, I must insist that I am next," Carlo grumbled, looming close in the small, crowded Elven dwelling.

Bertus stifled a laugh as Mirsa responded. "Your title means nothing here," she cautioned, eyes twinkling, "But I'll allow it."

"Excellent," the Blademaster nodded. "Hurry up, dwarf. Some of us have other duties to attend to."

"Do you even know how to hold her?" Rhysabeth-Dane's singsong tone belied the daggers in the gaze directed at Carlo.

"By the neck. Supporting the neck, I mean. I've done this before," Carlo scowled, motioning for the dwarf to hand over the child. "Twice?" he added as he accepted the yawning infant, cradling and rocking her, his gruff demeanor softening. "I can see..." Carlo sighed. "She's beautiful."

"No, no," Alanna lifted her hands and took a step back as the Blademaster held Maisy out in her direction. "Not right now. Maybe not ever."

"She is quite lovely," Anneliese agreed, taking her from Carlo. "A strong, fine child." She hesitated a moment before tracing a finger along the infant's jawline, tickling her to a fidgety wakefulness.

"I do need to go," Carlo frowned, and turned to Kevon. "Re-provisioning and recuperation will take a week, minimum. I'll do all I can to keep it short. My men would leave now if you pointed the way to the scum that took your sister, but I know it's not that simple." He withdrew from the room, closing the door behind him.

"Took your..." Bertus put a hand on Kevon's shoulder, shaking his head. "Alma's gone? What of Martin?"

"He was in league with Holten," Kevon shrugged, eyes glistening. "I didn't want this to cloud our reunion."

"He survived..." The color drained from Bertus's face.

"Pholos was right."

"He's dead. They both are."

"Holten and Pholos?" Bertus asked. "Then how did Martin manage to…"

"There was another Mage," Kevon explained, moving away from his friend to take a seat across the table from where Anneliese had settled with Maisy. "He arrived and escaped through Darkness, taking Alma and Martin, leaving Obsidian Reapers."

"I've heard the stories from Carlo," Bertus shuddered. "He'd rather face a bull orc, or one of those armored leapers. Someone that can use those against us? Damnation."

"Someone who can travel freely through that other Plane is likely to do so often," Mirsa offered. "Perhaps we can work off of that assumption."

"Anything will help," Kevon nodded. "It'll be difficult dealing with M'lani's family, if I'm worried about my own."

"You heard Carlo," Bertus sighed. "Time is short. We have to be prepared."

CHAPTER 2

"It's fitting that you have it," Bertus held out the Dwarven replica of his ancient sword. "It is a wonderful blade, no question. It was just on the smallish side for me."

"I don't know how to use it," Rhysabeth-Dane shook her head.

"You're as good with a crossbow as I am," Bertus corrected the dwarf. "Your world has changed so much since we met. You'll learn."

The Rider accepted the scabbarded weapon, drawing the blade free to get a feel for it. "Heavy," she grunted.

"Not for long," Bertus assured her. "Though later, it will carry a different weight."

"We'd better hurry to dinner." Rhysabeth-Dane re-sheathed the sword and tucked the scabbard into her belt, wriggling until it hung with a degree of comfort.

"Last decent meal for some of us," Bertus agreed. "After you?"

"We have barely finished mourning the lost," Aelion lamented. "And now the rest of you prepare to depart."

"The sacrifices the Children of Light have made," Kevon spoke in deliberate tones, using the name the Griffinsworn gave the elves, "Deepen the bonds between us. Your continued support…"

"M'lani desires it," the elder inclined his head a few de-

5

grees. "The way is clear. Your ship could not contain those who have volunteered to accompany you."

"If we had ships to carry them..." Kevon shook his head at the thought. "Our path is not as clear as we hoped. Your people that journeyed with us to Kelanoth are well known to us, and would be our first choice."

"Understood. The Hunters will be ready to sail with the morning tide." Aelion turned and slipped back down the wooded path that led back to the Elven city.

Kevon rejoined the others around one of the campfires, and accepted a plate of food from one of Carlo's soldiers. He regarded the servings of fresh fruit and vegetables with mixed emotions.

"They're not chimaera skewers," Alanna remarked, noting his reaction. "But they're not fish, either."

Nodding, Kevon bit into a chunk of Heartmelon. The clean taste lacked the bite of marinade the Griffinsworn prepared it with, but it still evoked memories of the Highplain. Ghostly echoes of tribal music swirled through Kevon's soul, flashes of dancers whirling and stamping around a bonfire intruded on the somber present. He shuffled the memories aside, and continued to eat.

"You're certain of this?" Kevon asked Mirsa as the celebration dwindled down to his friends and Carlo's officers. "I know Bertus wasn't keen on..."

"Alacrit must be made aware of what is happening," Mirsa protested. "It is time he lends us more than token aid." She looked at Maisy. "I won't sail with her," Mirsa shook her head. "I won't leave her, but I will not stand by and do nothing. Let me do this much."

"We've only got the power to send two through, with the Magi we have left. Weaponless, on top of that," Kevon sighed.

"Limited by steel, not weaponless," Anneliese argued. "I will escort them."

"That's an idea," Kevon agreed. "Carlo?"

"You can't get them directly into the palace," Carlo shrugged. "Alacrit has seen to that, they tell me. The inn between the Guild and the gates, then?"

"I remember it," Kevon agreed. "I can guide both Sendings. You would have time to collect your thoughts, and make your way to the palace grounds. Maisy, though..."

"It will take extra power to send her through with us," Mirsa thought aloud. "I don't like the idea of assisting with the spell I'm a target of, and holding her at the same time."

"I'll carry her through first," Anneliese offered. "You follow behind, moments later. We will visit L'mort's gift on any of the Dark Magi we encounter."

"Leave it to the Huntmistress to sweeten violence with poetry," Captain Yusa chuckled, sloshing a mug of grindleberry wine. "I like it."

"It makes sense," the Mage Reko agreed, flickering into view on the log next to Yusa. "The difficult Sending first, so that we can gauge the strength we need for the second one."

"We could stay longer, Send you after them," Kevon suggested.

"We've waited long enough." Bertus shook his head. "You think they're holding Alma to the north. You'll need an extra sword."

"We've felt surges of Dark magic in that direction, several times," Kevon explained. "It's the only clue we have."

"Find your sister. Bring her back," Mirsa's voice cracked. "We'll all be together soon enough."

Kevon nodded, squinting into the fading evening sun. "Meet back here at first light."

CHAPTER 3

The harness Anneliese strapped Maisy into held the child snugly on the Huntmistress's back, opposite her full quiver of arrows. The elf bounced and stretched, exploring her limitations with the temporary rig, eliciting contented gurgles from the cossetted infant.

"Ready?" Kevon asked.

Anneliese turned to Carlo, stepped forward, and embraced him, nuzzling and kissing for a few moments. Releasing him only when he was flush with embarrassment, she swept up her bow, plucked an arrow from her quiver, and pulled the bowstring back to a relaxed half draw. "Ready," she sighed.

Kevon tried to contain his grin, and began focusing for the Sending. The runes flared in his mind, and he pictured the inn. He focused on the corner near the table where he and Bertus had jested with Waine about a silly gift some of the Warriors in Navlia had given him. He wrapped the rising emotions into the spell, forcing the unfocused energy into the glowing runes, along with borrowed power from Mirsa and Reko. He gave the spell one last mental push, and the world bent, Anneliese and Maisy twisting and vanishing.

Mirsa stumbled as Kevon exhaled, releasing the magic.

"Are you ready?" Kevon asked Mirsa.

"I..." She turned to Bertus, locking eyes for a long moment, a gesture nearly as telling as the scene only moments ago with the Blademaster and the elf. "Yes."

The magic built once more, Mirsa flooding Kevon with power, then shutting herself off as the spell grew toward completion. Kevon drew on Reko's reserves until Yusa wobbled beside him. He funneled all of the gathered energy toward the runes in his mind, and reinforced it with most of the reserves he still held. He focused on the same spot in the inn across the sea, where Anneliese had been Sent only moments ago.

As Mirsa's form began to twist, she raised a hand and reached out. Kevon completed the Sending, and the Mage spiraled from view. Kevon glanced toward Bertus, who was lowering his own outstretched hand.

"You're sure about going with us?" He asked the younger Warrior, stepping forward to steady himself with a reassuring hand on Bertus's shoulder.

"They'll be as safe there as anywhere," Bertus shrugged. "Let's get your family to safety."

Carlo leaned on the foredeck railing, taking in the salt breeze. "I wasn't sure how things would go with Yusa," he admitted to Kevon with a chuckle. "I'm used to military ship captains. Giving orders, rather than making suggestions."

"He's on our side," Kevon agreed. "*They're...* on our side."

"Watch your heads!" A nearby crewman called out the warning, and eyes turned skyward.

Carlo stepped to one side, and a large fish smacked the deck where he'd stood. It flopped twice, and lay still. Wet *smacks* sounded across the rest of the ship, and as the impacts stopped, some of the crew set about collecting the bounty that had rained from the sky.

"Looks like your griffin are going to do their fair share this time," Carlo smiled. "We won't have to slow down to cast the nets."

"They're not my..." Kevon began, but Carlo had already turned to leave.

One of the Unbound griffin screeched as he landed beside Kevon, and began tearing into the fish he carried. Three others landed as Kevon backed away, hissing and flapping wings, before quieting and converging on the shared meal.

"Everything all right?" Carlo asked, reaching out to steady Kevon.

"Still to the north," Yusa called, stepping out of his cabin, scowling at the griffin-filled deck.

"Closer," Kevon agreed, taking a deep breath. "But only just."

"Have you decided how best to dispatch them, when we arrive?" Carlo released Kevon, and turned to look at the open sea ahead.

"With no idea of their defenses..." Kevon shook his head. "Our best chance is to get close enough for Rhysabeth-Dane to scout out what she can. We should only use magic to speed our journey for another day or two, at most."

"We could work the winds under a veil of Conceal-ment," Reko suggested, his image appearing beside Kevon. "It would be a strain..."

"We want to hurry, not rush." Kevon interrupted. "There are other things that we can do to prepare." He peered upward, and whistled, a piercing note.

After a moment, several of the wheeling specks above changed direction, one circling wider and faster than the others. Brightwing tucked his wings and dove, flaring and spinning in a tight spiral that took him and his Rider below the level of the deck. After skimming a curlicue on the choppy surface with an extended talon, the griffin swooped up over the railing. Squawking his intent at the loitering Unbound, he landed as they tore the remains of a fish apart and retreated to other corners of the deck.

Rhysabeth-Dane leapt from Brightwing's combat sad-dle, tucking her shoulder and rolling as she hit the deck. She wobbled as she finished the motion, standing and drawing her Dwarven-forged blade to point at Kevon. "I haven't been up there for nearly long enough! *What do you want?*"

"Ahh..." Kevon blinked at the dwarf, still easily twenty feet from where he stood. "I was wondering if you could gather the Unbound, and scout ahead while…"

"Oh." The Rider swung her left arm out to check the hissing griffin's advance, and sheathed her blade. "Certainly." She hopped up on the stirrup, and swung into the saddle with a far more practiced motion than her earlier dismount. She closed her eyes, and stroked the griffin's neck feathers, leaning into whisper to her mount.

Brightwing tilted his head, maintaining eye contact with Kevon. The griffin opened his mouth in a silent hiss, clicked an extended talon at the Mage twice, and crouched to spring off of the deck.

Rhysabeth-Dane rolled with the motion, one hand latched onto the saddle grip, the other thrown above her head and back, evening out her balance as the griffin's wings started beating. Her squeals of elation twined with Brightwing's squawks, fading in the distance and flurry of the departing Unbound.

The deckhands had the foredeck cleared of debris before the griffin were out of sight, dwindling in size to the north. By the time Kevon and Carlo reached the area they had set aside for infrequent training, groupings of dwarves were already squaring off in pairs at near the railing.

'Today, I'm going to win," Kevon chuckled, drawing daggers, and turning to face Alanna.

"Maybe, but not against her," Carlo rumbled. "You need to focus more on your swordplay."

Kevon frowned, replacing the weapons as he followed the Blademaster to an unoccupied corner. He drew his sword, ignoring the nearly magical tingle that ran up his spine, having long attributed the feeling to the remembered history he and the sword shared across the Planes.

"You going to make your move?" Carlo asked, turning his shield toward Kevon, his sword held low and away, tracing small circles in the air as he swayed back and forth, anticipating the rhythm of the combat yet to come.

"I don't have the advantage, yet," Kevon answered, circling, blade held in a two-handed grip, across his body. He slowed as Carlo's shadow drifted across his feet. "Or do I?" Kevon's grip shifted, flashing the reflected light of the mid-morning sun into his opponent's eyes twice in half a breath's time. The resulting squint was all he needed.

Carlo raised his shield to counter the initial strike, slamming the ornately decorated plank to the side. He stepped forward into a kick at Kevon's front leg, but the Adept was already on the move, whirling a reverse strike at Carlo's right side. The Blademaster whipped his sword up, deflecting the oncoming blade to a higher path. He followed through on his kick, stepping forward, ducking, and flattening the arc of his shield as he spun.

The iron-bound edge of the shield struck Kevon in the side at just better than half-speed. With a twist of his wrist, Carlo shifted the angle of the shield, the other edge pivoting into Kevon's right arm. Kevon retained his grip on the sword with his left hand, and back-flipped away, putting two sword-lengths between himself and his mentor.

"Ow," Kevon complained, stretching his side to feel for more serious damage. "I think I prefer knife practice to…" He trailed off as he noticed the other groups next to them turned toward the center of the deck.

"Knife practice, indeed," Carlo remarked as he stepped alongside Kevon, who had turned to watch the spectacle in disbelief.

Cartwheels of glinting metal fangs and flashing arcs of ancient steel ebbed and flowed in an intricate dance that had captured the attention of all the combatants. Neither Alanna nor Bertus appeared to be holding anything back, yet neither could penetrate the defenses of the other. The ringing of the parried attacks grew louder as the intensity of the 'practice' battle increased, until it seemed both were using more than their full strength.

Pressed toward the edge of the widening circle of their practice arena, Alanna flipped back, crouched, and leapt over

Bertus to the center of the deck.

Bertus swung at her, but met only empty air as she passed out of reach.

Rolling and twisting, Alanna landed a good fifteen feet beyond Bertus, and began a crouching advance, daggers held in a menacing backhanded grip.

"Uhh..." Kevon looked at Carlo. "I know she's good, but..."

"That's unnatural. Both of them." Carlo agreed.

"What was that?" Kevon turned to the Stoneguard standing a few feet away. "You said some..."

The dwarf turned to spit over the railing, mumbled something, and pushed his way past to go belowdecks.

"I'll talk to the boy," Carlo shrugged, stepping forward and barking for Bertus to stand at attention. Kevon slid around, calling out to Alanna, who shook her head and blinked, as if leaving a trance.

"What's happening with you?" Kevon probed, sliding his hands down her arms, guiding the clenched daggers into their sheaths. "Does that have something to do with the healing M'lani performed?" As she relaxed and released her grip on the weapons, Kevon stepped in closer, encircling her with his arms, leaning into her wind-tousled hair. After a few long breaths, he answered his own question. "It couldn't be. Bertus was not there, and he seems to be under the same influence."

"I wasn't going to let him win," Alanna whispered. "But he just kept speeding up, so I tried harder."

"You don't move that fast when we..." Kevon thought back to their most recent practices, where every 'win' he'd achieved had been a slight one, in a certain technique, before Alanna had moved on to the next lesson. "You've been letting me win?"

"Would you have continued your training if I hadn't?"

"I... don't know," Kevon confessed. "I used to do the same with Bertus, but lately he's been earning his vict..." He trailed off. "Only Kylgren-Wode has been training with Bertus since the Glimmering Isle. What do the dwarves know?"

"It may be best if we cleared the deck so the others can continue," Carlo rumbled, guiding a shaken Bertus past Kevon and Alanna. "We can see what the librarian thinks when she returns."

"I cannot detect anything different about either of them," Reko's image slumped in defeat.

Nice touch, Kevon thought. *The personality lessons are helping.* "I was holding my sword when they were at their most active, and could not discern any magical activity."

"I felt nothing from my vantage, not much further away than you were." Reko agreed. "Any unconcealed magic would have caught my attention."

"We were both using metal weapons," Bertus pointed out. "You wouldn't be able to tell anyway."

"Right." Kevon shook his head, "Neither one of you are Magi, though. This is something that we've never seen. We've been training more than ever, but this just does not happen."

"It has before," Rhysabeth-Dane asserted. "I've seen records of it."

"Well, then?" Alanna shifted toward the diminutive Rider.

"It was long ago, when I first began my duties in the library. I'd have to go back and study them further to be sure."

"Anything you could tell us may be helpful," Kevon assured her.

"That is not always the case, young man," Rhysabeth-Dane stood, and turned to leave the cabin. "A little knowledge can be deadly."

CHAPTER 4

"**N**ow where did you come from?" the inn-keeper pointed at Anneliese with the barely glowing end of the poker he'd just withdrawn from the fireplace.

"A moment, sir," the Huntmistress lowered her drawn bow and stepped to the side, keeping the weapon ready. "We'll be leaving soon."

"You'll..." the confused man's voice softened as he heard Maisy cooing behind the elf's back. "I see. No need to..."

He jumped as reality twitched, and Mirsa popped into existence. The Master Mage steadied herself on a nearby table, then reached out to take her child from the sling on Anne-liese's back.

"Leave her," the elf advised. "We may need more focus to reach the palace."

Mirsa nodded, and spotted the innkeeper for the first time. "Are the streets clear? Has the city been under attack?"

"The dark ones a-attack only the palace, m'lady," the innkeeper stammered. "The streets are s-safe during the day, but dawn is hours distant."

"Your eyes say we are not welcome to stay here until then," Anneliese relaxed her stance even more. "Have you good reason?"

"There are no Magi left besides the dark ones, outside the palace walls," he whimpered. "Buildings burn when folk hide them. Please..."

"We will not endanger you." Mirsa shoved the sleeves of her robes back past the elbows, and moved toward the door.

"It is not far from here."

The Mage summoned up the symbols for Fire and Concealment, joining them in her mind as she opened the door to the street. She slipped out into the shadows, and after a quick glance around, reopened the door for Anneliese. The Huntmistress stepped out and around her, taking the lead. Mirsa felt clumsy, footgear scuffing on cobble as she hurried to keep pace with the silent shadow ahead of her.

A strangled cry came from the entrance to an alleyway ahead, and a black robed figure slumped partway into the moonlit street. The hissing and clicking of the Reaper that stepped over the fallen Mage twisted into a gurgle as two more feathered shafts buried themselves in the creature's champing maw. The clatter of tumbling chitin subsided, and the night returned to stillness.

The glow from the castle gates shone down the street, extending the near noonday brightness half a block or more depending on the angle of the floating sphere. Anneliese led Mirsa toward it when the patrol guiding the spell was off to the side and the brilliance was confined to the mouth of the street ahead, and ushered her behind obstacles when the full force of the light aligned to shine past their location. When they had moved close enough that the risk of encountering Dark Magi was minimal, the Huntmistress pulled Mirsa out into the open as the light grew brighter.

"Ware!" Anneliese called, her bow held up and out to her right, her left hand waving empty to the guards on the wall. "We seek shelter and an audience with the prince!"

Mirsa pulled back the hood of her cloak, revealing her unmistakable vibrant red locks. "Mirsa Magus here, we bring news from the east!"

The light around them sharpened, as if focusing to verify their claims.

"Inside, quickly!" a voice called from the top of the wall, and the once familiar clunking of the gate mechanism preceded the slight outward swing of one of the gates.

"Lady Mirsa," the Guard Commander bowed as the gate creaked shut behind them. "We have no one to spare to escort you across the courtyard. I must return to the wall. You will be able to show your guests inside?"

"Assuredly," Mirsa answered, calling up a miniature version of the lights she saw gleaming over the wall at regular intervals. "This way, Huntmistress."

"That will be all," Mirsa smiled, remembering the look on the steward's face as she'd told him that Anneliese would be staying, but that they would share her quarters. "Send someone to fetch us for breakfast."

Maisy began to fuss as the door closed, and after loosening two ties, Mirsa scooped her up from the harness, babbling at her as she swept around the room in arching patterns before flopping into a cushioned chair. "Some of us can't wait for breakfast, can we?" she cooed, adjusting her robes.

Stirred from her fitful sleep after what felt like only minutes, Mirsa gathered the pillows that she'd placed to keep Maisy from moving, and watched her peaceful breathing.

"The palace is awakening," Anneliese murmured from her chair in the corner.

Mirsa strained to hear the faint sounds of activity echoing through the stone hallways, deflected for the most part by the heavy oak door. "So it is," she chuckled, sliding a finger into Maisy's hand, the involuntary clutching of the infant's grip drew an even larger smile across her face.

The Huntmistress rose, and walked to the doorway. Uncharacteristic impatience shaded her actions. Sullen pacing gave way to earnest listening at the seam of the door frame, hand held back toward Mirsa to command silence.

"The palace has withstood the Darkness this long," Mirsa reminded her. "It will stand a bit longer."

"Events realms apart are affecting all of Kærtis," Anne-liese countered. "Aside from the Dwarven Hold, this may be one of the most defensible places in all of Ærth. That may mean little in the days to come."

A long knife whispered free from its sheath. Mirsa had only a moment to wonder where Anneliese had gotten it before the knock sounded at the door.

"Enter?" the Mage's voice cracked as she stood, and the Huntmistress danced back a few steps, toward where her bow leaned against a table.

"Breakfast is..." A silken voice announced as the door swung open, revealing a nobly adorned elf. "Huntmistress!"

"A servant of the palace, now, are you?" Anneliese sheathed her knife, and as she smoothed her garments, all evidence of the weapon faded from view.

"Of course not," the newcomer deflected with a smile. "Reports of an elf accompanying Mirsa Magus into the palace in the dead of night made their way to me. I made a point of being the first to know who it was." The envoy, a handsome elf that Mirsa had not seen around the palace before, turned his smile to Maisy. "I've not been introduced to you, or your mother."

"Mirsa Magus, if you have the correct room," the Master Mage glowered, shifting the child as she turned. "And Maisy."

"Beautiful ladies, all." The envoy's words lingered a moment too long on his tongue for Mirsa's taste. "Allow me to accompany you to breakfast?"

"We'll only be a moment, Torit," Anneliese slid forward to close the door, a forced smile causing the corners of her eyes to crease.

"Not a friend?" Mirsa asked, stifling a yawn.

"Hunters and politicians rarely see things the same way," Anneliese shrugged. "Torit... is beyond that."

"Old lover?"

Anneliese's eyes flashed with an expression Mirsa had not yet seen from the elf. The Huntmistress nodded. "Before you were born." A sigh escaped her lips. "Before Carlo was born, several of your generations ago. And he still acts as if..."

"You were young..." Mirsa offered.

"I wasn't even that young!" Anneliese exclaimed, eyes widening in unguarded expression.

"A moment of weakness, then."

"Twelve years of weakness?" The Huntmistress bit her lip, watching the Mage's expression from the corner of her eye.

"There is something to be gained from every perceived mistake," Mirsa shrugged, clutching Maisy closer.

"The stories I could tell," Anneliese nodded. "You'd not have the days to hear them all."

"Then we'll have to settle for only your very best," Mirsa laughed. "Let's go, I'm famished."

CHAPTER 5

"**W**e've stayed true to the course, re-adjusted this morning to where Reko last felt the Dark magic," Yusa reported to Carlo. "He's uneasy though. There's a strangeness about that even I can sense."

Kevon nodded. "We're close, but not overly so. Plenty of time for our company to tear itself apart."

"With ample help from my countrymen," Rhysabeth-Dane added. "The nonsense I heard this morning at weapons practice reminded me of some of the reasons I left the Hold."

"How so?" Carlo asked.

"The Stoneguard need to wear their helmets more often," the Rider laughed. "Telling stories like that. As if Bertus and Alanna were bogeymen from old folk tales."

"What stories?" Relaniel stepped between some of the others, and turned to sit near Rhysabeth-Dane.

"Ehh," the dwarf started to shrug off the question, but saw the interest in the elf's eyes. "It was... a children's story. *Ororo*, an old word, a strange one. It can mean either 'half of', or 'more than', depending on how it's used."

"Doesn't seem exactly practical," Yusa observed.

"Which is why it's an *old* word, *ruta*," Rhysabeth-Dane spouted, glaring at the ship's captain. After a moment, she continued. "Some of the Stoneguard have been avoiding Bertus for weeks, afraid that he might be..."

"One of those things?" Kevon shook his head. "I've known Bertus for quite a while. This is the first time anything has seemed different about him."

"None of the books I brought would mention it," she added. "I was being practical when I packed. My parents never felt the need to fill my head with such nonsense, either so…"

"That's not a road we need to go down," Kevon assured her. "Between us, we've seen more unusual things, magical and otherwise, than most civilizations. We'll figure it out."

"The…" Relaniel began.

"That's different," Reko commented.

"Agreed." Kevon winced, his stomach knotted at the oily feel of restricted Water magic touching his mind. "This could be more important. Spread out and find it."

Reko's illusion-form dissolved, and Yusa's eyes swiveled up, as if he was listening to something only he could hear.

Carlo frowned, but led the charge out of the cabin onto the deck.

The light drizzle that had begun before their meeting was now fat drops that soaked through untreated cloth with every impact.

Rhysabeth-Dane whistled, and snatched her jacket from where it hung at her belt. She whirled it about like a street per-former, spraying droplets in every direction, but sliding into the dry garment in mere moments. She vaulted the rail to the lower deck, rolling as she hit with only the slightest wobble. She sprang to her feet, and bolted toward the open area on the foredeck.

Brightwing swooped down over her head, flapping once more so that he could clear his Rider's sprinting form. An in-stant of tucked wing, and a timed backbeat brought the griffin to a near perfect stop less than a dozen feet ahead of the speed-ing dwarf. Brightwing crouched, screeching at a nearby crew-man.

Rhysabeth-Dane leapt, planting both hands on the griffin's leonine rump and shoving off for extra height. She cleared the cantle of Brightwing's saddle, and threw her arms around his neck, squealing.

The griffin shrieked, leapt, and the two were airborne

and away in the space of a breath.

"She stayed on, that time," Alanna shrugged at Kevon. "That's something."

"Something..." Kevon echoed. "Something's wrong..." He looked around at the rising waves, squinting into the building storm. "This different Water magic, it's too sudden. We're not moving quickly enough to feel this much of a difference so soon."

"It's coming to us," Reko rasped, his image flickering into existence beside Kevon. "And whoever is bringing it is about to arrive."

A wave washed over the bow, and a deckhand sloshed through the uprights in the railing, and off into the sea.

"Tie off!" Yusa shouted. "Get below, unless you have business up here! Someone get to the pumps! We're taking on water!"

Yusa rattled off several more commands, but his voice caught in his throat as one of the Unbound dropped his lost crewman in a soggy heap less than two paces away.

"I thought they would all be above this," Kevon remarked, leaping to grab the unconscious man before the rocking of the deck could slide him back into the tempest below.

"There are no ships close enough to be the source of this," Reko announced, droplets of rain winking from view as they passed through his projected form. "This must be coming from below."

Alanna tore her eyepatch from its place, and gazed at the deck, beyond it. "One of your pumps is unmanned," she commented. "A foot of water in the hold, leaking in from starboard."

"Easy sailing has done this to the crew," Yusa growled, taking hold of the recovered sailor. "They'll not get so soft again." He dragged the man below, with the help of another deckhand.

"Myrnar," Alanna cautioned, glancing another direction. "Half a dozen."

Kevon spotted the wave, shouted a warning, and dove back toward the cabin, dragging Alanna behind him.

"They're getting closer," Alanna announced, leaning over the edge of the cot where she'd fallen. She sat and raised her eyes, scanning all around. "This is the center, and the seas are calm not far from here in every direction."

The granular Water magic grated at the edge of Kevon's senses, increasing in intensity. "It's the myrnar, somehow. They mean to sink us."

"Stop them."

Alanna's words clicked in Kevon's mind. His frustration at the loss of his sister, the revealed allegiance of her husband, and the newfound puzzles that were Bertus and Alanna had been wearing at Kevon more than he realized. This unprovoked attack provided the spark to ignite his fury. "Yes."

Kevon flung the door to the cabin open, and stormed out into the rain. The icy rain droplets hammering against his face became the first link in the chain of Water magic that he began crafting. His senses expanded, and the wave that loomed to the port side spread, flattened, and slid around the ship, calming the rocking motion to almost nothing. He pushed his focus downward, but the segmented magic distorted his concentration, and the ship listed to starboard. The interruption forced the Mage to regroup the patterns of magic around him, closer to the surface, where the aberrant energies wielded by the myrnar were less dense.

"How can I help?" Alanna's voice cut Kevon's angry shout short.

"Where are they?"

"Thirty yards that way," she answered, pointing down and just off the port side.

"The net." Kevon closed his eyes, spread his palms wide, and smoothed the sea as best he could, stilling the boat once more. "Go."

Alanna leapt to the railing that separated the upper deck from the lower, took a few steps, and bounded to the stairway railing, halfway between decks. She bounced and spun, rolling as she touched down near the port side net. Daggers flashed, and she cut the tethers that kept the rolled net from shifting while it was not in use.

The last binding parted, and Kevon shifted his attention to the dozen or so rocks that weighted down the net. A tangle of Movement runes formed in his mind, and he threw the rocks as evenly as he could manage, the net trailing behind. He glanced at Alanna, who was again looking down through the ship. He adjusted his Movement spells as she pointed toward the front of the boat, then back toward starboard. When she made a fist, and punched straight down, Kevon expended the rest of his magic to force the net down as hard as he could. Alanna slashed the rope that the crew used to retrieve the net, and it slithered over the edge.

The storm slackened, and Kevon could feel the constrained Water magic fade to nothingness.

"All but one of them," Alanna confirmed. "And she's injured."

Kevon banged a fist on the Captain's door. "Reko! Come out here and help Alanna secure the prisoner!"

CHAPTER 6

"Different than I remember it," Anneliese commented as they entered the dining hall, their first venture into the main area of the palace.

"This is all new," Mirsa confirmed, finally taking time to peer at the newly added layer of interior stone wall. She leaned in to look at the mortar joining the stones, and drew back in alarm as her finger almost brushed a metal shaving protruding from the masonry. "Another layer of magical defense? How many times have the walls been breached?"

"Once, since you left," Alacrit entered the room, flanked by half a dozen guardsmen, and a pair of Master Magi. "One too many for my taste. Precautions have been taken to ensure they never get as far as they did that night."

"Worse than the incursion we repelled?" Mirsa gasped at Alacrit's answering nod. "I had no idea. We'd assumed that most of them followed us to the coast. It seemed to us that was the case."

"The superior wards on the reliquary were all that kept it from being breached," Alacrit explained. "Over half of the residences on the upper level were compromised, mine included. If it had not been for my guards..."

"But there are..." Mirsa's face twisted in horror, and she clutched Maisy tighter to her bosom.

"Nearly a hundred perished. Twenty nine were ambassadors, dignitaries, and high ranking Magi," Alacrit's voice took on a hard edge. "They mean to destroy us."

"Dawn breaks, and the darkness fails once more," Torit

interjected. "I'm sure the ladies would hear more cheerful talk this morning."

"We're no strangers to violence and death," Anneliese shrugged. "Though I do prefer to wait until after breakfast when I'm not on the Highplain."

"My apologies. What manners we still possess we owe to Ambassador Torit," Alacrit bowed. "The palace was... less than cordial when he arrived weeks ago."

"Manners are not something so easily unlearned," Torit deferred. "A minimum of coaxing was required to reveal them again. Shall we?"

"Proceed."

At the prince's order, a single servant removed the lids from the ten silver dishes that lined one end of the great table. Long handled serving utensils were placed in each. The serving maid bowed, and returned to the kitchen.

"We've been short on help, but have learned to make do." Alacrit took a plate from the top of the pile, and began filling his plate. When he had finished, he spoke again. "Please, help yourselves."

"Better than ship food, but not chimaera flank," Anneliese observed as she followed behind Mirsa, dishing up uncharacteristically simple fare from the platters before them.

"It's nice to have meat again, after so long on the Isle," Mirsa countered. "Waine would have loved the time you all spent with the Griffinsworn. The stories he would have spun from that..." She stepped past the serving area to where the chairs were situated, and set her plate down across from Torit, two spaces away from Alacrit at the head of the table.

Maisy started to fuss, but Mirsa held her close, swaying back and forth a few times before taking her seat. The infant yawned, and dozed back off again.

"Mirsa Magus," Alacrit began. "I apologize for not being able to greet you as you arrived. It..."

The Mage at his right elbow leaned in and whispered something in his ear. The monarch's eyes widened for an instant, and he nodded.

"The child was unexpected, was it not?" Alacrit asked, gaze locked on Mirsa.

Mirsa coughed, avoiding choking on a bite of griddle-cake by the narrowest of margins. "I… ahh… Unplanned, yes," she answered. "We'd been expecting her for seasons."

"Of course," Alacrit amended. His voice softened a degree, though his stare did not. "The father. You mentioned Waine? The Adept that accompanied Kevon and Carlo to the west?"

"I don't see what…" Mirsa shook her head. "Yes, he is her father."

The Mage at Alacrit's right whispered to him again. The prince mumbled a response, and both of the Magi stood and left the room.

"She's a pleasant child, then?" Alacrit cut a slice of steak, and slipped into casual conversation as if the last few minutes had not happened.

Mirsa finished about half of her plate before the incongruity of Alacrit's behavior coupled with the semi-claustrophobic pressure sparked by the iron-laced masonry that surrounded them broke her calm demeanor. "I'm sorry," she blurted over the idle chatter between Alacrit and Torit. "What was that earlier? What did they tell you?"

"A small thing," the prince smiled. "They are arranging your new living quarters. Trivial matter, really."

Furthest thing from trivial, Mirsa thought, *considering my suite was as I left it, seasons from my last visit.* She smiled and nodded, but her stomach clenched, food became the furthest thing from her mind. A near irrational fear for Maisy's safety flooded her mind. She closed her eyes and rocked the child, breathing in the familiar scent, calming her racing pulse.

"We're here at your leisure," Mirsa affirmed. "We do have news from across the sea to discuss."

"I surmised as much," Alacrit nodded. "In good time."

The Magi returned with two servants. One began tidying up the serving area, while the other hung back, watching. The Magi took their seats and resumed the meal, so over-eager to catch up on missed conversation that it turned Mirsa's stomach.

Anneliese read Mirsa's expression, and they stood as one.

"If your majesty pleases," Mirsa began.

"You may take your leave," Alacrit responded, waving her off. "I find myself occupied until midafternoon, and will send for you when I am free."

Mirsa's unacknowledged glare spoke the volumes her clenched jaw would not allow. After a moment, she inclined her head, and stepped away from the table.

The servant who had returned with the Magi stepped forward, followed by a pair of Alacrit's guard. "I'll show you to your new lodgings," he stated, stepping past Mirsa and Anneliese without waiting for their response.

Setting off at a pace the servant was required to slow down for, Mirsa followed, glancing back at the trailing escort.

They made their way past the inner residences, toward the barracks and stables. As they passed beyond where the extra layer of new stonework extended, Mirsa felt a mixture of relief and apprehension.

"Here we are," the servant gestured toward a half opened door.

Mirsa opened her mouth as if to speak, but could not think of a single phrase that she would not regret later. She nodded, and pushed the door open.

"Junior officer's quarters," Anneliese remarked as she spotted the two double bunks and small desk. The room was similar in size to a standard cabin on any of the ships they'd been on, though the stacked beds took up more space to ac-commodate the larger frame of the average soldier.

"Moving us to the stable would have been too overt an insult," Mirsa's eyes locked on their piled belongings in the back corner of the room. "As it is, we're not important enough to merit the extra layer of protection they deem necessary for themselves."

"All of this would be fine if our purpose here was not to reaffirm Alacrit's support for Kevon," Anneliese remarked. "Perhaps our journey will not bear the desired fruit."

"I pretended understanding when Alacrit put us off before, before he was ready to handle what the Dark Magi might bring against him," Mirsa's cheeks grew flush as she spoke. "A war rages about the palace, and still he denies us?" She rocked her fussing child a few moments. "Unacceptable."

Torit and a handful of advisors spilled into the meeting hall, followed by the now familiar escort of Magi and guardsmen.

"Sorry for the delay," Alacrit's wooden apology did nothing to lessen the smoldering energy that encircled Mirsa, undetected by the Magi on either side of the prince. "Motherhood has changed you, it seems..."

"War has not tempered your character, as we had hoped," Mirsa sniped, her blue eyes rippling with subtle green hues, the few stray strands of her hair describing lazy waves through the air as she moved her head.

The elder Mage to Alacrit's right recognized the power he could not feel, and recoiled.

Giving purpose to the Water magic swirling around her, Mirsa slowed the flow of liquid in the Mage's body. He staggered, clutching at Alacrit's sleeve for support. "Calm yourself," she commanded. "If I wished to harm you, you could not stop me. I have no des... i..."

Mirsa flapped the collar of her cloak, sweating through what should have been near complete control of all water in the area.

"Dispense with the foolishness, children," Anneliese shook her head, steadying Mirsa with her free hand.

"The rigors of war have hardened my men, much as your adventures abroad have tempered your skills."

Releasing the runes she had bent to her will, Mirsa felt the heat surrounding her dissipate in response. "So it seems," she nodded to Alacrit.

"To the matter at hand?" the prince asked.

"My friends and I are not as welcome as we were in the past," Mirsa began.

"Recent security protocols," Alacrit waved his hand as if to wipe away her concern. "Your old quarters had not been addressed yet, as you'd been away."

"I know things must have been difficult, following the incident in Eastport."

"*Incident?*" Alacrit laughed. "Not calling for Kevon's head nearly cost me my throne, perhaps my life. My agents had to spread doubt as to the veracity of the claims, as I vowed to find the truth of the matter. There are some who still think it more than just a story."

"You know the truth, have known it for seasons, at least," Anneliese frowned.

"I still know little of you," Alacrit countered.

"Granddaughter of Aelion, the Eldest," the Envoy began. "Chief Huntmistress of the Glimmering Isle. Slayer of a hundred chimaera, Benevolent…"

"*Two…*" Anneliese muttered. She shook her head. "Be silent, Torit. This does not concern you."

"I decide what concerns him," Alacrit replied. "As one of my most valued advisors."

"There are things you should know about him, in that case."

"Your concerns may be the same reason I value him so much," Alacrit snapped. "Let us dispense with the trivialities."

Mirsa waited a few moments to see if Anneliese's composure would return, but continued anyway. "Kevon and the others have journeyed across the sea in your name. They have slipped beyond the boundaries of reality, to gain divine counsel."

"Heresy," spat the younger Mage at Alacrit's left.

"M'lani sends us her love," Anneliese glared at Torit.

"I'm sure she does," the Ambassador grimaced.

"They managed the crossing near the Throne," Anneliese offered.

"Impossible. It's…" Torit's usual smug expression softened to one of uncertainty, confusion.

"True. On my grandfather's honor."

"This changes things…" Torit turned from Anneliese to Alacrit.

"This changes nothing," Alacrit smiled, shaking his head. "Generations of history upturned on such a dubious report? I think not."

"You must consider the possibility that we are wrong," Torit argued. "That the *Ele…*"

"*I will do no such thing.*" Alacrit's tone took on a dangerous edge. "There is much you do not know. Nothing that needs aired in present company."

"*Baya* scum," the younger Mage spat, then turned and left the room.

"The fire of youth," Alacrit laughed. "His temper belies a deep devotion to our cause."

"Perhaps we should continue this later," Anneliese suggested, turning toward the exit, steering Mirsa as though the suggestion was already a foregone conclusion.

Guards scrambled into position, following as the Huntmistress led Mirsa and Maisy back into the hallway toward their quarters.

"What was that about?" Mirsa pressed Anneliese after they were in their closed room, and Maisy was snugged down for a nap.

"Something I thought was a rumor," Anneliese pressed her palms to her temples, and slouched down against the barred door until she sat on her heels.

◆ ◆ ◆

"So these…" Mirsa scrunched her nose. "These… *Eleri*, they're protecting us?"

"They must believe they are," Anneliese shrugged. "I heard the rumors first when I was young, barely a Hunter. It was on my first visit to Kelanoth. One of the Griffinsworn was behaving oddly, suspicious of our group. While I was learning to prepare Chimaera for a feast, one of the Meek mentioned that he'd suspected that the man was *Eleri*, an 'observer'. He pretended it was in jest, but something was not right."

"That's it?" Mirsa asked, tension lifting from her face. "It doesn't seem…"

"Then in Eastport, shortly after I became a Huntmistress," Anneliese continued. "Aelion accompanied us to the mainland, which is unusual to begin with. City officials were pleasant to deal with, except one. He was cold, short with all of us, my grandfather in particular. Whispers in the taverns named the official as *Eleri*, but I heard no proof."

"They might exist?" Mirsa shrugged. "I don't see…"

"Since then, I've heard things, little more than rumor. None of the information verified any other part. It is a scattered picture of a possible organization that is based on fear." Anneliese answered. "Though, taking recent events into consideration…."

"What fear?" Mirsa asked, rocking Maisy as she paced around the room.

"The fear of being manipulated, by beings not of this world." Anneliese stood, shaking her head. "If this is the same group that Torit and Alacrit have joined, it would appear they have become the thing they claim to oppose."

"Beings?" Mirsa scowled. "Not of this world. Monsters? How would monsters influence them?"

"Beings taking the form of Men, or the other races," Anneliese clarified. "Tricksters that mean to shape the course of events to their will. They, and their descendants were the primary focus of the *Eleri*."

"And you knew of them all along?"

"A fanciful story," Anneliese whispered. "An interesting puzzle to add pieces to as they appeared. Never a fact."

"And now, they're potential allies, or fanatics to avoid at all cost." Mirsa groaned, and lay Maisy down to nap. "Let's try and map out what we know of them."

CHAPTER 7

"**I**t's awake," Yusa snarled, splashing a bucket of seawater on the restrained myrnar.

Their captive writhed, testing its bonds, and hissed what could only be expletives in its native tongue.

"Common," Kevon ordered, stepping in front of the bound sea creature. "Do you speak Common?"

"Mmmann…" Their captive's lips struggled to form the unfamiliar words. "Die."

A Movement rune formed in Kevon's mind as he felt the Water magic reorganizing. He forced the sea creature's jaw closed, sealing lips and gill flaps with his Art. "None of that," the Mage cautioned.

The myrnar glared at Kevon in defiance, wrenching the magic to its will, until its body betrayed it. Magic in the area normalized as the creature thrashed and convulsed.

"You'll talk," Kevon continued, adjusting the shell necklace about his neck. "Or you'll die."

The myrnar's eyes locked on the necklace as it caught its breath.

"You recognize this?" Kevon stepped closer, tugging the charm toward their captive. "Then you know whose favor I've earned."

The myrnar's face contorted, revulsion sculpting its alien features. Dissonant Water magic tinkled at the edge of Kevon's senses, building with each writhing motion of the captured sea-creature.

"There's someone she hates more than us," Reko observed.

"So, we need to figure out how best to use that." Kevon added. "Watch her."

The dark-robed illusion nodded once, and flickered out of existence.

"We'll wait here, then," Yusa called after Kevon as the Mage hurried back up the stairs.

◆ ◆ ◆

"Allies, you say?" Carlo grunted. "I don't see how you'll be able to..."

"The magic," Kevon interrupted. "The different feel to it, so much like the other three Seats... It might be close. The Elven and Dwarven people stayed close to their Seats of Power, the myrnar may..."

"Half of these *Seats* I've visited have been in bone-strewn caves hanging off the edge of cliffs," Carlo roared. "The next one is likely as not to be at the bottom of the sea!"

"Ahh..." Kevon recoiled at the thought. "You could be right." He slumped onto a stool and leaned back against the cabin wall. "What should we do?"

"We've got scouts in the air, surveying the mission we're already committed to," Carlo began. "We've got a hand-ful of trouble we don't need trussed up in the hold. We don't know if keeping her is leverage to prevent attacks, or if it marks us as a sure target." The Blademaster sighed. "She's a dis-traction we can ill afford."

"Over the side, then," Kevon sagged further, his tunic grating against the rough wall. "Dead or alive? She has enough power to turn the seas against us."

"Does she?" Carlo chuckled. "If you were bound in her place, you'd have destroyed the ship by now. You fear her power because you don't understand it. I don't understand your power either, but I can tell that either you or Reko would best her in single combat."

"If we release her, she remains a threat," Kevon mused.

"Her group may avoid us, less intent on revenge." He stood, and shook his head. "There is plenty of blood to be spilled on the path we walk. No need to add what can be avoided."

"Here, now," Kevon protested, setting down one of the sea-filled buckets he'd brought from above. "Enough of that."

The captive myrnar's gill flaps settled back against her neck, and the ferocious rows of teeth disappeared behind her false smile.

"You're drying out. Hold still." Kevon poured the bucket with far more care than the previous applications of water. He slowed as the myrnar craned her neck to expose a dry patch, and obliged with a slosh of the bucket.

Rivulets of brine dripped from the sea creature's stringy hair, delivering gradual moisture to her upper arms and torso. She shivered as he spilled the rest of the bucket over her tail.

"I'm letting you go," Kevon announced, handing the empty bucket to Yusa, and retrieving the second full container. He knelt near the heavy-lidded captive amid protests by the captain. "Do you understand?"

After several heaving breaths through her mouth, the myrnar's eyes opened halfway. "Not... die?" she whispered, turning her face toward Kevon.

"No," Kevon shook his head, peering into the bright blue-green eyes that seemed so out of place in the whorls and lines of puckered scars that adorned her face. "You're not going to die."

The myrnar closed her eyes, and appeared to relax for the first time since she'd been spewed from the sea on a geyser of Reko's creation.

"I'm going to cut these off," Kevon pointed to the knife he'd drew from his belt, and then to one of the leather ties that tethered her to the hold beams. "Be still." He sliced through the first tether, and took a step back while the myrnar stretched and rolled her wrist. "I'll cut the other one off, now," Kevon continued, stepping around the myrnar's tail to her other side at a measured pace, pointing toward the remaining bond.

"Still," the myrnar agreed, giving a slow nod of her head, closing her eyes in a gesture that Kevon decided to take as trust.

Kevon cut away the remaining restraint, and sheathed his knife. He picked up the filled bucket, and sat it next to the released prisoner. "Here. As soon as you are well, we will take you above to release you."

The myrnar opened her eyes, and dipped her hands into the bucket. She splashed herself with cupped handfuls of the water, and massaged her forearms and wrists with the contents of the bucket. She patted and smoothed her gill flaps with dampened hands before turning her attention to the undersides of her breasts.

Kevon averted his gaze as the myrnar drenched her chest with half of the remaining contents of the bucket, and rubbed with upward kneading motions.

"Not watch?" she trilled, the first laughter escaping her lips since her capture. "Man... sweet."

After a few moments, Kevon turned and knelt to face her. "We're releasing you if you help us, or not. It would be... sweet... of you to answer a few questions before we do."

The myrnar trailed a hand in the bucket, flicking the surface to make soft *splishing* noises. "Ask."

"What lies to the north, where we sail?"

"Black stone. Danger. No go." Her voice did not convey much of a sense of concern, but Kevon did not blame her.

"We have little choice," he sighed. "What danger, exactly? Can you tell us more?"

"Not go, not know," she said, pointing to herself. She tilted her head, and took Kevon's hand. "You stay, stay here," she pulled his hand and pressed it beneath her chest, closing her eyes and humming an enthralling tune. "Stay..." she whispered, caressing his hand, then releasing it.

"I can't, we… c- can't…" Kevon stammered, confused by the gesture, and his body's reaction to it. He shook his head. "Questions. You know… who gave me this?" He pointed to the shell necklace.

The myrnar's lips pulled back in an involuntary snarl.

"It could help us," Kevon whispered. "Please?"

She squinted, and closed her mouth. "Sweet… man." She spoke after a moment. "Princess… there." She pointed to port, to the west. "Not far."

"Thank you," Kevon pointed at the bucket. "Are you ready to go?"

The myrnar upended the rest of the bucket over her head, squealed, and extended her arms toward Kevon.

Kevon stepped in, knelt down, and slid one arm around the mermaid's back. She arched her tail, and he slipped his other arm under her a third of the way down her lower body. As he lifted, she relaxed, and her tail section drooped and bowed, almost as if she had knees.

The myrnar turned her head toward him, but Kevon shifted his grip so that the mermaid's teeth were angled away from his neck. He stepped between two wary sailors, and hurried into the stairwell that led to the deck. He slid left and twisted to ensure the myrnar cleared the doorframe, catching his shoulder as he did so. Ignoring the scrape, he trudged up the stairs, and out into the warm sun and salt breeze.

The mermaid trilled with excitement as Kevon carried her down to the lower deck, wriggling and chirping at the attention her passage attracted. She undulated, and he felt the crescent of raised scars on her right side shift lower through his tunic, and the soft curve press into his chest. The smile he caught in the edge of his vision was a grotesque mockery of the glare Alanna shot him from across the ship.

"Here you are," Kevon blurted, depositing the myrnar near a break in the gunnel rail.

The mermaid clutched the rail with both hands, maintaining a wobbly balancing act on her semi-rigid tail. With a swift whirling motion, she was outside the railing, arms fully extended, back arched as she hung out over the sea.

"Wait!" Kevon called, extending a hesitant hand toward the rail.

"Yesss..?" the myrnar asked, drawing herself back toward the boat, her torso undulating in a distracting fashion.

"Why?" Kevon asked, staring at the myrnar. "Why did your people attack us?"

The low rumble was an unusual sound coming from the mermaid, as she leaned in closer, her smile widening until Kevon could see more than one row of teeth. Almost as if she were struggling to restrain herself, she spoke an octave lower than she had been. "Man..." she began, and the guttural tone, the distended jaw, plucked a chord in the Warsmith's psyche that jangled 'danger' as surely as the hint of altered magic he detected at the same instant.

"Sweet..." she purred, eyes narrowing closed. She released her grip on the railing, and the wave that swept alongside the ship seemed to hesitate for a sliver of time as she melted into it, and was swept back down into the otherwise calm sea.

Muscles already tensed from the encounter screamed as Kevon felt the constrained Water magic build below the ship. "How can she?!" Kevon howled as his fears seemed to coalesce around them. Reko let out a strangled battle-cry, and began forming Water and Movement runes.

Opening himself up to the pull of the sea, Kevon embraced the symbol in his mind, as the power spilled in and swam through him. Ready to thwart any water based attack the myrnar could bring to bear, Kevon's grasp on the power wavered when he felt the strange magic spiral away to the south. "She's..."

"Gone." Alanna finished, looking through the boat to where Kevon could only detect faint traces of the mysterious power. "Should you have let her go?"

Kevon shuddered, and with a modest effort, funneled the maelstrom of Water magic surrounding him into the cool void of the iron ring he wore on his right hand. "She didn't move against us," he sighed, relaxing as the press of the sea retreated to its normal seductive whisper. "Yet."

CHAPTER 8

"Yes, I am certain," Anneliese reassured Mirsa as they dodged through the service passageways near one of the kitchens. "I walked these halls before any of you were born."

"The only gardens I ever saw were on the northeast side of the palace," Mirsa argued.

"I'm sure it's still there," Annelies countered, turning yet another corner, and opening an iron-bound door. "Careful."

Mirsa sidestepped through the doorway, pulling Maisy closer to her as she did. "There's…"

"Nothing much until we get outside," Anneliese interrupted, glancing at the other door as she closed the one they'd just come through. "This next door, a short hallway, and a pair of latched iron gates."

"And I wonder why no one ever told me about this," Mirsa sighed.

"Alacrit's grandfather brought me here when he was but a prince himself," the Huntmistress smiled. "It's not common knowledge."

"Another youthful adventure?" Mirsa asked, leaning against the wall in the hallway after inspecting it for the anti-magic coating.

Anneliese shook her head as she closed the second door and worked her way back over to the first of the gates. "This was much more recent than even Torit."

Alacrit's grandfather was a recent acquaintance, Mirsa thought, head swimming with the temporal implications of such a statement. She added another hundred years onto her previous estimate of the elf's age, then tiptoed through the narrow opening as Anneliese held the gate open.

"I had no idea," the Master Mage breathed as a slice of the garden came into view through the gate around the next corner.

"The passage across from this leads up to the royal residences," the Huntmistress explained, unlatching the last gate and holding it open. "Guards patrol this twice a day, but this whole end of the palace is high atop a cliff face. Difficult to breach. We're unlikely to be disturbed."

"I'm disturbed enough with this entire visit," Mirsa admitted, peering out of the exit into the garden. "This should help a little."

"Mmm..." The elf did little to hide her disappointment as she stepped out into the sunlight. "They must be still recovering from imp attacks," she observed. "And have not been able to replant some of the rare varieties."

"Perhaps things have changed since you were here last," Mirsa offered, inhaling the fresh, fragrant air. "This is still beautiful."

"It is not as I remember," Anneliese admitted. "The pathways were pebbled, this stonework is new."

Mirsa strolled along the path until she reached a stone bench. She sat, taking cover from the midday sun under the cover provided by the wooden lattice and climbing foliage. "Torit will not bother us here?" she teased.

"I do not believe Alacrit's grandfather brought Torit here," the elf smiled. "Beyond that, I guarantee nothing."

"The *Eleri*," Mirsa pressed. "Is Torit the first of your people to join their ranks?"

"One of the reasons we are not as close as we used to be," Anneliese mused, sliding into place beside Mirsa, and reaching for Maisy. "Torit doubted the old ways. He had spent too much time in the company of men, whose memories are shorter, passed down more frequently than our own."

"Until Kevon and the others returned with their tales, I would have agreed with him," Mirsa admitted, handing over the sleeping infant. "These beliefs are going to be strongly held," she whispered.

"Doubtless," the Huntmistress nodded, rocking the child back and forth, the small shadow flickering in and out of view against the backdrop of Anneliese's shadowless form.

"Wait," Mirsa's face scrunched as she felt familiar magic tickling the back of her mind. The hint of restrained Light magic faded, and Maisy's shadow returned to full view. "What were you just doing?"

"I forget her shadow needs no training," Anneliese apologized. "An exercise we do with our young that teaches and tests them at even such an age."

"What I just felt was a taste of magic like what surrounds your Seat of Power," Mirsa exclaimed.

"Magic," Anneliese chortled. "I've never had a problem handling steel."

Mirsa peered at the elf for a moment longer before continuing to ask about the *Eleri*. "What could have led to the start of this, if they are obviously wrong?"

"They have lists of suspected targets," Anneliese considered aloud. "Strings of unexplained coincidences over time?" she asked. "Someone designing 'coincidences' to manipulate them?"

"Seems unlikely," Mirsa frowned. "A long, sick game with no reward. Difficult for an elf, impossible for any of the other races."

"The creators?" Anneliese suggested.

"Only one of the creators even knew that this place remained," Mirsa shook her head. "He and his followers are not that subtle."

"Even Torit would be able to detect the darkness attached to a follower of L'mort," Anneliese agreed. "But I've not been convinced of our theory of coincidences."

"Six of them," Mirsa stood and paced toward the center

of the garden. "Balancing the elements, completing the world. Could there be more that we are not aware of?"

"Making the *Eleri*... correct?" Anneliese sighed. "This is getting us nowhere."

"I just want to make sure that we're... wait." Mirsa pushed out with her magical senses, testing the area ahead where some of the wards that covered the rest of the palace and surrounding grounds seemed to weaken. "I could almost perform a Sending from here. Or *to* here," she added.

Restrained Light magic brushed against Mirsa's consciousness once again.

"There is light below," Anneliese remarked. "Faint, but it is there. I cannot see more than that."

"Like Alanna," Mirsa's eyes grew wide. "You can see like Alanna does!"

"A mere glimmer of her ability," the Huntmistress shook her head. "And here, less even than that."

"There's got to be a way in," Mirsa cracked a smile. "Let's find it."

◆ ◆ ◆

"This is amazing," Mirsa said, excitement causing her voice to waver. "Permanent Light stones, and a focal Sending enchantment. Anyone of any power who knows of this place should be able to come and go at will."

"A dangerous thing to have here behind the walls," Anneliese cautioned. "A dangerous secret to know."

"None of my peers could have known of this, and kept it secret," Mirsa declared. "Myself among them. I... should be able to keep it now," she amended.

"This was done in recent years," the Huntmistress observed. "I would have noticed the passage in my adventures before. None of the wood here has darkened with age."

"We shouldn't stay here," Mirsa decided. "If this is recently built, it will not be long forgotten. Just knowing of it is an advantage we should take for what it is."

"We should make our way to the parapets," Anneliese suggested. "It is a worthy view, alone reason for us to be in the garden."

With a last wistful look at the inlaid, spell infused stone sigils ringing the small room, Mirsa followed Anneliese through the narrow winding stairwell that led back to the guard tower.

"It is not the splendor of the Glimmering Isle, nor the loftiness of the Seacliff Camp lookout," Anneliese observed, "However, it is not without its own beauty."

Mirsa leaned over the ledge of the unshuttered window, and her eyes danced over the sparse farms that blended into the forest to the south. Toward the horizon, she thought she could see the edge of the frontier, shrouded in wavy lines of heat distortion. She pushed off, her hands rasping across the dusty, unfinished stone surface. She stepped between the stairwell and Anneliese, who rocked Maisy, whispering an Elven lullaby.

"You can see Kron from here!" she exclaimed, pouncing onto the westward facing window ledge. She squinted, trying to trace the exact border where the fields snapped to ordered attention beside their less organized neighbors.

"It was not always so," Anneliese cooed, pressing her lips to the sleeping infant's forehead. "The surrounding countryside was more productive and organized in my youth, before the farmerfolk organized in the west."

"And that's a bad thing?" the Mage asked, closing her eyes and leaning forward to savor the breeze that whispered past her, freshening the warm, stagnant air in the tower.

"Balance in the world is a humorous thing," Anneliese smiled. "There are more artisans, now that food is easily obtained elsewhere. Craftsmen here have wrought many a thing of beauty. But, the less work men have to do to survive, the more they turn to politics, theft, and war."

"You've seen a lot of that, then?" Mirsa asked, shifting to

sit on the window ledge, looking back toward the Huntmistress.

"Not even my people are immune," Anneliese stepped back and sat cross-legged in the far corner of the small room. "When I was young, a handful of Hunters abandoned our ways, exiled themselves from the Isle of their own accord."

"Something happened..."

"One of their number believed that men were the reason M'lani had not returned," Anneliese explained. "By the time word reached us, he and two disciples had carved a path of destruction through the lands east of Alcron, and ascended to the Highplain. The Griffinsworn fared better than the lowlanders, defeating Talmurn's followers. For a time after that, he was the thing to be feared in the shadows, rather than the chimaera."

"How did they..."

"We followed his trail into the upper lands, and convinced the Griffinsworn of our intentions," Anneliese spoke evenly, a faraway look in her eyes. "Over the course of three seasons, four of my sisters fell, including my Huntmistress. After the last attack, unbound by my superior, I tracked him to his lair, and took M'lani's gift from him."

"I'm so sorry," Mirsa crossed the space between them, and sat down beside her friend. "That must have been difficult for you."

"The taking of any life has a price," Anneliese nodded. "Even if the balance is not paid by the taker. My remaining sister and I spent the next eight years helping the Griffinsworn rebuild, doing whatever we could to regain their trust."

"So long away from home," Mirsa traced a finger along the line of Maisy's nose. "I can't imagine it, not with her to take care of." She sat back and sighed. "Then again, my home here is not what it once was."

"We spent as much time learning their ways as teaching them ours," Anneliese offered. "It was there, after the loss of my mentor, that I became skilled enough to advance to Huntmistress."

"I've learned a great deal since I've left here," Mirsa admitted. "And there is much more that we hope to learn."

"What there is to be learned here," Anneliese frowned, "May not be what we came for. That is not to say it is not worth learning."

"Torit, then," Mirsa decided. "He seemed uncomfortable with your announcement about M'lani, and may be ready to talk about the *Eleri*. Alacrit appears to be much more involved, less likely to be swayed."

"Though trying to influence the newest member of their organization is unlikely to please the prince," Anneliese cautioned. "It does seem to be the correct action to take."

Mirsa scooped Maisy up, rocking her as she began to fuss. "Then let's take it."

CHAPTER 9

"**W**e need to stop the ship," Rhysabeth-Dane announced.

"So you're the captain now, are you?" Yusa asked, chuckling.

"I agree with her, though my reason may differ," Reko whispered, nodding to the dwarf. "The Water magic here is too much like it was when we were attacked, but stronger as we go. I can tell the focus of the effect is to the west, but we will be at a disadvantage if we travel further north."

"What did you see?" Kevon asked the Rider.

"A dark island rising out of the sea," Rhysabeth-Dane began. "Miles of twisted open land between the shore and the stronghold in the center. The ground seems to move from above but..."

"What is it?" Kevon pressed.

"Obsidian Reapers, like the one you defeated beneath the Highplain," the dwarf continued. "Wandering in and out of caves hidden in the contours of the landscape. Attempting to cross, or even landing there would be foolish."

"I like her reason better," Reko admitted, dissolving into Mage-smoke with a shrug.

"There is no clear path to the stronghold?" Kevon pressed. "No bearing that would conceal our approach?"

"We circled the whole island," the Rider sighed. "There was no cover that would give us any advantage. I dared not get closer to the stronghold for fear of being spotted. We were the only things in the sky."

"Charging headlong into the problem may not be the

answer, I'm afraid," Yusa chuckled. "Shall we set course for the east side of the island? Further away from Reko's problem while we see what can be done about the other?"

"No." Kevon's hand went to the string of shells at his neck. "The mermaid said that the Myrnar Princess was to the west. I'm betting they have remained near their Seat of Power, like the dwarves. We'll chase another of our objectives while this one confounds us."

"Your sister?" Yusa asked. "What…"

"I'm no good to her dead," Kevon grimaced. "And the Myrnar are as likely as anyone to lend aid in recovering her. More likely, in fact." He released the charm at his throat. "Reko can help you set your course. Rhysabeth, you'll need your notes on the book for this meeting. I've got to rest."

"They look agitated out there," Alanna commented as Kevon closed the cabin door. "It's not about me, I assume. A welcome change."

"It's a pity you can't hear through walls, too," Kevon grumbled.

"A few more adventures," Alanna slid her eyepatch into place, winking her ensorcelled eye before it disappeared behind the Enchanted barrier. "And I just might. In the meanwhile…"

"There is no way we can approach the stronghold where we believe Alma is being held," Kevon reported. "We're diverting to where we believe the Myrnar Princess may be, to ask for her help."

"It'll be nice to see her again," Alanna grinned, her expression triggering Kevon's memories of their first encounter with the sea-folk. "The perfect blend of regal beauty, and animal savagery. It's not easy to balance the two. I'm more inclined to savagery, myself."

"I'm well aware," Kevon answered, nodding, then turning to sit at the desk by the door. He shuffled Rhysabeth's summary notes into a stack, moved aside a small sea-chart, and began writing a list of his own.

"What are you doing?"

"Preparing for our meeting with the Myrnar. Trying to come up with something to offer in return for the help we're going to request," Kevon sniffed back the beginning of a tear. "Trying not to think about what Alma is going through."

"That's not how we prepare for a meeting with the Myrnar," Alanna whispered in his ear, halfway across the room without the faintest noise to mark her passage. "If you remember, as I do." The assassin's fingers worked the knots in Kevon's shoulders with an insistent gracefulness.

Kevon glared at the stacks of documents on the desk before him, and drew in a deep breath. He relaxed and leaned back into Alanna, recalling their first night together, before they met the Myrnar in Eastport. "I will always remember," he answered, tilting his head back to look up into her eye.

"It sounds like you'll need to be *much* better prepared for this negotiation," Alanna teased. "We'd better get to work."

Kevon clasped Alanna's draped arm closer to his chest, twining his fingers with hers. The movement shifted her still form tighter against his back, and elicited a sleepy murmur in his ear. He wriggled against her soft warmth for a moment, and settled back into his own slumber.

CHAPTER 10

"Mirsa Magus?"

The Master Mage peered through the barely opened door at the slice of unfamiliar face, and the voice that accompanied it. "Yes?"

"We've yet to meet, I'm Blademistress Chelani, friend of Blademasters Carlo and Marco."

"Of course! He's mentioned you," Mirsa let the door swing open. "Please, come in."

"I'd heard your standing at court had fallen," Chelani scowled, looking around the room, "This is more than you should have to endure. You are welcome at the Guild, should it suit you."

"I have no doubt it would be more pleasant than this, Blademistress," Mirsa smile in the Warrior's direction sagged after a moment. "There are things we still need to accomplish here, I'm afraid."

"Alacrit has changed, these last seasons," Chelani lamented. "The press of the dark ones account for much, but there are whispers of wrongness that cannot be explained away so easily."

"Such as?" Anneliese interjected.

"I have reports of increased frontier skirmishes with orcs, where improper deployment has left many of the allied dwarves dead," the Blademistress hesitated. "Some of the Dwarven units have separated from our forces, building their own fortifications, and holding their lines by themselves."

"The southerners won't take that for long," Anneliese shook her head. "They will see it as the Dwarves gaining a foothold in their territory, possibly a greater threat than the orcs."

"Only one of their factions has held fast, wherever they are assigned," Chelani continued. "The…"

"Stoneguard?" Mirsa asked. "That is no surprise. I'd guess that none of the casualties have been theirs?"

"Not even a handful, but some," Chelani nodded. "You are familiar with them, then?"

"I have not seen them in battle, but have heard many stories, and spent a good deal of time with them," Mirsa admitted.

"One of their brothers was chosen to lead the Strider faction of one of the tribes on the Highplain of Kelanoth," Anneliese added. "After less than a season there. They have amazing potential, but often act like children."

"That's true of most Warriors," Chelani replied. "What worries me is that there has been no action by the prince to improve the situation. These reports are not through official channels, but they are from reliable sources. I'd thought to bring this to Alacrit's attention, but heard that a Hero had returned to the palace."

"As you've seen, my influence here is… tenuous, at best," Mirsa shrugged. "I can speak to Alacrit if you would like…"

"I will deal with Alacrit," Chelani grimaced. "I thought you might be able to get word of this to Blademaster Carlo. The arrangements were his doing, at least in part. He should know what is happening, and… about Blademaster Marco."

"Marco?" Mirsa asked. "What of him?"

"Slain, in the attempt to cleanse the city of Dark Magi," the Blademistress's eyes lowered. "Things have not been the same since."

"He sounded like one Carlo put all of his trust in," Anneliese offered. "I will tell him when we see him next."

"We may have to rejoin him sooner than expected," Mirsa sighed. "Conditions in the palace are not quite as hostile as outside it, but nowhere near what we expected."

"Again, if you have need of us while you stay, or as you

leave, you have only to ask," Chelani bowed, and turned to leave.

"Be well, Blademistress," Mirsa called after her as the door closed.

"The sooner we break Torit," Anneliese mused, "The sooner we can leave this place."

"Then let's begin."

◆ ◆ ◆

"I'm afraid I can't help you, ladies," Torit protested, glancing from Anneliese to Mirsa, and back. "You've known me since we were children."

"Well enough to know that something has changed," Anneliese countered. "Alacrit's actions reek of this nonsense. You should know better."

"What I know has been called into question," Torit shrugged. "Given recent history, the lore of Men begins to make sense. With even their dull senses, they see more than we do, because they *look*, they *question*."

Anneliese shook her head at Torit. "Our friends have seen..."

"Have they?" Torit countered. "If you came to me, telling of a meeting with M'lani, I would accept it. Without question. You would be wise enough to discern a goddess from..." A wave of disgust and anger washed over his features. "Your friends have been deceived."

"Deceived by what?" the Huntmistress probed.

"You think you can trick answers out of me, make me look a fool?" Torit laughed. "Have you anything to convince me of your claims?"

"Our friend, the woman Alanna, was healed by M'lani," Anneliese began. "She was given the gift of true sight."

"The girl Marelle?" Torit sneered. "Did you see her ruined eye? Did anyone? When..."

"How did you know her name?" Mirsa broke in. "Only a

few of us..."

"She is a suspect, then." Anneliese announced. "That answers several questions."

"N-no..." Torit stammered. "That's not..."

"How involved is Alacrit?" Anneliese pressed. "Does he lead them?"

Torit glared at Anneliese, silent.

"We're finished here," the Huntmistress chuckled. "We'll get no further aid, considering the things Alacrit and the *Eleri* think of our friends. I suggest we leave before this wretch can report to his master."

"I serve the truth," Torit protested. "I..."

"Have no time for this," Mirsa finished. "If you care anything for Anneliese, you will hold your tongue until we are clear of the city."

"If you value M'lani's gift," Anneliese commented as she turned to walk past Torit. "You may want to examine the source of the truth you serve."

Torit watched as they walked out, saying nothing. Minutes later, he hurried off to find Alacrit.

CHAPTER 11

"Here." Reko whispered, not bothering to form his customary illusion-self.

"Agreed," Kevon announced. "Have them lower the sails." He watched Yusa move about the deck, helping and hollering at turns.

Expanding his awareness, Kevon could better sense the differently framed magical energy that centered below them. He could feel the edges of the boundary sloping off in the distance, and shuddered at the image that came to mind; an insect alighting atop a soap bubble.

Do we know what we are doing? Kevon thought, projecting the thoughts into the abbreviated magical shorthand he used to communicate with Reko. *You see the danger we're in?*

Focused properly, the forces below could destroy us in an instant, Reko's thought-forms slid through Kevon's awareness. *My feelings on not being able to access that energy are mixed.*

"What now?" Carlo asked, craning his neck to scan the calm seas first to port, then starboard.

"If Yusa will have the dinghy lowered, I'll wait there, a little away from the ship." Kevon answered. "I don't expect they'll be long."

"*We'll* wait," Alanna corrected. "Are you ready?" she called down to the main deck.

Rhysabeth-Dane rested her forehead on Brightwing's beak, stroking his neck feathers and murmuring in comforting tones. "Wait here, all right?" she half-commanded, straightening up to look into her mount's eyes. The griffin clicked its tongue in a show of mild displeasure, but settled on the deck and began to preen.

The dwarf pulled the bound ledger from her satchel, and flipped through it before strolling over to the smaller craft that was being prepared for launch. "*Am I ready?*" she muttered, hopping down into the dinghy as soon as it dropped below the level of the deck.

Kevon and Alanna joined her, and waited as the crew continued to lower the smaller boat into the water below. "Nervous?" Kevon asked as they released the ropes and the dinghy began to drift away from the ship.

"I saw the one you let go," Rhysabeth-Dane shrugged. "They're not even as scary as chimaera."

Kevon bit his lip and squinted at the librarian for a moment. "You... didn't fight any of... the chimaera..." he clarified.

"I could now," the diminutive Rider announced, hand moving to her sword hilt. "They're not so tough."

"Yes," Kevon chuckled. "Perhaps you could. Kylgren-Wode says your technique is improving steadily. I regret not being able to watch you practice more."

"It's a touchy subject after..." the dwarf's eyes met Alanna's, and darted away.

"Neither Bertus or I have sparred since..." Alanna confessed. "It..."

"The two of you likely have the least need for practice," Kevon waved a dismissive hand. "We should focus on the matter before us. I feel something happening below."

Alanna leaned over the side of the boat to peer downward, a recent change in the use of her ability that Kevon welcomed. "Four, approaching at unnatural speed," she announced.

"On course to surface a comfortable distance away, *there*?" Kevon pointed to a patch of sea that lay as far away from them as they were from the ship, opening his eyes and relaxing his magical senses.

"It appears so," Alanna confirmed.

The shackled forces overlaying the regular Water magic

in the area jangled in an alarming fashion over the next few seconds, and Kevon gathered what power he could in advance of a possible confrontation.

Four heads broke the surface of the water no more than twenty yards from the boat, without sound or splash. Tension remained in the surrounding magic, but the frantic disruption had subsided. The figures rose from the water to chest height, two burly mermen with jagged-tipped spears in the lead, and two slimmer figures trailing behind.

"Honorable myrnar," Kevon began, standing and bowing as the newcomers advanced. "We seek the counsel of your queen. I carry a gift from her Highness, given long ago for..."

Alanna's hand on his leg made him pause. "*He knows...*" she whispered, gesturing to the lead myrnar.

"Much has changed," the Myrnar Ambassador commented. "But you remain constant."

"We are constant, again," Alanna laughed. "It is good to see you."

The merman emitted a warbling growl, answered by a questioning trill from one of the trailing myrnar. A sidelong glance and low hiss was all the response needed to send both of the scrawnier myrnar diving, and eddies of constrained Water magic whirling about Kevon's mind.

"Not so constant as I assumed," the queen's consort amended as he drew closer and saw the changes time and trial had wrought on Kevon and Alanna. "There is more light in your face, but things are rarely so simple."

"They seldom are," Kevon agreed. "How have you and your mate fared?"

"That is a tale she must tell," the myrnar answered, exaggerating a shrug, peering sidelong at Rhysabeth-Dane. "Is that a delver with you?"

"Dwarf, if you please," the Rider corrected, huffing.

"My apologies," the ambassador inclined his head. "I have simply never seen one of your people out upon the sea."

"*I suppose he's never seen one riding a griffin, either,*" she mumbled under her breath.

"Easy..." Alanna cautioned, placing her hand over Rhysa-beth-Dane's.

"She approaches..." the merman announced, a few breaths before Kevon felt the disturbance below the surface of the water. The silence thickened as they waited.

The lack of concern as the strange energies hurtled to-ward them from below grated against Kevon's sensibilities, but he remained calm. He flinched only inwardly as the Myr-nar Queen slipped from the depths to take her place beside her mate.

"Your Highness," Kevon tilted his head toward the newly arrived monarch. "It is good to see you again. I only wish circumstances were not so dire."

"An unexpected pleasure," she purred. "A pity that we have no time to enjoy the reunion properly. My people are at war."

"With those to the southeast?" Kevon asked.

"Does he always know the right thing to say?" the queen asked Alanna.

"We've had our share of disagreements," Alanna replied. "He's not always wrong?"

"There is enough light in you," the mermaid blurted, reaching out a hand to stroke Alanna's hair. "More than enough, without this falsehood. Did you not know this?"

"I..." Alanna flinched, then settled back into position and smiled. "I've been dyeing it... It is something I have won-dered about."

"This war..." Kevon peered, wide eyed, at the leader of the Myrnar. "How bad is it?"

"Three rogue factions have refused to consolidate under my rule, since I claimed the throne," she explained. "The lar-gest of them, most bothersome because of its nearness to the heart of our kingdom, has recently begun open hostilities with our people, and increased its interference in the world above."

"We were the target of some of that interference," Rhysabeth-Dane volunteered. "They tried to sink the ship until we netted some of them and grabbed another one to question."

"I'm relieved you were able to stop them," the queen sighed. "They have over-harvested their region of the sea, and have had to range further and further to sustain themselves…"

"They were hunting us for food?" Kevon's eyes glazed over as the conversation he'd had with the captive mermaid took on shades of disturbing he'd not been aware existed.

"Few ships pass through their territory unharmed," the queen lamented. "Did they try and lure you overboard with song, or feigned distress?"

"They turned the sea against us," Kevon's arm around Alanna clasped her tighter to him. "If Reko and I hadn't acted quickly to disrupt the waves…"

"I was not aware they had turned any Mystics…" The queen turned to look at her mate, and then back at her advisors. "This changes things. Not only do they pose a greater danger to the surface, but they may be able to gain enough strength to threaten the rest of the kingdom."

"I'll gather our forces myself," the queen's consort announced, and vanished beneath the waves, one of the smaller mermen diving with him.

"I'm sorry," the queen shook her head, using more of her body than a surface-dweller would for the same gesture. "You come to us for aid, and we must put you off to deal with horrors of our own. Where are my manners? What do you require of us? What news of my sister's murderer?"

"She's avenged, at long last," Kevon announced. "I defeated my former Master, but he fled, and regrouped. Our most recent battle claimed the lives of many, but he numbered among them."

Red rimmed gill flaps tensed, then settled back, undetectable along the mermaid's neck. "Did he… suffer?"

"Unimaginable pain," Kevon nodded. "There was

enough retribution for your sister, and a good amount of his other victims. Not all of them, but quite a few."

"I could not ask for more." A tear slid down the side of the queen's face. "Whatever you require of us, we shall strive to accomplish."

"My sister is held captive on the island northeast of here. Surrounded by demons from beyond this world, we cannot even approach the island, let alone storm the tower at its center."

"I cannot spare the Mystics it would take to get you there," the myrnar answered. "Not as we gather them to put down our brethren to the south. I know time is important, you need to save her while you still can..."

"Use us."

"What?" The queen recoiled at Kevon's sudden request.

"We stood against the renegade Mystics the last time they attacked. There are only two of us, but we use different magic, can accomplish different things with it. We could even serve as a distraction, or lure them out into the open..."

"I cannot ask you to do this."

"We offered. My people are in as much danger from the renegades as yours, perhaps more," Kevon fumed. "I'd prefer a peaceful resolution, as we tried to work toward, but peace is not always the answer."

"I did not take you for royalty when we first met," the queen curtseyed, or whatever passed for one half immersed in the sea. "I apologize."

"I'm no prince," Kevon protested. "Our interests align. I don't want to get eaten, and I do want my sister back. We can help each other to both of those ends."

"We may, at that," the queen agreed. "I will reserve my judgement on your lineage until later."

* * *

"He did *WHAT*?" Carlo roared.

"Said you could be bait," Rhysabeth-Dane laughed. "I think Brightwing and I will go flying for a while."

"It wasn't..." Kevon started. "Exactly what I said..."

"We'll be in a better position than we were before," Reko's image stood next to Kevon, arms crossed. "The Myrnar can move behind us under their own power, not alerting the other Mystics to their presence until it is too late."

"Who's to say they will even bother with us again?" Carlo grumbled.

"They don't have a choice," Alanna shook her head. "They're hungry."

A wave of realization swept through those assembled, even Reko's illusion-form was visibly uncomfortable.

"They're a threat to any ship that sails these waters," Kevon announced. "We'll do what it takes to stop them. Then the Myrnar will help us get to Alma."

"It sounds simple enough," Carlo shrugged.

"Only it never is." Kevon paused before he opened the door to exit Yusa's cabin. "Wake me when they give the signal."

CHAPTER 12

"**W**here do you suggest we go now?" Anneliese asked, pulling the rough cloak's hood further past her ears.

"The Warrior's Guild," Mirsa whispered, rocking Maisy to keep her quiet. "There are some guardsmen there, but many I believe hold more loyalty to Carlo than Alacrit."

"Let's find someplace near it that you can hide for a time," Anneliese suggested. "You are well known to them, I am not. Perhaps I can make contact and arrange for a quieter welcome?"

"We'd best hurry," Mirsa agreed. "I don't want to be out on the streets after dark."

Mirsa ducked into a shop and began looking at bolts of fabric, asking reasonable questions, but trying not to stand out as she stalled for time. She purchased two yards of medium-grade linen, and let the shopkeeper's daughter fuss over Maisy for a few minutes before Anneliese returned.

"I spoke with one of Marco's students," Anneliese explained as she steered Mirsa through the late afternoon crowd toward the Guildhall. "He will handle everything, we will not be disturbed."

The door opened as the trio neared it, and Mirsa recognized the Adept immediately. "Rex?" she asked.

"Yes, ma'am," he answered, ushering them inside and down an unfamiliar corridor.

"I was saddened to hear about Blademaster Marco," she offered. "I'd only met him a handful of times, but he was always a gentleman."

"Thank you, ma'am. Things haven't been…" Rex cleared his throat, and opened the door to a room. "Quite the same since…"

"I understand. If there is anything we can do, please ask."

"No one's been able to…" Rex shook his head. "You're better off just hiding. Stay here as long as you like, I have two other Adepts I can trust to keep this quiet, and your needs met. No one else will bother you."

"You don't know how much this means to us." After a quick glance, she leaned in and kissed the Warrior on the cheek.

"You and yours have a better chance of fixing what's wrong here than those that have been here all along," Rex shrugged. "Get settled in, I'll be back in a while with food."

"We're not in much better position here than at the Palace, if Alacrit is determined to keep us here," Mirsa sighed after she closed the door behind Rex. "He'll have the gates guarded until dusk, and I'd rather not test the streets after that."

"We had less ground to cover when we arrived," Anneliese agreed. "With suitable weapons, I feel confident against the Reapers. It's the Magi that concern me."

Mirsa paced with Maisy, bouncing the child to keep her fussy cries to a minimum. "If we're stuck here, we should at least get a message to the Dwarves," she decided after depositing her daughter on the lower bunk and wedging the blankets around her.

Rex knocked on the door, and opened it, bringing a small platter of meat, bread, and cheese. "This is what they had handy," he apologized. "Dinner will be ready in a few hours."

"Weapons."

The Adept paused only a moment before nodding to Anneliese, "Any preferences?"

"Soon."

"Yes, ma'am." Rex took a moment longer to scrutinize

the Huntmistress's lithe form. "I'll see what I can find."

"Recurve?" Anneliese asked, peering at the oddly shaped bow.

"You'll like it," Rex assured her. "I did alright with the sword, didn't I?"

"A touch light, but it will do." The Huntmistress rested her hand on the hilt of the scabbarded weapon. "I'll need supplies to rework those arrows, as well."

"I can get some tonight without raising too much suspicion," Rex offered, "but the best thing would be to get them in the market tomorrow."

"Whatever you think is best," Anneliese sighed. "You have done more than we had a right to expect."

"Tomorrow will be fine," Mirsa agreed. "Half the contents of the royal armory wouldn't help us out of here tonight, without a good plan."

"I'll get them to you before noon tomorrow," Rex bowed on his way out of the room.

"So this plan of yours?" Anneliese asked Mirsa, after the Adept had gone. "What will it entail?"

"I'd like to see how Alacrit reacts to our disappearance before deciding that," Mirsa frowned. "A simple escape to the Dwarven Hold via Eastport would be preferable, but predictable."

"If it were not for the little one, we could cut through the forest," Anneliese shrugged. "What we lost in speed, we would gain in directness. We would not have to deal with chance encounters, either."

"We'll keep it in mind," Mirsa mused. "I didn't accompany the rest of you to Kelanoth, but I've had my share of hardship, and difficult travels." She chuckled.

"Something amuses you?"

"With the resources we have at our disposal," the Master

Mage shook her head, "Our best avenue for escape is back inside the palace grounds."

"The underground chamber." Anneliese frowned. "It is something to consider. Untested, but a possibility."

Mirsa's thoughts slid to the chamber, and the rune-work that lined the floor and walls. She concentrated idly, letting her reserves flow into the unfocused spell.

The runes tightened, and drew the additional power they needed from Mirsa. The world spun, and before she could react, she found herself sprawled across the patterned stone of the chamber.

"It's her!"

Mirsa looked up, and saw the Prince's *Eleri* advisor, and two other Magi near the room's entrance. She could feel runes of Fire and Movement form as the advisor's subordinates began chanting. *I should be flattered they are speaking the words to enhance their spells*, she thought. Her hand shifted to support her, and brushed against one of the sigils that circled the stone pattern. The runes snapped to attention in her thoughts and she half shouted, half screamed the words that focused her remaining power enough to complete the spell. "*Raio Pert!*"

Magic from across the room clutched at Mirsa, restraining her and almost choking the tail end of her words to nothingness in the moments before her own workings took effect. The burst of flame crossed half the distance between the attacking Mage and Mirsa's position before her surroundings blurred and shifted.

The transition was easier, but only just. Mirsa's already sprawled form collapsed on the floor of the room in the Warrior's Guild, and Anneliese moved to check on her fallen companion.

"That won't work, after today," Mirsa announced, groaning with exhaustion. "We could use it if we snuck in. I think walking to Eastport would be easier, now."

"You were discovered, then?" Anneliese frowned. "This may work to our advantage. Alacrit will pull more Magi to watch over the room, and weaken his forces elsewhere."

"Discovering the weakness in time to exploit it is another matter altogether," Mirsa sat up and rested her head in her hands. "I fear he will compensate with extra guard patrols if his Magi are spread thin."

"Leave our escape to me," Anneliese offered the weary Mage a hand up, and helped her back to her bunk.

CHAPTER 13

"**W**e've come too far," Carlo grumbled. "I don't like it."

"They should have attacked by now," Kevon agreed. "Most of us haven't slept for the last two days, we'd be hard pressed to hold them off if they did strike now." The Adept's eyelids drooped as he spoke, and Carlo shook his head.

"Take your rest the next shift. I don't believe they would dare an attempt on us at midday."

Kevon glanced across the deck to where Alanna was working with Rhysabeth-Dane, exaggerating attacks in slow motion, and instructing the Rider in responses and counters. Their eyes met for a moment, and she flashed him a smile.

"Now, the same attack, but full speed," Alanna suggested. "Sidestep or parry it, then counter as you see fit."

Rhysabeth-Dane nodded, and stepped back to wait for Alanna's movement to begin. She swung her blade upward, from left to right, almost as if she was drawing it from its sheath, and the dull gray Dwarven metal sparked against the assassin's blade, opening her guard enough for the dwarf's counter-stroke. A flick of her wrist, and Rhysabeth-Dane's blade was arcing back on the attack.

Taking advantage of the angle of the upward stroke, Alanna tucked and rolled under the dwarf's attack as it began shifting downward. Before the attack was fully extended, Alanna was behind the Rider, reaching around to position her knife at her opponent's throat. She leaned in to whisper in Rhysabeth-Dane's ear.

Sturdy fingers closed over Alanna's thumb and forefinger where they grasped the dagger, the rest of the small hand positioned between the blade of the weapon and Rhysabeth-Dane's neck. Before the contact registered in the assassin's mind, the grip tightened and the dwarf's arm swept across her body, extending and twisting with the movement her attack had already begun.

Rhysabeth-Dane stepped forward and rolled her shoulder.

Alanna cried out in confusion as she dropped her weapon and spun over the dwarf's shoulder. The assassin bounced once on the deck before she rolled back to a menacing crouch, another dagger appearing in her hand from a concealed sheath.

"Better," Alanna admitted, straightening up and sheathing her weapon. "You've gotten so much stronger since we started."

"Since I started riding, really," Rhysabeth-Dane corrected, retrieving the fallen dagger and handing it to Alanna, hilt first. "The sword work along with the extra riding has helped things along."

"Kevon surrendered when I used that move on him," Alanna laughed. "He never thought to..." she looked at Rhysabeth-Dane's hand, grasping it as she took the weapon. "You're hurt."

"Small cut from when I grabbed you," the dwarf shrugged. "It'll be fine."

"Please have someone dress it, at least," Alanna peered at the wound a moment before releasing the dwarf's hand. She glanced up to where Carlo watched, and Kevon beckoned. "I... have to go. Keep up the good work."

"They should attack soon, as early as this evening," Kevon told her as she reached the upper deck. "We're under orders to rest until then."

The afternoon was more *and* less restful than Kevon liked. The anticipation of the upcoming conflict, the crushing weight of the sleep he'd denied himself, and Alanna's slumbering warmth beside him kept Kevon balanced a yawn away from needed oblivion.

They approach.

Kevon startled awake at Reko's whispered announcement in his mind. "They're…"

"I see them," Alanna squinted at the corner of the cabin. "Faint, and distant yet, but many more than last time."

Rouse the others, Kevon projected his thoughts through the illusion form to Reko. *We'll meet you on deck shortly.*

After shrugging into his tunic, Kevon stood, arms held out as Alanna buckled on his swordbelt. "If it comes to that, we're probably lost," he grinned.

"If it comes to that, and your sword is in the cabin, you will be lost," Alanna swept her hair back and knotted it into place before outfitting her own armaments. "Besides, you just need to hold them here until our allies arrive." The assassin adjusted her wrist sheaths, and motioned to the door. "Shall we?"

Yusa barked orders from the helm, shaping the controlled chaos that roiled over the decks. Sailors swarmed the rigging, reefing sails. Soldiers secured safety lines to the railing and readied crossbows. Elven hunters clustered on the upper deck, at a watchful rest, bows strung. Unbound griffin swirled overhead, the vortex guided by Rhysabeth-Dane on Brightwing.

"I'll move down on the foredeck, and focus on keeping us upright," Kevon announced, stepping up alongside the captain. "If you stay here in reserve, you can watch for the unexpected, or opportunities to attack in the first moments before reinforcements arrive."

The request prompted a blank stare and shrug from Yusa, but Reko flickered into existence a moment later.

"Too many of them to 'spout up onto the deck, I suppose?"

"Or up to the griffin," Kevon answered. "I'd prefer they didn't get a taste for Myrnar, if possible."

"So we're rolling with the first few waves?" Reko's image flickered, a new affectation that usually indicated discomfort.

"If we calm the sea right away, they may retreat too quickly, difficult for the other Mystics to combat when they arrive," Kevon confirmed. "Focus on locating the renegade Mystics, in case we have to engage them our..."

"They're almost here," Alanna interrupted. "Move."

Kevon was halfway across the lower deck when the first swell hit. *This one started deep*, he thought, *or I'd have felt...*

The crystalline Water magic raked across Kevon's mind as if in response to his unspoken wonderings. "There it is," he laughed aloud, leaning against the sloping deck, sliding toward the starboard rail. The ship began to right itself, and Kevon crouched and leapt the last few feet to the gunnel rail as the deck lurched to port. He wrapped himself around the top rail, and twined a leg around an upright to keep from flopping over before he opened himself to the sea's call below.

The salt tang filled Kevon's mouth as he took in the power. The icy cool of the northern ocean coursed through his veins, threatened to fill his lungs with its vast insistence.

The ship listed further to port, threatening to capsize in moments if nothing was done to prevent it.

No. Kevon drew a small bank of water up to cradle the far side of the vessel, arresting its tilt and beginning to right it. He could feel the rapid withdrawal and recrystallization of the rogue Mystic assault, a swell building to starboard, rising twice as high as the ship's main deck, advancing to sweep them from their places into the rough sea. He raised his eyes to peer over the rail, nearly straight up into the sky, where dozens of griffin circled. *No.*

Kevon felt the rhythm, the movement of the wave, and used its own energy to shape it into something that would not result in their destruction. The wave crested, nearly doubling over on itself, and crashed back down into the sea, striking a glancing blow along the side of the ship, tipping it into the wall of water Kevon still cupped against the other side of the vessel.

Subtle.

Reko's recent mastery of sarcasm amused and frustrated Kevon, who still struggled to hang onto the railing. He reached for his safety line, but Alanna was already securing it. He closed his eyes, and dove deeper into the magical battlefield that surrounded them.

Abandoning his mortal senses, Kevon *became* the surrounding sea. He could feel the trailing Myrnar forces, the inbound reinforcements, swimming at top speed without the aid of any magic, about a minute away from the ship's position. They sculled and slid through the currents in formation, with steadfast purpose.

The renegade forces were further away yet, but would be upon the vessel in a third of the time. Constructed currents sliced through the sea, carrying knots of Mystics and their allies through the sea at impossible speeds. The restrained Water magic formations writhed and clawed their way forward as if the currents themselves were starving predators.

Kevon blunted the next attacking wave with as little interference as he could manage, still not wanting to alert the enemy to their true strength before their own people arrived to impose final judgement. He slipped and slammed into the railing as the ship began to right itself from the last lurch to starboard. His head banged against one of the uprights, and his concentration faltered. His connection to the sea slipped from his grasp, and blood dripped from a cut over his left eye.

Enough. Reko's voice cut through roar of the growing maelstrom that surrounded the ship. *We hold here.*

The sea's power danced before Kevon's aching head, draining away as he reached for it. He was unsure if the boat was as unsteady as it seemed, or if his injury was making it worse, but he kept reaching for the suddenly elusive energy, and failing.

Runes formed nearby, and Kevon could feel the power that Reko used, currents that the Mystics could not track pounded them as they neared the surface, disrupting their attacks for a moment.

The Mage focused on his friend's thought forms, ignoring the throbbing, stinging distraction that threatened to engulf his entire head. He poured his own energy into the spell, until his connection with the sea reasserted itself. He broke off contact with Reko, and turned all of his attention to the surrounding water.

The influx of power brushed aside his discomfort, and filled him to overflowing. Two measured breaths, and the surface of the sea for hundreds of yards in each direction contorted, calmed, and settled to a mirror smoothness.

Trusting Reko to handle the renegade Mystics, Kevon turned his attention to the column advancing from the north. He focused on the section of sea that his Myrnar allies sped through. Deep in the grasp of the Water magic, he channeled the sympathetic magic surrounding him into a spell that pulled the entirety of the Myrnar ambush force toward the ship at better than twice their previous speed.

Within the space of two breaths, the Myrnar Queen's Mystics began their portion of the offensive. As Kevon felt the new magic crystallizing, he ended his spells that controlled the surrounding seas, and focused his senses on the theater of battle below.

Whorls of constrained energy sluiced about, writhing and striking like a burlap sack full of adders. The lead formation of the newcomers boasted two Mystics, and three other myrnar. It struck out first, sliding through the nearest knot of renegades, leaving still forms sinking into the depths, and the taste of blood in Kevon's mouth.

"It begins," Alanna confirmed.

Kevon nodded in acknowledgement, but was lost in the

increasing complexity of the battle.

Aside from the group which Kevon assumed contained the princess's consort, no Mystics accompanied the Myrnar warriors in their attack formations. Where renegades clustered in ragtag mobs of a dozen or so each, one Mystic per group, the royal forces operated in smaller squads of half the size. Twenty or more of the six myrnar teams cut through the water, each guided by a Mystic further removed from combat, flanked by more soldiers. The Mystics guiding the battle formed a hemisphere in front of another cluster of myrnar, and at their center, Kevon assumed, the queen.

Two more of the groups of renegades were dispatched within the first minute of the renewed conflict. Already far less organized than Kevon's allies, the renegade forces broke and began retreating deeper to the south. The granular Water magic from the formation of Mystics surrounding the princess spiked, and two of the smaller formations converged on each of the four fleeing pods of mer-folk. Traces of the renegade Mystics' magic winked from Kevon's awareness before the pursuers broke off to allow the remaining survivors to escape without the aid of magic.

That was too easy, Kevon thought, as he labored to shove aside the connection to the waters below. His awareness unlinked from the sea, and the world was tiny again. A feeling of insignificance swept over him as the ship's normal movement resumed.

"It's over." Alanna stood and released the knot that secured her to the railing. "We should tend to the wounded."

"Wounded?" Kevon scanned the deck, and spotted a sailor tethered to the mast writhing in pain, unable to stand. "Oh."

"There are more below," she retorted, dropping the end of her safety line and sprinting for the doorway that led down to the lower cabins. "Some of the crew got knocked arund worse than you."

His own safety line released, Kevon managed three

steps toward the wounded sailor before his body acknowledged the magnitude of the exertion the magic had required.
His senses faded as he stumbled to his knees, and he was unconscious before his head *thunked* into the deck.

CHAPTER 14

"**P**erhaps tomorrow."

"No break in the numbers of the Dark Magi?" Mirsa asked as Anneliese stowed her weapons by the bunk.

"A number of them lie broken," the Huntmistress shrugged. "More gather."

"The daytime guard patrols have been more than doubled," Mirsa sighed. "It's only a matter of time before we're discovered here. I'd hate to cause trouble for our supporters."

"Surrender is an option," Anneliese's nose wrinkled as she spoke the words. "Our welcome is bound to be less cordial than last time, but I doubt we'd be killed on sight."

"We'll hold here a few more days before giving up," Mirsa decided. "Our allies may yet manage something."

"If nothing else, you might be able to slip out in the armory wagon compartment they described, and I can smuggle Maisy out the following evening."

"I won't be separated from her," Mirsa shook her head.

"I had to suggest..."

A quiet knock interrupted Anneliese's explanation.

"Yes?" Mirsa called through the closed door, as Anneliese readied her sword.

"Ladies?" Rex opened the door a crack. "We've arranged something."

"You're sure they will cooperate?" Mirsa asked, peering

at the handful of farmerfolk that crowded around a table near the fireplace in the common area of the Guildhall.

"We've more than paid for the cost of their cargo, and are only taking a small portion of it," Rex explained. "A wagonload of alfalfa headed for Eastport. We've offloaded bundles for use in our stables here, and have restacked the load around a tent large enough for the three of you."

"Perfect!" Mirsa exclaimed.

"Far from it," Rex countered. "The tent had to be small to begin with, to allow the bundles of fodder to cover it properly. The lumber that was added to reinforce it was more than expected. You will fit, you'll not be comfortable."

"Anything that gets us out of the city without more bloodshed," Anneliese shrugged, "Is desirable."

"You'll load before first light, only hours from now. I'll wake you myself before then."

The polished orc-tusk dice tumbled onto the brightly embroidered leather mat, with hushed clicks against their fellows and the worn play surface as they settled to rest.

"Three boots," Alacrit announced, moving the carved green figure the remaining spaces to the castle at the end of the path.

"Naturally," Torit frowned, then turned to observe the page that approached from the far end of the chamber.

The messenger circled around and approached Alacrit with a fearful expression. He attempted to close to within whispering distance, but the prince waved him back. "You have no news the Ambassador should not hear."

"Very well, sire," the page nodded. "One of the gambits has produced results. Your guests will be returned to the palace before breakfast is served."

"Excellent news, to be assured," Alacrit chuckled. "It means I have lost a wager to my friend here, but that is a small matter."

"You'll be retiring, then?" Torit slid his chair away from the table and prepared to stand.

"If you tire of losing," Alacrit grinned. "I could stand another round."

"I have no great love of sleep," Torit shrugged, leaning forward to rearrange the tokens on the board. "Preference of champion?"

The prince's eyebrow arched. "I favor the brigand."

"I'm sorry we're so cramped in here," Mirsa whispered as the wagon lumbered down the street. "You didn't even have space to keep any of your weapons with you."

"Ahh…"

A chill ran up Mirsa's spine as she detected a hint of *something* in the elf's voice over the muffled street noise. "That's not the reason?"

"Forgive me," Anneliese's discomfort was evident in the twinkles of sunlight that poked through the stacked bundles of wheat as the cart jostled over cobblestone. "I couldn't risk a battle if we were found escaping. Killing Dark Magi is one thing, the prince's men is quite another."

Maisy coughed and began to fuss, and Mirsa clutched her closer, adjusting the cloth that covered the infant's mouth and nose. She shushed and rocked as much as she could manage in the tight space that the beams around them kept from filling with the bundled sheaves of grain.

"So you…"

"The farmerfolk were nervous," Anneliese whispered. "I'm guessing we're to be delivered to Alacrit."

Mirsa could feel the Huntmistress's hand brushing a stray stalk of wheat from the side of Maisy's head.

"It's where we need to be, for now." A momentary gap in the shifting cargo illuminated the elf's face, showing a recent affectation – a mischievous nose scrunch. "If these clods try anything but that, they've made a huge mistake."

The wagon turned, and Mirsa could feel the pressure shift as they started up the slight incline to the Palace, rather than the eventual descent that led to the East gate.

"Remember," Anneliese continued, "Surprised. Indignant. Anything but violent. We'll get through this."

Real emotion fueled Mirsa's measured hysteria. Paired with Anneliese's restrained aggression, the two managed to negotiate a full refund from the farmerfolk, after being 'discovered' and forced from their hiding place. Allowing that to calm them further, they found themselves escorted from the palace courtyard to the Great Hall by less than a dozen men.

A flick of the elf's eyebrow as they rounded the last corner managed to calm Mirsa's jangled nerves a bit, but only just.

I'd imagine she wants to handle this, Mirsa thought as they were brought before Alacrit and his advisors, Torit closest among them. She cradled Maisy tighter, and clenched her jaw in defiance.

Anneliese stepped forward, her timeless Elven features conveying an air of stern displeasure. "What right have you to hold us?" the Huntmistress asked Alacrit, in a calm, measured tone.

"What claims do I need to make?" the prince stood, smiling. "Here, in *my city*, in the heart of the lands I rule?"

"You court war, Highness," Anneliese responded. "This war may be avoided. It should be avoided, for the one that follows cannot."

"According to you?" the monarch sneered. "Forgive me if I have reservations about your judgement. Fanciful stories you've peddled since you last arrived..."

"Orclords and flying demons were *fanciful stories* not so

long ago," Mirsa reminded Alacrit, who paused at their mention. "Perhaps ours is the counsel you should heed."

"Companions of the *heretic!*" Alicrit's Mage advisor spat, not hiding his contempt.

"I…" Alacrit's voice wavered. "No. None of these things would have happened if not for his heresy. You speak of outside forces that only few even claim to have seen, and expect our full faith and support?"

"If you're not going to help us, we'll be on our way." Anneliese turned to Mirsa and gestured back the way they had come.

Guards shifted to cover the exit without prompting.

"What do you hope to accomplish by holding us?" Mirsa asked. "We were sent to gather aid, not your ire. If Kevon has lost your support, the loss of three more is meaningless."

"So is it war, or apathy?" Alacrit mused. "What will the heretic bring to my door when he hears of this?"

"I was not speaking of Kevon," Anneliese whispered.

Clearing his throat, Torit stepped between Alacrit and the Huntmistress. "I believe you were going to invite the ladies to breakfast."

"It would be the polite thing to do," Alacrit sighed. "I…"

"Yes, it would," the ambassador agreed. "Lady Anneliese, would you be so kind as to make sure no harm befalls these gentlemen, who will escort you to the dining hall?"

"I will behave, though I dare not speak for my companions."

"You cannot appreciate my position," Alacrit frowned, dabbing at the corner of his mouth with his napkin, and pushed his plate away. "None of you."

"I am as close to a neutral party in this as there may be," Torit volunteered. "Ours is a recent friendship, but I have come to understand much about you. I also know Lady Anneliese, and have been fond of her since before you were born. Further, the way we are all behaving will not last, will not end peacefully."

"We will stay." Anneliese turned to look Alacrit in the eye. "Your men will return my weapons. I will be allowed to wear them at all times. We will not be escorted about like prisoners. These are our conditions, but we will stay."

"Give your weapons...?" Alacrit sputtered. "As if we..."

"As a gesture of respect, nothing more," Anneliese clarified. "I..."

"She could take the weapons of any man here, with ease," Torit explained. "She defeated the scourge of the Highplain, Talmurn, before this castle was built. Before she came into her true power as a Huntmistress. The winds of Death blew through the ranks of the Griffinsworn, and she stilled them. The walls of this castle, of this city, could not contain her if she did not wish to stay. I suggest you do as she asks."

"That is not..."

"My place to say?" Torit interrupted Anneliese. "No matter what any of us believe, no one would be served by an escalation of the conflict in this room. Not Alacrit, his throne, his Order. Not Kevon. Not our people. Can we at least agree on that?"

"I concede that a life at court has not left you completely addled," Anneliese allowed a hint of a smile to creep onto her face.

"Sire?" Torit turned to look at Alacrit.

"Allow the greatest threat that has graced these halls to wander about them unhindered, fully armed?" the prince frowned.

"Unhindered. Fully armed. Thinking pleasant thoughts. Yes." Torit's voice wavered, a break from his usual calm.

"I..." Alacrit's eyes danced about the room, as if searching for an excuse to deny the request. They settled on Anneliese, and their gazes locked. "Very well. But we still have much to discuss."

"*That's why we came, now isn't it?*" Mirsa muttered under her breath, sliding a cut square of griddle cake through the leftover yolk of her last egg with her wooden fork. Maisy fussed, reaching over the plate, hand grasping, clenching, and unclenching.

Alacrit leaned to listen to whispered counsel from his *Eleri* advisor before amending, "The south gardens are of course, forbidden."

CHAPTER 15

"**A**t last, he wakes."

Kevon sat upright in his bunk, clutching at the rough blanket that slid as he moved. "Majesty," he mumbled, and reached for the pounding in his head that threatened to relieve him of consciousness once more. "You needn't have…"

The Myrnar Queen pressed her hand into the blanket that covered her lower half, and rivulets of water streamed through her fingers to drip and pool on the floor. "After all you have done, this is but a minor inconvenience."

"There is more that we need to ask of you," Kevon groaned, reaching for his folded clothes on the bedside table.

"As is your due," the queen pressed. "Kevon, if not for your assistance, we might not have engaged the renegades as swiftly as we did. They might have sensed our approach, and prepared. Losses on both sides could have been far greater."

"Esinane has already made arrangements."

Kevon startled at Alanna's voice, and turned to see her leaned against the wall behind him. "Esinane?" he asked.

"In your tongue, it means 'coral heart'." the queen answered. "My sister was Phulamda, the 'moon hyacinth'. She should have been here, in my place."

"What arrangements?" Kevon pinched the bridge of his nose to distract from the growing ache behind his eyes.

"We should be nearing the Black Isle in mere hours. Three of our best scholars have arrived, and work now with the Sky Delver," Esinane explained. "They should be finished with their translation before we return with your sister. In addition, the Court Mystics who are not on their way to us prepare the palace for our arrival."

"Send for Carlo and Yusa, will you?" Kevon asked, turning to Alanna. "We have a more immediate arrival to prepare for."

◆ ◆ ◆

"I think we should accompany you," Reko's fist pounded the table, startling even Yusa.

"You make more sense staying with the ship this time," Kevon argued. "Yusa can maintain order even as you assist the Mystics with whatever defenses are needed."

"A dozen men is not nearly enough!" The Mage's form blurred as his voice rose. "There are many times more Obsidian Reapers on the isle than you faced on the beach. You will need your full strength."

"Eight Hunters have volunteered," the Elven commander announced. "They will not remain on the ship."

"We don't know what extra surprises they will bring to bear on us once we begin our attack," Carlo rumbled. "It would not be prudent to extend our full strength into the unknown, but the elves will be welcomed."

"It remains unknown," Alanna grimaced. "Though still an hour or more distant, the tower blocks my sight as nothing I have yet seen."

"That may change as we approach," Kevon shrugged. "Having you with us is not negotiable. Bertus, Carlo, and I will round out the incursion force. The rest of the soldiers accompanying us will hold the base of the tower, guard our escape."

"I will ask for volunteers to stay with your men," Esinane offered, "to aid, and signal the retreat."

"The men will be honored to fight alongside them," Carlo bowed to the Myrnar Queen. "We should make preparations."

◆ ◆ ◆

Kevon stepped from the dinghy onto the black sands of the island. A score of Reapers lined the ridge ahead, scuttling over the crest and back beyond it, fearful of the waves that had taken a great number of them out into the depths. Their clicks and screeches set his nerves on edge from even this distance.

"If they don't know we've arrived, they will soon." Carlo shoved the craft back toward the ship with his boot. He turned and readied his crossbow. "We need to get to the tower."

Reaching for the power that lapped at his feet, Kevon used the sea's magic to send the transport and its two remaining occupants scudding over the waves back toward the ship. He pushed the energy aside to a manageable intensity, without fully releasing it, and pivoted to face the advancing line of darkness. Crystalline Water magic tickled his senses, and he could feel the waters behind him swelling.

"The Mystics are here!" Kevon called to the troops scattered around them. "Form up."

The power spiked, and Kevon heard the trills and hisses of the Myrnar forces as they surfaced. He stepped up alongside Carlo and grinned. "Hold on." Alanna's fingers curled into his as the wave swept them up toward the waiting demons.

Carlo yelped and fired, his bolt smashing into a Reaper's eye as the group sped above and past the charging monstrosities, buoyed on a squishy cushion of water and magic. The shape of the wave shifted, the outer edges surging forward and down. Myrnar warriors with spears leapt from the safety of the hurtling mountain of water to skewer leapers and reapers that came too close to the core of soldiers and Elven hunters resting in the calm trough of the wave.

The wave lurched, the magic behind it faltering. Kevon swore, and brought his own power to bear on the group, fumbling with the complexity of the spell he sought to work. He felt the restrained Water magic shift to compensate, and saw the Mystics move higher behind them, near the wave's crest.

"Be ready, lad!" Carlo shouted over the roar of the wave, as the tower ahead rushed toward them.

Still connected to the magic, Kevon fired jets of water from the crest of the wave toward three large imp-like creatures that had flown up out of reach. Two struck true, stunning the flying demons, sending them tumbling to be swept up with the rest of the creatures of darkness that lay before them.

The chaos at the base of the tower came into focus as they drew nearer. Scores of the darkly gleaming reapers rushed toward the tower, while similar amounts fled the wave's approach. Hordes of leapers and leaper knights milled and hopped about with the flow of the larger reapers, crowding the walkways that led up to the dark stone plateau where the tower sat.

Bring a dozen men, Kevon thought, drawing as much power as he dared from the wave, and through its connection, the sea miles beyond. *Great plan. Reko will never let me hear the end of this.* The Mystics' spell faltered again.

The runes flared brighter in Kevon's mind, as he closed his eyes to concentrate. Behind the company of soldiers, an oval window opened in the wave. Kevon shifted the mass of the water from behind to above and below, in preparation for their impending stop. The strange magic the Mystics wielded shifted to compensate, and Kevon reopened his eyes.

"It's time." Alanna's whisper cut through the maelstrom as she gave his hand a quick squeeze and released it, reaching for her weapons.

Trusting his allies to handle the landing arrangements, Kevon readied Water magic attacks for the waiting throng. Half of the volume of water they rode on separated and slammed against a cluster of Reapers, knocking them off the edge of the tower's escarpment. The remaining liquid buckled beneath them, lurching upward to arrest their momentum before splashing down on the freshly cleared area, devoid of the magic that had conveyed them so far.

Kevon pitched forward, at just the wrong angle. He shifted his weight further, and turned his right shoulder. As he hit the ground, he looked up to see an iron-shod boot hurtling toward him, worn by a rattled soldier.

This should make things more difficult, Kevon thought, and closed his eyes, bracing for impact.

The chaos intensified. Kevon tumbled over and the momentum carried him back to his feet. The soldier behind him dodged between Kevon and Alanna, drawing steel and squaring off against a leaper knight a few paces beyond.

The kick the soldier leveled against the grotesque beast served to check the man's forward motion, and send his foe tumbling off the ledge to fall several dozen feet to the shattered obsidian landscape below.

"Form up!" Carlo bellowed, handing his crossbow off to a junior officer. He fixed his shield and drew his blade. "Secure the entrance!"

Still awash in Water magic, Kevon threw blasts of the puddling liquid at several nearby enemies. A small wave off-balanced one reaper, and it stumbled into the swung scythe of its neighbor. Another splash of water in the face of an orc distracted it enough to give the fighters who had spread to the outside perimeter the opportunity for a finishing stroke. As the borrowed magic dried up, Kevon felt more of the workings of the Mystics behind him, by the base of the tower.

"Move!" Alanna sidestepped and kicked a leaper out of the air before it could tumble into Kevon.

As Kevon turned toward their destination, he could see the scope of the magic the sea-folk wrought. A misshapen globe of water squatted on the entrance to the tower, swarming with myrnar bristling with weapons. Four Mystics held station two thirds of the way up the bulging sphere, backed against the tower wall. Two Myrnar soldiers with long pikes flanked them, jabbing with impossible speed at anything that came near. The balance of the merfolk warriors lined the edges of the construct, hacking and thrusting at the swarming creatures of darkness.

This wasn't the plan, Kevon thought, joining the measured dash for the tower, his mind racing far faster than his feet. *Four were to return to the sea, two remain here to...*

Kevon realized what had happened as the waters ahead parted to admit them to the doorway beyond. *There are only four left. The enemy is much stronger than we suspected. They're all staying.*

Alanna and Bertus had breached the simple wooden door by the time Kevon and Carlo made it through the tunnel. Carlo turned to address the remaining three soldiers that followed close behind. "Hold here! Pray for reinforcements," he added as he followed the others into darkness.

CHAPTER 16

Kevon reached into a pouch and withdrew the Light globe, infusing it with power. Shafts of brilliance erupted from the charm, spearing between the gaps in his grasping fingers. Bertus and Carlo raised hands and shield to protect their eyes, while Alanna strode forward, not even acknowledging the dazzling sphere.

"There is no one left on this floor, she commented, angling for the staircase on a far wall. "I'd still avoid *those*."

Kevon twisted his wrist to shine more light in the direction Alanna gestured, and the beam dimmed, cloudy tendrils snaking back up the shaft as it hit the sculpted stone alcove. He played the light across different areas of the room, directing the fitful illumination over half a dozen of the depressions that surrounded the darkened room. He pressed out with his senses, and recoiled as his suspicions were confirmed. Much like the portal arch that had been below Gurlin's tower, these Enchanted areas could open gates to the Dark realm, but it seemed they would act like his Light sphere, powered at will by a very small amount of energy. He focused his will on the sphere, determined not to let his mind wander and be used by the foul enchantments that lay all around. He wondered what Alanna's advanced sight had shown her about the gate enchantments, if she felt even a fraction of the disgust he did at their vileness.

"Quickly," Carlo followed close on Alanna's heels, eyes darting to each new shadow thrown by Kevon's light. "The others are counting on us."

Kevon moved in behind Carlo, shifting out to the side so

that the light shone in front of Alanna. Bertus followed, his ancient sword drawn, manner far more calm than Kevon could manage.

"Torches," Alanna motioned with a tilt of her head toward the sconce at the top of the stairs.

"Be ready." Kevon lit the torch with a small burst of power, and shoved the Light orb back in his pouch. The subdued flame diluted the darkness. The dull black walls of the hallway were only just visible, but did not dim further from shadows thrown by the passing of Kevon and his friends.

The hallway opened up, and Kevon lit the two torches that flanked the opening.

"Oh." Alanna moved off of the groove she'd stepped onto, back toward the lit torch on the left.

"Blood?" Bertus asked after crouching and touching the tacky substance in the shallow carved trough. "Eww. Not normal blood."

Kevon started to step over the muck-filled depression, but noticed the curve and twist of the carved channel, and recoiled. He reached back into his pouch to grasp the Light orb, and focused on its stabilizing rune to force out the image of the Dark rune that threatened to manifest itself against his will. "I have to go around," he whispered.

"What kind of unholy..." Bertus wondered aloud as he realized what Kevon had meant.

"Let's hope we never find out. We should search these rooms, anyway, right, Alanna?"

"Bedrooms, empty, from what little I can see."

"More stairs, then," Carlo gruffed. "Hurry around, then."

"Who lit the?" The creak of the door opening registered in Kevon's mind just as the unfamiliar voice began to speak. "Intruders!"

The call rang hollow on the oppressing walls, and a clattering ensued from above.

"You'll never..." The Dark Mage's words cut short as Alanna's thrown knife *thunked* hilt-deep into his chest.

"You'll never, either," Alanna retorted as she leapt over to the falling body to wrench the blade free. "But I think this is where things get bad."

Kevon sprinted around the perimeter of the corrupted rune, gathering as much focus as he could from the orb as he withdrew it from his pouch. "Hah!" he shouted, pulsing a bright beam from the orb straight at the upper eye of the reaper that charged down the stairs at Carlo.

The beast faltered, and the Blademaster blocked its clumsy attack with his shield. He swung the shield wide, at the same time he whipped his sword in an underhanded arc, severing its other scythe-arm at its elbow joint. Before the reaper could recover, Carlo spun around, leveling the shield into an attack that cracked the monster's carapace and knocked it backward on the rough ebony steps.

Bertus leapt past Carlo, pinning the reaper's remaining arm with his boot, and plunged his Dwarven blade into the beast's shrieking maw. He leaned on the sword, and levered it from left to right before pulling it free of the quivering carcass. "I thought you said these were tough," he teased as he wiped the blood off his sword in the creature's leathery underarm.

"Mmm," Carlo grunted, stepping over the remains. "That one might have been house-trained."

The team dispatched two leapers and a leaper knight before they reached the top of the staircase. Kevon could feel the Dark sigil behind them pulsing with hunger. Gut-wrenching magic ebbed and flowed in time with the symbol's magical heartbeat in his mind, distortions that could only be portals began taking shape somewhere above them.

"No!" Kevon screamed. "We have to reach them!" He shone the focused beam from the Light orb down the narrow hallway, and illuminated the writhing mass of leapers that roiled their way.

Reinforcements, not escape routes, Kevon thought, shifting his focus to the Fire rune that formed of its own accord in his mind. *Small comfort.* He stepped ahead of the others, waited until the wave of creatures was within range, and unleashed the power he'd accumulated for this purpose. "*Phes movra,*" he intoned, and the rune in his mind glazed over with a sparkling ruby sheen, snapping into crisp clarity. The power slid through the focusing symbol with ease, manifesting in a swirling cone of fire that spread from his hand to smash against the middle half of the front of advancing leapers. He chanted louder, and the wide end of his fiery whirlwind sloshed back and forth across the panicked mass of demons. He fed all the anger and frustration he'd felt since Alma's abduction into the spell, and his eyesight blurred as the power of the spell grew. Charred leapers *thudded* to the floor before him, as injured ones deeper in the ranks squealed and tried to flee. Kevon stepped over the fallen beasts, drawing ambient Fire magic from their corpses and the glowing obsidian walls to maintain the faltering stream of flame. The walls frosted and cracks spread like delicate spiderwebs as he advanced, hurling the last of his power in a wide burst at the broken attack force before him.

Kevon choked on the smoke that rose off the still forms all around him, and held the Light orb aloft as the glow from the flames subsided. He drew his sword, reversed his grip, and drove the blade through the neck of one of the leapers who tried to crawl back to its fellows. The beast twitched and was still. Kevon braced his right foot on its shoulder, and pried the blade loose with a grunt. "Let's go."

Bertus and Carlo slid past Kevon, dispatching a handful of the incapacitated leapers as they went.

"There," Alanna said, pointing at a closed door on the left side of the hallway ahead.

Carlo kicked at the door, and it buckled, but did not give. Bertus stepped in beside him, and the two struck in unison, tearing the door free from the jamb, sending it whirling across the small room beyond.

"Thank you for rescuing us!" one of the two young men in the room stepped toward Carlo.

"The horrors they..." the slender brunette woman choked on the words as she staggered, steadying herself on a high-backed chair.

"There, there," Carlo dropped his shield, and held out a hand to the sobbing girl. "The door locks on the inside, the discarded robes..." the Blademaster motioned to the pile of crumpled black fabric in the corner. "We're Warriors, not idiots."

Bertus flicked the tip of his blade up and across, slicing the nearest Mage between the earlobe and jaw nearly to the tip of his nose. The stricken Mage convulsed as he fell, and was still.

"The light is fading," the other Mage warned from behind his fallen brother. "Only those who embrace the Dark will survive."

"We'll take our chances," Carlo snorted, advancing past the motionless body, sword at the ready. "Where is the real prisoner?"

"You'll never make it to her," the woman laughed, snatching up a gnarled staff from behind the table where she stood. She took two steps back and a portal opened between her and Bertus.

A familiar keening, a leathery rustling, and a cloud of taloned fury burst into the low torchlight. Bertus slashed with his sword, three, five, seven times. Half a dozen imps lay dead or dying on the ground around the snarling Adept, but another dozen circled the room, poisoned claws glinting in the wavering light.

Kevon stepped through the doorway and threw the Light globe across the room, where it shattered on the stone wall. The stored Light enchantment fractured, releasing its layered energy all at once. The flood of power disintegrated the imps nearest to it, and weakened the Dark portal enough that it collapsed in on itself.

Blinded by the flash, Carlo stopped, standing perfectly still.

"Keldra will sacrifice the..." the Mage's boast was cut short when Carlo's sword pierced his ribcage.

Opening his eyes, Kevon lunged and slashed the two remaining imps out of the air.

"She's still alive, here, and we need to speak to a guy named Keldra." Carlo pulled his sword free of the Mage and rubbed at his eyes. "Anything else we should know?"

The remaining Dark Mage grimaced, and dropped through the floor. The small Dark portal she'd escaped through closed with the barest whisper of sound.

"Well." Bertus wiped his blade on the bedsheet of the nearest bunk, and surveyed the contents of the room. "That was something."

"I have a feeling we'll see her again," Kevon agreed. He snatched up one of the smaller volumes that rested on the table, ignoring the large tomes that had runes inscribed on the leather covers. He slid the thin text inside his tunic, and turned toward the door. "Let's keep going."

Alanna winced as she fished a knife out of a reaper's still twitching maw. She glared at the others as they returned to the hallway. "There's two more in that one," she groaned, pointing to the still form slumped against the wall further down the passageway. "A little help?"

Kevon and Carlo moved past the fallen reaper, peering ahead into the gloom. Bertus sighed and retrieved Alanna's knives, handing the gore-stained blades to her as she made her way over the charred carpet of leaper corpses.

"I am really ready for today to be over," she whispered as she slid the blades across the thigh of her breeches, and sheathed them at her wrists.

Carlo kicked open another door, a small alchemy lab that was not in use. Kevon slipped in and scanned the room, but could not identify anything that would be of immediate use. He shook his head at the Blademaster, and ducked back out into the hallway to follow Alanna and Bertus up the next curling stairwell.

"I'm guessing Keldra is up there," Kevon pointed to the top of the spiral staircase that twisted around the dark stone column in the center of the room.

"These are worse than the ones below," Alanna murmured, gesturing to the darkened archways carved into the walls of the chamber.

They are portals, too? Kevon wondered at the larger indentations, unable to feel their magical potential because of his connection to the sword.

"Nothing coming out of them yet," Carlo grunted, pushing past Kevon for the stairway. "That could change. Hurry up."

"They're almost here!" a familiar female voice complained, cut off by a deeper masculine laugh.

Kevon pressed his finger to his lips as they neared the top of the spiral.

"I can flood the chamber below, but the *mess...*"

"They've killed *everyone!* We must flee!"

Peering around the central column, Kevon recognized the escaped Mage from the chamber below.

"Nonsense. I have only to summon... Lilion?"

"Should have listened to her," Kevon chided as he stepped into view. Lilion's shuddering form crumpled to the floor, skewered by one of Alanna's thrown knives.

"I don't listen, I command." The Dark Mage flung a crooked finger in Kevon's direction. "Get them."

Two of the largest reapers Kevon had seen stepped out of the shadows, between Keldra and the invaders. They turned toward Kevon, scythe arms waving in a hypnotic fashion as they began their slow advance, central mouths chattering.

"Someone needs to stop that guy," Bertus called out, squaring off against the Dark portal opening behind them.

"Fine," Kevon agreed. "You've got the portal, these two handle the reapers, I'll kill the Mage. Did Yusa say what was for lunch?" He dodged behind a column, out of view of the approaching nightmares, smiling at Alanna's glare.

"Just hurry," the assassin huffed, drawing a short sword that she rarely used, after flinging half a dozen smaller daggers at the onyx behemoths, to little effect.

Kevon leapt from the cover of one column to the next as the reapers passed by, too engaged with Alanna and Carlo to bother pursuing. He shot a last glance at Bertus, who slashed at a young bull orc, and kicked it back through the portal it had barely emerged from. Scanning the shadows for other dangers, he ran headlong for the door Keldra had disappeared through.

"Stop right there!" Keldra shouted, holding a carved ivory dagger left-handed in a reverse grip, the point aimed at Alma's neck. "She comes with me, or she dies." He fumbled in a cloak pocket for a brass key, and stepped around to the other side of Kevon's sister's limp form, poking the key at the matching lock on the gleaming shackle that bound her to the wall.

"You can't make it over here, kill both of us, *and* save her," Keldra sneered, gesturing to Martin, who had risen from his chair and moved to awaken Alma.

"No," Kevon let his brandished sword droop, closed his eyes, and tried to blink away the glowing brilliance that cascaded into his mind's eye. "I can't."

He felt the cool steel of the weapon's hilt through the dampened lattice of wrapped leather that enhanced the grip, but the sigils persisted, glowing white and azure against his murky field of concentration. The symbols for Light and Wind burned with impossible clarity across Kevon's soul, and as he focused on each in turn, he caught a glimpse of their authors. Fleeting images of the exceedingly feminine M'lani, and the avian changeling M'phes whispered across his consciousness, and Kevon started to see the power and simplicity of the gifts he'd been entrusted with.

"There must be some arrangement..." he began, stalling in hopes that every moment would bring another sliver of magic he could shape with the new foci he grasped. He lowered the sword further, trying to put his adversaries at ease, but taking care not to break contact with the Enchanted steel.

"There will be no..." Keldron spat, turning the key, releasing one of the restraints that bound Alma. He coughed, and a look of horror washed over his face.

Kevon grunted with the effort, shoving every bit of willpower he could through the Wind rune, stifling the air in Keldron's mouth and nose, doing his best to suffocate the Mage before the trickle of power ran out.

The choking Mage dropped the knife and key he held, lunging for the staff leaning against the wall nearby. With a stuttering flourish, he twirled the staff, pointed it off to the side, and staggered through the resulting portal.

Martin's eyes flickered to Kevon, to the portal, and back to Alma. He let Alma's hand fall, and lurched around her toward his last avenue of escape.

Alma's foot shot out, and Martin stumbled to the floor only half the distance to the dwindling tear in reality.

"Don't! I..." Martin curled in on himself as the portal closed, leaving him stranded. Shuddering, he startled at the sounds of movement near him, and peered up at an approaching Kevon. "Wait!"

"No time." Kevon's boot lashed out and knocked the traitor unconscious.

CHAPTER 17

"The Dwarves are behind Kevon, and only two have even met him," Mirsa countered. "They're not known for making rash decisions."

Alacrit studied the dice, and moved his green figure ahead the one space to where her blue piece stood. "You completely dismiss the possibility that outside forces are interfering?"

Mirsa peered at Alacrit's roll, did the math in her head, and nodded as he moved her figure backward two spaces, just one move away from the pursuing Dragon piece.

"While the two of you quarrel, you lose sight of all else," Torit advised, rolling the three dice he selected from his collection. "Pitched a shoe," he lamented as he returned the white horse die to the stable area of the board, advanced his brown Warrior token a single space, and took two gold markers from the central pile.

"Our enemies would prefer we fought," he continued, rolling the red Dragon die that sat in front of him. "Because it makes us more vulnerable to them. All our effort attacking each other mean less defense against the true threat." Torit moved the Dragon forward to Mirsa's space, and pointed to the breath symbol on the upward face. He looked at the shields remaining in each of the other play areas, and smiled. "It defeats you both. Had you chosen to move further and not attack, your Highness, you may have overtaken me."

Alacrit frowned as Torit rolled his dice and the Dragon die the remaining three times it took to escape to the fortress at the end of the board, and sighed. "Life is more complex than a game, my Elven friend."

"Yet much can be learned from each to be used in the other," Torit argued. "Balancing risk and reward. Perspective. The strength of alliances... Common courtesy." He watched for the Prince's expression, tight-lipped.

"Reset the board."

◆ ◆ ◆

"I am not required to tell you anything."

"I am the only living being allowed to bear steel in the Prince's presence besides his personal guard," Anneliese shrugged. "Along with Torit, I represent the greatest potential allies this Realm can possibly court. Your faction is small and weak. There is little I could learn from you that I had not forgotten before you were born."

"You spoke to the ambassador about others meeting with..." Arucan motioned to a nearby chair.

"Our matron," Anneliese offered, waiting for a moment before taking a seat. "You are too learned to take such a claim seriously, of course."

"We exist to discern the deeper truths," the Mage countered, taking a seat across from Anneliese at the small table. "Through consistent observation and comparison, rather than regurgitated folklore."

"From your studies you must be intimately aware of the other Planes, and their links to this one."

"Early Magi were deluded," Arucan shook his head. "They discovered the Primal Planes and crafted a story to tie them together, stealing from Elven and Dwarven superstitions with little regard for logic. Most of that nonsense has been stripped from the texts we now use."

"Take care what you judge by its age," Anneliese cautioned. "Be it a person, or an idea."

"I have heard many tales," Arucan sighed. "Lesser *Eleri*

have left our ranks in confusion over them. I do believe that there are influences that steer the tides of history, I have seen them myself. We suspect these are far from divine."

"The *Baya?*" Anneliese asked. "Your flavor of unexplained interference makes much more sense than ours," she mocked.

"Our records uphold that point of view," Arucan half-shrugged. "Our agents have been trained to spot *Baya* for generations. Verification is more complicated, usually when one of their spawn shows signs of unusual power, and has to be eliminated."

"*Ororo...*" Anneliese whispered.

"One of the terms we've adopted from the Dwarven lore, yes." The Mage paused. "What do you know of it?"

Anneliese smiled. "I've been across most of the Realm. Little surprises me." Her mind wandered to the tale Mirsa told her of Bertus and the Stoneguard back on the Glimmering Isle.

"We're already watching you," Arucan folded his hands on the table in front of him. "Your friends. Our network is larger than you realize."

"If only you sought the truth," Anneliese lamented. "What allies we could be."

"Is Bertus the only one you suspect, or has the *heretic* gathered others to himself?"

"I have learned all I need of your madness," the Huntmistress slid out of her chair and turned to leave. "Know that anyone who tries to harm Bertus or any of our company will meet a swift end."

CHAPTER 18

"There may be good in him, still."

"Alma, we're not taking him with us. We have no room for prisoners, no time to drag him with us back to the sea."

"I know." Alma glanced at Martin's inert form, and averted her gaze within moments. "I could not stand that."

"Are you alright to walk?" Kevon pushed the water skin she held up toward her mouth from the bottom. "Drink some more."

"I'm just a little weak," she stood, wobbling. "I'll be fine. I can walk anywhere as long as it's not through *there*," she added, looking in the direction Keldra had escaped.

"It looks like the stairway down to the level below is clear," Alanna announced.

"I didn't think you could see through..."

"Carlo just signaled," the assassin smirked. "Let's go."

Kevon held Alma's arm as they threaded through the carnage of broken reaper carapaces and severed orc limbs that told the tale of the battle that had raged outside while he faced Keldra. The party picked their way down the corpse-strewn stairwell and was halfway between the spiral from above to the simple stairway that led below when Kevon felt the Dark magic begin.

"Run." Kevon whispered.

His warning scarcely preceded the clicking and screeching that rose from the portals opening in each alcove around the curve of the structure. "RUN!"

Alma screamed as she saw the first reaper emerging

from the darkness.

"Clear the way!" Kevon shouted, hefting Alma over his left shoulder, and drawing his sword before sprinting ahead.

Carlo smashed a leaper in the face with his shield, and kicked the beast into an oncoming reaper just as Kevon reached him.

"*Down down down!*" Kevon huffed, following Alanna as she darted between Carlo and Bertus to the stairwell, knives drawn. "Watch the rear, but push through!"

As Kevon neared the floor and the giant Dark sigil etched into it, he could feel the magic shifting. "No..." he groaned, the purity of the Light symbol anchored on the sword kept him from losing his mind as the Darkness warped reality in front of him.

The area ahead grew murky, and Kevon stopped beside Alanna at the edge of the distortion that covered the entire symbol. A familiar malice clutched at his mind through the gigantic portal.

Surrender.

The single concept hammered into Kevon's mind with enough force to stagger him. His arms and legs lost their steady, practiced stability.

Accept.

The gentler command screamed through his awareness, blurring his focus further, and his grip loosened on his sword.

"No." Kevon clutched the sword tighter, and let the meager reserves he'd accumulated flow into the pristine Light rune that he was sure had protected his enhanced senses from obliteration. A sphere of pure light formed near the ceiling over the center of the Dark rune, and the haze that flowed over the stone floor began to shrink and burn away. "Run!" He stumbled onward, his strength returning in the golden glow from above as the portal and the aberrant will on the other side of it retreated.

Bertus and Carlo were close on his heels as he turned down the stairway to the bottom floor. Kevon glimpsed a handful of reapers clogging the top of the staircase behind them, screeching at the cleansing light. Estimating their speed and his reserves, Kevon withdrew his magic from the spell, and pressed downward in relative darkness.

Kevon called up a dimmer light as they reached the bottom of the stairwell, again near the ceiling and the center of the chamber, taxing his meager magical reserves as little as he dared.

"Almost there," Alanna called out in encouragement, sprinting ahead.

The magic took Kevon by surprise, the smaller Dark portals opening all at once. Streams of shrieking imps poured through from all directions, clogging the air with flapping shadows and a fetid, leathery stench.

"Hah!" Alanna leapt through the chaos, slashing and kicking at any of the already smoldering demons who dared cross her path.

Carlo and Bertus hacked and bashed at imps on either side of Kevon and his unconscious sister, advancing through the wake Alanna's passage left.

Halfway to the exit. Three quarters. Both Kevon's weary body and mind felt a sense of elation as they neared their goal. The fumes from the disintegrating creatures started to build up, and Kevon choked on the acrid taste. The light faltered.

One of Alanna's daggers clattered to the floor. She threw her other at a nearby imp, and drew her sword again, clutching her left arm to her side. The weapon's tip traced an elegant swath of destruction to the edge of the doorway.

"Get her through!" the assassin screamed, turning her blade back toward the center of the room.

Kevon pushed a final burst of magic into the Light construct behind them, and staggered out of the tower into a different flavor of mayhem.

CHAPTER 19

"I'm not asking," Anneliese clarified. "I'm telling. We have delivered the message we came to, and have gained many unfortunate answers to questions best left unasked. There is nothing left for us here. We depart in the morning, with or without your leave to do so."

"I daresay my personal guard will be more at ease," Alacrit acknowledged. "The past few days have taxed their nerves. Torit thinks that we cannot stop you without unacceptable losses."

The prince frowned a moment longer. "I'll allow it, on one condition."

"This is not a negotiation."

"Hear me out," Alacrit cautioned. "My intentions are true, though you believe them misguided. I seek only the knowledge that would unite our paths once again."

"You refuse to listen," Anneliese fumed. "How can you claim to seek…"

"Torit will accompany you," Alacrit announced. "He will be allowed to send messages, unhindered, about what he observes. In return, until he finds cause, our order will not pursue you."

"Preferable to Arucan, I suppose, though of less use," Anneliese mused. "If he does anything to stand in our way…"

"Excellent." Alacrit snapped his fingers at a nearby page. "Fetch the ambassador. Have him meet me in the parlor. I fancy a game or two before he leaves."

◆ ◆ ◆

"No good will come of this," Mirsa warned as they neared their quarters.

"Separating Torit from this madness is a victory," Anneliese offered. "However slight. He should regain his sense soon after we depart."

"I'm sure Carlo will be eager to meet him," Mirsa teased. "I wonder how the others fare. Yusa is the only one I can track reliably, and I can sense him much in the same direction as when we arrived, if further north."

"I can't imagine the captain surviving if the others have not," Anneliese reasoned. "This bodes well."

"You're right," Mirsa agreed, dismissing the maid fussing over Maisy with a smile and a wave. "We should worry about reaching the Hold, focusing the aid of the Dwarves in advance of Kevon's arrival." She closed the door to their room behind the departing servant.

"We need to reach the Hold sooner than later, to tell them what we have discovered," Anneliese frowned. "I may know a way," the Huntmistress paused. "You still have your charm of concealment?"

Mirsa reached into her pocket and drew out the wooden amulet, feeling her mystical senses cloud as she touched the Enchanted talisman. "Yes, it needs to be reinforced, but…"

"Do it." Anneliese suggested. "Keep it close, make sure it will work when you need it. It will be soon."

Mirsa sat on the bunk, and let her mind explore the magical construct embedded within the smooth wooden talisman. She wrapped her thoughts around it as she clenched it tighter, and let the magic within her seep into the symbol, pushing harder as her reserves shrank. She could feel the magic accumulate, a thin film covering the sigils that described the enchantment powering and directing it in its duties. She opened her eyes minutes later, as the last of her power drizzled into the thought-form.

"It will hold for now," Mirsa shrugged. "I can devote more time to it as needed."

"If you are certain it cannot be breached, it will suffice." Anneliese clarified. "I'll let you know when it becomes important. Now, we should prepare for the morning."

Anneliese folded a spare set of clothing and stuffed it in a knapsack which she sat beside her weapons that already leaned against the wall. "While you finish your preparations, I'll gather supplies from the kitchen."

Mirsa frowned as the elf slid out of the room, and peeked out after her, calling to a nearby page to fetch her a set of saddlebags. She arranged her belongings in piles, singing a gentle lullaby to Maisy as she condensed the things they would need for the trip into heaps of organized disarray.

The bags were filled to the point of difficulty to buckle closed when Anneliese returned empty handed.

"I thought you were..."

"They will deliver the rations to the stables before we leave tomorrow," the Huntmistress reassured her. "We should not need half of what I requested, but for sake of appearances..."

"Another Rune chamber?" Mirsa asked, wondering at her friend's cryptic words. "Some way to ease a Sending to the Hold?"

"Nothing so simple," Anneliese chuckled. "Perhaps not as reliable, but worth the risk, I think."

"We'll leave it to you," Mirsa conceded. "We could not have come this far without you. I trust you will not be betraying us into the hands of anyone more sinister than Alacrit?"

"I have no plans to do so," Anneliese feigned a pout. "We had to rescue Torit."

"We'd best avoid telling him that, I assume,"

"Naturally."

"A grand day to depart, if there is such a thing," Torit exclaimed, smiling as Alacrit frowned at the statement. "No attacks overnight, clear skies, the morning dew should be burning off as we reach the gates."

"Splendid." The prince's monotone response echoed the disinterest in the morning meal he'd shared with his 'guests'.

"Cheer up," Mirsa teased. "The last time you saw my friends and I off, we raided the armory. This time we're only taking horses and food."

Alacrit's forced smile broadened as his *Eleri* advisor appeared more distraught. "I cannot see you off, but wish you well. He stood and stepped over to Torit, holding out a clenched fist. "Do not forget who you are." The monarch slid the contents of his closed hand into Torit's, and strode out of the room, flanked by advisors and guards.

Torit stood there a moment longer, and smiled at the feel of the figurine in his hand. He slipped the green Brigand token into a pocket, and began cajoling nearby servants into hefting the bundles that needed carried to the stables.

"What was that?" Anneliese asked as they padded down the hallway.

"I believe my friend is through playing games," Torit shrugged, and lengthened his strides to catch up to the page that scurried ahead of them.

CHAPTER 20

"**W**atch her," Kevon commanded the injured soldier who leaned against the tower just outside the entrance. He deposited Alma at the man's feet, next to the wavering arch of water that loomed over them. "Bertus, Alanna, hold the entrance!"

Without looking back, Kevon charged out into the open, slashing at a leaper that stood over another fallen soldier. As the beast lunged, he kicked, deflecting the leaper into range of a Myrnar spear.

Crying challenge, Carlo leapt over his downed subordinate, and blocked the scythe-stroke of a reaper with his shield. He spun the shield up and to the right, clearing the way for an underhand thrust of his sword into the demon's maw. Two more soldiers charged, shoving the dying beast toward the edge of the escarpment, and over it onto the rocks below.

Kevon turned to survey the line, now more solid since he and Carlo had returned. Elven Hunters had cast aside bows, and stood shoulder to shoulder with Carlo's men, their short bladed swords dripping with ichor.

"We're going to have to walk out of here, aren't we?" Carlo growled, peering up at the Myrnar Mystics, who were beginning to show the strain of their efforts. "They're not going to be able to signal…"

Eyes already closed, Kevon could feel the slight warmth of the midafternoon sun, and the light that carried it whispering against his skin. It echoed against the brilliant symbol etched in his mind, anchored by his connection to the sword.

He gathered all of it he could, and focused at the edge of his awareness, creating a globe of light far above the tip of the dark tower. Once the mental framework was in place, Kevon flung all of the magic he could muster into it, focused through the sigil burned into the blade. The flash from above threw the surrounding army into a panic, and fed back into Kevon's reserves. He pushed again, expending more will, and the orb flashed brighter. One last push, and the light from the orb exploded and faded, leaving brilliant streaks across the sky that mirrored the ones in his mind.

"If they don't come now, it's not because they couldn't see that," Carlo rumbled, reaching out to steady the now wobbly Kevon. "Just a while longer, men!" he barked to the others, who had paused to look up at the spectacle above.

Carlo's soldiers and the Elven Hunters resumed the battle with renewed vigor, but it was clear that the skirmish, along with the losses they had already sustained, was taking its toll. A weary soldier's misstep onto a patch of blood-slicked stone caused him to slip forward into the reach of an advancing reaper. With a low slash, the demon hooked the offending foot, and dragged the stunned Warrior into the chaotic frenzy of the enemy line. The bloodcurdling screams faded into the click-clack of chitin against stone and sword, and were gone.

Stepping ahead to fill the gap in the line, Kevon drew the sword and cleared his mind. He danced between one of the senior Hunters and one of Carlo's remaining officers, blending the unit tactics the Blademaster taught with the more fluid, reactionary movements he'd learned fighting chimaera on the Highplain.

The press of dull reaper armor and pale leaper leather rippled forward, as the rear ranks clambered over their fallen brethren in leaps and lurches.

Kevon alternated flashes of ichor-drenched steel and sigil sharpened magic, weaving slashes of Light and Wind into his slowing movements. Sweat and gore dripped into his eyes, stinging, distracting. He twisted his blade, and kicked a convulsing leaper off onto the pile. He stepped back to take a breath, and wipe his face on his sleeve. "We can't keep this up much longer," he called to Carlo over the scream of another falling soldier.

"Won't have to," the Blademaster yelled in response. "Look!"

The wave was still a handful of breaths distant, but larger than the one they'd arrived on. Scores of tiny figures dotted the churning mountain, spear-wielding Myrnar lining the edges. Kevon felt the peculiar magic as he gazed at the oncoming wall of water.

"Final push!" Carlo roared, stepping to the inside, assessing the situation with a more critical eye. "Shore up the left flank! Bring the injured up! Clear the entrance!"

The shadow of the approaching wave loomed over them, and Kevon blasted the trio of reapers ahead of him with a wash of Light magic. He stepped in to where Alma crouched, tying off a tourniquet on one of the injured soldiers. "I'm not sure how this is going to…"

The wave shifted and crashed down on the enemy lines, and wrapped around the battlefield, merging with the remaining water and myrnar near the tower entrance and reforming. Myrnar spearmen lined the outer edges, while Mystics organized far above in the towering construct. Other myrnar poked free of the wall of water, beckoning to the soldiers isolated in the now silent funnel. The injured were passed to the waiting arms of mermaids and mermen, who held them clear of the water wall, moving to higher positions with strong flicks of muscled tail sections.

"That's all of the wound…" Kevon's words caught in his throat as myrnar began snatching the soldiers that had brought their fellows, outcries of surprise breaking the new stillness. He felt he magic around them shift from the gathering draw it had been, to power coiling for something, and soon. "No! It's all right! Everyone, to the sides!" Kevon secured his blade, and stepped to where a mermaid waited, arms outstretched. He turned his back, raised his arms, and found himself soaring up the wave-wall, laughter hissing in his ear.

He felt the forward magic collapse as the curtain of water opposite them spilled inward, filling up the space they'd all just occupied for what seemed like an eternity. The sides followed suit, and he could feel the water supporting them shudder and buckle forward onto the failing column. Containment of the front section of the water eroded, and massive amounts of the rescuing wave slid off the escarpment, flooding over the corpses of fallen demons and soldiers alike. The water supporting them lurched forward twice, and the magic recrystallized, feeding off the momentum of the directed failure. Kevon could feel the focus of the magic shift from the taxing shape-maintenance of the previous moments to a cursory guidance, moving with the contours of the land back in the direction the rescue had come from. As they neared the sea, and Kevon could spot the ship in the distance, he felt the portion of magic that had focused on recovering and reconsolidating water from the trailing edge of the wave lessen. The terrain ate up more of the wave, lowering the survivors at an uncomfortable rate.

"Almost there, men!" Carlo shouted, to weak cheers over the grinding surf.

Kevon glanced low to the left and spotted Alma, passed out in the arms of her Myrnar handler. The trip back had taken only minutes. The shift in magical focus and downhill momentum had helped, but everyone was exhausted from the trip up and the battle in the interim. Only the Elven Hunters seemed immune to the exertion of the previous hours; resting, but alert.

The soft splash into the warm afternoon sea was a welcome shock. Artificial currents swept the company to the edge of the ship, where soldiers and Hunters climbed up waiting rope ladders, and began hauling up the wounded in baskets.

"Miska... Welha...?" Relaniel called, peering over the rail as the last of the wounded were lifted aboard.

"Lost," Alanna stepped to the elf's side, and wrapped a supporting arm around her. "Along with five of Carlo's men. I don't know how many myrnar..."

"Too many..." the slender noble trembled as she spoke, glaring at the ranks of leapers and reapers that milled about at the water's edge. "This is not how it was meant to be."

"No, it's not," Kevon agreed. "Those Magi should not have been that strong, that young. Their leader, I could understand. The layered enchantments around the tower explain much of it, but the ease with which they used it..."

"The darkness is stronger," Alanna whispered, glancing around. "It was worse at the tower, but seeing the corruption clearly there, I can recognize its influence here."

"You can feel it here?" Kevon pressed, his concern shifting. "Does it intensify when you look toward the tower?"

"Not really," she answered. "It's just an underlying taint that may have been here already, but I'm seeing now for certain. I hope it gets better the further we go from here." She reached into her pocket and withdrew the Enchanted eyepatch and slipped the strap over her head, preparing to snug the covering into place over her healed eye. "This helps, but using focused darkness to blind myself from more of the same..."

The assassin stopped midsentence, pulling the patch free of her field of vision. "We need to get clear of this island, and quickly."

Kevon followed her gaze upward over the island to a smattering of dark specks that spread across the sky, shifting as they drew closer. "Yusa! We need to move! Look to the skies!"

The ship lurched as the crew began hauling anchor. The captain listened to Reko for a moment before shouting orders to the few men who were not carrying wounded. Sails unfurled where men were there to handle them, and where they were not. Kevon felt magic spiking at various points about the deck, Reko's magic responding to Yusa's murmurs between his shouts.

The growing streaks in the sky resolved into winged shapes, scores of what must have been the thick imp-like creatures that they had seen earlier blanketed the horizon, oblivious to the afternoon sun.

Kevon's hand went to his sword-hilt, a habit from his Warrior days he had tried to break himself of. Light and Wind runes gleamed in his mind, a welcome change from the jolting pain he'd grown accustomed to. "Rhysabeth-Dane! We need the Unbound to..."

As he spoke the words, one of the older griffin that spent most of its time onboard the ship looked at him and squawked. Kevon glanced back to the sky, and the Unbound elder followed his gaze, squawking again. The beast stretched its leonine haunches, clawed at the deck with its talons, and launched itself over the railing with a shriek.

Following the griffon's arc up into the sky, Kevon saw the formation of the airborne Unbound shift into a cyclonic spiral. The formation that reminded him of the moment he had returned to the Highplain from the realm of M'phes, the goddess of Wind. The Unbound had responded to him then, or to his sword. He hadn't been certain of which.

She'll need Brightwing, he thought, *She'll want to lead them against this.* Kevon squinted as he looked up, and spotted the Rider's mount right away, an unusual occurrence at best. For an instant, he thought he could feel something of the griffon's mind, but dismissed it as the dwarf approached from the upper deck.

"Looks bad," she commented, gazing at the sky to the north. "I'll call Bright..."

The griffon slammed down on the deck before them, its last powerful wingbeat nearly slapping the two of them together, as Alanna had danced free of the landing zone.

"Be safe," Kevon called as the dwarf mounted her steed.

"Just buy us some time. I don't think they will be able to follow us long distances without landing."

Brightwing leapt from the deck without his usual predatory glare in Kevon's direction, and climbed swiftly into the sky, bearing his Rider to the front edge of the swirling formation. As they reached it, Kevon felt another twinge, and the flight shifted from their holding pattern. Tetherfoot and Greybeak swooped out on the edges, shepherding the younger Unbound toward where the battle awaited them in the north.

Startled at recognizing the names he had never heard before, Kevon recoiled, and the sword-hilt slipped from his grasp. The connection to the Wind rune broken, he watched the scene above with a sense of detachment.

Glints of light and dark circled and dove, clashing and separating, some dropping from the fray and plummeting to the jagged landscape below. A dozen or more of the fallen forms appeared to be griffin.

"We're underway, but the Unbound are taking heavy losses," Reko's illusion-form flickered into being next to where Kevon watched the battle. "They are too far away to assist. I worry about the dwarf."

"As do I," Kevon agreed. "I'm not so sure they are too far away. Help me."

The cowled figure nodded and faded, tendrils of Magesmoke dissolving in the afterimage of the vanished projection.

Kevon felt the offered power, and lay claim to it before retaking the hilt of his sword.

The battlefield leapt into surreal clarity as Kevon directed the borrowed energy into Wind and Light runes. Strained wingbeats and battle-screeches filtered through the magical link, splitting his concentration between the immediacy of his surroundings and the chaos that filled the northern sky. He shifted his focus through the rune to the battle, and found Rhysabeth-Dane astride Brightwing. *We need her, need them*, he thought, and centered his attention on the Rider and her steed.

Before Kevon could act, one of the gargoyles dove at the Rider from above. Brightwing screeched and dove himself, unable to outrun the smaller, swifter demon, but buying precious seconds before the inevitable clash. The moment stretched. Kevon could see and feel Rhysabeth-Dane clutching at the combat saddle, tensed in the stirrups of the evading griffon, when they made their move.

Brightwing spread his wings, and leveled off. With a powerful, uneven downbeat, he slowed their downward motion, and lurched to the side, curling his wingtips under to reduce his aerial profile.

Drawing her sword from its saddle-sheath, Rhysabeth-Dane twisted in the saddle, and severed half the wing of their pursuer with her backhanded stroke as it passed them.

Folding his wings back into dive position, Brightwing followed the flailing gargoyle lower. He raked into its sides with his front talons, and gouged through the thick leather at the base of its neck with his beak, tearing muscle and crushing bone. Squawking in triumph, he planted his leonine hind claws in the middle of the creature's back, and shoved off, beginning the ascent back to the main battle.

Shocked back to action, Kevon refocused on the battle. He used blasts of Wind magic to slow or deflect gargoyles that were ready to deliver killing blows against the more powerful, but less agile Unbound. He meddled with the battle for a dozen breaths, making a difference in a score of different skirmishes before the distance and intensity of the magic he worked drained the reserves of both himself and Reko. The power dwindled, and his enhanced view of the battle zone wrenched backward, settling back into his own eyes aboard the fleeing ship. Contact with the sword, and the still-glowing Wind rune gave Kevon a vague sense of what was happening, but he was unable to draw enough power from anywhere to continue the fight.

"They'll have to do the rest on their own," he sighed, releasing the sword and grasping the railing.

"The Unbound outnumber the gargoyle demons two to one," Alanna remarked before sliding the eyepatch into place. "The battle is all but over."

"The few wounded have already been tended to," Rel-aniel reported as she approached from the passage that led below. She looked to the approaching forms of the Unbound, and her voice softened. "We'd better prepare to deal with more."

CHAPTER 21

"Is this necessary?" Torit scoffed, fidgeting with the smooth iron charm that hung from a leather strip around his neck.

"It is," Anneliese replied, adjusting her own. "If Alacrit's Magi are searching for us right now, it might appear that we are losing a battle. You and I have already been defeated, and now Mirsa and her child."

The Mage produced two Enchanted talismans, one on a leather strap like her comrades, the other on a small strip of stretchy woven fabric. She placed her charm around her neck, and fitted Maisy's around her ankle, snug enough to stay on, but loose enough that it did not affect circulation. The child giggled and kicked, but the charm held fast.

"The Prince's contacts in Eastport will spot us, even with these," the Ambassador sighed.

"They'll be looking the wrong direction," Anneliese laughed. "Eat quickly, we have to be back to the last fork, and well beyond it by nightfall."

"Leaving the road, with the horses?"

"Torit, your complaints have not gotten more tolerable with the passage of time," Mirsa snapped. "We've taken a risk being this exposed since we left the forest."

"We can trek through the foothills, and angle around unseen to our destination," Anneliese explained.

"Resting here a day longer would be a good idea," Mirsa

suggested later that evening as they struck camp near a small stream. "We should use the moonlight to travel as far as we can. The territory beyond can be hazardous, the idea of sleeping there is more frightening to me than what could be following."

"Gnomes," Anneliese explained before Torit's argument could begin. "She's afraid of having her child snatched by gnomes while she sleeps. I'm sure I could keep watch and prevent it, but gnomes... unsettle me."

"I would feel much better about all this if I knew anything about where we were headed, what we were doing," Torit sat on a rock, and sighed. "This is not what I am accustomed to."

"And I fear I shall grow *too* accustomed to your whining, again," Anneliese rummaged through her pack and produced a handful of apples. She tossed one to him and laughed. "Not something I want to repeat."

"Ancient history is usually one of my favorite subjects," Mirsa caught her own apple, and glared at Torit. "It's becoming less so."

"Perspective, young one," Torit's eyes seemed to twinkle as he smiled at the Mage's taunt. "Shall I snare us a rabbit?"

"Going hungry might be a nice change of pace," The Huntmistress's barb was softer spoken than Mirsa expected. "Please."

"Ladies," Torit pulled a length of cord from a pocket, and strolled up the game trail that ran alongside the stream.

"Has he always been so..." Mirsa struggled to find the right words after Torit was out of earshot.

"Always."

"And the two of you were?"

"As I said, I was young, and he was wiser in many respects." Anneliese sat down next to Mirsa, and offered to take Maisy. "It was not all bad. There are a few things I sometimes wish he'd teach Carlo."

Mirsa bit her lip, suppressing a giggle.

"I'm glad for this time alone," Anneliese continued. "I don't think he will remove his wards to betray us, but he still believes our destination has not changed."

"Kevon might return to Eastport," Mirsa shrugged. "He can't stay there long, not since he was there last. He's more apt to go to the Dwarven Hold."

"After this next stretch of travel, Torit will know we are not behaving as the *Eleri* believe we will. That moment will be the true test of his loyalties."

"You can deal with his loyalty, or lack of. *Yes you can,*" Mirsa half spoke to Anneliese and half to Maisy, touching the infant on the nose as she finished. Her eyes widened as she continued, "Mommy just wants a hot bath and some people who aren't just pretending to be nice to us, *doesn't she?*"

Grinning at the child's squeal of delight, Anneliese nodded her agreement. "That will be most welcome."

"True to my word," Torit announced, swinging two fat hares from the cord slung over his shoulder, returning to camp just before dusk. "I don't think I should have to..."

Her skinning knife already free from its sheath, Anneliese motioned for their companion to bring his kill over to her. She looked at the prepared fire-pit, and Mirsa's still form beside it, eyes closed. Flames blossomed from beneath the stacked fuel, and the Mage relaxed and stepped away.

"You'll have to gather sticks for a spit," the Huntmistress told Torit as he handed over his kill. "We were not inspired by previous examples of your hunting prowess."

"Of course," Torit admitted. "There are several snarls of brush along the streambed that should provide... I'll return soon."

"We won't need any more sage to season them with," Anneliese commented, sniffing one of the carcasses before untying them from the cord. She sat one aside, and pinched the other by the scruff of the neck. Making a quick, shallow cut, she sat her knife down and stuck her fingers into the incision, pulling in opposite directions, shucking the fur and skin off with a practiced motion. She popped the ankles and sliced through tendons with her recovered knife.

"We'll be over here," Mirsa whispered, averting her widened eyes. She carried Maisy to the other side of the firepit, where the smoke was less, and ignored the rest of the elf's food preparation techniques.

"You should always appreciate where your food comes from," Anneliese teased as she returned from burying the unused parts of the rabbits.

"I appreciate not having to do that." Mirsa balanced the skewered carcasses on the improvised spit above the now-glowing coals.

"There are many things that make more sense in the light of recent events," Torit walked around the outskirts of camp, swinging Maisy in his arms to contented gurgles.

"That is good to hear, and even better to see," Anneliese remarked as she took a seat near the fire. "The weeks ahead should go by easier for it."

"I fear the weeks ahead will be rough for all of us," Torit spoke in low tones as he approached the others. "Alacrit's men have been gaining more influence in Eastport, and I'm sure word has gone ahead of us, if not from him, from others in the organization."

"We'll be fine," Mirsa chuckled as she turned the spit, and then stood to take her daughter.

CHAPTER 22

"I don't care how tired the men are of fish," Carlo's voice took on a knife's edge as he talked to his lieutenant. "We're waiting until things are right before we move on. The men are recovering, they're not hungry, just bored. Give them something to do."

"Yes, Commander." The man excused himself, and brushed past Kevon as the Warsmith entered the cabin.

"So, when are things going to be right?" Carlo growled as soon as his subordinate was out of earshot. "*I'm tired of fish*," he added with a whisper.

"Soon," Kevon assured the Blademaster. "The preparations have taken longer than expected. Over half of the palace below has been prepared for our arrival, but the way to the Seat is still not open to us. The myrnar have been working hard to do this much. What I have seen of it is amazing, and the escorts have been getting better. I haven't nearly drowned in two days."

"Lovely." Carlo stood and peered out of the cabin's single window. "If we could just get those bandaged catbirds off the deck, things around here would almost be pleasant."

"The Unbound are more upset at this arrangement than we are," Kevon argued. "But they are..."

"The only reason we're still here." Carlo interrupted. "So you've said. I think we would have done well, had the flying demons reached us, but that is neither here nor there."

Kevon stood in silent frustration.

"But soon?" Carlo asked.

"I'm going to speak with Yusa and Alanna next," Kevon

explained. "The palace crew thinks if they work through the night, the escort team should be able to get us there late tomorrow."

"Then weeks more of waiting." Carlo sighed. "Best get started, eh?"

"That's my preference," Kevon's hand strayed to the hilt of his sword. "More runes whispering across my mind? Can't wait."

"You see now why the Guilds have maintained separation."

"This much power is not something I would choose for myself," Kevon hissed. "There is no one else to do this."

"I know, lad," Carlo groaned. "But I'm here to help you when you need it, or stop you, if..."

"It won't come to that. But I'm glad."

"As am I." Carlo clapped Kevon on the shoulder, and headed for the door. "Go talk to your friends. I have to see a dwarf about some birds."

Following the Blademaster out onto the deck, Kevon looked to where he felt Reko's illusion being maintained, and saw the hooded figure talking with Alanna.

"Yusa is even more concerned about it than I am," Reko cautioned as Kevon walked into earshot. "We'd both prefer wading through chimaera to being helpless under the waves."

"You've seen what they can do with waves," Kevon slid his hand into Alanna's as he arrived. "They've been practicing since. It's not this side of the portal we have to be concerned about."

"The Mystics have escorted you to the Palace and back what, six times?" Alanna asked. "I'm not worried."

"Seven," Kevon corrected. "They have been training a pair of Mystics for each of us, and each team has managed the trip at least twice, with increasing skill each time. Besides, we're not exactly helpless."

"As much time as I have spent on the sea, you'd think I'd be better at controlling it," Reko lamented.

"Be thankful you are not," Kevon laughed, "Or it would drive you mad. You'd have to convince Yusa to take up another profession." His laughter stumbled to a stop as his connection to the sea twinged in response to a gentle roll of the deck. "I may need a break from the sea after this," he added.

"Blasphemy," Yusa chortled, joining them. "A longer stretch than most are used to, it has been, but rather this than ashore. Planning our adventure below, Reko says?"

The image of the hooded Magi nodded and wisped out of existence.

"Tomorrow afternoon, if their progress below holds," Kevon reported.

"Ahh... yes..." Yusa looked to the side as if listening to something only he could hear, and frowned as he turned back to the others. "We find ourselves without an extra Mage to spare below, to reopen the portal. Reko is concerned. Will we have to stay behind?"

"I've spoken to the myrnar about this," Kevon shook his head. "They have never attempted a portal opening, unaware it was possible. When we are ready to cross over, we'll open it, and see if the Mystics can maintain it."

"If they can," Alanna released a soft sigh. "They will be able to do the same thing as you open a return passage."

"That's the hope," Kevon agreed. "Even if Yusa and Reko stayed behind, it wouldn't be practical for them to wait below until we returned, not knowing how long it would be."

"It's not a climb down the face of a cliff, through bone-strewn caves," Alanna shrugged. "But it's not a nice hike up a hill, either."

"Just think how pleasant the next one will be," Kevon laughed. "Sandwiched between helpings of Dwarven generosity."

"Even I can't see that far ahead." Alanna squeezed his hand. "We should focus on what is in front of, or *below* us."

"I'm going to focus on a hot meal, an early watch, and then a warm bed," Kevon watched as a riderless Brightwing led a flight of recovering Unbound up and away from the lower deck, toward the midafternoon sun. "I may speak to Rhysabeth-Dane first if she has a moment."

"I may join you for two of those." The assassin's fingers slipped from Kevon's grasp as she turned and headed to the passage that led below.

Letting his mind wander over the possibilities for a moment, Kevon made his way down past Carlo to the foredeck where the Dwarven Rider tended to the injured griffin, changing bandages and smoothing ruffled feathers. He watched as she finished applying a fresh poultice dressing on one of the griffin's braced wings, speaking to the beast in matter-of-fact tones throughout the process.

"I could never do that," Kevon chuckled as Rhysabeth-Dane's latest patient squawked and hopped off to mingle with its fellows.

"They trust you well enough with steel drawn," the Rider commented as she packed the remaining supplies back in her satchel. "More so now. Even Brightwing."

"It's not the same," Kevon shook his head. "Their deference to me is a gift. I didn't earn it, not like you have."

"I'm done for today, but help me tomorrow," Rhysabeth-Dane suggested. "You can work on earning it."

"If I can," Kevon smiled. "I came to ask you about the translations."

"I've refined them as much as possible in the last few days. Difficult without context, but these Myrnar scholars have picked out some nuances that I would have missed. Symbols that are close, but have different enough meanings it may matter." She slung her satchel strap over her shoulder and patted the flap down smooth. "I have probable translations, and several pages of possible substitutions, once we figure out how to put it all together."

"Are any patterns emerging?"

"Not reliable ones. Two or three words link up and make some kind of sense before it breaks down, or we need an untranslated word." She frowned. "I may need to reexamine my original Dwarven translations for nuance, as the myrnar did."

"Well, you should have time for that," Kevon reassured her. "We should be leaving for the Water Seat tomorrow."

"You wouldn't catch me down there if Brightwing could fly it. Wrong shade of blue."

"I would prefer someone else went in my place," Kevon agreed. "There is nothing to be done for it. Tell me, have you eaten yet?"

CHAPTER 23

"You look like you have a question," Mirsa grinned at Torit as she dismounted.

"No questions, just observations," Torit grumbled. "Eastport is three days sane travel behind us, if I'm not mistaken. The only slowing we have done in the last two and a half days has been to feed ourselves and change your spawn."

"Funny you should mention that, it's your turn." Mirsa unknotted a dry cloth from the leather ties on her saddle, and handed it and Maisy to the Envoy. "There's a nice pool just downstream from here."

"The one bright spot in my new life," Torit commented as he accepted, and bounced the drowsy infant. "You, young lady, bear me no ill will, and have not deceived me."

"It's all for your own good," Anneliese laughed, swinging down from her mount. "Are we camping here?"

Mirsa looked around and shook her head. "We may reach a suitable site by dusk, but I can press on overnight if the weather holds, the moon is still full enough to light the way."

"We're close enough that he must know our destination by now," Anneliese whispered when Torit was out of earshot. "We're taking the most direct route."

"After we rest," Mirsa decided. "Another night and day of hard riding, another night sleeping on the ground. He'll be ready then."

Stifling a yawn, Anneliese nodded. "I think we're all about ready."

❖ ❖ ❖

"I thought as much," Torit shrugged when Mirsa awoke two days later and told him the news. "Though my trips to see the Spires were always from the northern route. I've not been since they fell."

Just how old are they? Mirsa's mind reeled as this newest clue to that question entered her thoughts. *I don't remember offhand how long ago the Spires fell, but it must have been generations of Dwarves ago.* "I would have loved to see them intact. You do get a good close-up view of one though."

"The pass can't be more than half a day's ride further, correct? The rate we've been going, we'll be in the Hold by nightfall."

"If we can keep it. The horses got some good rest last night, but may not hold out that long today."

"The horses never would have held out this long if you were not with us," Anneliese corrected Mirsa. "Known to you or not, their strength has been sustained by magic. If your strength holds, so will theirs."

"That's never happened..."

"You are used to traveling with Warriors carrying more steel, and being swept along with them at their pace," the Huntmistress interrupted. "Your charm may have kept you from seeing what you did, but it did not prevent it."

"Then we'll reach the Hold tonight. I'm sore and grouchy, but I know where there's a hot bath and fresh bread that will make things better."

An hour down the road, Mirsa thought about what Anneliese had said, and clutched the amulet that rested against her chest. Encircling it with folds of her tunic, she felt her magical awareness emerging from the required haze she had been mired in since they had gone into hiding. The Movement rune shone dim in her mind, pulsing in time with the hoofbeats from all three horses as they loped along the track toward the Dwarven Hold. The working reminded her of the run she had made with Kevon, Bertus, and Carlo when they were fleeing the Orclord. This was light, easy, and had an almost musical quality. The fluid motions of their steeds fed back into the spell, pulsing outward at each rhythmic footfall. The elegance and intricacy of the spell alarmed her, and she released the amulet to fall back against her skin. As the rune faded out of her mind, she closed her eyes and focused on the music of the run.

"This is a good place to rest," Mirsa announced, sliding down off her mount at the mouth of the pass. "We're making better time than I expected."

"It's not even midday," Anneliese agreed, dismounting her own steed. "There's no stream here, we'll have to use most of our water for the horses."

"I believe these horses could outrun you, Huntmistress," Torit gasped as he joined them. "I was ill prepared for that."

"As soon as the horses are watered, you'd better be prepared." Mirsa handed the envoy her skin of water, and loosened the straps on the harness that held Maisy against her chest.

"*Muhr-Sa!*" Bargthar-Stoun held his arms out wide, and gave the Mage a crushing hug as she approached him. His attention shifted to her companions. "*Palha...* Elf? Oh... pup?" He stepped closer to Anneliese to get a better view of Maisy. "Oh... you... Bertus?"

"No, she's not Bert..." Mirsa clutched the Dwarven King's hand. "You've been learning Common."

Grinning and making a pinching gesture between his eyes and Mirsa's, the monarch laughed. He guided his pinching fingers to Mirsa's forearm, catching a bit of flesh and squeezing twice. "Talk later," he announced. "Eat now."

"You see what our problem is," Mirsa spoke through a mouth half filled with warm, crusty bread, unable to choose between communication and consumption. Remembering her manners, she covered her mouth with her hand and finished chewing.

The dwarf seated opposite her began translating, but the king waved him off.

"*Rego mala nut pah,*" Bargthar-Stoun started, then began again. "Prince, not…"

"He doesn't scare us," the translator finished. "We cannot be defeated here, miss."

Torit snorted. "So we just dig in, and wait for the others?"

"You could craft a game board, to pass the time," Anneliese suggested.

The Ambassador's hand moved to the carved figure in his pocket, his fingers tracing the blunt features. "Perhaps I will."

CHAPTER 24

"**I**'m not sure I can go further," Yusa leaned against the damp, glowing moss in the pocket of air they had stopped in, while their Myrnar escorts and support Mystics maintained the spells that kept the atmosphere from dissolving into the sea, or collapsing upward to the hallway's ceiling.

"You can't stay here," Kevon advised, sniffing the air. "It's starting to smell *stale*, I think the air would foul if we were to remain much longer."

"Besides, the moss will die if it dries out, like it has above." Alanna pointed to the dark sections of dried moss on the ceiling. The arch of the carved coral hallway serving as air storage for moments like this had deprived the moss overhead of the moisture it needed to survive. "It will take ages after we depart for these passages to recover."

Kevon nodded as his escort motioned for him to proceed. He took a few deep breaths, exhaled to a comfortable level, and stepped into the water that led deeper into the Myrnar palace.

Prickles of sensation, layered physically and magically, pressed in on him as he crossed the barrier. The restrained Water magic, so much more potent here, near the source, screamed for attention. The combination of the proximity of the Seat, and the expert manipulation of its energy threatened to birth an additional physical sense that subordinated the previous five.

As he moved from the 'safety' of the air pocket, gravity shifted, and Kevon's body fell forward, suspended prone near the floor of the passageway by the magic. *It's like being wrapped in a thin, wet, transparent tarpaulin,* Kevon mused as he fought the urge to gasp. He could feel his companions positioned above and behind him, and felt the ripples of the air pocket collapsing upward into its 'storage' state.

He pressed his lips together as hard as he could, and wrinkled his nose, bracing for the next leg of the journey. *They're bypassing two previous checkpoints they've used, if I remember correctly,* he thought. *This will be new territory for me as well.* Craning his neck to look forward, he grasped the hilt of his sword. He pressed his left arm flat against his side, tightened his upper body, and relaxed his legs.

The lurch took him by surprise, even though he had been expecting it. The light brightened and dimmed as they rushed through one passageway after another. Glimpses of armed and armored myrnar flanking connecting hallways flowed past Kevon as they rushed deeper into the palace. After the second splotch of darkness, the passage opened up into a grand hall, lit brighter than the afternoon above they'd left not an hour before. His vision spun as they raced down and around a pillar, along a spiral staircase. *Ramp, not a staircase,* Kevon thought as they whipped out of the bottom turn and flashed across the open center of the hall toward the opening at the far end.

Too long... Kevon's chest convulsed, the air within it depleted past usefulness. His lungs burned, the pain shattering the focus that even holding the sword granted. Tears sprang to his eyes, and remained pressed against them by the same forces that kept the surrounding liquid from his skin. Layers of water and magic twisted and blurred his vision. He blinked, a futile attempt to clear trapped tears from his eye-sockets. At the center of the chamber, the focal point of the palace's illumination, darkness took him.

"We should rouse him," Yusa muttered. "Even this much air will only last so long."

Kevon startled awake, gasping and clutching at his chest. "Can't brea..."

"We know," Alanna pressed a hand over Kevon's on his chest. "We just woke up a few minutes ago. The myrnar... misjudged this last section. They have already apologized."

Climbing to his feet, with Alanna's help, Kevon saw more myrnar in one place than he ever had, gathered in the throne room ahead, surrounding the Seat at a short distance. The light ahead seemed muted, overpowered by the brilliance of the great hall behind them, and the damp, still-glowing walls of the drained antechamber they occupied. Glancing back to the larger room they had passed through to get here, Kevon could see two or three times as many of the sea-folk gathered as were surrounding the Seat. Small knots of myrnar kept station, and the sounds of underwater clicking and chirping they used when not speaking Common above the water drifted through the magical membrane that kept the sea from spilling in on them.

"No doubt this is taxing the Mystics," Kevon could feel the strength of the barrier building and ebbing, balanced between a number of the Myrnar Magi. "Likely why they have hurried us. We should go, now."

"You don't look steady enough to stand, let alone swim," Alanna observed.

Kevon pointed to the increasing number of distortions forming in the membrane that led to the throne room. "It doesn't matter. Reko? Are you ready?"

Feeling the other Mage's spell begin as an affirmation, Kevon reached out to the barrier, passing his hand through it. He began forming runes of his own in his mind. Unable to tap into the crystalline Water magic emanating from the Seat ahead, he used its near-perfection to pattern his Water rune after. Kevon reached between and beyond the latticework of restrained energy to tap into the latent magic contained in the sea around them. He used his own reserves to invite, contain, and then begin shaping the slow, almost viscous sympathetic magic.

As Kevon began to focus his spell at a point before the Seat, he felt Reko's spell end, and then the other Mage's strength and skill were there again, guiding, enhancing, and steadying the complex working that blossomed before them.

The Seat of Water seemed to flicker, and disappear. The coral behind it changed to a smoother, lighter shade of blue that wavered back and forth to its original color.

"It's open!" Yusa cried out. "We have to move now!"

"We can't yet!" Kevon groaned through gritted teeth. "The Mystics haven't…"

The barrier between the air and water became even more chaotic, and Kevon felt the effort needed to keep the portal open halve, then fade to nothing.

"They can't keep both spells going for long," Kevon announced, ending the effort directed at the portal, but maintaining his link to the Water rune. "Into the water!"

Before Kevon was even halfway through the Myrnar barrier, he realized his mistake. He had not accounted for the pressure that crushed in on him, that the Mystics had shouldered for he and his friends the entire time. He redirected the focus of his Water rune to compensate, and reinforced it with a Movement rune that he joined with its fellow in his mind. He felt Reko crafting an Enhancement rune, and once it was fully formed, the effort became bearable.

Forward.

Reko's illusion-formed thought sounded grim in Kevon's water-filled ears.

Gathering power around himself, Kevon directed his art and the sphere of pressurized sea-water around the three of them toward the occluded Seat, and the portal.

CHAPTER 25

"I'm not convinced these dice are exactly balanced," Mirsa scolded Torit.

"These are Dwarven-wrought stone, not the carved ivory we are used to," Torit explained. "I submitted the designs, but had no hand in the production. You are welcome to play something other than the Mage, if it troubles you so."

Frowning, Mirsa looked at the five dice that sat before her. "I'm still not convinced this variant is better," she remarked, snatching up the largest of the cut cubes, and leaning in to study the remaining four. She selected the spell die with the flame design chiseled into it, bypassing the one marked with a gust of wind. The lighter colored cubes that remained were marked with a horseshoe and a talon. Her hand hovered between them, and she grimaced as she reached for the latter. "The griffon is unpredictable, but I don't know if I can catch you without it."

She slid the unused dice to the side, and leaned over the board to roll. "Wait, there is a carriage here." She returned the griffon die, selected the Wind die, and placed two of the small gold tokens before her in the larger pile to the side of the board. "I'll pay the fare."

"A reasonable strategy. The dragon is right behind you."

Mirsa rolled the cubes between flattened palms, and cast them onto the playing surface. Two boots came up on the large die, and the spell dice showed their namesakes, Fire and Wind.

"A respectable roll. You will be far less powerful next

turn."

She picked up her figure. "Four movement, two from the carriage. No other contracts." She moved her character ahead four spaces, to the spot behind Torit's Brigand. She removed the large die from the board and placed it with the two others.

"Didn't quite make it to me, but you have no attack this round, so it doesn't matter much," Torit observed. "You can use the Wind spell to move ahead of me."

"I could," Mirsa agreed. "I would rather use it to move you behind me." The Mage lifted Torit's figure, and placed it behind her own. She placed the Wind die off to the side, next to the other spell dice on the library section of the board.

"Ah."

"And the Fire spell will knock you back an additional space." Mirsa discarded the Fire die with the other used spells, and Torit slid his figurine to the empty space.

"I'd hoped we would both be two spaces further, but no matter," Torit shrugged. "Pursuit?"

Mirsa nodded and rolled the large Dragon cube, counting off and calling out the wings and flames that came up. "Three, and two."

Torit moved the Dragon token forward three spaces. "I'm in range, thanks to your clever play. No defense this round. Two damage." The Ambassador slid two colored markers from in front of him off to the side. "Well done."

After choosing his own dice, Torit rolled. "Three swords, two coins, one defense. No carriage, no other contracts.

"Very productive," Mirsa teased. "My turn?"

"Of course."

Mirsa selected her large die, and the lighter one marked with a horseshoe. "Can't ride them both," she lamented as she rolled.

"Two boots, and the Flame." Torit observed.

"Better than it could have been," Mirsa shrugged, collecting the Fire die from the library and adding it to her collection. She slid the Mage figure two spots forward to a town square. "I'll hire a mercenary, too." She dropped six coins in the pile beside the board, and picked up one of the dice from the tavern area.

"Pursuit."

Torit tossed the Dragon die, and sighed. "Three wings, five claws." He moved the Dragon token forward the two spaces to the one his Brigand occupied. "So six claws. One defense. Five damage. Three remaining."

"You might be able to get a healing potion in town," Mirsa suggested as Torit made adjustments to his tokens.

"Again?" Anneliese asked, striding into the room, Maisy slung at her side, balanced on her hip. "Always this game. Do you not know that you have been summoned?"

"Shame. She was finally winning." Torit swept all of the tokens on his side of the board into a pile. "Perhaps later?"

Mirsa opened her mouth to protest, motioning to the jumbled pile of mixed tokens, but shook her head and stood, reaching for her daughter. "The throne room?"

◆ ◆ ◆

"...*Bad man.*" Bargthar-Stoun concluded the rant of broken Common and Dwarven he'd been spouting for minutes.

"It sounds bad," Mirsa agreed, looking to the translator. "News from the frontier? Heavy losses?"

"Not only that," the dwarf confirmed, "The way Alacrit's men are deploying. They're being drawn back while our forces press forward. Our translators have heard rumors of transfers to operations further north.

"How much further...?" Mirsa questioned the dwarf. "How recent is this information?"

"We learned of it yesterday, from a Stoneguard a week off the frontier," the translator answered. "The men believed the orders came from Alacrit himself."

"They'll scour Eastport for us first," Anneliese mused. "That should take them under a week once they arrive. If we're just hearing about this now, it may have been going on for some time. I doubt that forces of any size are there yet, but we cannot assume that for long."

"And after Eastport..." Mirsa's breath caught in her throat.

"They will head here," Torit announced. "They are aware of the connection your Kevon has to the Dwarven people. There is no other reasonable destination in the area." The Ambassador turned to focus on Bargthar-Stoun. "How are your defenses?"

CHAPTER 26

T he mossy glow and the different flavors of magic that wedged the portal open faded as Kevon and his friends passed through it. He felt a slight ripple as the opening closed behind them, and their link to the other side vanished. Feeling Reko's ebbing contribution to the spell keeping the water from crushing them, Kevon redoubled his own efforts. He scanned the expansive seascape for any indication of what to do next.

Rays and all other manner of flat fish swept over the open areas of the seafloor, dodging between coral formations and various outcroppings of sea vegetation. A dim, diffuse light permeated the expanse, not as bright as the Light realm, or even the Plane of Wind. Some of the plants erupted into ethereal brilliance as passing fish disturbed their fronds. Other creatures produced their own steady or intermittent light as they whirled about in intricate patterns. Gargantuan forms lumbered about in the expanse above, plaintive rumbling groans and slow swishing tails marking their passage.

No buildings, no landmarks, nothing to point anywhere, Kevon thought, squinting as if it would help cut through the distortion of the relaxing liquid that enfolded him. The only constructed *thing* in sight was the coral throne behind them, a pristine echo of its twin on the other side.

Yusa tapped Kevon on the shoulder, and pointed upward. Nodding, Kevon focused his will and the magic responded.

The trio slid upward, the magical sphere leaving a trail of light in its wake as it disturbed minute, unseen life that glowed in response. A school of bright green and red fish split as their paths intersected, and flowed around them, reuniting and doubling back to follow them upward for a few moments before continuing on their way. Kevon directed their passage around some of the larger fish that were in their path, and steered wide of a predatory looking form that circled above and to one side of them.

Slowing as he felt his reserves draining. Kevon looked to Alanna, who was still sweeping her gaze about in all directions, looking for some goal that might be reached in time. Their eyes met, and she shook her head, reaching for her throat.

Too far from the Seat to attempt a portal back, not enough magic between us to manage, he realized. *Got to do something.* Gathering all of his energy, and reaching out for more from Reko, Kevon drew the sword. As he focused part of his magic through the blade's Light rune, the rest he expended in a rush even further upward, a shooting star flashing through the endless sea they had bumbled into.

Kevon's magic ran out, and the sword dimmed as the currents from outside the protected sphere washed over them, even more relaxing than before. His heart pounded, and lungs burned. There was nothing left to be done. He returned the sword to its scabbard, and with a series of awkward motions, made his way to where Alanna suffered in kind. The same darkness as before settled in over Kevon's vision, and there were no rescuing myrnar to bring him out of it. He reached out a hand to brush against Alanna's cheek, looked into her panic-stricken eyes, and gasped for breath.

The savory warmth filled his lungs, quenching the fire that burned within. The bubbles he exhaled dissolved into the water, neither rising nor falling, but evaporating into nothingness. He tried to expel the foreign sensation, but every breath brought the sea in deeper.

So this is what death is like, he thought as the relaxing warmth enveloped him, and his eyes closed, his sensations beginning to separate from his self.

Tap. Tap. Tap.

Kevon opened his eyes to a smiling Alanna. Her unbound hair danced in the currents like sea fronds, but she was alive, and not struggling. She tapped him again and pointed to Yusa. The captain was waving his arms, flailing his legs, trying to move closer to them.

Air was like land in the Plane of Wind, Kevon thought. *Water must be like air here. I don't dare think otherwise,* he concluded, remembering the near disasters they'd had before.

Overwhelmed by the discovery that he was not dead, Kevon pulled Alanna close and buried his face in her neck, kissing and sobbing, shaking from exhaustion and relief. She held him tight for a long while before letting go.

So we're not going to drown, Kevon thought. *What next? I can't talk.* He wondered if an illusion form would make enough noise to communicate with, but did not have enough energy to even attempt it.

Pointing to Alanna and Yusa, then his own eyes, Kevon thought for a moment. He used his hands, fingers outstretched, to form a crown about his head. *Help me look for the creator,* he thought, as though it would help convey the message.

After a moment, Alanna responded. She placed her hand on her chest, then pointed to her temple. She pointed down, then brushed the fingertips of her right hand across the upturned palm of her left.

Somewhere on the floor below, Kevon nodded as he realized what she meant. He looked above, and wondered if there even was a surface to reach. Peering back down through the teeming sea life below, Kevon twisted his arms about in the water, reorienting himself toward the seafloor they had left minutes ago. Kicking and paddling to begin the return journey, he looked back long enough to see his companions were following before increasing his efforts.

The way down was more crowded than the journey

up had been, with many creatures diverting to approach and study Kevon and the others before departing. The path ahead was clear, but fish of all shapes, sizes, and colors swarmed around them, most stopping a dozen paces or more away. Some more adventurous, tiny fish darted closer, even between the companions before hurrying back into the shifting kaleidoscope walls composed of their fellows.

It's good none of these have been hungry, Kevon thought as he veered to avoid another tentacled behemoth that undulated along on a trajectory that would have come close to theirs. Scores of fish that circled on the side Kevon swam toward scattered in a brilliant visual cascade of motion and color. He relaxed for a few moments, taking in the animated beauty that surrounded them.

Alanna twirled past him, a fingertip tracing along his neck and chin before she resumed the graceful waving motions that propelled her through the water with apparent ease.

Mimicking her actions, Kevon slowed, the water around him punishing his lack of experience with the technique. Craning his neck to watch Alanna's movements closer, he began relaxing his hands and wrists, allowing the fingers to spread when he moved them forward. Stiffening his arms and cupping his hands as he pushed back to provide forward momentum proved more effective, the relaxation slowing him less as he practiced.

Attuning himself to the slight variances in pressure, he refined his technique. He held his arms close as he pulled them forward, then outward and back, flowing into an inward and back motion before repeating the steps again.

Yusa lurched past, his froglike swimming motions synching with the flares of Water magic Reko pulsed in time with his partner's movements.

They neared the throne, and Kevon felt a wave of relief as he touched down on the seafloor and flipped around to rest his feet upon it, reorienting so that the ground was *down* again.

Dizzy from the physical exertion and the massive perspective changes, Kevon stood, muscles buzzing, and closed his eyes. He allowed the water around and within him to work, pressurized ripples working the tension out of his body, easing him into relaxation. After several deep breaths, he felt so at ease that he felt as if his mind could slip free of his body and swim about on its own.

Startling back from the brief meditation, Kevon spotted Alanna nearby, scanning the distance for their objective. As her gaze wandered near to him, she shook her head.

Nothing, he thought, not nearly as frustrated about it as he would have been minutes before. *We really should try and find...* He stopped mid-thought as Reko's illusion-form appeared at the edge of his vision near the throne. Kevon and Yusa both turned to look at the magical projection of the Mage.

The dark robed figure pointed at the arm of the coral throne, took the three short steps toward it, and reached out to touch it.

Half-expecting something to happen, Kevon cringed as the image ran its hand along the surface of the seat of power. His apprehension redoubled as Reko turned back to them, and swept his arm back in an inviting gesture toward the throne.

I'm not sure I want to touch one of them, Kevon thought. *Not sure I want anyone to touch them. We haven't yet, and that's fine with me.*

Face rapt in wonder, Yusa took two slow steps toward the throne.

Kevon waved his arms to dissuade his friend, and launched himself on an intercept course between Yusa and the divine monument. He clutched at the captain's wrist, pulling Yusa back and himself forward. He wrenched his friend's arm upward and to the side as he twisted his own body into position between Yusa and the throne. His back foot slid through the moss-streaked sand as he braced himself near the base of the Seat. Kevon pushed back and released, waving his spread palms to and fro, shaking his head at his friend.

Pointing at Kevon's chest, Yusa began a series of gestures. He touched his eye, then swept a pointing finger in a wide circle. He finished with his hands wide, palms up, shaking his head, mouth agape.

Kevon closed his eyes, and shook his head in agreement. *I don't see anything,* he thought, clenching his fists in frustration. He opened his eyes, and prepared his response. Kevon's foot tapped against the seafloor, stirring whorls of silt that danced up around his ankles before settling back to the bottom. He waggled a disapproving finger at the motion, and stopped the tapping. *Don't be impatient,* he thought, looking at Yusa. He pointed to Alanna, who was still gazing off into the distance, then to his eyes, then in a slow arc around. He finished with both hands, spread fingers lowering in front of him, eyes wide. *Alanna's looking. Calm down.*

CHAPTER 27

The tremor shook the realm, blurring the lines that Alanna had drawn in the seabed.

A wave of breathlessness, or whatever passed for that in this place rolled through Kevon, and he fought the urge to cough. It was the third such event since they had arrived, and the strongest yet.

His gaze slid from the distorted star figure before him, past the trio of nested squares, to the warped semicircle and the arrow that described its direction. He approached the squares, and drew his own lines nearby, a crude drawing of a castle.

The corner of Alanna's mouth clenched in a partial frown before she shrugged at Kevon's interpretation.

Yusa held up three fingers, and pointed to the drawings between them. He held up three fingers again, and pointed to himself, Alanna, and Kevon.

Frozen in place for a few moments, Kevon's mind squealed in protest. He had thought of that when Alanna had discovered and drawn the third landmark, but was loath to voice that option. They were in such a strange place, far from home and safety, even if they managed to portal back to the Myrnar palace.

We're not splitting up, Kevon thought as he shook his head. *I'd rather...*

Another tremor hit, and the light from above dimmed by half. Over the space of the next few moments, it brightened back to nearly what it had been, as the three companions gasped and choked on the water that had turned bitter, acrid to the taste, and burned in their lungs.

Looking at the few squiggles that remained of the drawings between them, Kevon clutched his chest, and breathed deep of the restored seawater. He held up three fingers, and shook his head, holding up one instead. He waited until the others nodded in agreement.

Making another attempt, Kevon formed a Water rune, shaping it with the guidance of the contained magic of the Seat behind him. He spread his senses as far as he could manage, but the underlying power of the realm was a constant distraction, one that built faster the further Kevon probed with his mind. Within moments, he would not be able to sense anything through the noise. He released the spell, and sagged from the effort.

When Kevon opened his eyes, Yusa was pointing at the throne. The Warsmith turned and looked at the Seat of power, feeling the lines of force that emanated from it, persistent yet intangible. He stood, taking deep breaths of the seawater that tasted far less nourishing than it had been when they arrived. *We have to do something,* he thought, as he took the half-dozen steps to the side of the coral throne. Kevon braced himself as he reached out to grasp the arm of the divine Seat.

The power tore through him, too slippery for him to grasp onto with his Art. Pain, more ephemeral than physical, slashed through his mind as the lines of force reoriented at random angles. Pushing through the agony, Kevon clutched the arm of the throne with both hands. His entire being *sloshed*, filled to the brim with the deluge of energy that spewed through and beyond his grasp as fast as it rushed into him. Flecks of darkness danced across his vision, as he struggled to remain conscious. *Where. Is. She?* The desperate question whispered over the maelstrom in his mind, the only thing that kept him clinging to both the throne, and sanity.

The lines of energy containing the Water magic shifted again, as if in response to the question. They splayed outward, and spun about in a mad vortex.

Unsure of what the new fluctuations meant, Kevon wrapped his arms around the section of throne he had gripped. He held on, hoping for clarity as the vortex wobbled and stretched in his mind. The power continued to rush through him, leaking away at a pace that outstripped his mind's ability to measure. With every passing moment, it seemed he slipped closer to madness. The movements of the lines were even starting to make sense, to point...

Kevon coughed, choking on the bitter breathing-water that filled his mouth and lungs. Splotches of light swam into his vision, expanding, merging, blurring, and sharpening into the form of Alanna, who shook him with desperate force. His head pounded with every heartbeat, every shake, every breath, every stray thought. His vision swam in and out of focus with the throbbing, with only one speck of clarity in the swirling soup that was his new reality. He blinked to try and focus on Alanna, and wipe away the aberrant dot against his field of vision, but it remained, through his eyelids, beyond Alanna, far beyond where he should be able to see.

He raised his hand to point, and had to look down to be sure the limb he could not feel had responded to his orders. His eyes rasped as though surrounded by a carpenter's gritcloth as they tracked down to see his hand pointing to the mark in the distance. The pain shocked him, and he twitched. The resulting cascade of agony flooded through him, delivering him back into enfolding oblivion.

Dim light filtered in through the gap in Kevon's eyelids. A soundless groan, and a yawn full of swirling water resulted in only gentle aches, and he opened his eyes. The illumination from above had waned further, the water tasted and smelled impure in a manner Kevon could not put to words. Rhythmic tugs at his armpits were Yusa and Alanna swimming at his sides, towing his limp form along with them. A too-familiar looking form darted through Kevon's field of vision, flashes of pink and grey flesh twirling in a playful arc below the companions. He tensed, and felt the hands at his arms release.

Waving arms to right himself, Kevon's horizon shifted, and he recognized the misshapen semicircle that Alanna had drawn looming in the distance, a giant clam that dwarfed all of the distant figures swimming around it.

The mermaid that had skimmed past his gaze moments ago circled back around, her fluid motion calling extra attention to her lack of basic covering that the myrnar in the Plane of Enchantment usually maintained. She bobbed before them a few moments before emitting a warbling chirp, a cheerful sounding note that emanated as she flared her gill flaps, and motioned for them to follow her.

As Kevon followed the arc of the mermaid's passage, he noticed the twinge in his vision near the center of the giant creature ahead. The answer to his question, their destination, was close at hand. He probed his reserves, and found them nearly full. Forming a Water rune, he encapsulated a sphere around himself and his friends, and with a mental shove, maneuvered the bubble after their shapely escort.

He felt the tremor on the skin of the sphere as he concentrated on its maintenance. The light flickered, but did not dim further. Kevon's spell provided relief from the choking alteration of the surrounding seawater, a welcome benefit. The myrnar leading them was not so fortunate. Panicked chirps sounded from her, and several other directions where Kevon could see clustered myrnar. She clutched at her throat, and her gills flapped in frantic waves for the space of several agonizing breaths.

Still gasping, but no longer in acute distress, the mermaid beckoned once again, and sped for the distant seafloor near the midpoint of the edge of the clam's warped shell.

Tapping into the Enhancement rune that he felt Reko form alongside the Water and Aid runes already glowing in his mind, Kevon wrestled the power to his will. The unseen life the bubble passed through flared brilliant green, more evident now in the lower light from above. As they neared their escort, Kevon extended the bubble around her, jostling them as velocities equalized.

Alanna paddled forward, beckoning to the mermaid, who appeared to be on the verge of panic. She took the myrnar's hand, and pointed forward to the approaching landscape.

Twisting the magic to swerve around knots of congregated myrnar, Kevon brought the sphere close to the center of the edge of the gigantic shell. He slowed their motion and ended the spell near the lower lip, nearly forty paces from the seafloor.

The currents around them changed as Kevon ended the spell, and the mermaid chirped her excitement. Pulling Alanna's hand, she led the group between the barnacle encrusted lips of the giant clam.

CHAPTER 28

"**H**ow is Torit dealing with his solitude?" Mirsa asked Anneliese as they met in the hallway, headed toward the throne room.

"He complained yesterday of boredom, requested his game board, and a visit from you."

"Taking it better than I would," Mirsa admitted. "I would be..."

"He knows that his loyalty is suspect, at best," Anneliese clarified. "I think the actions Alacrit is taking have turned him more toward our side, but he understands and supports Bargthar-Stoun's position on the matter. At least until this conflict is resolved."

"You were summoned?" Mirsa asked as they rounded another corner.

"I was. They wanted to discuss siege defense strategies. You?"

"There is a transport coming in. I felt it from my room earlier. The drumbeats have been easier for me to detect, now that I know it's what they are."

"There are bound to be more recalled troops on the transport, they may need help deciding how best to deploy them," Anneliese mused. "Some of the Dwarven crossbowmen, especially the Stoneguard, rival even our hunters. One of the chambers below is a practice range."

"The two fallen spires that lay across the pass coming into the Hold are obvious places to place them, I would think?" Mirsa asked.

"Yes, there are more than enough troops to have them

shoulder to shoulder across both," Anneliese confirmed. "I'm not convinced that would be the best use for them. There are access points further out along the pass that are smaller, higher up, not as vulnerable. Having small groups there to assess the risk, make decisions, and eliminate key targets before they close on the Hold if needed..."

"Really? How far back up the pass? How many?" Mirsa's could not contain her surprise at the new information. "We hadn't spotted them either trip."

"Three, though the furthest is just large enough for one scout," Anneliese clarified. "I wonder if you would be comfortable in the middle section, estimating the magical threat that might be arriving with them, and disrupting it if needed."

"Where will you be?"

"The innermost outpost, where the final decision will have to be made," Anneliese shrugged. "A handful of well-placed arrows, and a retreat to the near spire to reinforce the Dwarven archers. It should not come to that, but tensions may be running high."

"I'm not sure how much disruption I would be able to provide," Mirsa admitted, "But I have some ideas I'll need help with that may work." She cringed as they entered the passage that led through the smithing district, her nerves twanging with each hammer-strike. "I've managed to tune this out when we're further away, but there is no way to keep it out when we're this close."

"The transport has arrived," Mirsa announced. "The drums have stopped. I wonder what news they bring today."

Mirsa fidgeted as they walked down the last few corridors to the throne room, wondering if she should have brought Maisy instead of leaving her with the Dwarven nurse. She'd spent more time apart from her daughter since they had reached the Hold than she had since she was born, but the Dwarves were always so playful, eager, and kindhearted. There was seldom a reason to refuse an offer to watch her.

"Ahh. We should find out..." Anneliese stopped as she

saw the look of concern on Mirsa's face. "What?"

"The drums have started again."

"Sending out a crew to pick up another load of soldiers?" Anneliese guessed. "They usually rest overnight before returning, it's unusual, but haste may be…"

"Those drums would fade," Mirsa argued. "These are the drums that help the transports stop on the return journey."

"Another incoming transport so soon?" Anneliese wondered aloud. "What could that mean?"

The guards normally standing at attention on either side of the doors to the throne room were peering inside as Anneliese and Mirsa rounded the last corner to their destination, their pole-axes held at stray angles that made the Mage stop well short.

"What's happening?" Anneliese asked, keeping a safe distance herself.

Both guards turned and hoisted their weapons to a loose approximation of their correct placement. One of them shook his head, the other shrugged, a muttered *'meh'* escaping his lips.

"Are we… okay to go in?" Mirsa asked, creeping closer.

The other dwarf shrugged, and exchanged glances with his partner.

"*Okay,*" the other guard made a small gesture with a clenched fist in Mirsa's direction.

"Is that…?" she asked as Anneliese imitated the gesture to smiling nods.

"I'm guessing it's a yes." The Huntmistress chuckled as she led the way through the oversized doorway.

A semicircle of armed Dwarves stood near the concealed passage that led below to the landing area, arguing with Bargthar-Stoun. The king gestured toward the hidden passage, and roared a command in his native tongue. Half of the group turned to obey, the remaining four took a step back, and looked at each other.

"*Should we interfere?*" Mirsa whispered.

"Anything we can help with?" Anneliese called, startling the entire group, along with Bargthar-Stoun. "Sounds like trouble."

"*Muhr-sa!*" the regal dwarf called out, pointing through the opened passage the others were starting to file through. "*Come!*"

"I've never been down there before, have you?" Anneliese asked, breaking into a jog.

"Never," Mirsa answered as she hurried along behind her friend.

Anneliese moved to the right as they started descending the staircase that wrapped around the central pillar of the landing area, putting herself between Mirsa and the metal railing that skirted the outside edge. She pulled the Mage close to her side, so that there was a suitable distance between Mirsa's head and the iron baskets that held the light-rocks against the wall at heights the Dwarves did not have to worry about.

Dwarves were still unloading supplies from the transport sledge that had just come in. *Armor and weapons, likely from their fallen brothers,* Mirsa thought as she saw the gear being piled against the wall. *We'll need it here soon enough.*

"Different tunnel?" Anneliese asked, pointing to the troops stationed two tunnels away from the sledge. "Are they boarding it up, or reopening it?"

"It looks like that is the disagreement," Mirsa guessed. "It's been boarded up, I don't think they know who is coming through. Who would they expect but more of their own? Who else knows…" Mirsa bit down on the words as they escaped her lips. "*Martin has been through the tunnels,*" she whispered.

CHAPTER 29

"**M**artin and his friends are the worst things that could come out of that tunnel," Anneliese agreed. "A few boards aren't going to stop them, but might damage someone else. I think we could take Martin and whoever else he brings with him."

"Hey!" Anneliese shouted over the cadence of the drum below. "Clear that passage! Move back! Set up a perimeter!"

Dwarven translators looked to their ruler for a nod of approval before shouting orders in their own language. Hammers and axes made short work of the remaining boards that extended across the opening. The resulting debris was tossed aside, beyond the line of Stoneguard and regulars that formed up in a semicircle twenty paces from the entrance. Crossbowmen climbed onto crates, the other sledge, and up the stairs to get better vantage points.

Anneliese readied her bow, easing an arrow into place and drawing it back just enough to hold it to the bowstring. "You might want to get ready."

The cadence of the drums slowed, as the assembled crowd seemed to grow more agitated. Mirsa looked overhead to make sure she was clear of lighting baskets, and took two steps forward to get a better angle on the unfolding action. The Fire rune in her mind roared to life, as a tongue of flame leapt into existence over her upturned palm. Without conscious thought, she fed the heat that washed over her hand, arms, and face back into the spell. The basic technique prolonged the spell and protected her from the damage at the same time.

"Something's…" Mirsa turned back to Anneliese, her expression contorted with worry. "It sounds… wrong." She closed her eyes and focused on the irregular beat that rippled through her mind, still too far away to be heard with her ears. The tempo rose to a frenzied, uneven pace. Feeling the intensity of the odd magic growing, Mirsa opened her eyes, and saw the thin stone rollers near the entrance to the passageway start rotating into the room, rather than outward from it as they had been. She could feel the transport getting closer, accelerating, rather than slowing down as it should.

Anneliese stared at Mirsa's face for a moment. "Pick up the beat, boys!" The Huntmistress called to the Dwarven drummers that were beating on the launch drum below. "I don't think our new friend is slowing down!"

"Oh!" Mirsa exclaimed as the shaking in her mind lessened. The frenzied drumming that emanated from the tunnel came to an abrupt end. The remaining waves that rolled through her were solid, and steady, much easier for her mind to adjust to. Her estimation of the approaching transport grew less certain with the sudden absence of approaching magic, but she knew it could not be more than a dozen breaths away.

"Shouldn't it be here by now?" Anneliese growled, echoing the thoughts in Mirsa's mind. "I think we sh…"

A low grinding sound rose over the cadence of the drums, and some of the Dwarves arranged below advanced toward it, others stepped back.

"I don't like that sound," Mirsa commented, sharpening the focus of her spell as Anneliese pulled back into a full draw.

The murmurs below grew in volume as the new grinding noise, though closer, faded as it approached. The broken semicircle of Dwarves straightened into two lines on either side of the entrance, lining the rollers that led up to the tunnel's dock. "It's one of our sledges!" one of the translators below called up. "We can't see anyone in it!"

The Dwarves lining the track stepped back as the sledge

ground into view, its bow crumpled and splintered, runners at an odd angle. The tail end of one of the supporting rails dragged against the side of the channel the rollers were housed in, metal sparking against the stone every few feet.

Mirsa gasped at the sight of the rubble that filled the cargo hold of the sledge, and her spell dissolved. The last flash of firelight left a haze of warmth that raised a sheen of sweat on her face before it dissipated. "What is..."

"*Skergiz*," Anneliese whispered, keeping her drawn bow trained on the slowing transport. "You have something besides fire we can use on it?"

"That's a..." Mirsa squinted as she peered through the railing at the contents of the sledge, realizing that not all of the greenish-grey mounds within were boulders. As she shifted to look around some of the iron uprights, she gasped as she made out the outline of the reptilian form. She guessed it was nearly twice Anneliese's height, and weighed as much as four armored Stoneguard.

"We'd better get down there and check it out," Anneliese sighed, edging down to where Mirsa stood. "I really hope it's not *Ateraz*."

"You know him?" Mirsa squeaked, backing down a step."

"*Ateraz* is their warrior Caste," Anneliese explained as she made her way down the staircase. "Before I was a Huntmistress, my superior and I had a run-in with a skergiz, an *Ateraz*, she said. We were all fortunate to have survived the encounter. I believe I could defeat it now, but there would be losses."

The Huntmistress motioned the Dwarves that surrounded the transport away as she stalked up the ramp to the platform above it. "I'm going to put my weapon away," she cautioned as they drew near. "To put it at its ease. You should have something prepared, but not visible."

Mirsa focused on a Movement rune as Anneliese returned her arrow to its quiver, re-slung her bow, and made sure the blades at her sides were free of obstructions. The Mage located a handful of medium sized boulders, and spread her concentration among them, ready to shift her focus to one and lob it if the need arose.

Stepping up to the edge of the platform with Anneliese, Mirsa added another Stoneguard to her estimation of the creature's weight. The bases of the skergiz's legs and tail were as thick as her torso, and well-muscled. Its chest heaved in long, slow breaths, its clawed hands flexing as if it were dreaming of rending flesh. The head, something between that of a snake or a lizard, would have appeared intimidating anywhere else. Attached to the brawny shoulders that rested above the creature's huge chest, it seemed a little understated.

The skergiz's eyelids flickered, and it moaned in pain.

"Who are you?" Anneliese demanded, her voice filling the now-silent chamber. "Why have you come here? What is your faction?"

Taking in a few short breaths and another long one, the skergiz hissed as it tried to begin forming words. "sCommon... sssmall," it managed after a few attempts. "Katarit... cassste... Tamaraithhh..."

Mirsa saw the tension drain from Anneliese as the Huntmistress heard and absorbed the skergiz's words. *I've never seen her transition from a state of fear to one of relief, but I'm certain that is what just happened*, she thought as Anneliese motioned for everyone else to relax.

"Be at ease, Tamaraith," Anneliese said, hopping down to the sledge. "You are among friends." She turned to the nearest translator. "Bring water, meat, firewood. Bring a healer. Bring all of your healers."

CHAPTER 30

The defect in Kevon's vision that marked their objective dissolved as they moved further into the odd structure. The pulses of magic that he used to supplement his swimming motions echoed behind him as Yusa and Reko followed where the myrnar led, hauling Alanna.

Grotesque looking fish with glowing bulbs that dangled near their mouths from above their eyes slid to one side or the other as the party slipped deeper into the undulating darkness.

Ripples of luminescence sped along the ceiling as the pressure of their passing activated the moss that hung in ragged clumps from above. The delayed illumination threw warped shadows ahead of the group, distorting the appearances of myrnar and other sea life that drifted within the space between the moss-strewn ceiling and the pink mottled flesh that undulated below.

Their Myrnar escort slowed as they approached a thick curtain-wall of moss. The pressure wave that followed them sloshed ahead, lighting up the ceiling moss, but the thick barrier moss only rippled, absorbing the light cast on it from above. She angled toward an opening flanked by Myrnar males larger than Kevon had ever seen.

Challenging thrums flared outward from the guards, who moved closer to the center of the opening, barring passage. The answering trill was ignored, and repeated.

The ground trembled.

Bracing for the accompanying suffocation, Kevon

clenched his teeth and squeezed his eyes shut.

Their escort repeated her request, a plaintive note threaded into the melody.

Opening his eyes, Kevon felt no sting, tasted no bitterness. He breathed deeply of the pure water, and watched as the guards drifted aside and the mermaid towed Alanna into the chamber beyond.

Two pillars of hanging moss flanked the entrance, thick as oak trunks, dazzling in their brilliance. Another set of the same pillars, spread wider, lit the other side of the room, where the halves of the enormous shell curved and met. The grooves visible on the ceiling and back wall converged toward the center of the room, and the occupied throne that sat before the focal area.

In a flash of mottled yellow and brown, the shiny mountain of chitin that lay beside the gleaming seat sprang forward and to the center, clicking claws as large as a griffin at the oncoming group.

Kevon shifted the focus of the spell he had been using to propel himself through the water, and as it began to resolve into something suitable for attack or defense, the magic slipped from his grasp, going dull in his mind. His vision blurred, as though he'd been slapped across the face. He reached for the power again, but as it eluded his grasp, he recognized the futility in a matter of moments. Glancing aside at Yusa, he looked for a hint of what Reko was doing, but without the Mage's ability to whisper in his partner's ear, there was not even an errant expression to judge. Feeling no other magic in the area, he assumed Yusa's alter-ego was in much the same position.

Their Myrnar escort slowed, holding onto Alanna's hand until she shifted upright before releasing her and shifting to the side. Kevon and Yusa swam up next to Alanna, and regarded the gigantic crab that still scuttled and snapped before them.

A wave of icy calm shuddered through Kevon, and the

mammoth crustacean before them cowered, its body dropping nearly to the spongy floor, its claws drawn back close to its mouth, clenched motionless. It tiptoed back to its place, revealing a smaller, almost translucent version of itself opposite the throne, and the objective of their journey.

M'drea, Kevon thought, taking in the spectacle before him as the matron of the Myrnar rose out of the carved pearl throne with a flick of her tail. He lowered his gaze, trying to drink in her visage with his eyes, without offering an overt challenge.

The creator's silhouette was much the same as a myrnar, but most of the similarities ended there. Her lower half, instead of smooth gray, was covered in small blue-green scales that flashed in the light as she rippled forward. Scattered scales seemed to glow on their own, independent of the angle they held toward the pillars of light. Her tan, lightly muscled midsection was strong, yet feminine. Her shoulders and upper torso were partially obscured by the shifting mass of a luminous creature. An opaque jellyfish that glowed soft blue fluttered in the currents, clinging tight to its master. Dazzling blue eyes, too vivid to be human, were the only feature in her olive-toned face that marked her any different than a gorgeous woman, until her hair fell across it. Captured currents of aquamarine flowed from M'drea's head, falling about and below her shoulders. The tips of her animated coiffure were swelling breakers of glittering sea-foam.

The twined locks of the creator's hair surged and shrank within the confines of its outlines regardless of her movement, and Kevon felt his gaze drawn to it. He raised his eyes to meet hers, and felt his spirit beginning to drown in her majesty,

Currents at Kevon's back propelled him forward toward her. He writhed in panic as she raised a sinewy arm, and extended webbed fingers. Her pale blue lips parted, revealing rows of teeth, reminiscent of a myrnar, but smaller, staggered, curved and cruel.

Alanna reached out and grabbed his hand, but the currents adjusted and pulled them apart with a tender insistence.

Fear built in Kevon's mind as M'drea closed the distance between them, and her size became more apparent. She was twice as tall as Kevon, and her outstretched hand was large enough to encircle his head.

She reached for his face, and he could see the small flesh-colored suction cups that covered her fingertips and the underside of her palms.

WHO HAS MY CHILD BROUGHT TO ME?

Kevon startled as the voice pounded into his mind, an amalgam of lapping waves, crashing surf, and screaming gulls. The pain subsided as he broke contact with M'drea, her outstretched hand slipping from the side of his chin.

The creator's eyes flashed at Kevon's response, narrowing as her lips curved upward, her mouth opening wider in an expression that could not be mistaken for anything but hunger. Her shoulders rolled forward, and half a dozen pale, whiplike tentacles lashed around from behind her body, snaring Kevon, drawing him to her.

Both Alanna and Yusa moved to his aid, but were knocked aside by other tentacles that emerged from behind M'drea's back.

WHY ARE YOU DOING THIS?

The question built like an ocean storm, punctuated by thunderclaps in Kevon's mind as his captor held the sides of his face in both hands, her eyes mere inches from his.

I'm not doing anything! He thought, writhing in her clutches. *If I can't find a way to talk to her, she's going to kill us all!*

M'drea's eyes widened, and she relaxed the tentacles that encircled Kevon. Floating back a short distance, she removed one hand from Kevon's face, sliding the other down under his chin, her touch gentle, but firm.

KILLING... DEATH IS L'MORT'S GIFT, NOT MINE.

The words poured into Kevon's mind, a waterfall descending from a dizzying height.

Your words, hurting... Kevon thought in response, his mind on the verge of shutting down.

You are FRAGILE, M'drea boomed. *You cannot be responsible.*

We were sent by M'lani, Kevon explained. *She wanted us to speak to all of you, about L'mort.*

I sensed him in you, M'drea's words flowed over Kevon's mind as a brook babbling over smooth stones. *As I should. You are Man. Men are no more. How have you come to be here?*

The Plane of Enchantment endures, Kevon's thoughts turned to the journey he'd begun years before, leaving Laston, meeting his friends. *It was not destroyed, as you all thought. It is... locked away, impossible for you to enter.* Memories of L'mort's attempt to cross over in the caverns below Gurlin's tower filled his mind, and M'lani's grip on his jaw tensed.

L'MORT KNOWS OF THIS? Her angry query crashed against Kevon's mind in thunderous waves.

Gently, Kevon reminded her. *He has had agents at work in our Plane, expanding his influence, and the walls between his realm and ours weaken, as yours grow thicker. M'lani has sent us to you to gather strength to protect ourselves from him. If he should cross over into our...*

He grows more powerful with mere influence in your Plane, M'drea thought in return. *We were ever only there at the same time, in balance. If he were free to wander there himself, it could mean the destruction of us all. The disruptions plaguing us now would grow unbearable. The tremors started out as a nuisance, but require more and more power to suppress, each one stronger than the last.*

M'drea released Kevon, and her tentacles shot out, wrapping around Yusa and Alanna, who had swam back into range, ready to rescue Kevon. She pulled them close, reached out and cupped each of their faces in one of her hands. She smiled, concentrated for a moment, and set them adrift, retracting her tentacles until they were hidden behind her once more.

They will let us continue to speak, M'drea continued, resuming her contact with Kevon, cradling his face in her hands with a far lighter touch. *Tell me what else you know. Show me.*

Many men are in league with your brother, Kevon thought, as he gazed into M'drea's eyes. His vision softened and blurred as her face drew closer to his. The feeling of losing himself returned, stronger than before. Images of the battle in Eastport flooded into his mind, shifting to memories of belowground skirmishes under the Highplain, the extermination of chimaera nests linked to the Dark portals. *Those aligned with him have fashioned gateways between realms, allowing creatures of darkness to invade, infest, overwhelm. We have destroyed several gateways, but do not know how many more exist. We are losing.*

The semblance of control Kevon had over his thoughts dissolved as the memories flowed through him, contorting from one nightmarish scene to another. He held on tight to the buckboard of the wagon as they barreled over the cobblestone path that led to the palace gates. Soldiers to the right circled an obsidian reaper, and Carlo barked commands from the fray. Kevon ducked as they rode between the opening gates, and leapt into a crouch, slowing in the sudden darkness. The stale air moved, followed by a rasp, and a scream. He rushed forward into the full light in time to see the Orclord stuff the rest of Waine into his mouth. The shield of Light and Wind flashed upward, tinted blue-green. He could see himself as if from above, drowning alongside Mirsa as he struggled with the magic in his mind.

Kevon clawed his way back to himself, head pounding, and slipped into the duel with Alanna in the heart of Eastport, as the city burned around them. He dodged several attacks before she connected, knocking him backward, sprawling on top of him. His vision wavered, darkening as her clothing shifted to bedsheets, her aggression slowing into a primal rhythm. Her face remained constant, her hair a mix of brown and gold, her green and gold eyes locked on him, while the surroundings swirled. An inn-room in Eastport became the steerage on a ship, which faded into a moonless night sky. He tried to blink the memories away, but saw flashes of an abandoned smithy, the inside of a hide tent, a palace suite. Some were places he'd never been with her, but that had not stopped him from dreaming.

Enough, Kevon pleaded as M'drea slowed the memories, and began cycling back through them.

Battling to reassert control of his own mind, Kevon forced images of M'lani and M'phes to the surface, and M'drea lingered over the Alanna memories for a moment longer before shifting focus.

Touched by my sister, M'drea commented, allowing Kevon's consciousness to surface enough to see her eyes shift away to gaze at Alanna beside them. *She is special, and not just to you.*

M'lani restored her sight, Kevon agreed, *She's been special to me since we met. That's all I care about.*

The image of M'lani grasping the blade of Kevon's sword surfaced, and slowed, fading as the goddess began to release him from her grasp. *This is why you came?*

Yes, Kevon thought in response. *M'lani requested that we...* the words rang hollow in his own head as the suction-dimpled fingertips slipped from the side of his face.

Motioning for the sword, M'drea smiled at Yusa and Alanna in turn.

Kevon drew the blade, and held it out, hilt first.

The sword shifted as M'drea grasped the hilt. Before contact was broken, Kevon could feel her magic draining into the void that the other creators had filled with their immense power, the same void that had taken him ages of agony, discomfort, and uselessness to fill before the sudden change at the dark tower.

The streams of captive water that formed M'drea's flowing locks blurred, mixing with the surrounding sea. The unmaintained seafoam ends dissolved as the tentacles behind her back splayed out in a quivering fan formation.

Foul tasting water followed the silent rumble that rocked the room. Kevon choked on the now-familiar taste, evidence of L'mort's growing power even here.

Covering the grasping hand with her other hand, M'drea closed her eyes in concentration. Her tentacles sagged downward, tops and ends first, settling into a silhouette of wings before she retook active control, and drew them back behind her. She slid the covering hand partway down the blade, pausing at the two spots Kevon had felt that the previous enchantments by the other creators resided, before turning back toward him and offering to return the sword.

The sea around Kevon snapped into sharp detail as he took the sword by the blade, and the newly imprinted rune filled his mind. The awful taint that the last tremor produced was receding, freshened by waves of magic flowing from M'drea. One of the guards outside turned to peek at the meeting, poking his head past the curtain for no longer than a handful of heartbeats before returning to his vigilant posture. Alanna's breath and heartbeat were rapid, panicked, but slowing as the moments passed.

Sheathing the weapon, Kevon maintained contact with the hilt, and the added awareness connected to it. Though it demanded nothing more of him, he could detect an emptiness in the blade verging on hunger. It slipped away as soon as he focused on it, and Kevon turned his attention back to the matter at hand.

M'drea beckoned to Alanna, and Kevon could feel the currents form, gentler than those that had pulled him into her grasp.

Swimming forward, Alanna closed her eyes and bowed before the goddess, who reached out to lift her chin with a gentle touch.

Be welcome, child, M'drea thought. *There is much of my sister, M'lani, in you. Kevon has shown me the bestowing of her gift, among other things.* Letting her words sink in, she continued. *With the realms in the state of chaos they are, his foremost thoughts are of you. He is simple. Your thoughts are guarded, layers of conflict and restraint, so deep. Take care not to lose yourself in them.*

Those layers of restraint have kept me alive, Alanna responded. *If Kevon knew...*

Kevon released the hilt of the sword, at the shocking realization that the sword may have been allowing him to hear the conversation. The voices faded from his mind. *She'll tell me when she's ready,* he thought.

M'drea pulled Alanna into an enveloping embrace. She curled her shoulders inward, lacing her back tentacles around until only the assassin's lower legs were visible before releasing her and moving on to Yusa.

Wrapping himself in Water magic, Kevon slid over to Alanna's side and took her hand, watching Yusa's interaction with M'drea. *I wonder what they are talking about.*

You sure had plenty to tell her, Alanna squeezed his hand in response. She ran her thumb along the edge of his, and lurching, inappropriate scenes slipped through his mind.

You can... We can... Kevon projected the fresh memory of the embrace they'd shared after they nearly drowned toward Alanna. Her eyes closed, lips parted, and head tilted to the side as the vision engulfed her. He sank into the reenactment, shifting around into her embrace. After a few moments of the echoing kiss, he withdrew the mental projection. *Soon enough. There is time.*

They untangled, and watched the end of M'drea's interaction with Yusa, with only stray thoughts clouding their minds.

The goddess of the Myrnar drifted back from Yusa, and turned toward her throne. The whiplike tentacles that protruded from either side of her backbone writhed with purpose, pinching areas on the surface of the fleshy floor, pulling her forward, releasing, and sliding forward again in a hypnotic fashion. When she neared the pearl throne, she turned with a flick of her tail. The tentacles extended back, wrapped about the back and legs of the seat, and pulled her into a seated position before coiling behind her, unseen.

Settling his hand back onto the sword's hilt, Kevon projected his thoughts once again. *Can you hear me?*

I can, my child. Can they?

Can you? He thought at the others.

Of course we can. Reko's gruff tone slid through the water, a perfect imitation of his image's usual voice.

You can hear me! Can you hear her?

Not since she let go, Yusa's disappointment was evident in his thoughts. *Why can I hear you?*

They can hear me, but not you, Kevon reported. *It must be the sword. I feel connected to everything.*

I must stay here, and gather more of my creations closer so that I can protect them from the chaos my brother inflicts on my realm, M'drea announced. *Return to the Plane of Enchantment, and do what you can to restore the balance, in my name.*

I will, my lady. Kevon turned back to the others. *Are you ready?*

She said we can visit when this is all over, Yusa answered. *We can leave.*

Projecting the memory of their carriage ride through Eastport to the Myrnar embassy into his consciousness, Alanna smiled and squeezed Kevon's hand.

Focusing on the new Water rune enchanted into the blade, Kevon gathered a trickle of latent Water magic, a small fragment of the otherwise bound energy that flowed through the realm. He used the rune's clarity, building on the spell, extending his senses out of the living structure they floated in. Plotting out the best path, he filtered the energy through the glowing sigil, and the spell took hold. Bubbles coalesced around the three of them, and they zipped out of M'drea's chamber. The trio slid between the guarding myrnar and their mermaid escort, skimming just over the wavy surface of the living floor. They burst out into the open, and the clam-shell palace shrank behind them as Kevon pushed the spell further.

For long minutes they spiraled up toward the light, far enough above that Kevon could feel the lines of magical force that centered on M'drea below them, and stronger still, around the coral Seat that they had emerged near.

We'll be back to our realm before we know it, Kevon announced to his friends, to mixed responses as he shifted formation, aimed them down toward their destination, and dove full speed.

CHAPTER 31

"How does our newest guest fare?" Torit asked, gesturing to the table where the game sat, reset, ready to play.

"You're not even supposed to know about him," Anneliese frowned, holding her position near the door.

"Ah," he chuckled. "My translator friends are eager to practice their Common, and far less skilled in court-craft than my usual adversaries. A handful of different details from each one, and I can deduce the rest of the goings on around the Hold."

"I'll instruct them to hold their tongues, have them replaced."

"Had I ill intentions, I would not have revealed what I know," Torit admonished. "Our fates are joined. Even the skergiz."

"That may be," Anneliese conceded. "Until everyone is convinced, you remain here."

"Does the king play?" he asked, a smile creeping back onto his face.

"He's rather busy of late," the Huntmistress answered as she turned to leave. Pausing in the doorway, she added, "I'll ask when I see him next."

"Your recovery seems nearly complete," Mirsa commented as she led the Dwarves bringing in armloads of wood for the roaring fireplace. "Do you need more to eat?"

The skergiz stirred, shifting on the pile of cushions arranged near the fire. "Food... Sstill." Tamaraith stifled a yawn.
"Sso warm. Made fire... good."

"Made fire..." Mirsa sat in a chair a few feet further from
the fire than Tamaraith, and waved away the Dwarves that had
stacked their wood near the fireplace. "You are not used to
'made fire', are you?"

"Home..." Tamaraith began, "Mountain, warm. Ssun,
warm. Here... only ssun warm."

"Mountain..." Mirsa nodded at the skergiz. "Anneliese
has told me some of your people. They live near the volcano
near Alcron. Where you live depends on which faction is in
power at the time?"

Tamaraith closed his eyes, shifting on the cushions
again to warm himself from a different angle. "Common...
sslow. You... fasst. Head... pain."

Mirsa covered a chuckle. "I'm sorry. I'll slow down." She
waited for a nod from the skergiz before continuing. "Your
warm mountain... how close did you live?"

"Ahh," Tamaraith's eyes glinted in the reflected firelight
as he turned to bathe his face in the heat. "Katarit lead. Live...
most near. Ateraz... next?"

"Your caste are in control, and live closest to the mountain, where it's warmest?"

"Were," the Skirgiz confirmed, turning back to look at
Mirsa. "Tamaraith here... many sseasonss."

"You can't be sure who is in power now," Mirsa nodded.
"Your society is always shifting."

"Trialss... change leaders... change... where live."
Tamaraith clarified. "Win, warm. Losse, cold. Cold... sslow,
weak."

"The ruling castes live closer to the mountain, the volcano, where it is warmer," Mirsa mused. "The extra warmth
gives them an advantage, lets them gather more strength, to
stay in power."

"Yess." Tamaraith twisted his tail around closer to the

fireplace. "Made fire... for sskergiz... not fair. Counssil only."

Moments passed before she made sense of the statement. "Wait, you weren't allowed to build fires, only the top caste?" Mirsa shook her head. "That doesn't seem..."

"Counssil... all casste leaderss..." the skergiz explained in halting fragments of speech. "All sstay, warm mountain, made fire. Lead uss."

"I think I understand it better now," Mirsa scooted the chair back a foot, and wiped away the thin sheen of moisture that had formed on her forehead. "What about you? Why were you on the southern end of our realm? Why so far from home?"

"Katarit and Egitur... ally," Tamaraith answered. "Katarit... trade, Egitur... *sassathir...* build?"

"Expanding your influence across the sea," Mirsa acknowledged. "There were two of you?"

"More," Tamaraith countered. "Two fourss Katarit... two fourss Egitur," he described, flexing his clawed hand wide, wiggling the three fingers and opposing thumb in sequence.

"There were... sixteen of you?"

"Four fourss... many of us," Tamaraith agreed. "I am... lasst."

"With the amount of troops you have recalled, we will need more food stores if there is any action against the Hold," Anneliese told Bargthar-Stoun through the accompanying translator. "Prepared rations at all of the outposts, for extended rotations. You have routes to Kron, correct?"

"We can get a wagonload from Kron every four days," the dwarf told her, after conversing with his king.

"How many wagons do you have?" she asked, then shook her head. "Never mind. Send them all. Grain. Salt. Firewood. Cured meat and cheeses. It will be expensive."

"*Yah,*" Bargthar-Stoun nodded as he received the translated request.

"Now?" she asked, eyes widening as she addressed the king.

Pointing at a following page, Bargthar-Stoun shouted orders until his subordinate stumbled out of the room at a run.

"Water," Anneliese continued. "You have access to plenty of fresh water, and little enough stored around the Hold. That may change, prepare for it. Fill every barrel that you can, distribute them as you will do with the rations, for emergencies."

Wasting no time, Bargthar-Stoun directed another page to relay the order.

"Watch rotations. Your men know how to fight, and they fight well," Anneliese admitted. "The troops here, ex-cepting the ones recalled from the south, do not know how to wage war. Enforce schedules. Make them sleep, keep them rested, prepared for what is to come. You have the strength of position, fortification, combat prowess. If Alacrit moves against you, he has the advantage of numbers, and magic. I'm not worried about the numbers, because of your strengths. If we can stop the magic, we win."

"*Yah.*"

"They spent years running, hiding, fighting orcs beyond the southern frontier," Mirsa exclaimed, pacing as she related the story to Anneliese. "He's been on his own for over a year, hiding and foraging, before he stumbled on the entrance to the transport line. It took him nearly a season to clear the col-lapsed section of the tunnel enough to get through."

"He'll be a good ally to have when we need to deal with the Skergiz," Anneliese commented as she readied for her evening patrol. "More so if his faction is still in power by then." She finished fussing with the arrow, and slid it back into its quiver. She caught up her unslung bow, and rubbed the top of Maisy's head.

"I'll have to talk with the skergiz tomorrow, if he feels well enough," the Huntmistress concluded, making her way to the door of the chamber she, Mirsa, and Maisy shared. "After this watch, and some sleep. I should take my own advice."

Anneliese wove her way through the halls of the residential area, taking the wider passages for as long as she could before ducking into a service tunnel that led to the upper routes that connected the lookouts above the Hold and further down the valley. She ducked to avoid hitting her head on light-stone baskets, and slid to either side as Dwarves moved heavy casks of water on sturdy handcarts from one place to another.

As she progressed further down the tunnels, the bustle lessened, and the only Dwarves she passed were soldiers and Stoneguard, who greeted her with nods and grunts. She continued down to the end of the last tunnel, and climbed the tight spiral staircase that led to the lookout platform. She tapped the occupant on the shoulder as she sat down next to him, and he murmured something in his native tongue, nodding as he stood to leave.

Sliding down the short stone bench to where her predecessor had sat, Anneliese looked out over the curve of the narrow valley below, and the thin slice of sky above. Patchy, dark clouds crowded the dim wedge above, obscuring all but a few faint stars. After scrutinizing the area below for several minutes, she uncorked her water skin and took a long drink. She wiped her mouth and replaced the cork, setting the skin aside and resuming her vigil.

The wind shifted, and the remaining stars winked out, dimming the scene below to all but Elven eyes. She spotted the glimmering reflection of moving steel minutes later, at the far end of her assigned area. A single glint a first, then three, then ten. By the time she could see fifty armored soldiers marching under cover of the unusual darkness, the sounds of their passage drifted up to her keen ears. Even at this distance, she could tell it was more than fifty.

The darkness obscured all but the occasional flash of reflected starlight from polished steel, she could not make out any individual targets for the nocked arrow she'd drawn and aimed without thought. Growling in frustration, she unstrung her bow, spun off her spot on the bench, and dashed down the stairs.

Alacrit's men had arrived.

CHAPTER 32

*R*emember, we can't breathe the water on the other
side, Kevon thought to his friends, putting off
opening the portal back to their realm for a few
moments longer. The water around him buzzed, and he coun-
teracted the effects of the following quake without thinking
about it, stabilizing the pressure, and filtering out the vile
taste before it could invade their senses. The Water rune Enchanted onto his blade flared brighter in his mind as the magic
worked, dimmed as the need subsided.

Measuring the reserves he still held, Kevon judged them
sufficient for the task ahead, and signaled the others. He
gathered the energy to open the rift that would take them
back to their own reality. He triggered the spell, and the gateway sliced open.

Energies from the other side braced and expanded the
rift, and Kevon relaxed, holding the rest of his power at the
ready. He took a deep breath, encircled Yusa, Alanna, and himself with Water magic, and propelled them through the opening.

The magic of the Myrnar Mystics enveloped them, and
whisked them to the antechamber outside the throne room,
refilled with air. Kevon and his friends sprawled onto the
damp coral floor.

Kevon heaved the water from his mouth and lungs,
coughing and gasping for air. *It was too much to hope it would
retain its breathable qualities for long enough to readjust,* he
thought, as soon as his head stopped reeling. He looked to the
side, where Alanna leaned against the wall, retching up more

than water. Yusa stood beside her, patting her on the back, exhibiting no discomfort.

"Reko used Water magic to clear my lungs out," the captain explained as he met Kevon's gaze. "He thought you would do the same."

Summoning the energy to follow Yusa's advice, Kevon filtered the power through the sword's Water rune. The remaining liquid slid out of his mouth and nostrils. The stagnant air in the room ignited fresh waves of new pain through his chest as he took his first full breath of air.

Stings, doesn't it? Reko laughed in Kevon's mind as Yusa placed his hand on Kevon's shoulder. *I didn't feel it, but Yusa thought it. We've still got whatever it was she gave us, so that we could talk with her. Useful. I hope it lasts.*

Alanna's vision has not diminished, Kevon thought after recovering from the initial surprise. *Perhaps this will remain as well.*

Alanna's breathing eased, and she sprawled backward, away from the wall and the puddle of stomach contents near it. "Is it strange that I want to go back?" she whispered, forcing a smile.

"When all of this is over," Kevon sighed. "I'll see what we can do. Until then, we should get back to the ship. Can you walk?"

"I... yes, but why...?" Alanna asked as Kevon helped her to her feet.

"We missed a lot when we came in. I doubt a small delay will hurt anything at this point." Kevon grasped the hilt of his sword, and took hold of his magic and the Water rune to work it with. He seized the membranes of water that encapsulated the room, and took control of them with his Art. *Follow me,* he thought to Alanna as he led her by the hand out into the grand hall where scores of myrnar swam in intricate whorls.

How are we supposed... Alanna's thoughts faded as the air in the room followed, bulging out into a bubble that surrounded the party as they strolled out into the majestic chamber. Swimming patterns changed as the sea-folk realized what was happening, and altered course to investigate.

"You were successful?" the Myrnar Queen poked her head and shoulders into the moving bubble and queried Kevon. "You... have returned with... far more power." Her tone carried differently than before, her eyes fixating on Kevon with unusual intensity.

If I didn't know better, Alanna whispered into Kevon's mind, *I'd say she was...*

Shushing her thoughts with his own, Kevon spoke. "M'drea is suffering, drawing her subjects to her to shield them from the chaos that assaults her realm. Her influence here has waned, weakening her realm in turn."

"She is proud of the job you've done with the renegades," Yusa offered. "Though she asks you reach out to them to try and establish peace, help them relocate to somewhere they can live in balance with the sea rather than in competition with it."

"The more of you that perish in conflict here, the weaker she grows, the stronger our adversary becomes," Alanna added.

"And I thought she had a lot to say to me," Kevon joked. "This method of travel is not taxing, but it will take us a good deal longer to return to our ship. Will you show us the way through?"

The queen withdrew, and began swimming across the chamber. Ranks of myrnar parted as she approached, and a trail of the sea-folk gathered behind the bubble. More than one curious youngster poked at the surface of the creeping bubble, then whirled away, swimming into the chaotic vortex of smaller myrnar that paralleled the sedate procession of adults.

Esinane led the group to the far end of the space, then up and around the spiral ramp that accessed the level above. She paused several times, gesturing to coral friezes or ornate statues, making sure to point out all of the beauty they had missed on the trip down.

"I've loved the sea most of my life," Yusa sighed. "The surface will seem empty now that I've been here."

"I think you'll appreciate it even more," Alanna argued. "Just knowing all this is down here, to visit on occasion."

They made it down the hallway to one of the checkpoints they had skipped when they had rushed to the Seat. As the bubble surrounding the three of them met the bubble stored in the domed hallway, the air burped and hissed, freshening, but increasing in pressure.

Frowning, Kevon extended the borders of the spell to readjust the pressure in the bubble. The next few hallways were simple, functional, and went by without gesture from Esinane.

The extra air from the intervening checkpoints had pushed Kevon's spell out far enough that maintaining it was a constant distraction.

I know that's not the way out, Kevon thought as Esinane turned an unfamiliar corner.

It's a way, Alanna thought back, glancing in the direction the Myrnar Queen was headed. *It's the best way.*

Around two more corners in the descending passage, Kevon understood what Alanna had seen.

The gallery was at least the length of the great hall that stood outside the throne room, though not as deep or wide. Two rows of statues flanked the walkway. Likenesses of myrnar, male and female alike, towered over the group, more than three times as tall as they would have been in life.

Kevon moved quickly, not wanting exposure to air to damage the vivid varieties of manicured moss that covered the statues, giving them an eerie, lifelike quality. He marveled at his surroundings as he shifted the stagnating bubble of air along the floor of the gallery.

When they reached the end of the room, Esinane poked back into the bubble. "Your friends are waiting above. Go to them. Rest. We shall speak more tomorrow."

The Myrnar Queen bowed out of the air bubble, and gestured to the passage ahead.

Inclining his head to the retreating ruler, Kevon led the others through the passage to the entrance. The light from the moss inside faded, and the dark murk of the sea closed in on them.

Stand steady, he thought to Alanna, then turned to speak to Yusa. "We may lose some of our air as I shift focus. Keep hold of enough for us to breathe, and try not to fall."

Feeling Wind magic form around them, Kevon turned his attention to the Water spell he'd been maintaining. Elongating the bubble around them upward, Kevon allowed water to drain in around their feet, then twisted small currents to his will, welling up beneath them with supporting force, but churning to the side and down, maintaining a turbulent floor of water. As soon as the three had their footing, Kevon drove the spell upward.

As he'd suspected, keeping the bubble intact at speed was more than he could manage. Water crashed in against the sphere of Wind magic Reko maintained, compressing the trapped air into smaller bubbles that floated upward. Kevon split his concentration just enough to filter some energy through the Wind rune on the sword, and offer it to Reko in support. The minimal effort, while distracting, was far less so than the spells he'd been maintaining moments earlier.

Growing more confident with the Water magic below him, Kevon sped their ascent. Light blossomed above, brightening and spreading. The sea took on a shade of blue that strove to match that of M'drea's realm, but could not quite. The few fish they sped past were dull, grey, and fled when they spotted the unnatural trio.

The shadow of Yusa's ship took form as they neared the surface, and Kevon veered toward it.

There was a soft *pop* as the bubble of air surrounding them broke the surface, and Reko ended his spell. The fresh sea air washed over them, and Kevon took a few deep breaths before shouting for a rope ladder.

CHAPTER 33

"Esinane is coming aboard," Alanna murmured, nudging Kevon. "Get up."

"This is the first time I've slept in three weeks," Kevon protested, snuggling closer, closing his eyes.

We weren't really there for three weeks, she thought at him, arching her back and stretching. *Getting tired was different there, too.*

I'm telling people I didn't sleep for three weeks. You do what you want.

Alanna sat up, severing the contact that still allowed the silent communication between them.

"I'll go meet her," the Assassin yawned, "And make a bunch of promises you'll have to keep."

"I'm awake."

"Then get dressed," she teased, trailing fingers over his hand, projecting an image into his mind that was quite the opposite.

Kevon sat up, and reached for the clothes stacked on the table near the bed. A fresh outfit, not damp, not crusted with dried brine. He dressed at a comfortable pace, savoring the feel of the dry fabric as it moved across his skin. He stood, buckled his sword on, and turned to head for the door.

"Are you...?" he asked the lump of blankets, stopping as they murmured at his fragment of a question. *I did tell her to do what she wanted,* he thought, to himself for a change.

"Just in time," Carlo announced as Kevon closed the door to his cabin. "She's waiting with Yusa."

"Thanks," Kevon nodded as Carlo held the door to the Captain's quarters open. "Your Highness. It is good to see you again."

"And you," Esinane replied. "I trust you have been made aware of our situation?"

"We have. Carlo informed us shortly after we arrived," Kevon answered. "This many factions breaking away, in so short a time. Those conflicts, the lives lost, may have been what was making things worse for M'drea."

"Messengers have been sent to every faction, pleading for peace," Esinane splashed herself with a handful of bucket water. "We cannot do L'mort's work for him."

"I will speak with Alactit, and see what he knows of the seas on the far side of Purlon," Kevon suggested. "Alanna says that your people have not explored that far, but braving new waters might be what brings your people back together."

"You have been helping my people since we first met," Esinane whispered. "When you were little more than a minnow. Restoring our heritage, avenging my sister, and now..."

Kevon stepped forward and knelt before the queen. "The honor has been mine."

"She... touched you?" Esinane asked, trembling.

"She did."

"What was she like?"

"Beautiful... and terrible," Kevon frowned. "As they all have been. The only thing more frightening than the power they possess..."

"Is... what?" Esinane asked, reaching out to touch the side of Kevon's face.

"Knowing the fear, the dread they feel," Kevon closed his eyes, recalling his meetings with M'lani and M'phes. "If they are so afraid of what is to come, what chance do I..."

"No," Esinane lifted Kevon's chin until he opened his eyes and looked straight into hers. "You have been my champion for some time now, but since you have returned..."

"What?"

"All of my people feel it as I have," the queen struggled to find the right words. "Something changed in you. Her touch... brought out something I had already seen, and they cannot stop talking about it. If you were to be at negotiations with the wayward factions, they would surely see it too."

Recalling the effect M'phes's touch on the sword had with the Unbound, Kevon understood what was happening with Esinane. "Our path lies elsewhere, for now," he explained. "You know I will do whatever I can. We'll have to keep in contact, and see what can be done. Until then, you will be your own champion. Let the others know what is at stake. Speak from your heart. They will listen."

Kevon took the hand that held his face in his, and shifted his other hand to the hilt of the sword. He sensed some interaction between the myrnar and the Water rune on the sword, but could not be certain of it. He kissed her hand, and released it as he stood.

"They will listen," Esinane smiled. "They must."

"I am so tired of looking at books," Rhysabeth-Dane closed the text she had been studying when Kevon entered the room. "Brightwing and I are just going to fly until we get to where we're going next. Okay?"

"I take it your research time has been productive?" Kevon laughed.

"The more sense I make of those words, the less sense everything else makes," the Rider sighed. "There's still no order that I can see, and one fifth of the text is completely untranslated, compared to the rest that *might be* accurate. I need a break."

"We need someplace to dig in, collect our thoughts. Someplace stable. Solid. Steadfast." Kevon watched as Rhysabeth-Dane's gaze turned into a glare. "We're heading to the Dwarven Hold."

CHAPTER 34

L eaping back from the orc's attack, Kevon slashed
with his sword, and the tip left an arcing trail of
light. He sliced through hide and bone, severing
the creature's arm. He twisted, leaped, and kicked the writhing abomination into the wall behind it.

A scream sounded in the distance, and he turned to
look down the hallway. In the feeble torchlight, he could see
a woman being dragged through a doorway. He lunged at the
orc, impaling it, and wrenching the blade free before sprinting
toward the continuing screams.

Kevon reached the door. It was closed, barred from the
other side. He kicked near the handle, and the wood shuddered. He kicked again, and it groaned, but did not give.

Drawing latent Earth magic from the stone bricks all
around him, Kevon snapped a final kick at the door, releasing the focused Earth power at the point of impact. The door
splintered, the bar behind it exploding from the resulting
force. Kevon rushed forward into the murky oaken haze, and
listened for the screams.

As the dust cleared, the light dimmed, rather than
brightening. Between his own ragged breaths, Kevon heard a
distorted *thumping*, but he could not pinpoint where it came
from. His heart raced, pounding a violent melody in his chest,
and Kevon picked out the rhythm pressing in on him from all
directions; a grotesque parody of his own heartbeat.

The Dark magic pressed in on him without warning.
It raked its icy claws through his soul, sapping his strength,
stealing his magic to fuel its own twisted desires. Reality

warped further, and the gateway rune etched into the floor opened. Kevon slipped into the void, his own cries for help muffled by the enfolding oblivion.

Another heartbeat, not his own, pattered nearby. The darkness lightened to streaked black, flashes of green and gold winking through. Kevon struggled as the void warmed and softened. Familiar lips pressed against his own. Confusion mingled with relief, as he returned the advances, his lips working from her mouth, to her earlobe, to her neck, drawing a shuddering sigh.

That was some nightmare, Alanna's voice whispered through his mind. *It's safe to wake up now.*

Kevon opened heavy-lidded eyes, and saw the blur opposite him that was Alanna. He shifted in the sweat-soaked bedroll, and her hand slipped from his, breaking contact.

"I know you haven't been sleeping well," she frowned, wiping the moisture beaded on his forehead away from his eyes. "This is the first time I've seen why."

"You shouldn't have to see that," Kevon shrank back, unsure how to react to the invasion of his dreams, the revelation of one of his deepest fears.

"Your darkness is ahead of us. There is still something to be done about it." She slipped out of bed, and pulled her tunic on. "Rhysabeth-Dane is landing. We should go find out what she's seen."

"Lines of troops past Eastport, scattered right up to the entrance to the Hold," the Rider exclaimed. "They don't look like they are there to help, even to talk."

"Planning a siege, if not laying one already," Carlo rumbled. "Anneliese. Mirsa. Maisy. This can't mean anything good for the three of them. That many troops in the area could only be Alacrit's men. If he has moved on the Dwarves, you can bet we're no longer his favored champions."

The Blademaster crossed his arms and paced the length of the cabin. "Alacrit has not left the safety of Navlia," he decided. "We should change course to reach there as soon as possible."

"We could be in Navlia in the space of a heartbeat," Kevon argued. "Let's make sure that is the course we want to take. If we went, it would be foremost to rescue our friends, would it not?"

"Aye," Carlo confirmed. "Of course, it would."

"All right," Kevon continued. "If Alacrit is moving, it is most likely because of us?"

"Yes," Carlo grunted. "What's your point?"

"There are only two things that could have happened," Alanna chimed in. "He either has them held captive, or they have escaped!"

"Of course, they would have escaped," Carlo's voice took on a defensive edge.

"Assuming they have escaped," Kevon asked, "They would have gone to..."

"The Hold," Rhysabeth-Dane concluded. "They would be welcomed there, protected. If they have added themselves to the Hold's defenses, it would take quite an army to breach. A siege would be ineffective, though they have no way of knowing that."

"So, they're at the Hold," Carlo relaxed, somewhat. "So how do we get through that army between us?"

"I... may have a way," Kylgren-Wode grinned.

"You're sure there is an entrance here?" Kevon asked as the dinghy lowered into the sea beside the ship.

"Near those trees," Kylgren-Wode nodded. "I have been there more than once, moving provisions."

"Fair enough." Kevon took hold of the hilt of his sword, and the dinghy leapt forward, propelled by coerced waves, to bear them to the shore. He looked behind them to the other landing craft, where Reko plied his less focused Art to the same task, at less than half the speed.

Summoning a medium sized wave to carry the shallow bottomed craft up past the tide line, Kevon released the sword, and the magic, as the dinghy slid back a few inches and stopped.

Carlo, Kevon, Bertus, Kylgren-Wode, Alma, and a handful of Dwarves climbed out of the boat, unsteady at first on the solid ground.

"No one for miles," Rhysabeth-Dane called out as she and Brightwing touched down nearby. She marched toward the group, her low slung sword scabbard leaving snake trails in the damp sand beside her footprints.

"We should be in the Hold in a few hours," Kylgren-Wode fidgeted as he took a few steps out to meet the Rider. "You should fly in to one of the upper outposts after dark."

"I'm going to try and find a good hunting ground for the Unbound first," she shrugged. "It may take a day or two."

"Oh. Well, I..."

"Don't worry," she teased, hugging the ambassador. "I'll hurry." She turned and whistled to her griffin, and Brightwing took a flapping leap, closing half the distance between them. Landing, swinging his hindquarters around, gouging up great plumes of sand with his leonine hind paws, he presented his side, with stirrup, to his rider.

"See you soon, Kyle," she called over her shoulder, and climbed back into the saddle. Brightwing crouched, lunged, flapped, and was airborne within the space of two breaths.

Yusa, the remaining Hunters, and most of the rest of Carlo's men were climbing out of their dinghy by the water's edge. The captain shouted greetings over the splashing of the surf, and turned to speak to his first mate.

Four Stoneguard picked up the dinghy they had just arrived in, crew and all. They jogged back down to the water, jostling each other with the craft as they ran, raising shouts from the shaken rowers.

Kevon followed the Dwarves, and stood, waiting, until the last of the men who were coming with them had stepped ashore.

"Head for Eastport," Yusa told his second in command. "Pick up one or two local crew, take jobs that you can do in a week or less. When we're finished here, we'll meet back there, or deliver a message with the flying dwarf."

"Aye, captain." The sailor shook Yusa's hand, and stepped back into the dinghy. "Casting off."

The sea surged, and washed up and around both boats. Kevon directed the flow with the Water rune glowing in his mind, turning and pushing both craft until they were halfway back to the ship before ending the spell and allowing them to finish the journey under their own power.

Kevon watched the last of the Unbound disappear in the distance, then turned to Kylgren-Wode. "Lead the way."

They passed the clump of trees that they had been aiming for, and hiked a little further into the foothills, to a jumble of boulders that rested against the side of the mountain. Kylgren-Wode walked up to a boulder that was only a bit taller and wider than he was, and felt around the bottom. He lifted, with a slight grunt, and the face of the rock swung up and out, the squeak of pulleys and counterbalances coming from the opening passage.

"It's not a barn," Kevon remarked, ducking to enter the passage, lighting the way ahead with a gesture and a trickle of power through the sword.

The tunnel, comfortable by Dwarven standards, was cramped, causing the men and elves to stoop until they reached the supply station. The chamber opened up, lit by green stones encased in the wrought iron baskets. A small transport sled with an attached drum sat on a platform above the lowered track.

"There's water here," Alma announced, tasting a trickle from a brass tapped cask.

"Smoked fish, dried seeds and berries in the pantry," Kylgren-Wode pointed to a doorway off to the side of the chamber. "Eat something, I'll get the sledge back on the track." He moved over to the far wall, where two ropes led to hand crank winches bolted into the stone on either side of a thick metal post topped with a swing arm. He cranked the winch on the left, winding in rope that ran up and along the wall to another pulley, to a point near the end of the swing arm. Another rope anchored to the same point stretched to the far wall, where a counterbalance groaned upward. The end of the arm reached a point above the sledge, and Kylgren-Wode dropped a bolt into place to keep the winch from unwinding.

As he moved to the other winch and began lowering the block and tackle down toward the sledge, two Stoneguard and four of Carlo's men crowded around the craft, lifted it, and walked down the ramp to where the stone rollers started before lowering it back down.

"Usually down here by myself," Kylgren-Wode muttered, dropping the other bolt.

"This won't hold everyone," Kevon pointed out. "Not even a third of us."

"If you, Carlo, Alanna, Alma, Yusa, Relaniel, and myself take the transport to the Hold," Kylgren-Wode began, "I can return for another load right away."

"How far away are we?" Kevon asked.

"A quarter of a day, or three days walk, at least," the dwarf answered. "Four trips should take around two days."

"Three days walk?" one of the Elven Hunters asked, eyeing the raised stone walkway above the recessed channel the sledge rested in. "Two days run? Less?"

"Stoneguard have run it in two days..." Kylgren-Wode volunteered, "But..."

"Less!" the Hunter laughed. "We run!"

"Make sure you have enough food and water," Relaniel cautioned. "Run safely."

Murmurs of excitement ran through the ranks of the

Dwarves, and Carlo's soldiers as the Elven Hunters sprinted into the darkness. The Stoneguard pressed into the pantry, filling pouches with rations and skins with water. The Blademaster's subordinates looked at him with pleading eyes.

"Some of you can't run because of injuries. I expect others to stay behind to help with them."

Warriors scrambled, reprovisioning and dashing out of sight down the tunnel. As the sound of fleeing footsteps subsided, four soldiers and two Dwarves remained to wait for the next transport.

"No sense waiting around," Alma shrugged as she corked her filled waterskin. "I'll drum."

CHAPTER 35

D warves scattered as Anneliese sprinted through the service tunnels toward the Hold. She ducked around lighting cages, and slid past a worker pushing a cart of supplies as she dashed into the connecting passage that led down to the residential area.

"Troops coming down the canyon!" she called out to the first translator she saw. "Find..."

"Another transport coming in?" Mirsa asked, hurrying in from another hallway.

"No, I don't think..." Anneliese frowned. "There are armored soldiers marching on the Hold," she explained. "They're moving slow, but I still need to get back to the Spire crossing outpost before they reach that far. Raise the alarm!"

"All right! Go. Go!" Mirsa pointed back the direction Anneliese had come from. "I'll try to meet you up..." The Mage squinted at the rhythm pounding at the back of her mind. When she regained her focus, the elf was already gone. Shouts in Dwarven were ringing up and down the hall, and she had to step back against the wall to remain clear of the growing chaos. When a gap opened up, she fell in behind a squad of Dwarven regulars headed toward the throne room.

Jogging to keep up with the flow of foot traffic, Mirsa cringed as the marching Dwarves stepped in and out of time with the *thudding* in her mind.

There has to be another transport coming in, Mirsa thought as she neared the throne room, and her headache intensified. *No other explanation,* she amended, following the guard detachment into the empty chamber, and into the passage behind the throne that led down to the transit station.

"He knows that the royal army approaches?" Mirsa asked Bargthar-Stoun's translator as she stepped in beside them, behind three lines of Dwarves that stood between them and the tunnel where the transport rollers were just starting to turn, reacting to the strange magic that she had felt from four levels above.

"We can deny the army entrance," the translator answered, then pointed toward the tunnel ahead. "This is another matter."

Mirsa jumped as the station's drum sounded, and the rhythm took shape, vibrating along her skin, seeping into her mind. The rollers leading out toward the inbound transport slowed, stopped, and began to reverse their direction. She glanced aside, and saw the stone cylinders of an adjacent tunnel spinning up to a blur, absorbing a fraction of the pulsating magical flowing from the drum to perform their intended function, warping the flow of the enigmatic energy just enough for her to notice.

The drumming from the tunnel whispered into the chamber, overlaying the magical pulsing that Mirsa sensed. The shifting delay between the two jumbled into her already disordered thoughts. The patterns between the approaching beats and the stationary ones began an intricate synergy, a countdown in her mind that would culminate with the transport slowing to a stop within the space of a few breaths.

Ratt.. tatt tatt... The beat of the lighter oncoming drum ended on a crisp note, and the station drummer responded with a flurry of smaller beats, and one last resounding strike to the center of the large drum.

The humming of the spinning stone cylinders faded, nibbled away by the squeals of stone on wood as the ensorcelled surfaces of the path contacted the bottom of the transport. The arrested motion served as a braking force that brought the sledge to a stop as soon as it cleared the tunnel arch, well short of the unloading platform.

"Bertus," Mirsa whispered, then called out with more force, her voice cracking as she dodged between Dwarven guards whose weapons were festooned with bright red ribbons, marking their metal surfaces for caution on her behalf.

The front line of the Dwarven blockade stepped forward, weapons brandished as Bertus stood in the front of the sledge, then backed off as he leapt over the side, casting aside his scabbarded sword. "Mirsa," he breathed, rocking on his heels as the Mage charged forward into his arms.

"Behr-toos," Bargthar-Stoun stepped forward through his watchful retinue, hand extended in greeting.

"Your Majesty," Bertus responded, returning the greeting, still clutching Mirsa with his left arm. "It has been too long. I'd like you to meet my friends."

"Anneliese is still three levels above us, and further down the service tunnels, in an outpost above the canyon," Mirsa wheezed, her lungs burning from the dash through the Hold's halls and stairwells.

"Show me?" Kevon asked the translator who had been pacing them.

"*Aso falhu tes leffen bolto*," the dwarf called to a nearby Stoneguard. "*Nanao.*"

"O-kay," the armored dwarf turned around and waved for Kevon to follow before sprinting through the crowd, bellowing warnings in his native tongue.

Kevon closed the distance between them at the bottom of the third flight of stairs, shortening his stride to keep from tumbling into his new guide. They burst out into the cramped tunnel, and the Stoneguard jostled a knot of his fellows aside, cursing at them. He lowered his shoulder and made some room before hefting his shield and pulling his axe from its belt loop.

Eyes widening, Kevon thought the worst until the dwarf

slapped the flat of his war-axe against his shield boss. The Stoneguard clanged the two together half a dozen times until everyone stopped, looking toward the sound to see what was happening.

Into the sudden silence, the dwarf shouted three words of command, and the center of the passageway cleared as everyone stepped to the side.

"Go."

Kevon nodded down at the grinning dwarf, and leapt down the hallway. Movement runes sprang into his mind, and he latched onto them, enveloping his limbs with the spell rather than using it to push off with every step in such narrow confines. Each motion stretched into the best version of itself, and time seemed to slow as his concentration deepened. He sprinted down the passage, easing the spell when he had run far enough that the path was still opening up, rather than already cleared of obstacles. He dodged around several slower dwarves before spotting Anneliese poking her head out into the hallway.

"Kevon?" her face contorted in surprise. "Where is..."

"No time," Kevon gasped, the effort catching up to him as the magic faded. "Alacrit's army is here?"

"I haven't spotted them from here," she answered, leading Kevon back up to the overlook carved into the fallen spire. "They've dumped five barrels of lantern oil, and we have torches at the ready."

"We shouldn't need the torches," Kevon answered, leaning against the carved railing of the stone walkway. "Can you clear the dwarves out of here?"

Moving down the length of the repurposed spire, Anneliese whispered to each of the dwarves she met, touching shoulders, gesturing back toward the passageway. Each crossbowman released the tension on his weapon and marched down past Kevon without comment, until he and the elf were the last two present on the entire walkway.

"So we wait?" she asked, leaning over the edge near

Kevon.

"We do," Kevon smiled. "How have you been?"

"Busy," the Huntmistress answered. "Simply knowing you complicates things."

"My apologies," Kevon chuckled. "I trust it has been at the very least, entertaining?"

"At least," she agreed. "How fares my Commander?"

"Irritable, more so than usual," Kevon reported. "Something only time can correct, unless I'm mistaken. We'll see about getting some of that time when Alacrit's men arrive."

Nodding, Anneliese resumed watching the far end of the canyon below.

"Prepare yourself," the elf announced, minutes later, her hand moving to her unslung bow. "They're here."

"Good." Kevon drew his sword, and held the blade aloft by the tip and the crosspiece. He funneled a stream of power into the Light rune that glimmered its soothing perfection across his mind. The symbol sprang into brilliant clarity on the far side of the blade, then spread to the entire face of the sword. The glow radiated outward, lighting up the oncoming troops with a slice of bright midday glare that threw the long shadows of dusk.

Comfortable behind the dim side of the blade, Kevon raised the weapon higher. He split his concentration, and whispered the Wind rune to full strength, bending the magic to carry and amplify his words.

"Who *DARES* march upon the Dwarven Hold?" he thundered, the sound shaking loose dust from the steep mountain faces above.

The already disordered ranks coming around the corner far below milled to a stop, save a single soldier, who marched on, undeterred. He closed half the distance between the halted army and Kevon's position before stopping himself.

Squinting, Kevon could see that the soldier stood at attention. He twisted the existing Wind spell to carry sounds from below to his ears.

"...can be heard by my entire army, that you can hear our Prince's demands."

Kevon widened the spell so that Anneliese could hear, pouring enough magic into the rune to increase the volume.

"The Heretic, Kevon of Laston, of late, Hero of the Western Vale, is summoned to plead his case in a tribunal convened between the Warrior's Guild, the Mage's Guild, and the royal house of Kært. Failure to comply with this order will be recorded as willful defiance of a Royal Decree. Any power harboring the fugitive Kevon is hereby instructed to release him to our custody, or void any Accord held with Kærtis. You have until midday tomorrow to accept these terms and surrender the outlaw." The soldier paused a few moments. "Signal your acknowledgement of this message."

Kevon dimmed the sword, gradually cutting off the flow of magic to the Light rune burned into the blade. He ended the spell, and sheathed the weapon.

Gripping the railing with both hands, Kevon envisioned a Fire rune, and pushed a spark of magic into it. He ignited the oil pooled below, and accelerated the spread of the flames, goading and collecting the rising heat energy to redirect back into the spell. The ranks of re-illuminated soldiers milled about at the edge of the firelight, but the lone emissary stood, unflinching.

Coaxing the fire below into a solid sheet that stretched up almost to the bottom of the fallen spire, Kevon shifted the focus of the spell, and began shaping it further.

Taking hold of the Wind rune on the sword, through his grip on the hilt, Kevon wrestled the flames and spaces into a moving picture of the pursuit of the Orclord from Gurlin's tower in the Western Vale. The flames spread up and out as the beast drew closer, reaching ever closer. Four fleeing figures bobbed in the foreground, an aura of flickering panic surrounding them.

The perspective of the scene shifted, wheeling to the side, as three figures sank out of view, and one stood taller. A flaming hand flung outward toward the lumbering giant, and spikes of flame spewed up from the burning oil to transfix the shuddering construct.

The image melted into a solid sheet of flame before twisting into another blazing scenario. Dark shadows swirled above a lone figure, winged beasts that resolved into griffin as they spiraled in for a landing. Scores of the shadowy figures descended, gathering around the still figure. The flaming image drew forth a sword of fire, and the shadows leapt, the hissing of the flames intensifying as they leapt into the air to ascend out of the scene.

The fire merged again, wiping the images within from sight. Kevon reached back further in his memory, and let the image within the flames form on its own. The figure strolled down a hallway, turning a corner. The world spun, and he was pinned against the wall, held in place by a delicate creature who let him escape after a few kisses. The flames whorled into a moving carriage, and dissolved into the front of an elegant seaside embassy. The doors opened, and the viewpoint slid through them, from chamber to chamber, down stairs in a divided amphitheater centered on a round table. A Myrnar female slid out of the rippling flame on the other side of the table, baring teeth and flaring gills, her open mouth devouring the scene as it expanded. The lower teeth became cheering men, crowding together. The upper teeth dissolved away, save two, who shifted into armed Warriors, circling each other for advantage. They danced and struck at each other until one offered his hand in friendship. The crowd below circled in, surrounding, and the sizzling shape of a heated brand emerged from them, becoming the entire focus, then fading away.

The flames dropped to natural levels, the oil below all but burnt away. Kevon released the Fire rune, and wiped the sweat from his brow before drawing the sword, activating the Light and Wind runes once more. The false daylight played over the stunned troops, and Kevon spoke, his words given unnatural weight by way of the Wind enhancement.

"None that know me condemn me," he began. "Alacrit's actions, in this, are misguided, at best. I must be sure this tribunal is indeed what he wishes, rather than something forced by small men who think my life is a danger to their narrow view of our realm. Until such proof of claim is delivered, this Hold is under my protection. Any violence done against these people will be met with savage reprisal. However, groups of four or fewer men will be greeted with water and supplies, as we are not your enemies. What say you to this?"

Kevon twisted the spell back around to listen for the answer.

"We shall pitch camp here, and send for word from Alacrit," the soldier responded. "I will lead the first group in the morning to meet our Dwarven hosts." He raised his sword in salute, turned on his heel, and marched back toward the straightening lines of his fellows.

Letting the magic drain out of the Light rune, Kevon allowed the sword to dim again before returning it to its sheath.

"What was all that about?" Anneliese asked, her expression unreadable in the faint starlight.

"I need to delay them for a few weeks," Kevon shrugged. "Let's go."

CHAPTER 36

"The Dwarven King's throne is the Seat of Earth, isn't it?" Kevon wondered aloud as he walked back down the service tunnel with Anneliese. "I could feel it as I ran by. The throne room, the transit lines, even the forges that..." he trailed off, trying to remember the sensation he'd felt as he'd sprinted by the smithing district.

"The Dwarven people are closer to their own type of magic than the others, aren't they?" he asked Anneliese. "You and some of the Hunters have a minor connection to it, and what Aelion did to heal me was amazing, but the dwarves have woven this into their lives. They are more connected to it, more aware of it than even your enlightened people?"

"It would appear so," the Huntmistress admitted. "Shedding our shadows, the occasional Healing, a shade of the Vision," she remarked. "Nothing so practical as the dwarves maintain."

"The Vision..." Kevon turned to look at the elf. "What is... hold on." He looked down the hallway to where dwarves were gathering around Carlo.

"Give me some room!" the Blademaster roared, and the circle around him widened enough that he could step forward to meet Kevon. "Alacrit's army... It's bad, isn't it?"

"I talked with them," Kevon smiled. "Demanded that they provide proof that Alacrit's demands are not just pressure from the Warrior's and Mage's Guilds."

"There are other factions at play," Anneliese warned. "Alacrit has fallen in with the *Eleri*, and his actions have become unpredictable, dangerous."

"My little speech should keep them busy for long enough," Kevon assured them. "With you two, Mirsa, the extra Hunters and Stoneguard we have brought back..."

"And you..." Anneliese peered at Kevon.

"Oh. We're... leaving in the morning," Kevon explained. "No way of telling when we'll be back."

"Mirsa said something about a skergiz?" Carlo scratched his head and started walking back down the passageway, through the crowd he'd just escaped. "That'll be worth looking into. As tough as orcs, I've heard. Don't see them around here much, gets too cold for them in the winter."

"Sker-what?" Kevon asked, following his mentor down the tunnel.

"Bargthar-Stoun is getting information as soon as anyone knows anything," Mirsa assured Bertus, holding onto his arm to prevent another attempt to exit the throne room. "Kevon, Anneliese, Carlo, scores of Stoneguard, hundreds of regular troops. You'd be a welcome addition, but before we have all the information..."

"All right," he conceded. "How are you? How is Maisy? What happened in Navlia?"

"Calm down," Mirsa whispered, leaning into him. "We're here. We're safe. Navlia... was odd. Alacrit has strange notions that something is horribly wrong with you, among others. He thinks that... Bertus?"

Unable to hide his look of alarm, Bertus began to explain. "I thought... the Stoneguard thought... back on the Glimmering Isle, they called me something... *oro*..."

"*Ororo*," Mirsa finished. "What happened?"

"I thought I'd done well with my training, that I'd gotten stronger than I knew, faster." he continued. "I've been holding back since then, afraid of what others might think of what has come to me naturally."

"You have been training," Mirsa stepped back to look him over, and ran her fingers up his arm and shoulder. "You are so much stronger than the skinny Novice that left Navlia for the Western Vale. There is much to be said for all the progress you have made in the seasons between then and now."

"There's more," Bertus sighed. "We were sparring. Alanna and I paired off, and she was coming close to beating me, so I fought harder. So did she. By the time they stopped us, everyone knew there was something different with both of us."

"The *Eleri* believe that the *baya* and *ororo* are threats that need to be eliminated," Mirsa stepped back inside the curve of Bertus's arm. "They don't know any better. We'll show them."

"I'll take you back to the throne room," Anneliese offered. "The king will want to speak with you, show you his collection of axes, drink a few pints of ale."

"There are few things I'd like more right now," Kevon admitted. "I can feel my way back down. The Seat doesn't exactly... pull... but it's hard to ignore. Are there any areas between here and there I need to avoid?"

Anneliese shook her head. "You might stop by the smithing district and spend a little time watching, but you can do that at any time. The king should be your first stop."

"I'll do that," Kevon nodded. "Thank you."

As Kevon disappeared down the hallway, Anneliese touched a passing dwarf on the shoulder, speaking a few words in their rough tongue. The Dwarven woman smiled, nodded, and scampered off.

"What was that?" Carlo asked.

"Having my things moved to different quarters. I've been staying with Mirsa and Maisy. That's no longer practical.

I'm sure she and Bertus will want some privacy."

"That's nice, thinking of them," the Blademaster nodded.

"Mmm," she nodded, taking Carlo by the hand. "I'll show you the dining hall. We can relax over a cup of firemoss tea."

"Kind of late at night for firemoss tea, isn't..." Carlo spotted the Huntmistress's raised eyebrow, and stopped himself. "Yes, ma'am."

"The dwarves kept turning me this direction," Relaniel sighed as she sat down at the table with Carlo and Anneliese. "It's good to see familiar faces again."

"Familiar faces... wait here a moment." Anneliese sprang to her feet and sauntered to the food counter, and talked with one of the dwarves behind it. She stood and waited while the server prepared a small platter of cut fruit. Accepting the tray, she stopped a dwarf that was discarding his rinds and returning his dish. She asked him a question in halting Dwarven, and he nodded. She steered him back to the table, and handed the platter to Relaniel. "Follow this gentleman."

"I don't know what..." Relaniel protested as Anneliese took her by that hand and helped her to her feet.

"You will," Anneliese laughed. "Trust me."

Relaniel followed the dwarf as he trotted through hallways and down stairwells to a lower level of the Hold, and the lines of the surrounding construction grew more severe. Near the end of a long hallway, two guards stood on either side of a sturdy looking door.

"*Leffen mharla sopil leffen,*" her guide announced, bowing before turning to scurry away.

One of the guards nodded, and looked over the tray Relaniel held. He pulled on the door, and peered inside. Nodding again, he motioned for her to enter.

The elf's eyes adjusted to the low green light as she stepped into the small chamber, and she sighed. "Anneliese will answer for this."

"Relaniel, my love," Torit stirred from his bunk, yawning. "Is it morning already? I was not expecting you."

"I haven't been *your love* in thirty years," Relaniel corrected Torit. "You're in a Dwarven *prison*? Is that what this is? Father *was* right about you."

"Oh, my dear," Torit stood and gestured to the small table and chairs. "We do have much to catch up on."

The torch sputtered down to a smoldering nub, and Kylgren-Wode swore under his breath. He sat for a few minutes, letting the exhausted light cool before replacing it with a fresh torch from a chest in the corner. He pulled a hunk of flint from his pocket, and struck it until the new torch lit. He sat back down, arranged his blanket, and leaned back against the piled rubble.

He looked out over the sculpted rail of the upper outpost balcony. In the near darkness, he could make out only the silhouette of the Lhurridge Range to the west, Mount Elenna in particular, looming close, it seemed, because of its size, but still a distant landmark. Dark clouds in the sky above kept many stars from shining through, dimmed the entire nightscape, and prevented him from seeing what he waited for; a sign of Rhysabeth-Dane. The dim light from above was just enough to show the three dark shapes that dotted the barren valley below and behind the Hold, the broken pieces of the spire that had extended far above this outpost before the last war. It was too dark to see the twisted gouges the fragments had made when they fell. The scored stone collected water that the surrounding rock face did not. Moss and sometimes flowering plants grew in those wounds, an odd reminder of the violent past that Kylgren-Wode had seen only a handful of times before.

He turned back to the stone bench, and scooted it further back against the piled stones that blocked the stairwell that led up to nothing. He glared at the torch for a while, and drifted off to sleep.

A flurry of wings and scraping of claws woke the dwarf, his torch blown out by the sudden wind.

"Easy, boy, hold on..." Rhysabeth-Dane stroked Brightwing's head with one hand, as she pulled herself over the railing into the outpost with the other. She leaned back over to unstrap her saddlebags, and slipped. Brightwing extended a wing, smacking his rider in the shoulder, knocking her back upright.

"Hey, there..." Kylgren-Wode approached the griffin, hand extended. "Thank you for bringing her back."

Brightwing hissed, but allowed Kylgren-Wode to scratch between his eyes for a few seconds before he launched into the night sky and winged off into the darkness.

"You're freezing," Kylgren-Wode felt Rhysabeth-Dane's hand and pulled her close, taking her saddlebags from her and wrapping the both of them up in his blanket.

"N-night f-flying," Rhysabeth-Dane chattered, snuggling closer to him. "Y-you know what I r-really want right n-now?" she asked, gazing into his eyes.

Kylgren-Wode grimaced. "To see your library?"

She nodded and shivered, closing her eyes and shrugging deeper into the blanket around them.

"Let's get you warmed up first," he whispered, guiding her back to the bench. He sat between her and the cold stone debris, rearranged the blanket so that it covered them better, and closed his eyes to the sound of her gentle snoring.

◆ ◆ ◆

"The first group of soldiers should be here in the next hour or two," Kevon reported, speaking to the translator near

Bargthar-Stoun's throne. "I don't know how much extra water or supplies you can spare, but any amount will demonstrate our goodwill, and lengthen the delay I need to finish my next task."

The Dwarven King nodded at the translation.

"It sounds like Avolentz is leading the army now," Carlo volunteered. "Excellent soldier, loyal to a fault. I think he's somebody's nephew. Not a lot of ambition, no imagination, but nothing rattles him. If he says he'll hold off, you can take him at his word. That would be great news."

"We're going to cross over into another realm, this soon?" Yusa asked. "Reko says that we're standing close enough to open a gateway now."

"Not before we meet with Alacrit's men," Kevon answered. "I'd also like to talk to this skergiz that everyone is talking about."

"Rhysabeth-Dane has him cornered in his chamber, looking at the book," Kylgren-Wode reported. "He wouldn't fit into the library, or they'd both be there."

"She found the Unbound a home?" Kevon asked. "That was faster than she though it would be."

"They left her," the dwarf chuckled. "They headed straight for Mount Elenna. Brightwing couldn't keep up, not with her on his back."

Kevon reached for the hilt of his sword, running his fingers over the leather laced grip, contact with the metal skipping through his mind. "I have a feeling I could call them back if we need them. Did Brightwing stay behind?"

"I heard him roosting above the broken top-spire," Kylgren-Wode nodded. "I think. We might clear the stairway, add a railing, put down some straw. Make a proper roost for him."

"I'm sure they'd like that," Kevon smiled. "So she thinks he can help with the book?"

"She does," Kylgren-Wode answered. "She left to find him as soon as she heard he was here."

"I doubt I'll get a word in, then before we leave," Kevon

chuckled. "Might fare better when we return."

"How does the king feel about all of this?" Kevon asked the translator.

Bargthar-Stoun grinned, and pointed to the tapestry that Kevon and Alanna had inspected earlier, the one depicting a man with a flaming sword, towering above ranks of Dwarven legions, leading them into battle against hordes of orcs.

I think he has a job for you, Alanna thought, and Kevon could picture the wry look on her face without turning to look at her.

He squeezed her hand. *Behave.*

"We won't know how to handle this siege without meeting with their representatives, will we?" Kevon asked Carlo.

"I would not start planning anything until I knew who we were dealing with." Carlo agreed.

"I'm going to go to the Smithing district, then," Kevon announced. I almost couldn't sleep last night thinking about it."

That's not what you were thinking about, Alanna teased, the words sliding into Kevon's mind with a mental sigh.

Kevon squeezed her hand again, and released it, stepping forward to bow to Bargthar-Stoun.

"You will let me know when the soldiers approach?" he asked Alanna as he turned to exit.

"Of course," she frowned.

Now she's upset, Kevon thought. *We really should talk out loud when we're not alone. I don't know why she...*

"Thank you." He strode out of the throne room, following the ripples in the restrained Earth magic back toward their source.

CHAPTER 37

Lost in the chorus of hammers, Kevon stood, swaying to the rhythm of the bellows. His muscles twitched at every *clang* against the gray steel before him, as if his arms believed they were swinging the hammer themselves. Ripples of captive Earth magic reflected and refracted, bouncing off walls and ceilings, whirling and combining in a convoluted dance that his mind projected over the reality he saw with his eyes.

"You're not even aware of it..." he whispered, to a sidelong glance from the Dwarven smith he was facing. "It's all instinct, like the Elves."

The dwarf ahead of him tossed his steel back into the forge, and Kevon moved on to watch another, drawn on by the increasing complexity of the forge-music.

An older smith drew Kevon's attention. He worked at a smaller, sculpted anvil, with an array of different shaped hammers that he exchanged for one another after a tap or two. Where other dwarves had long beards, dark with streaks of gray, his was close trimmed, silver, with two lines of black that dropped from the corners of his mouth. The dark streaks ran down to his chin, and swept back, widening and thinning as they reached his neck. His hair, a full mane of lustrous silver, was knotted behind his head, kept back from the close-up work he was doing.

Sliding around to get a better view of the project, Kevon saw the curved light silver-gray shape the smith held with finger-sized tongs.

The smith dunked the delicate looking piece of metal

into a nearby cup, and swished it around before pulling it out and testing it with his fingers. He bent the two pointed ends, curled around to within less than an inch of each other, halfway again toward the other. He released, and the piece flexed back out to its normal shape, the points curved parallel to each other. He set the finger-tongs down, and ran the head of a fine wire brush through the small holes that sat just below each point. The smith took a thin wire, and stuck it through one end. He picked up a half-finished leather and mail gauntlet, and slid the piece over an uncovered middle knuckle. Continuing to thread the wire through to the other side, he pinched the sides down, and worked the joint, making sure it did not catch or scrape. Satisfied, he pulled the wire free, and inserted rivets, pulling the nail on one side, then the other, before working the joint slower. He sat the gauntlet aside and used a larger pair of tongs to pull another glowing lump from the small forge.

The dwarf craned his neck, rubbing it with a hammer-calloused hand. He looked at Kevon, studying his build, and offered the hammer he'd just picked up.

A thrill shot down Kevon's spine as he took up the hammer, and his magic left him. The hammer was smaller than he was used to, but the Dwarven metal had a good heft to it. He shifted into place as the Dwarven smith stood aside, and memories of his time on the Southern Frontier flooded back. The long hours, the sweltering heat, the pride of a job well done. He wrapped up all of his emotions, and swung at the glowing mass resting on the anvil.

Clink.

The sound jangled into the surrounding symphony. No sparks flew from the impact, and Kevon could not see where he had struck. *Clink. Clink. Clank.* A single glowing spark leapt from the anvil to the dirt floor below. Kevon thought he could see the beginning of a dent, but could not be certain it was not a trick of the light, a shadow burned into his eye from staring at the work.

The sounds around Kevon slowed as other smiths turned their attention to him. The elder smith patted him on the shoulder, and took the hammer back.

In half a dozen strokes, the metal was flattened out, close to the correct thickness, and turned with the recovered finger-tongs to pound into the right shape. Even the gentler shaping taps bore the telltale waves of magic that Kevon's strikes would have been devoid of. The smith tossed the flattened metal back into the forge. He winked at Kevon, and nodded with a grin that seemed to say, *Keep at it, you'll learn.*

Kevon bowed, and moved on.

"It's time," Alanna called later, over the din.

"Be right there," Kevon answered, watching the last decorative detail being etched onto a Dwarven war-axe. "Amazing," he breathed, standing upright and waving goodbye to the craftsman he'd spent the last hour watching.

"They can work miracles with that metal of theirs," Kevon sighed. "I can barely put a dent in it."

"They can't breathe water and speak directly into other peoples' minds," Alanna shrugged. "Probably."

I know, Kevon thought, taking her hand. *Too many talents have gotten me into trouble already, as we will see in greater detail, once we get outside.*

You could keep trying, Alanna thought in reply. A fleeting image of Kevon's bare chest, with muscle definition he had not maintained since he left the southern forges, slid through his awareness, accompanied by a hint of sultry hunger.

"You're far better at that than I am," Kevon admitted, squeezing her hand. "I'm of two minds about it."

"I'm of two minds about most things," Alanna commented. "As long as one of them approves..."

They continued in silence through the hallways up toward the entrance hall, sparring with suggestive images until Kevon whispered his surrender.

"Ready to meet our new neighbors?" Carlo asked, stepping alongside Kevon as they passed the dining hall.

"Ah. Y-yes..." Kevon stammered, still flushed from the walk. "Give me a few moments."

"There will only be four of them," Carlo continued. "It would be offensive to bring more than ten, foolish to bring less than six."

"The three of us," Kevon began, "Anneliese, Bertus, Mirsa, Kylgren-Wode,"

"We could let the Dwarves choose the other three?" Carlo shrugged. "Seems fair."

The others stood in the center of the room, near Bargthar-Stoun and his guard complement. After a quick greeting, Kevon relayed the plan to Kylgren-Wode.

The Dwarven Ambassador buried his face in his hands.

"*I. Go.*" Bargthar-Stoun declared, punching Kylgren-Wode in the shoulder.

"He wants Rhysabeth-Dane and Tamaraith to accompany us, too,"

"That will be quite the argument against attacking the Hold," Mirsa laughed. "All four Heroes, two of them Magi, three Warriors. Elves. Dwarves, including the king. Skergiz. Will the griffin make an appearance?"

"If it will help," Kevon smiled.

"Only three of you?" Carlo called as the trio approached. "I can tell it's Avolentz from here, who have you got with you... Is that Blademaster Vellamic?"

"It is, old friend," Vellamic answered.

"I was afraid that Alacrit would send only fools on an errand such as this," Carlo laughed, striding out to meet the approaching party.

"That remains to be seen," the older man jested in return.

Kevon fell in behind the Blademaster, hand resting easily on his sword's hilt, above the white ties that showed the weapon was peace-bonded. He grasped at the Wind rune on the sword, and shifted his senses upward, around the mountains to where Brightwing circled the back side of the Hold. With a gentle tug of the power, he made the griffin change course, on a heading that would pass over them.

"It has been too long," Carlo stepped forward to clasp arms with the Warrior. "This is Kevon."

"You're the young man most of this fuss is about?" Vellamic's released Carlo's arm to accept Kevon's. "Doesn't look like a troublemaker, Carlo."

"I appreciate that, Sir." Kevon laughed. "If you can convince Alacrit of that, again, I would be grateful." He extended his hand to Avolentz. "I believe we met last night?"

"In spectacular fashion," the soldier agreed, crossing his arms. "Though I do not find as much joy in this task as Blademaster Vellamic. I am here at Alacrit's request, to secure your surrender. This delay was not planned. The men are set to begin a siege, and instead we consider drawing aid and comfort from potential enemies?"

"We are not your enemies." Kevon stepped back to a respectful distance, folding his hands before him. "Since our arrival here I have heard stories of Alacrit's behavior that cause me worry, for my friend, ally, and patron. As you can see, we have gathered the support of the Dwarven people, the Elves, even the Skergiz aid us in our fight against the darkness, a battle that Alacrit has fought on his own for many seasons. His mistrust of these allies has endangered the entire Southern Frontier."

"You speak of *trust*," the Mage behind Avolentz and Vellamic spat. "You are surrounded by those you should not trust, and their accursed spawn!"

Vellamic shot Carlo a wide-eyed glance, paired with a crooked smile.

"Two of them stand in your midst, now!" The Mage stepped around his companions to level accusing fingers at Bertus and Alanna.

"Arucan, is that you?" Anneliese called from the group that stood behind. "We've been through this before."

"You are not above reproach," Arucan shouted, clenching his fist. "Daughter of Aelion!"

"We have not come to hurl insults," Kevon chastised the Mage. "But you have come to try and claim something you don't have enough strength to take. You lack the advantage in position, troop strength, and sheer magical power. Your only hope of avoiding defeat is to convince me to go willingly. I've outlined my terms."

"Vellamic and I agreed to this meeting," Avolentz stepped forward to speak. "Arucan was opposed. I find enough merit in your statements to warrant a message back to Alacrit, asking for the proof you seek."

"As do I," Vellamic agreed. "It was good to see you, Blademaster. I pray that it remains so."

"Fools, all of you." Arucan turned and stomped back down the canyon toward the encampment.

"Neither of you seem the sort to ally with one such as him," Carlo observed.

"Certainly not," Avlonetz agreed. "However, he is the representative approved by the Mage's Guild, as Vellamic is by the Warrior's Guild. Alacrit sent me as the voice of the army. Should the Guilds disagree, I have the final say."

"Of all the things I have heard of you, madness is not among them," Carlo admitted. "In the end, I trust the two of you will make the right choice."

"The choice we make will be the correct one," Avolentz announced. Looking past the group to the barrels and crates stacked near the entrance, he grimaced. "Keep your supplies. You may have need of them soon enough."

◆ ◆ ◆

"Carlo mentioned there was something different about the two of you," Anneliese pulled Alanna and Bertus aside as they returned to the Hold. "Arucan let it slip that they had been watching Bertus, and others around Kevon. "What do you know about this?"

"It's not something I notice until I do something that I shouldn't be able to," Bertus explained. "It isn't that I can force myself to move faster, hit harder. It just happens when it needs to."

"The feeling has increased since I was healed by M'lani," Alanna offered. "More since we met with M'drea. I know how much I am capable of on my own, and how much I owe to whatever this is. I realize now that most of the strength that got me through my father's death was borrowed, or given to me from *somewhere.* Without it, now, I would be stronger than I was before. With it… I have a place among the rest of you."

"If what the *Eleri* believe is true," Anneliese took Alanna by the hand, "This is not something you can lose. It is a part of who you are, and always has been. Of course, you belong with us. Never doubt that."

"What do these *Eleri* believe?" Bertus asked. "Why are they singling us out?"

"I would prefer to be certain, rather than alarm you with guesses," Anneliese admitted. "In light of what the Mage said today, I should talk with my father."

"Ready for your last meal in weeks?" Kevon asked, slipping through the front gate. "What?" he asked, looking at Alanna, Anneliese, and Bertus in turn. "Let's have breakfast. I'm hungry."

"We'll return as soon as we can," Kevon assured the others. "There is no way of knowing how long this reprieve will last. If they have enough Magi to Send a message back to Alacrit…"

"Mirsa is above, waiting for them to try," Bertus volunteered. "She said she probably wouldn't be getting much sleep."

"I can stay, Reko can help," Yusa shrugged.

"We don't know what things are going to be like on the other side," Kevon shook his head. "If we need to return before we meet L'drom, it could take both of us to reopen a portal."

"Agreed," Yusa nodded. "Shall we get to it?"

"Do your best to hold on while we are away," Kevon cautioned Carlo and the others. "We'll return as quickly as we are able."

Summoning all of the power he could manage, Kevon infused the Earth rune in his mind with energy, and pried apart the barriers between worlds. He followed Yusa and Alanna through the rift into the dark unknown.

CHAPTER 38

"**D**ark," Yusa commented as the others jostled against him, and the portal behind Kevon vanished.

"Musty," Alanna added.

Calling a sphere of Light into being, Kevon looked around at the cramped space. "Small."

"Cave-in," Alanna reported. "There are three small ones like this in that direction, one larger in the opposite. Through the larger, there is a village."

"To the village, then." Kevon decided. "So we're clearing this passageway?"

"I can't lift another rock," Kevon announced, collapsing between the cave-in and the rock pile he and Yusa had started near the wreckage of the broken stone throne. "It was easier with the magic."

"Rest, we'll start again soon. Reko says he will keep the light going." Yusa said from his resting place on the other side of the rock pile.

"I'm starting to get hungry," Kevon complained as his stomach growled. "Wait, can we get hungry in here? This is far more exhausted than we got swimming everywhere last time."

"We didn't get hungry or tired in the last three Planes," Alanna frowned. "We haven't been here yet. I don't know."

"Maybe they have food at the village," Yusa yawned.

"We want to take a little nap."

"We definitely did not sleep when we were in the other Planes," Kevon said, sitting upright. "Has something gone *that* wrong here?" He stood, and hobbled over to the cave-in to grab another rock for the pile.

"We're most of the way through," Alanna said, grabbing Kevon's hand as he limped back toward the cave-in. "Rest, and use magic to clear the rest of it, then we'll be ready to walk to the village."

"It just feels wrong," Kevon complained, slumping down beside her. "The air has a funny smell, the rocks are *heavy*... my back itches."

"There, there," Alanna said, scratching near the middle of Kevon's back.

"Much better..." Kevon arched his back as he felt her fingertips through the cloth of his tunic, almost as if they were pressing through the material to his bare skin. "That's... Mmm. Wonderful."

He ran his hand along her leg, and she mirrored back the sensation through her thoughts, many times more potent than it should have been. Kevon broke contact, and slid a short distance away from Alanna. "This is a dangerous place," he declared.

Exhaling, Alanna nodded in agreement. "Sensations here, more powerful than we're used to. We'll need to be careful until we understand it better."

Kevon did not need to be connected to Alanna to guess the thought that followed the caution in her statement. As soon as she understood, Alanna would find a way to use the rules of this realm to torture him in the most exquisite way possible. Her sultry wink verified his suspicion, and he tried to focus on the job at hand.

Rest. Gather strength. Stay calm. Kevon thought of all the things he needed to do, but the bead of sweat that started at the nape of his neck and slid down between his shoulderblades through the gap in his tunic collar was a powerful distraction.

The earthen wall of the tunnel bulged and shifted, dirt sliding down to the stone floor.

Standing, and wrapping himself in power, readying a Wind spell through the sword, Kevon watched the still-trembling patch of wall.

The sounds of digging, of powerful claws rending through the soil grew louder, and the disturbed area of the wall crumbled faster, deepening the pile of loose earth below it.

"It's a mole," Alanna stood and glanced at the wall. "A *really* big one." She circled the rock pile to stand behind it, and drew her short sword. "I don't like the idea of killing anything here, but…"

"We understand," Yusa agreed, stepping alongside her.

Mottled brown claw-tips gouged into the passage, widening a hole two feet in diameter before they withdrew. A long, furred nose poked out, snuffling. The claws raked again, widening the hole, and pulling the giant mole further into their already cramped prison.

"Stay back," Yusa shouted, and the Light spell Reko wove brightened and shifted closer to the intruding animal.

With a final push, the mole dragged itself through the opening. It tumbled forward, rolling one complete revolution before collapsing in a heap between its exit and the rock pile. It stood, snorting at the ground in front of it, and clawed at the dirt. It unearthed a pale, plump tuber, and gnawed on it, sitting back on its haunches, gripping its prize with its front claws.

"I don't think it's going to hurt us," Alanna walked out from behind the intervening pile of rubble, and approached the creature.

The mole squinted, looking at her as she advanced. It closed its eyes and sniffed the air, tilting its head as her scent reached its nostrils. Unconcerned with her proximity, it continued gnawing on its recovered treasure.

Alanna reached the mole's side, and reached out to touch the creature's fur. She ran her hand down its back, sweeping away some of the dirt and dislodging pebbles that had been trapped from its passage through the earth. She repeated the movement, smoothing the fur, running her fingers through the long dense fibers to brush against its skin.

The mole paused its eating and shuddered, fluffing its fur back up in a cloud of dust, and a pattering of shed gravel on the ground around it. It turned to Alanna, nudged her arm with its nose, and resumed eating.

"Those are probably Dwarves in the village I see further down the tunnel," Alanna reasoned aloud, as she resumed her new scratching duty. "I believe they live in harmony with these creatures."

Kevon relaxed his grip on the sword, and joined Alanna, stroking the creature's fur while he contemplated their plans for escape. "Is his tunnel wide enough for us to climb through?"

"It's through softer soil, and already collapsed in places," Alanna reported, after peering through the wall.

"Could it help us dig through the cave-in?" Yusa asked.

"Those claws are really only good in soft dirt," Alanna judged, peering around the side of her new friend to get a better look. "He looks to be strong enough to move a heavy load, but it would take a harness and more cooperation than we can be sure of. I think we just take this visit for the distraction it is, and continue with our plan when he leaves."

The mole munched on the tuber, turning it in its clumsy paws until it was small enough to fit the remainder into its mouth. It stood, stretched, and shook itself out once more, resulting in far less dust and falling debris. With a yawn, it circled around the pile of rocks to the opposite side of the tunnel. It snuffled in a few places, and started digging into the soft earth, churning out a pile of rich smelling soil. It leaned deeper into its task, and after a few minutes was out of sight.

"Ready to clear the last bit of the collapse?" Yusa asked.

"Reko is getting impatient. Before, it was at least a little effort for him to talk to me. Now he can't shut up, or won't."

Walking closer to the edge of the collapse, Kevon knelt and put his hands on the stone. He formed an Earth rune, and allowed his mind's perspective to spread through the surrounding stone and soil. The jagged breaks above the tunnel in the stone ached, an unnatural shearing that Kevon could taste in the distance in all directions, a bitter, smoky sensation that drifted across his altered senses as he worked the magic. He fed more magic into the spell, and encouraged the rocks touching each other to merge. Guiding the joining, he coaxed the semi-fluid element back up into the ceiling of the passage, coating the break, reinforcing the weak spot that had broken to cause the stone slide. Dust and earth sifted out from the shifting mass of stone, and piled on the floor where it landed.

The light from Reko's spell crept further along the re-opened tunnel, illuminating much of the same kind of passageway they had already seen.

Hurrying past the repaired section, Kevon motioned for the others to follow him. Light glimmered ahead, from just around a corner.

"The same stones they use in the Hold," Yusa observed as they passed a cluster of the glowing green rocks. "I wonder how plentiful they are here."

"Wait until we reach the village," Alanna smiled.

"I'm getting really hungry," Yusa complained, minutes further down the brightening tunnel. "This village had better..."

"We're almost there," Alanna interrupted, pointing to the glow from around the next bend in the passageway.

The tunnel opened up into a cavern ten times the size of the throne room in the Dwarven Hold, three times as tall. Jagged teeth, the inside of an immense geode, pointed inward from the sides and ceiling of the cavern, all luminous green.

Trees flanked the entrance, sturdy knotted branches laden with apples, and leaves that tilted toward the near wall for light.

"Apples?" Yusa started for the nearest tree.

"We'd better make sure it's all right with the locals," Kevon cautioned, moving in front of the captain before he could reach his target.

"Oh…" Yusa exclaimed, noticing the dwarves jogging toward them.

"They won't know Common," Alanna chuckled. "Do any of you speak ancient Dwarven?"

Kevon stepped forward into the path of the oncoming villagers. "Greetings!" he called.

A smattering of something that resembled the Dwarven language poured from the newcomers.

Holding his hands up, Kevon waved in a frantic manner to show he could not understand. He mimed an eating motion, then clenched his stomach, grimacing as if in pain.

"*Covaninal?*" one of the dwarves whispered to another.

Nodding, the dwarf held out her hand, beckoning for Kevon to take it. Other dwarves circled around to Yusa and Alanna, holding outstretched hands and speaking in soothing tones.

"I think they want to feed us," Yusa said, not bothering to mask the excitement in his voice. He smiled, and took the offered hand of the dwarf in front of him.

The three allowed themselves to be led down toward the center of the village, past more trees, and a fenced in area that held large rodents. They walked past several stretched fabric huts that seemed to be made of material similar to what the dwarves wore as clothing.

The procession slowed at a small garden plot near the low center of the cavern, and the dwarf leading Kevon released his hand to stoop and collect two odd looking fruit from a small plant. He removed the thin husk from one, and wiped the silken strands from between the husk and surface of the fruit off, until they all dangled straight down. Pinching near the bottom center, he peeled a third of the flesh away, and handed it to Kevon. He broke off the other two thirds, handing them to Alanna and Yusa, giving the remaining pod and attached silk to one of his fellows before shucking and portioning the other.

"*Covaninal*," the dwarf said, pretending to eat a bite of the fruit, clicking his teeth together several times before handing the sections out again.

Sniffing one of the sections, Kevon thought he caught a hint of roasted pig, or baked apple, traces of campfire smoke. He placed his teeth on the smooth orange skin, and bit down.

Just beneath the skin of the fruit, which was not quite thick enough to be tough, was a thin layer of tangy sweetness. The off-white paste separated the outer skin from a softer, lighter colored inner skin. Beneath that were layers, like an onion, with less definition. A strong savory flavor rolled over Kevon's tongue, billowing through his nose. The texture and flavor of the *covaninal* lay somewhere between chimaera flank, roasted boar, and raw heartmelon, but he could not pinpoint the specific taste from moment to moment. Kevon nodded his approval to the others.

While the three stood eating, the dwarves conversed among themselves. Two of the villagers separated from the group, and scurried back toward the rodent pen. They opened a chest, retrieved saddles fashioned from the same coarse fabric, and loops of braided silk rope. The rodents crowded around, lining up to be saddled, squeaking with excitement.

Finishing the first slice of *covaninal*, Kevon watched the dwarves flick the ropes under and around the twitchy-whiskered mounts. They fastened the saddles with knots thrown into the cords with casual precision, the kind that develops over a lifetime of practice.

Saddles secured, the dwarves led their two chosen steeds out of the pen, and secured the gate. They mounted, and rode out of another entrance to the village cavern.

"Wonder where they're off to," Yusa commented, as he tore into his second section of *covaninal*.

Picking a stray strand of silk from his teeth, Kevon shrugged. "They seem friendly, maybe they ride to fetch L'drom." He accepted another piece of the orange fruit from a smiling dwarf.

"I can only see so far, in this place," Alanna admitted. "Where we entered, this village was at the edge of what I could see. There are two other villages I can spot from here, but the path to one is blocked, far beyond what we can clear. The riders are halfway to the other village."

Their hunger and thirst sated by the unusual fruit, Kevon started to feel the fatigue of the earlier exertion wearing at his spirit.

After acting out exaggerated drooping eyes, yawning, and tilting over to lay down, the three were led to one of the sturdier constructed tent-huts. Inside, an arrangement of ten hammocks fashioned from the silk of the *covaninal* plant and interlaced wooden frames took up most of the shaded room. With gentle shushing noises and gestures of direction, they let themselves be guided to the empty slings, and settled in to sleep.

CHAPTER 39

Woken by the gentle sway of the hammock, Kevon opened his eyes to the inquisitive gaze of two of his new Dwarven friends. "What!? What is it?" he asked, sitting up, to groans from his newly awakened companions.

Their benevolent hosts gestured for them to follow, and after a brief struggle to untangle from the luxurious hammock, Kevon and his friends followed the dwarves back out into the light of the village.

They walked down around the rodent pen to where a circular stone table was surrounded by a quartet of low stone benches. The table was littered with apples, tubers, and sectioned *covaninal*. Three other dwarves already sat, eating.

Kevon glanced back at the rodent pen. "The riders have returned, there are six mounts in the pen. I wonder how long we were asleep."

"Almost long enough," Yusa yawned, sliding onto one of the benches at the direction of one of their guides. "I hope we don't sleep through the war that may be happening back home."

"Agreed," Kevon sighed, sitting next to Alanna, across from the captain. "We have to figure out how to find L'drom, and quickly."

"These two here were the ones that rode out earlier," Alanna commented, pointing to a pair of dwarves that shared the table. "Maybe they know something."

Pointing to the pair, Alanna shifted her focus to the rodent pen, then the tunnel. She bobbed her hand up and down to simulate the riding motion of the furry steeds.

One of the dwarves smiled, and nodded his head. Chattering on in the unfamiliar tongue, he pointed to his mouth, then his partner's mouth, then outward. He put his hands up to his head, fingers spread wide.

"They... talked, to... crown?" Kevon squinted as the dwarf kept motioning. "I think they went and talked to L'drom. It's been the instinct of every people we've come across. He's probably on his way."

"Good," Alanna breathed, withdrawing the eyepatch from her tunic pocket. "The light in here is giving me a headache. It works differently than in our world, or in M'lani's realm. It has a different flavor that... is taxing. I noticed it when we were with M'drea, but everything here feels so much more..."

"More," Kevon agreed, biting into an apple. "You don't need a headache here if it isn't helping anything." He nodded to the rider who had explained their mission, and resumed eating.

After the meal was finished, the dwarves led the companions to a large pen on the far side of the village. The lights above were clustered closer together, brighter than the rest of the village. The pen had extra fencing inside it, two half-squares at nearly opposite ends of the enclosure, with extra boards lashed to them. The open-faced triangles faced each other across the length of the large rectangular pen.

"What is..." Yusa began to ask as four dwarves brought saddled rodents into the enclosure, and closed the gates.

The companions found themselves herded toward the center of the pen, where they waited for the others to meet them.

Two of the saddled rodents lined up facing toward one end of the pen, and the other two arranged themselves opposite their fellows.

"Hey! What...?" Kevon asked as one of the dwarves started to pull a stretchy band of bright red woven material onto his arm.

The dwarf poked Kevon in the chest, and slapped the red armband around his own upper arm.

"Oh," Kevon smiled, and slipped the band further up his arm to mimic the accessory's placement on the dwarf, who passed armbands out to Yusa and Alanna. "I think we're on his team, to play a game."

"Saddles on these rats are red, and the section of fence behind us is darker than the one ahead of us," Alanna observed, sliding her armband into place. "Learning the rules should be interesting."

The dwarf who had passed out the armbands picked up a leathery looking sphere, and pointed down toward the separated section of fence behind them. He gestured for the others to follow him downfield. Directing Alanna to a spot to the left, and Yusa to the right, he gestured to their side of the field.

"We stay on this side?" Alanna asked, pointing to Yusa, then herself, and gesturing around the area the dwarf had just covered. "Okay, what do we do?" she asked after he smiled and nodded.

The dwarf let the leathery ball drop to the ground. It deformed as it hit, with a soft *thunk*. It rolled once, and stopped. The dwarf pointed to the ball, then to their teammate astride one of the saddled rodents. He took two quick steps forward, seized the ball with one hand, and flung it to the mounted dwarf. The rodent lurched forward several steps before the dwarf could rein it back around to return the ball to the instructor.

"So *we*... give, *give*... the *ball*... to *him*..." Alanna tried to communicate, using established gestures along with a throwing motion to show her understanding of the instructions. "Oh. Him *or* you..." as the dwarf motioned to his fellow and himself. "Got it."

"You want us to jump? Wave our hands?" Yusa shook his head. "I'm not sure what..."

"Oh. He's pointing at the riders on the other team,"

Kevon observed. "Distract, scare their mounts? I'm not completely sure."

The Dwarven instructor led Kevon back to the triangle, and positioned him near the center of the open edge. He pointed to Kevon, and the area within the half square, and an equal amount of space outside the fence. Looking at the ground, Kevon saw the sunken boards that described the boundaries of the square.

"I stay inside here. Okay. What next?"

The Dwarven instructor pointed to one of the opposing riders, and made a throwing motion toward Kevon.

"They'll throw it at me?" Kevon asked, gesturing his question back to the nodding dwarf. "What do I do?"

The dwarf pointed to Kevon, made a swatting motion, and pointed to the ball he held in his hand.

"Hit it?" Kevon responded. "Okay."

The dwarf dropped the ball in the outer half of the square and nodded. He picked it up, and faked a throw to his mounted counterpart, then nodded again.

"Get the ball, throw it to one of you."

Dropping the ball inside the inner back end of the fence triangle, the dwarf shook his head, waving his arms back and forth.

"Inside here is bad?" Kevon asked, shaking his head. He picked the ball up and dropped it outside of the partially enclosed area.

The dwarf patted him on the shoulder, picked up the ball and walked back out to the center of the field, where one of the other players held the reins of his rodent. He tossed the ball to the opposing rider, climbed into his saddle, and mayhem ensued.

Kevon leapt to the side, swatting the leathery puffball out of the air, again. He staggered forward, recovered the ball, and pitched it to one of his riders. He stepped back and leaned against the fence, gasping for breath. He watched the bounding gait of the rodent steeds as his team's attackers crossed midfield to try and get past their opponents' defenses.

One of the Dwarven guards leapt in front of the ball carrier, waving his arms and angling the giant rat away from the goal. Its rider twisted and passed the deflated puffball in a wobbly arc to the other mounted attacker.

The dwarf wheeled his steed around, catching the mangled fungus in one hand. They charged around the other guard, and he threw the ball at the goal.

The puffball bounced, squishing to the side at an odd angle, and the dwarf guarding the goal misjudged, leaping to the wrong side. The disheveled ball skidded and slammed into the fencing, bursting into a shower of gray-brown spores.

The dwarf that had instructed Kevon and his friends dismounted, and helped the fallen goaltender to his feet. He stooped to collect the remnants of the ball, and tore them into four sections.

Kevon and the others made their way over to where the rest of the players were laughing and shoving each other in a good-natured fashion.

The rodents were gathered around, eating the tenderized inner flesh of the ball.

"They waste nothing," Kevon observed as the dwarves collected the cleaned skin of the ball, recognizing it as the material the saddles were made of.

"Not as obviously pleasant as M'lani's domain," Alanna commented, sliding her hand into his. "But not without its charms."

The warm thoughts Kevon radiated back to Alanna were shattered by the quake.

Saddled rodents shrieked and scattered as the ground buckled beneath them. The ceiling above cracked, dim fingers spreading through the glowing crystals from one of the tunnel entrances, a deformed hand that looked to crush the village in its cruel grasp. Shards of glowing green arced downward, streaking toward the stunned population below.

Alanna tore the eyepatch from her face, throwing it clear as she swept the scene above with her enhanced vision. She pulled Kevon past her and released, sending him staggering. "Stay there, Yusa," she called, tackling one of the nearby dwarves before he could be impaled by a glittering stalactite.

The rumbling subsided, and Alanna looked around. "See to the wounded rodent. There is more happening near the center of the village."

Kevon held the rodent's head in both hands, keeping it from turning to lick the gash that had been sliced into its right front shoulder. Two dwarves sat on its twitching limbs, and Yusa leaned against the saddle, draping his arms across the beast's heaving chest.

"It's going to be all right, isn't it?" Yusa asked Kevon.

"That poultice looks like it should work," he answered. "We need to trust they know what they are doing."

The rodent squirmed as one of the dwarves squeezed juice from a tuber into the wound, and wiped it out with a woven silk cloth. Sap from another stalk was dribbled into the cleaned gash, and the sides were eased together and covered with the prepared poultice. The sap seemed to act as a natural adhesive, binding the middle of the compress to the wound. The Dwarven medic tied the rest of the poultice down with crisscrossed silken ropes around the beast's shoulder and leg.

"Easy there... They're almost done," Kevon whispered to the panicked patient, stroking its neck on the left side to soothe it without releasing his grip. "We'll finish this up and go see if your friends are all right, okay?"

Reacting to his soothing tone, the rat's breathing evened out, and its muscles relaxed as it settled down on its left side. The Dwarven medic tested the fit of the poultice, and backed away, releasing the pressure he had been holding on the wound. The dwarves holding the rodent's legs eased up, rubbing its legs as they did to keep it calm. The medic circled around behind it, and helped lift its left side as it scrambled to its feet.

Yusa stayed behind to help remove the rodent's saddle and start leading it back to its pen, while Kevon vaulted the outer fence of the playing field and ran toward where Alanna had disappeared minutes earlier.

Rounding a corner past one of the stretched fabric huts near the center of the village, Kevon stopped as he spotted the crowd gathered in the path. He started forward again as Alanna stood upright in the center of the gathering and beckoned to him.

Kevon slid through the throng, moving silent dwarves to one side or the other with the touch of his hand. He reached the center, and knelt by the still Dwarven form with Alanna.

"He's gone," Alanna whispered. "I... don't think... it seems like... they are not accustomed to death."

"That would mean..." Kevon shook his head. "How could they be..."

"Think about it," Alanna brushed a stray lock of hair back from the fallen dwarf's face. "None of the other Planes we visited had any predators. No hunger, thirst, fatigue. Death has never touched them, been here, until now. These creatures are immortal, or have been."

"So what should we..." Kevon began as he stood. He reeled as the balance of the constrained Earth magic in the area shifted. "*Something* is happening," he gasped.

Alanna reached up to steady him as she stood. "Oh..." she breathed, glancing in the direction Kevon could feel the magic spiking. "It looks like L'drom is on his way."

CHAPTER 40

"You feel it too?" Yusa called, running to the edge of the gathered dwarves. "Is it him?"

"Coming through that tunnel," Alanna pointed at one of the cave mouths.

"I thought you said that one had collapsed," Kevon frowned at Alanna.

Go, see what is happening, Alanna thought to Kevon through their shared touch. *You can make it if you run. We'll stay with them.*

"All right, I'll go," Kevon answered aloud. He pulled away from Alanna and stepped in the direction she was pointing, and the dwarves ahead parted so he could pass.

Pulsing energy into the Movement rune he had readied, Kevon began running toward the entrance to the cave. He leapt over the fissures that zigzagged across the path, and sprinted into the passageway. He refocused as the tunnel narrowed, changing tactics to the ones he'd used in the Dwarven Hold's service tunnels. His body screamed in pain, exhausted from the exertion of the game, his spirit shattered by the loss his new Dwarven friends were experiencing. The ends of his magic, strength, and the passageway intersected, and Kevon collapsed in the dim corner of the obstructed tunnel.

Swaths of obscured Earth magic reverberated from further down the blocked passage, advancing, pausing, changing, and resuming in a tireless rhythm that became audible as it grew nearer.

Kevon scrambled back as the jumbled stone nearby began trembling in time with the sound and magic emanating from behind it.

Light from the other side speared through from the top of the rock pile, between huge fingers that poked out just below the ceiling, sweeping and shaping the stone downward as Kevon and Reko had done, with brutal force and practiced efficiency.

Through the initial swath, Kevon glimpsed L'drom, the huge figure looking somehow even more Dwarven with its enormous hands, appearing far too large for his body. His barrel chest, and strange furred trousers added an aura of overwhelming masculinity that his horned helmet only enhanced. His palms slammed to the floor, and he pressed outward, shaping the leftover rubble into the walls with an incongruous fluid motion. As L'drom's movements reached their apex, supporting beams grew out of his fingernails, intertwining and sprouting the occasional leaf as he spread his arms out and back down to the floor of the passageway. Twisting his wrists, he snapped the beams off all at once, dragging the broken nails along the stone floor to file them down, the pause in the distant rhythm Kevon had grown used to.

"Man," L'drom chortled in Common, leaning forward toward Kevon, balancing on his fingertips. "What is a Man doing in my Realm? You were the force I felt in the lower passages?"

The antlers Kevon had assumed were attached to a helmet drew closer, and Kevon could see the oversized moss-laced velvet covered headpiece was part of L'drom, as much as the shaggy fur of his ram's hindquarters.

"I am. We bring greetings from your sisters, M'lani, M'phes, and M'drea," Kevon began, climbing to his feet. "And grave accusations against L'mort."

"We?" L'drom asked, standing back to his full height, antlers scraping against the ceiling. "Let us return to the village beyond, so that I may meet your companions."

Unsure if it was the fatigue, L'drom's overwhelming musk, or the creator's imposing figure that caused it, Kevon remained silent for the rest of the walk through the passage.

L'drom stopped every so often to raise reinforcing beams to support the tunnel ceilings, the cracking and scraping of the creators fingernails against the floor of the passageway setting the Mage's teeth on edge.

"Tell me of the Plane of Enchantment," L'drom rumbled after greeting the others, and a throng of his dwarves as they exited the cave into the village.

"We were not destroyed, as you all had thought," Kevon explained. "Ages have come and gone. Wars between the races, where Men have prevailed. The Dwarven, Elven, Myrnar, and Skergiz people have been pushed back into tiny holdings, and have been nearly forgotten. Many of the creatures we have seen in your Planes are considered by most to be myth."

"Orcs and demons are on the rise, increasing the influence of L'mort in our Plane, shifting the balance of power here," Alanna continued.

"I have rebuilt my Realm a dozen times over in the past few centuries," L'drom thundered. "These quakes are L'mort's doing?"

"Centuries?" Yusa asked, pausing before forming his next words. "From what we know, it has barely been a generation, perhaps two. The realms of Light and Wind did not appear to be affected. Either it may have been far more recent, or their influences were not as compromised." Yusa spoke with a slow deliberateness, translating for Reko.

"The dwarves?" Alanna asked. "They have been confined to the Hold for ages. Your influence in our Realm must be weaker than the others."

"The Skergiz have been affected as much, maybe more," Kevon added. "The Plane of Fire may be in worse condition. I did not know to look when I was there last with Pholos."

"Something is amiss..." L'drom peered over those gathered to the mound where the fallen dwarf had been buried near the playing field.

"We showed them how..." Alanna wiped a tear from her eye. "They didn't know what to..."

"I remember how L'mort's gift was, when we lived in harmony," L'drom sighed, and seemed to shrink as he slouched back down to address them once more. "I was careful not to let it in when I returned here. Now... It has found its way on its own. The more mayhem he causes in your Realm, the more powerful he grows?"

"He is trying to become powerful enough to enter the Plane of Enchantment," Kevon explained. "If he manages that while the rest of you are weakened,"

"It would be the end of everything," L'drom nodded. "That cannot happen. You have visited others, what can we do to stop this?"

Kevon drew the sword, and held it out before him. "This is one answer we are preparing for your brother. M'phes gifted us a pair of dragon eggs."

L'drom reached out and took the blade, smiling as he touched it. "I see. Invoking our names gives you great power in your realm, does it not?"

"It does," Kevon nodded. "Recently."

"I feel you, melded into this," the creator wrapped his gigantic hand around Kevon's arm. "When it is completed, it will be a powerful tool in the fight against my brother. Guard it well."

"I will," Kevon bowed as L'drom released his arm, and returned the sword.

"We must restore the balance," L'drom continued, "Let us see what can be done."

CHAPTER 41

"Oof..." Kevon stumbled into Rhysabeth-Dane, almost releasing the hilt of the sword that kept the portal open. His concentration shifted enough that he could sense Reko bolstering the spell behind him. "You're all here!" he exclaimed. "The siege hasn't broken the Hold, then?"

"We haven't left," Carlo scowled at Kevon's question. "You've been gone for a few minutes."

"But we were..." Kevon thought about the days they had spent preparing for the return to the Plane of Enchantment. The bugling call L'drom had made, gathering his subjects from across his domain, the flights of riders that journeyed through the tunnels to retrieve more Dwarves. "We spent more time there than we did with M'drea, and we're back already?"

"L'drom's centuries of troubles could have been just the last few seasons here," Alanna suggested, rushing her words and guiding Yusa and Kevon off to the side. "We need to move."

"Right," Kevon agreed, concentrating on the Earth rune in his mind, steadying the portal that stood between himself and the Seat of Earth. "Nobody panic, we invited them."

Dwarves from the Plane of Earth spilled through the portal, coming through three at a time on foot, and two abreast on riding-voles. Bulging silken pouches dangled from saddles and shoulders, some larger, filled with rounded shapes, others smaller, angular, glowing through the loose-weave of the material.

"Find someplace to put them for now," Kevon called to Bargthar-Stoun. "We'll expand the Hold later to make room for them."

The parade of otherworldly invaders continued for the better part of an hour, trickling to a stop well before Kevon's bolstered magical reserves neared their limit.

"How are we going to feed all of them?" one of the translators asked at the Dwarven King's direction.

"*Covaninal*," Kevon answered, pulling a pair of the fruit from his pocket, after releasing the spell that kept the portal open. "With a little preparation, these will be feeding us all soon."

At the mention of the fruit's name, Bargthar-Stoun approached Kevon, eyes wide.

"These are just a story..." the translator sputtered. "If this is true..."

"Dwarves of old used to travel the world, leaving with nothing but a seed," Kylgren-Wode elaborated. "A plant would grow in an hour, provide enough for a meal, and relieve their thirst."

"More like six hours," Kevon shrugged. "It may work differently here though. The rest sounds about right."

"This could change the..." Kylgren-Wode stood with his mouth agape.

"Balance of power in the Realm?" Kevon smiled. "We hoped it would."

"The farmerfolk of Kron must never know," Bargthar-Stoun cautioned through his translator. "We will keep doing business with them, stockpiling what we can't use for later."

"I hadn't thought of that," Kevon admitted. "Quite reasonable of you to worry about the needs of Men, considering their threats of late."

"A few Men, controlling the actions... of an unknowing... many," the translator struggled with the king's sudden shift to eloquence. "We wish to be equals, nothing more. We will not destroy our neighbors to that end."

"We should have had him do the talking earlier..." Kevon scratched his head, trying to wrap his mind around the new information. "this morning?" He popped a section of fruit off and handed it to Bargthar-Stoun. "Now, we need to talk about living arrangements."

Kevon gripped the hilt of the sword, and began the spell. His senses spread through the bare wall at the end of the dining hall, next to the entrance to the kitchen. Nothing but stone and sediment lay beyond for hundreds of yards.

"This spot will do just fine," he decided aloud. He reached out to touch the wall, and his senses fled his body, immersed in the spellwork that twisted stone, shaped benches and shelves, sifting soil into evenly spaced depressions the length of what would become the room. Air pockets expanded as stone compressed, forming the walkways between the rows of raised planting spaces.

A gust of wind blew past Kevon as the first gap in the doorway appeared, and his hand shifted over to the wall to maintain contact. The muted groaning of the shifting stone grew in volume as the stresses increased. Material began to be displaced outward from the room instead of shifted or compressed within it.

Wrapped in layer upon layer of Earth magic, Kevon broke contact with the wall, and walked through the still-changing gloom. With a thought, he called up a sphere of light through his contact with the sword. The shift in focus hampered his Earth spell, and his senses receded to just more than normal. Surfaces smoothed and flattened as Kevon strolled down the center aisle of the room, coordinating the movement of Light and Earth around him.

Half of Kevon's reserves were depleted by the time he reached the far end of the new chamber, and released the mental grip he held on the Earth rune.

"This room should feed half the keep by itself," Mirsa commented, stepping alongside him.

"Nearly all," Kevon argued, "If staffed by the new arrivals. Two to three harvests per day. It will need light," he added, as he began heading back toward the dining hall. "I'm going to see about finding room for L'drom's volunteers."

"There was never a reason to continue adding residences," Kylgren-Wode explained. "We have not returned to the numbers we had before the wars, many of these have been unoccupied for generations."

"They'll be filled soon enough," Kevon smiled. "Your population more than doubled today, and if we don't make room, things will get far more difficult than I expect them to be already."

"You have our king's leave to continue adding to this wing. There are three levels below us that all end here," the dwarf pointed at the bare stone wall in front of them.

Kevon opened the door to the last room, and peeked inside, noting the dimensions of the empty chamber. "Sooner is better," he shrugged, trailing his hand alongside the wall of the passageway as he walked toward the end of the residence hallway. He infused the Earth rune with power, and began shaping the surrounding stone and into similar dwellings as he walked into the lengthening passage.

Tasting the grit of the increasing sand and dirt content that lay ahead, Kevon altered the spell to shape a curling stairwell down to the second level he'd formed as he had moved along the upper one. He'd grown used to the near darkness of the single light-crystal that Kylgren-Wode carried, having done most of the work with his eyes closed. He closed his eyes, sending his senses further out, and located a nearby underground reservoir. Using his fading strength, he formed a channel from the aquifer to where the residences ended. Slimmer conduits formed from that newly formed chamber along the outsides of the residences on either side as Kevon walked back toward the main part of the Hold.

"I'll need to rest," Kevon sighed, releasing the sword, and the spell. "Send word to Mirsa. She can have the same crew of dwarves help her light this area, and do what she wishes with the water. I'll return when that is done, to finish the other two levels."

❖ ❖ ❖

Yusa and Reko have expanded the stables to house the riding voles, Alanna thought to Kevon as he slid from his dream back into her arms. *Most of the ancients are settled into the new residences, but it is crowded. The army outside remains as it has been.*

So I can afford to sleep a while longer, Kevon responded, yawning. *The world will not crumble around us?*

You can try to sleep, Alanna's thoughts took on the playful tone that Kevon remembered from their last few days in the Plane of Earth, while L'drom gathered his people together to explain his plan. Her lips brushed against his earlobe, less vivid than it had been in the other realm, but pushing Kevon in a direction sleep was not.

With unnatural skill, Alanna mirrored her sensations back at Kevon. He could feel himself nestled against her from both of their perspectives, the tiny thrill as each breath he took shifted his body against hers. She nuzzled his neck, channeling her growing excitement into the link that M'drea had gifted them with.

All thoughts of sleep abandoned, Kevon shifted position, and began sharing his sensations back to Alanna. Though less skilled at that facet of their nonverbal communication, Kevon's efforts began a cascade of reverberating sensation that closed both of them off from the rest of the world.

Closing his eyes, Kevon opened his mind to Alanna's projected visions as guidance, moving in response to her desires. Her sighs and whimpers of delight intertwined with their precursors in eerie echoes as the lines between thought and motion blurred.

Alanna's motions slowed as their thoughts fed back through each other, building to levels that rivaled the enhanced sensory levels that were native to the Plane of Earth. The things beyond Kevon that her healed eye saw through him faded, as her thoughts coalesced around him, and the moment.

This, Kevon thought, his vision blurring from the tremor that tore through them. *Forever.*

Yes, Alanna answered, collapsing onto his chest. *Forever.*

CHAPTER 42

"We don't want to wait until we get back to the ship," Kevon shook his head, expending the last surge of power that connected the lower two levels of the new residence wing to the upper two. The stairs melted into and out from the stone wall to complete the half-recessed stairwell. He released the magic as the steps groaned the last few inches into place.

"You understand, don't you?" he asked Yusa.

"I'd prefer it were otherwise," Yusa shrugged, looking up at the last stone basket that bloomed from the wall. "But I'd not risk angering the king."

"You'll be there?" Kevon asked, as he felt Reko's spell end.

"We wouldn't miss it for anything." The captain reassured Kevon. "Go. We'll finish up here."

Kevon dodged around ladders that held dwarves putting glowing stones in the stone sconce-baskets that Reko had formed behind him. The hallways were full of ancients, the dwarves that L'drom had sent to the Plane of Enchantment. The volunteers had offered everything to help their master, to help tilt the balance of power enough in his favor; to save the rest of their realm from the disasters that had been plaguing them for centuries. By crossing through the portal, they had condemned themselves to an eventual death, vulnerable to L'mort's influence without L'drom's realm to insulate them.

The Ancients moved with a steady deliberateness, appearing relieved to have a rhythm to step back into. They had dealt with the shift in sensory concentration as best as they could, eschewing the various Dwarven foods they were offered in favor of the familiar, flavorful *covaninal* that many of them cultivated in the new gardens by the kitchen.

Half of the new floor of the residence was already filled, the new inhabitants filtering in behind the Magi as they shaped the rooms and added fixtures. Wooden stands for mounting woven silk hammocks were the most common items being hauled down the passage, along with fired clay pots filled with soil and *covaninal* seedlings. Ancients reached out and touched him as he walked by, murmuring greetings and words of encouragement in their native tongue.

I need to learn to speak some Dwarven, Kevon resolved, *As much as they have given to be here with us, they deserve that much.*

Kevon rounded the last corner that led back to the center of the Hold, and spotted Carlo and Anneliese.

"Almost all of our troops from the ship have arrived from below," Carlo announced as Kevon picked his way through the crowd to their side. "Is there anyone else you want to...?"

"No," Kevon shook his head. "It's not such a big event..."

"To us," Anneliese interrupted, "It is. To her, it is. Trust me."

"I need to..."

"You need to go with Carlo," she shook her head. "Bargthar-Stoun has requested your presence."

Nodding, Kevon followed the Blademaster deeper into the Hold, glancing back until the Huntmistress was out of sight.

"He says that many soldiers that had to take up farming will now be able to return to service, and the Stoneguard now have more Regulars to recruit from," Kylgren-Wode translated. "Our army will be at its strongest in a generation within the week. It will rival Alacrit's by the end of the season."

"I'm glad," Kevon tipped his head to the Dwarven King. "The ancients are settling into their quarters, and seem to be adapting to their new lives here."

"The upper Spire has been cleared so that Rhysabeth-Dane can get to Brightwing without risking a fall," Kylgren-Wode added. "She has taken extra supplies up there, and is having lighter saddles made from the new material the ancients brought."

"We may need her in the sky before too long," Kevon admitted. "But there is one more thing I need to ask of your king, and I need it soon."

"What is it?" Kylgren-Wode asked, not bothering to translate for Bargthar-Stoun.

"Alanna and I..." Kevon began, "Have come to realize that whatever happens in the world, whether it burns, or falls away into darkness..." He struggled for the words. "We... we may not be able to stop it from happening, but we want to face it together, as one."

Bargthar-Stoun nodded slowly at the translation.

"We have asked our closest friends to meet us here, in just a little while," the Mage continued. "We would be honored, if you would marry us."

The Dwarven King listened for few moments longer before standing and starting to shout orders to nearby pages.

"No!" Kevon called, waving to get Bargthar-Stoun's attention. "Please... nothing else needs to be done, just the few that are already on their way. We know how precious time is right now. A simple binding ceremony, a mug of ale," he shrugged. "It's all we need."

Bargthar-Stoun listened to Kylgren-Wode's translation, and nodded. He stepped between his guards, and across the short distance to where Kevon knelt. He extended a gauntlet-clad arm, and pulled Kevon to his feet. *"O-kay."* One more curt order, and a single page scurried out of the room toward the main part of the Hold.

The others arrived soon after the page returned with a

thin wooden box. The Dwarven King excused his guards, sending them to await Alanna's arrival.

Anneliese and Carlo stood with Kevon near the Seat of Earth, listening to Bargthar-Stoun and Kylgren-Wode argue in Dwarven.

"Nervous, boy?" the Blademaster asked as Kevon turned to pace.

"No..." Kevon stopped and shook his head. "There's really nothing to be nervous about, it's just..."

"My, my," Carlo chuckled, following Kevon's eyes to the entrance of the throne room. "You were saying?"

Kevon stood, mouth agape, unable to speak. A vision from the past swept into the room, ambling down between the ornate pillars of the room, coming into sharper focus with each step. Her dark tresses were held back from her face with a green bow, matched by the dress below it. The soft green fabric was different than he remembered; long enough to brush the floor, and instead of sleeves, thin straps widened into the remembered cut and drape of the dress he had first seen Alanna in. Her march down the aisle was a blend of her normal stride, and the prim, timid gait that he recalled from years ago.

By the time Alanna stepped up alongside him, Kevon was the clumsy, naïve youth he had been that day at the 'Dancing Sheep Inn'.

"You never said..." he breathed, "I didn't know you were..."

You're adorable when you're embarrassed, Alanna thought as she took Kevon's hand. *I've been waiting a long time for this, I think we're finally ready.*

Stylistic Dwarven script in light brown ink covered the backs of Alanna's hands, and wound up and around her arms, ending near her elbows.

Seeing Kevon's questioning glance, Alanna thought in response. *Matrons of all of the noble houses, their wishes for our enduring happiness. It's temporary, fades in a week or two.*

It's amazing, Kevon thought in response. *I start thinking I know these people, and they still surprise me.*

Bargthar-Stoun began speaking, and Kevon stood still listening for the translation.

"The Ancients asked a day ago what they could do for the three that had brought them here to this new home, the... lovers, and their friend. When they found out that Kevon and Alanna were not joined, they spoke with our elders, and together, fashioned this binding, to be used when they were joined."

"They knew before you did, lad," Carlo whispered.

The Dwarven King opened the thin wooden case, and withdrew the silken cord contained within. The light green weave of *covaninal* silk was stained with different colors, knotted in half a dozen places. White, light blue, dark blue, brown, red, and black knots lay equal distances apart on the cord that stretched two feet in length.

"Life, breath, blood," Kylgren-Wode continued, following Bargthar-Stoun's solemn intonations in Dwarven, as the King gripped each colored knot in turn. "Bone, spirit, and... void. These things... combine to form ourselves, and... our realm. Without any of these, we are not... whole."

Bargthar-Stoun draped the cord over Kevon and Alanna's joined hands. "These two... wanderers have journeyed... separately, and together. They are complete, but seek to be whole."

The king closed his hands over and under Kevon's and Alanna's as he waited for Kylgren-Wode to finish, looking at each of them in turn, then began speaking again.

"Kevon and Alanna have found in each other what they did not know they missed, unseen, untouched... unmeasured. Honoring that, as the... elements combine to form the world, these two will combine to form a family, joined when together or apart. Whole whether near or far. Do any here know why they should not?"

Bargthar-Stoun waited a few moments before wrapping

the cord around their hands three times, and tied the ends. The knot tightened, pressing their hands closer together, stopping well short of pain. He lifted the tied hands, cradled in both of his.

"I give you Kevon and Alanna." The translator concluded.

"Marelle," she whispered, eyes shimmering with unresolved tears. "It's Marelle. It's always been Marelle."

"I... give you Kevon and... Marelle?" the translator amended as Bargthar-Stoun looked on in confusion.

The king shrugged, and lowered their hands. *"Kiss?"* he suggested.

CHAPTER 43

The wagon rolls to a stop, and the driver sets the brake. "Think he's dead?" he asks, pointing to the body lying perhaps twenty yards off the road, half concealed by brush. "Should we check it out?"

"I'm not sure," she answers to neither question in particular, scanning the brush, and across the road below and to the left that leads to the sea. "Carlo wouldn't approve. He might check himself, if he'd come along..."

"We're well rid of them both," the man sighs. "And the coast has never been a problem before. If it were a trap, he'd be more visible from the road."

"He was more visible from the top of the last rise, further back," she cautions. "Less so now. Better for a trap?"

"Dedicated to his craft, that one, if it is," Rhulcan chuckled, tying off the reins and climbing down from the seat of the wagon. "I'll go have a look. Mind the crossbow."

"Do be careful, Father." Marelle readies the weapon, and looks around once more before watching her father's advance through the brush.

Kevon leaps down from the back of the wagon to follow Rhulcan, and spots the movement to the sea-side of the road. He calls out to Marelle, who continues to watch her father, oblivious to his shouts.

The bandit in the brush hooks Rhulcan's foot as the Merchant steps close to prod him with it. A brutal yank, and Rhulcan is on his back in the sandy soil, his longknife kicked away, a dagger to his throat.

"Put it down, or he dies!" the highwayman calls, crouching low over Rhulcan's limp form, leaning toward the thickest brush coverage.

"I put it down, you'll kill us both!" Marelle cries, firing the crossbow, striking the bandit in the thigh. "Father!"

The bandit slides the dagger across Rhulcan's throat, and struggles to stand upright over the gurgling corpse. "You'll live to regret that," he calls. "For a little while."

Marelle struggles with the bow, drawing it back with the foot strap, and fumbling with the replacement bolt. She draws down on the advancing bandit a second time, but before she can pull the weapon's trigger she is snatched backward off of the wagon by the second thug.

"Made a mess of things, didn't you?" her attacker hisses, spittle dripping from his sand-flecked beard onto her face. "It could have been quick. It could have been easy." An unsettling smile splits his features as his gaze drifts lower. "Could still be nice."

Laboring for breath, Marelle twists a hand free and snatches the dagger strapped to her ankle. "Father!" she wheezes, swinging the weapon up toward her leering assailant.

"No, no," he laughs, knocking the knife from her grasp. "Don't you want it to be nice?"

"Get your hands off of her." Kevon rounds the wagon and tackles the bandit, rolling with the man over and over down a small embankment. He leaps up from the tangle, and pulls his sword free of its sheath. With two swift strokes, he cuts the highwayman down before he can struggle upright. He starts to turn back toward the road, but notices the fallen corpse fading from existence. "What...?"

Kevon sprints back up the hill to the road where the bandit he just killed still paws at Marelle, taunting her and tearing at her dress. The other bandit limps to the back of the wagon and snaps the bolt in half, screaming from the pain as he pulls the bolt shaft free of the wound.

"Leave her alone!" Kevon screams, swiping at Marelle's

assailant without effect. His fists pass through the bandit's head as if he were an illusion. He draws his sword, and slices through bandit and wagon, again without impact.

"You haven't killed her yet?" the wounded bandit asks through clenched teeth, ripping fabric to tie a tourniquet.

"Naw, I think this one's sweet on me," he answers, pressing his forearm to her neck, freeing his other hand to fumble with his trousers.

Marelle pulls and claws at his arm, choking and gagging from the pressure on her windpipe.

"Please leave her alone…" Kevon falls to his knees, and pounds the ground in frustration, unable to look away from the horrors unfolding before him.

Marelle goes limp, her eyes rolling back in her head. Her assailant takes to opportunity to shift position, tear her bodice down further, and pin her hands out near her head before she can regain consciousness.

"Hurry up," his partner scolds, rifling through the mostly empty wagon. "There'll be trouble if anyone else comes along."

"Oh, this'll be no trouble," he whispers, leaning down to lick Marelle's neck, shrieking and cursing, jerking back with half an ear.

"Filthy wench," he shouts, his backhand snapping her head to the side, sending the severed lobe tumbling from her lips into the blood-spattered road dust. "Take my ear? Shoot my friend? I'll balance the scales, that's what you Merchants like, isn't it? Wake up. Wake up! I want you to see this."

The brigand grabs a fistful of Marelle's hair for leverage, and presses his thumb into her eye socket. Exhilarated by Marelle's renewed whimpers, he leans in close. "Stay with me, beautiful. We're just getting started."

The world fades to blinding white as the bandit's thumb stabs into Marelle's eye.

Just getting started.

◆ ◆ ◆

Kevon startled awake, and Marelle's whimpers continued, curling in on herself in his arms. Cold sweat drenched them both. He rolled over, and cast off the damp bedroll, snatching up his nearby tunic to place over her before he rose. He placed his hand on her forehead, and listened, but her thoughts were jumbled, disorganized.

He walked to the bath-chamber, shaking his head to clear the remnants of the previous evening's celebration from his mind, and splashed his face with cool water from the standing stone basin. He threw one lever wide open, and hot water coursed into the ornate stone tub. Easing its companion lever halfway, the water flow increased, the temperature becoming bearable. Kevon stood there for a few moments, making sure the blended temperature was constant, before returning to the bedchamber for Marelle.

"You never told me," he whispered as she blinked awake, halfway to the bath-chamber from the bed, cradled in his arms. "You hinted at it when we reconnected in Eastport, but you never told me."

"I... You were there?" Marelle's eyes opened wide, and filled with tears. "I meant to. I wanted to. *I will*. It was something Alanna could never do, show weakness, admit shame."

"She had her moments," Kevon admitted, easing her into the water. "But her strength was yours all along. Everything about her was you, or less than you, because she kept parts of you hidden."

Marelle shivered in spite of the steaming bath.

Kevon pulled the levers closed, and sat on the edge of the tub. "You'll get through this, you have already, and now I'm here. And I know. Just tell me what you need."

"All the things I need..." Marelle whispered, snaking a hand out of the tub to place over his. *I have. Right here.*

◆ ◆ ◆

"Reports on the siege?" Kevon asked, walking into the makeshift command center, munching on a slice of *covaninal*.

"Same as yesterday," Carlo growled. "He's keeping his word, but he may hear back from Alacrit at any time."

"Has Rhysabeth-Dane made any more progress with the skergiz?" Kevon asked Kylgren-Wode. "I have questions for him, time permitting."

"Tamaraith's grasp of Common has been a problem," the dwarf answered. "When we believed it was weeks before you would return, she was worried that the translation would take longer than we had. Since your return, it seems to be going slower."

"See if you can arrange something today or tomorrow? I should be free this evening and tomorrow morning, at least."

"Aye. I'll speak with her, and let you know," the dwarf confirmed.

"I'll also need to speak with the king about accommodations for the rest of Carlo's men," Kevon continued. "We'd like to have them grouped closer together, somewhere near the main entrance. I can arrange quarters, as I have done with the expanded residences for the ancients, but I won't do so without his approval."

Kylgren-Wode nodded, and marched out of the room.

"Mirsa and Bertus have been unavailable for some time," Kevon turned to look at Carlo. "Any insight from her or the elf, Torit, could provide information we could use to break the siege."

"A show of force could do that, as well," Carlo suggested. "A fraction of the power you have used in the last two days should give them further pause."

"Threaten to bring the mountain down on them?" Kevon shook his head. "Not the path I would choose."

"Not the path I am suggesting," Carlo grinned.

◆ ◆ ◆

"The dwarves are all right with this?" Kevon asked, fidgeting as Avolentz and his group approached.

"Anneliese is making sure that no guards are out on the spire," Carlo shrugged. "You're just fixing it, why would they be upset?"

"I..." Kevon glared at the Blademaster as the opposing general walked into earshot. "General Avolentz. Have you been in contact with Prince Alacrit?"

"Riders have been dispatched," the soldier answered. "You will know more when we do."

"I..." Kevon frowned. "May not want to wait. I have obligations to fulfil, but discussing this with Alacrit is becoming more important."

"What obligations would be of more import than complying with an order from the prince?" Avolentz asked, glaring.

"Repaying the hospitality of my hosts," Kevon answered. "Our kind took something from them long ago, I'd like to repair it."

"Your games mean nothing to me, heretic," Avolentz locked his gaze on Kevon. "I care nothing for what you do in those foul warrens."

Kevon nodded, and began the spell.

Avolentz jumped as the earthen walkway overhead between the meeting and his encampment groaned, scraped, and began to sag. "Repair? You're going to collapse the thing, cut me off from my men!"

"Easy," Carlo chided the soldier. "I'll vouch for your safety. Hold your tongue."

Earth magic filled Kevon's soul, and though his eyes pointed at Avolentz, his senses were elsewhere. Power enough to liquefy the stone of the broken spire passed through the stabilizing rune on the sword, and out into the world, shielded from detection by its connection to the weapon's iron. Soldiers and Magi alike scrambled back from the camp tents as stone rained down and pooled on the canyon floor. Kevon shifted the spell, and the pool crept to the right side of the canyon wall, began inching up the south face of the pass, toward where the Dwarven lookout remained inside the intact portion of the broken spire.

The stone changed as it flowed upward against the forces that fought to keep it down. Memories of what it used to be, both today, and ages ago swirled into the directed chaos that was the spell Kevon wrought. Smooth, twisted surfaces flowed in and out of the liquid stone as segments of the stone reconnected with their former neighbors and split again, without warning.

Phantom pieces of flowing stone surged up the advancing slick, keeping their forms longer as they grew closer to their remembered homes. The first piece clicked into place above the Dwarven lookout. The energy and concentration required to keep the spell maintained decreased as the spire grew back into the form it had been before. Relief surged through Kevon's spirit as the last few gallons of liquid stone oozed upward to form the tip of the twisted stone spire.

"I'm sure the Magi I have at my disposal could do much the same," Avolentz shrugged, his uncertainty plain on his face.

"I wouldn't ask, as we are still at odds," Kevon replied, beginning the spell again, this time targeting the broken chunks of stone from the three spires that had broken between them and the entrance to the Hold. The large pieces had served to narrow the approach to the Hold, giving a defensive advantage to the dwarves. Those defenses softened, and ran into puddles that began their own journeys uphill, against gravity to their appointed places.

More familiar with the process, Kevon managed to give the soldier a casual grin, even as the three separate workings taxed his concentration, and claimed a sizeable portion of his magical reserves.

"You are not completely without honor," Avolentz shrugged, and spun on his heel to return to camp.

"Are you all right?" Carlo asked, as they neared the entrance to the Hold, looking up at the spires, which were nearing complete restoration.

"Tired," Kevon answered. "They're far away, three of them, and I'm not in direct contact with stone that connects to the spell. Any one of those would have made it much easier, but it looks better this way."

"Let's hope that was enough to make them think twice before making a rash decision," Carlo laughed as the door before them swung open.

"It wouldn't take much to bring the spires toppling back down, if it comes to that," Kevon shrugged, winking at Carlo's horrified expression.

"The king will see you," Kylgren-Wode prompted as they entered the Hold. "Is it true? The spires?"

"Restored," Kevon grinned, attempting to hide his fatigue. "Give me a moment with Carlo, and I'll head down to the throne room."

"I'll send word, and join you after I speak with Rhysabeth-Dane," the ambassador bowed and turned to leave.

"Do you need to rest?" Carlo asked. "Would you like me to go with you?"

"No," Kevon answered, shaking his head. "Draw up plans for a new command center, and requirements for the lodging of our troops here. I'll have the approval before dinner."

"I believe you will," Carlo chuckled. "Good luck."

After a few deep breaths, Kevon started the march down through the Hold to the throne room. The waves of constrained magic from the forges seemed to refresh Kevon as he drew closer to them. By the time he rounded the last turn, it was no longer difficult to stand straight and walk with the purposeful stride he had maintained the entire excursion.

The guards nodded as he passed, as they had since he returned from L'drom's realm. The combination of his apparent part in the mural ahead, and the delivery of the multitude of Ancients from the dimension beyond granted him unfettered access to the Hold, as far as most were concerned.

"Hero!" Bargthar-Stoun called, rising from the throne and advancing to meet Kevon beyond the security of his guards. "Ahh... Spires, good?"

"I did fix the spires," Kevon nodded. "I hope that was acceptable."

"Men," the king ventured, "...afraid?"

"Their leader has courage," Kevon admitted with a shrug. "His troops looked a little afraid."

"Spires good... good." Bargthar-Stoun decided. "Speak, Hero."

"I've made room for all of your people, and the ancients, in the residences," Kevon began. "Our soldiers and some of the others are filling up the guest quarters, and would feel more at ease..."

"Homes... for men?" Bargthar-Stoun asked. "Where?"

Kevon pointed to a spot on the map between the main entrance hall and the stables, which he had already expanded to house the scores of riding voles that had crossed over with the ancients. "I'd like to put, 'houses', here, and move our command, our meeting place, here. Closer to the entrance."

"There, good," the king nodded. "Up, down, good. Meet there... soon?"

"We would be honored," Kevon answered. "Is there anything else we can help you with?"

"Watch army?" Bargthar-Stoun shrugged. "Big magic, spires good. *Covaninal* big good... Yes. Watch army."

"It is very good, isn't it?" Kevon laughed. "We will watch the army, and look forward to your visit later." He bowed to the king, and took his leave.

"Do you remember anything of the south, where the orcs were coming from, where they were the thickest?" Kevon clutched the side of his head, fighting the headache that was intensified by Tamaraith's broken, lisping Common.

"Tamaraith fight ssome, run more," the skergiz hissed. "Not Ateraz."

Kevon's gaze drifted to Anneliese.

"Their warrior faction," she explained. "Tamaraith is from the sect that champions trade and treaties."

"We could use a few more Warriors like him," Kevon sighed.

"If they could be made to see reason," the Huntmistress countered. "Bertus, Marelle, and I would be about the equal of an Ateraz War Leader," she estimated. "A battle I would avoid."

"Is there a way we could convince the Ateraz to help us?" Kevon asked.

"If Katarit, first faction," Tamaraith answered. "Could ssend Ateraz to help."

"First faction?" Kevon frowned. "What does that...?"

"The first faction is the sect that is currently in control of Skergiz society," Anneliese explained. "Leadership is decided by combat, between heads of factions. Ateraz normally lead, as the largest, fiercest."

"Someone from his faction would have to defeat the leader of their entire people?" Kevon asked. "How likely is that? What would it take? Is it reasonable to even try?"

"You'll have to try it eventually," Anneliese whispered. "They control the Seat of Fire."

"Of course." Kevon stared at the rough wooden table that sat between them, and the hulk of a skergiz that hunched over it. "We can't just sneak in and portal through. I've tried to open a gateway to the Plane of Fire, as Pholos was able to do. Even with focal runes, it has proved impossible. The Plane of Darkness remains the only realm that will allow passage without extreme effort."

"Because the Planes are so unbalanced," Anneliese agreed. "What are we to do?"

"What about him?" Carlo asked, breaking from his quiet observation. "He moves like he could be a Warrior. The fighting in the south has changed you some, hasn't it, Tamaraith?"

"Fighting... hard," Tamaraith argued. "Peace... better."

"If we can't get these men into your territory, there will be no peace," Carlo lectured, standing to address the skergiz. "No light. Only darkness. Is that what you want?"

"Darknesss cold..." Tamaraith hissed. "Ssun better."

"You need to help us, then," Carlo crossed his arms, and glanced over at Kevon. "If we fail, darkness may be all there is."

"What would it take for one of your faction to be able to defeat the champion of the Ateraz?" Anneliese asked.

"Meat," Tamaraith answered. "Fire. Fighting."

"We've got all of those," Carlo grinned. "And we can get more."

"You handle that," Kevon suggested, looking to Carlo as he stood. "I still need to speak with Mirsa about her time in Navlia."

"Send Bertus and Marelle, if you see them," Anneliese called after Kevon as the Warsmith exited the new command center.

"A *Sending* chamber?" Kevon asked, eyes wide. "Do you remember what it was like? Could we build one?"

"I suppose it could be done," Mirsa frowned. "We've got..."

"The transport system is great for some things," Kevon agreed, "It doesn't cross the seas, get us into Alacrit's palace, or any number of other things. To coordinate the fight against the darkness, we'll need this."

"You could sculpt the room," Mirsa cautioned, "The enchantments will take time. Layers upon layers before we will see any benefit. It will take the three of us a season or more to lay down such a large-scale enchantment."

"We don't have that kind of time," Kevon shook his head. "I can't stay here for two weeks, let alone two seasons. Neither can Reko. We'll have to recruit."

CHAPTER 44

"**C**an you picture it?" Kevon asked, gesturing to the center of the large circular room.

"I can, but my skill with Illusion is not..."

"I'll feed you power, stabilize your rune. You focus on recreating the Sending runes."

"All right."

The power built, and Kevon felt the Illusion rune take form in Mirsa's mind. He partitioned the power in his reserves, and offered half of it to her. As she accepted, he sharpened the edges of her thought-formed sigil, and waited for the illusion to begin.

Carved wood inlay rose up past the level of the flat stone floor. Layers of nested sigil shapes blurred, then reformed with crisp clarity. Abandoning the sigil support, Kevon began using his half of the power to move stone.

Inside the confines of the covered area, underneath the projected illusion, the earth softened and separated into different textures, colors, swirling in near-liquid form. After the sifted earth had separated into four puddles of light tan, rich brown, gray, and black, Kevon began shaping them to match the dimming illusion that hovered above it.

The inner sections of the runes filled with the creamy tan sandstone. The smaller pool of black stone split and surrounded those forms, wavering into thin lines that solidified into sharp relief. The gray stone flowed into the outer forms that puffed in gentle exaggerated outlines around the crisp inner runes.

The outer confines of the circle and the leftover gaps filled with the rich brown rock, giving the pattern a more vibrant, yet colder feel than the inlaid wood of the original.

"That's good," he said, withdrawing his aid from Mirsa. When the illusion faded, Kevon compressed each form, hardening it and leaving slight gaps between each type of stone.

"Easier to enchant if they're separated," Mirsa murmured in approval. "I'll have them bring up a load of that red sand from the lower levels, we can sweep it into the gaps, make it easier to concentrate on an individual section. The black lines will need to be focal enchantments, close to exact in form already. The inner shapes can be layered with power to draw from for Sendings, replenished as often as possible."

"Beginning the main focal enchantment may help out sooner than we planned," Kevon mused. "Just seeing it there makes me feel more confident."

"Agreed."

"Before we begin using it, before anyone outside of our group knows it exists, we will have to ward it." Kevon decided. He grasped the Earth rune again, and lowered the plain stone surrounding the interior circle by a few inches, except a narrow path that led from the circle to the doorway. "I'll have them mix clay with metal dust from the smithing district, and spread it here. A little Enchanting similar to that in the palace on the path and walls, and a metal bound door. That should prevent any enemy Magi from getting in here too easily, or at least getting out."

"It should," Mirsa grimaced, remembering the walls of the palace in Navlia treated with similar, though more obvious decoration.

"Do what you can here in the next few days," Kevon suggested. "Spend time with Maisy, relax while we're here."

Mirsa fell silent as Kevon stalked out of the room. *While we're here?*

◆ ◆ ◆

"If they haven't heard back from Alacrit in the first two days, it will be closer to two weeks," Kevon argued. "The closest place Magi would be stationed would be Eastport, and they're three days from reaching it, at least."

"Pulling half of our forces, and two units of Stoneguard while the Hold is under siege?" Carlo shook his head.

"It still leaves half of our Elven Hunters, tactical support from your officers, and three quarters of the Dwarven army to defend one door," Kevon pointed out. "I can try and recall the Unbound, Rhysabeth-Dane can use them for support if needed."

"What is so important that we need to leave in the next few days?"

"This war is happening," Kevon told the Blademaster, his thoughts straying to the mural in the throne room below. "We have to be ready. That means preparing a stronghold in the south, setting up defenses that can support an army, without being tied to the transit lines, or exposing them."

"I'd prefer we all went at once," Carlo grimaced.

"As would I," Kevon agreed. "We need a foothold in the south, and Alacrit to see reason in Navlia. We need access to the Seat of Fire, so we need to train Tamaraith to lead his faction. We need to be able to manage our deployed forces from here, faster than we can send messages by sledge. Those all need to happen soon. We can't *just* do one thing at a time."

"Anneliese should lead the mission to the south," Carlo sighed, leaning over the map on the table between them. "There's no one I trust more to do it."

"Agreed. They'll need a Mage, and that leaves Yusa." Kevon checked off the personnel roster in his mind. "We don't know how bad it will be there, but Marelle and Bertus have been training with Tamaraith. They're as ready for this mission as any of the Stoneguard will be.

"I'll call for volunteers, and reform the units. My men will follow Bertus."

"Anneliese will choose the right Hunters to take with her," Kevon mused. "Tamaraith's training will have to wait, but Rhysabeth-Dane has been wanting more translation time with him since he started. She'll get her wish."

"So I stay here, and monitor the siege?" Carlo asked.

"Oh no," Kevon chuckled. "You're coming with us to stop it."

If there was someone better to send, Kevon thought, *I would send them.*

I know, Marelle responded, returning his crushing embrace with a firm squeeze. *We'll be together soon enough.*

The assassin stepped down into the second troop sledge, and sat shoulder to shoulder with two of the Stoneguard she and Bertus had been training with, along with Tamaraith, for the last two days.

Yusa glared at them from the rear drum-seat, the only place in the transport free of the uncomfortable clank of Dwarven armor.

"They're far enough down the passage their drumming shouldn't interfere," Kevon told him after a few moments.

"You're coming back for us before you visit the next Seat?" Yusa asked, gripping the drumsticks.

"Well before that," Kevon assured him. "Establish a safehold, scout out the area. We'll be there before you know it."

Yusa nodded, and began drumming. The stone cylinders beneath the main body of the sledge groaned, and turned under the weight of the fully loaded transport, but inched the load forward, transferring their burden to the rollers already spinning ahead of them.

The drumming and accompanying waves of constrained Earth magic faded, and the stone cylinders spun down to silence before Kevon began the climb back up the stairway that led to the throne room.

"Thank you for your hospitality," Kevon shook Bargthar-Stoun's hand as the king greeted him on his way through. "We'll be leaving for Navlia soon, I think the soldiers outside will be on their way back there within a week or so."

"Good," the king nodded, an unusual heaviness clouding his features.

"Is something the matter, sire?"

The king gritted his teeth for a few moments before speaking. "You. Carlo. Behr-toos."

"Your Highness..." Kevon stepped back, shocked at Bargthar-Stoun's words. "If there is something we have done..."

"No," the dwarf shook his head. "You, Mirsa, Ann-leeze. Men... inside. Elfs. Have been... good... brothers?"

"We all feel the same about you," Kevon answered, relief washing over him. "We're doing everything we can to honor this newfound kinship."

"Men outside..." Bargthar-Stoun shook his head, lowering his eyes. "Not... fear? Not afraid... to fight. Only... sad. Sad... not brothers."

"I understand," Kevon nodded. "We will make Alacrit listen, and if he does not..."

"Your Highness," Carlo called, approaching from the main entrance back to the Hold. "We really should be going, Kevon."

"Yes," Kevon agreed. "We were just... saying our farewells. If it seems as if the siege will become something more, we will return to stand with you."

Bargthar-Stoun nodded, and watched as his friends departed. He waved off his guards, and headed for his chambers.

"She's already here," Kevon observed, as he and Carlo entered the Sending chamber housed below the stables.

"I've just begun the first layer of focal enchantmenton

the Sending rune," Mirsa sighed, taking a seat at the edge of the raised circle.

"We were planning on leaving now," Kevon explained. "Or soon, at least."

"An hour, at the most, and I should be recovered enough to help Send all three of us," Mirsa shrugged. "I wanted to spend some more time with Maisy before we left."

"You're ready, right?" Carlo asked Kevon. "Send me."

"I don't think it's a good idea for you to meet with Alacrit alone," Kevon cautioned.

"Don't Send me to the palace," Carlo laughed. "The Warrior's Guild. The new bunkroom next to the kitchen. No one will be there this time of day, too noisy to sleep. Security there is much better since they rebuilt the Guildhall."

"You can get a sense of where loyalties lie, before we arrive," Kevon agreed. "You can make sure the area is clear when we arrive later."

"An hour, then?" Carlo asked, stepping into the center of the circle.

"Yes, that should..." Kevon began. "You'll need to leave your weapons. Anything metal, really, or we can't Send you anywhere."

Frowning, Carlo unbuckled his sword belt, and marched to the edge of the room by the door. He removed iron studded armbands, steel reinforced greaves, and three daggers, piling them against the wall.

"An hour won't be enough," he growled. "Wait until sundown."

Kevon waited until the Blademaster returned to the center of the circle before nodding. "Sundown, then. Ready?"

"As I'll ever be. Get on with it."

"Good luck. See you around sundown."

Kneeling to reach out and touch the thin, dark design that he'd helped craft earlier, Kevon felt the hint of enchantment Mirsa had infused it with. He latched onto the symbol that wavered in his mind, bolstering it with the visual representation that surrounded Carlo. He fed power into the spell, using the guidance of the enchantment to keep the magic confined within the lines in his mind. As the magic grew in brilliance, Kevon split his attention, and pictured the destination. Memories of the Common area of the Guildhall pushed into his thoughts, but he tamed them, and centered his mental vision on the bunkroom Carlo had suggested.

The smell of stale sweat and fresh ale wafted through Kevon's mind. The warmth of the polished wood walls, the age-worn floorboards, balanced by the cool basin of water on the table near the door.

Kevon felt reality beginning to warp around him, and sharpened his focus. He shifted the effect toward Carlo, separating his emotions from the magic so that he would not be drawn along as well. The Blademaster twisted out of sight, and Kevon sensed the room in the same instant, as near to an exact match as he'd ever experienced with a Sending.

"He's through," Kevon announced as he ended the spell.

"Sundown?" Mirsa half-asked, already headed for the archway back into the Hold.

"Yes," Kevon answered. "See you then."

I've already said most of my goodbyes, Kevon thought, as he followed behind the Mage. *Maybe I'll see what Rhysabeth-Dane is doing.*

Mirsa hugged Maisy close once more before passing her back to the Dwarven nurse who had accompanied them to the Sending room. "Be a good girl for mommy," she called after her as they headed back toward the main part of the Hold.

"Tough decision," Kevon observed as Mirsa joined him on the raised Sending platform.

"When I took her with me last," Mirsa explained, "We had no reason to believe Alacrit would be hostile. Now..."

"Even under siege," Kevon reasoned, "This is the safest

place for her."

Mirsa shrugged. "I would have preferred our place on the Glimmering Isle, but..."

"Unless we hurry, nothing will be safe," Kevon agreed with her unfinished statement. "We'd better go. Carlo will be waiting."

Kevon opened his senses to the runes that surrounded them, and took up the power that Mirsa offered. When the world around him started to warp from the magic, he expanded the effect to cover Mirsa, and pictured the room he had seen earlier. More confident with the destination, the use of the focal runes, and his recent success, Kevon sped the spell to near-completion. He slowed as the power built to the right level, and eased it over the edge. The magic drained from his reserves, and the world shifted in a distended instant.

"You're not Carlo," Kevon observed as the man before him drew steel. He grunted as rough hands grabbed his wrists, and clapped shackles on them. The remainder of power in his reserves fled into the cold metal. His sword was taken, and Mirsa cornered under threat of a beating with iron clubs.

"Carlo's not invited to this proceeding," the leader scowled, leveling his weapon at Kevon. "Tell your pet Mage to come quietly, or don't. The boys wouldn't mind thinning the ranks, I'm sure."

"Mistress Mirsa, please, come this way," one of the club-wielding Warriors asked, lowering his weapon, stepping between her and the others. "Blademaster Carlo did not tell us you were..."

"He did tell you something, or you would not have known where and when to wait," Mirsa deduced, smoothing her robes. "I have no desire to bring this place down on your heads, you have been more than kind to me in the past. Do I have your word Kevon will be treated fairly?"

"Yes, ma'am."

"Good. Put those weapons away. Release Kevon. Take us where you mean to. We will not fight you."

"I'm afraid we can't release him until after the trial," the Warrior with the sword said, sheathing his weapon. "Your co-operation is... unexpected."

"Trial?" Mirsa crossed her arms and glared up at the leader. "He has passed every test you have put him through."

"You don't understand, Mirsa Magus," the Warrior shook his head. "Kevon is on trial for heresy, violating the tenets of the Warrior's Guild."

CHAPTER 45

"**N**othing, as far as I can see," Anneliese peeked around the corner from her spot beneath a concealed rock ledge. "The others should be here soon, bring up a few Stoneguard to watch this end of the tunnel. Stay low, wait for me."

"I'd rather go with you," Bertus argued. "Carlo would never forgive me if…"

"Carlo should not be the one who concerns you, young one."

"Yes, ma'am," Bertus grinned and began making his way down the narrow passage back to where the rest of the group was moving their transport sledge to a storage platform.

The Stoneguard unit had already stowed the transport, and were helping the two ancients they had brought along clear out the long abandoned supply post, making room for the goods they had brought to replace them.

"All right," he began. "Do the Ancients have everything they need? What about those pots?" He walked over to where the ancient dwarves were unstacking the empty pots they'd brought along for planting *covaninal*. "Hold up. Two Stoneguard… no. Three Stoneguard, down the passage, guard the entrance. You two," he pointed to two of Carlo's soldiers. "Grab those stacks of pots, follow the Stoneguard. There's a break in the rock formation halfway down. You can fill the pots from the dirt pile, and bring them back for the ancients to plant. And you…"

The Elven Hunter Bertus had pointed at perked up his ears.

"You're with me. Huntmistress Anneliese is unaccompanied in the badlands."

"That simply will not do," the Hunter echoed Bertus's tone of concern, and collected his arms before following the Adept into the passageway.

Bertus and his Hunter escort slid past the soldiers carrying filled pots, and circled round the rest of the empty pots and the mound of dirt that had seeped through the crack in the stone above over many years.

"She didn't want any help out here," Bertus commented as the Hunter followed him past the complement of Stoneguard near the tunnel's mouth.

"She wouldn't," the elf agreed, nocking an arrow, and easing through the narrow exit. "I suggest we keep low, avoid drawing attention to our location before we know what lurks here, even in the daylight."

"I doubt it will be as bad as the dark island," Bertus offered. "They had all manner of sorcery to bring those vile creatures right into their midst, and the means to control them. Nothing like that here, I'll wager."

"I wouldn't be so sure," the Hunter whispered back from his place just below the ridgeline. He motioned for Bertus to move up, and slid back down below the crest of the barren rock formation.

Bertus peered over into the landscape beyond the small rise, and his heart sank.

Clusters of orcs dotted the shattered plain, roving from one landmark to another, huddling in the shade of eroded stone formations, and clashing as they happened upon each other.

Near the edge of his vision, he spied a gang of orcs engaging what looked like a pack of Leapers. Light and dark figures danced back and forth, slowing, stopping, and separating over the course of a few minutes. As the remnants of the two groups fled, Bertus noticed the dark gray figures descending upon the carnage from the pale blue sky. Gargoyles such as the

Unbound had fought after the Dark Isle landed to feed upon the dead.

"Twice as large as the ones Kevon had helped the griffins defeat, at no small cost to their own ranks," Bertus estimated in a low voice to his Elven companion. "We'll not be able to set up a stronghold here, at the entrance to the transit system. If the creatures of darkness managed to breach our defenses, they would have direct access to the Dwarven Hold. This place needs concealed better, and we should raise defenses nearby."

A screech from above sounded, and was cut short. The convulsing carcass of a gargoyle crashed to the ground a few paces behind Bertus.

The Seeker drew his sword, and leapt the distance between himself and the flailing form. He landed, one foot on the beast's wing, one crunching down on one of its hind legs. Bertus drove the ancient blade into the creature's chest, silencing its ragged keening. He pulled a feathered shaft from its neck, and looked back at the Hunter.

The elf scanned the skies, bow at the ready, walking down the rough slope to where Bertus waited.

"You didn't shoot that, did you?" Bertus asked as the elf reached his side.

"I did not," the Hunter answered.

"She's going to yell at us, isn't she?"

"I've never heard her yell," the Hunter commented. "She is certain to be displeased."

Bertus wiped his sword on the gargoyle's leathery skin, removing most of the greenish-black ichor with two motions before returning it to its sheath. He grabbed the lifeless gargoyle by the neck and leg, and tossed it up over the crest of the hill, away from the entrance back to the passageway. "We'll wait for her inside, then?"

◆ ◆ ◆

Marelle, Yusa, and the others had arrived and unloaded their supplies by the time Anneliese returned to the chamber.

"You'll have to look to the skies, at least, if you don't plan on following my orders," the Huntmistress lectured as she stalked back in. "That gargoyle would have killed one of you."

"The area around here is too crowded with creatures of darkness," Bertus restated the concerns he had voiced to the Hunter. "We shouldn't draw attention to this entrance, rather build up something nearby that we can defend and use to launch attacks and scouting missions."

"Reko says he can attempt raising walls, if the terrain is right," Yusa volunteered. "He says he can feel the Seat of Darkness, though he is not sure which direction, or how far away. The journey here muddled his senses; he didn't feel it begin."

"South," Marelle shuddered, glancing sidelong at the murky distortion toward the south before covering her eye with the Enchanted eyepatch. "Not because of what I can see, but what I can't."

"The barrens seem to quiet when the sun is near its peak," Anneliese reported. "The creatures above have started to stir again. I will scout to the south tomorrow when the sun is high again, find the best place to raise a garrison."

CHAPTER 46

The unnatural silence in the Common area of the Warrior's Guild was punctuated with the occasional dark murmur from one of the clusters of brooding men. Serving maids slipped between the groups, delivering mugs of drink without their usual banter.

Bound at the wrists and ankles with iron shackles, Kevon sat in a chair at the edge of the sparring arena, backed nearly to the wall, apart from the rest of the men. He stretched, craning his neck, and glanced at Mirsa, alone at a table near the front of the room. He watched her listening to the surrounding conversations, wondering what courtly arts she prepared in his defense.

Heads turned as Carlo shoved his way past the Adepts standing watch between the Commons and the front entrance.

"I have every right to be here!" Carlo shouted, the display of fury sending those nearest him scrambling out of arms' reach. A semicircle of Warriors three deep formed between Carlo and Kevon, blocking the Blademaster's access to his former student.

"Hold," an unfamiliar voice called, following Carlo in from outside. "Blademaster Carlo is here at my request."

"Blademistress Chelani," the leader of the group that captured Kevon stepped forward to address the petite female Warrior.

"There will be order in this Guildhall," Chelani's voice rang clear and loud above the growing chaos of the agitated crowd. "I have no patience for heretics, Magi, or fools. Least of all, fools! Blademaster Carlo has asked me here as a neutral party, to make sure that justice is served."

"There is only one verdict for this heresy," the leader of the mob argued. "Justice will be done."

"Then you shouldn't mind me sitting in." Blademistress Chelani smiled, and stepped around the protesting Warrior, inviting Carlo to take a seat at Mirsa's table.

"So you're Bertus's Mage, aren't you?" Chelani asked Mirsa, motioning for a drink from one of the servers. "I haven't seen the boy in quite a while. I knew him from my travels in the south. I didn't get to know the Warsmith, who I understand was there as well?"

"His Mage?" Mirsa frowned, fretting with the hem of her robe. "I don't know that I would..."

"Word travels fast," Chelani chuckled. "*I* think that you would. I wouldn't blame you, either. If I were younger..."

Mirsa sighed, and leaned in over the table. "You might have a fight on your hands."

"I already liked what I'd heard about her," Chelani laughed, leaning over toward Carlo. "A few more mugs, and we'll be braiding each other's hair."

"She prefers elves and assassins for that," Carlo shrugged, "But go ahead and try."

"Really?" the Blademistress asked, her gaze drifting from Carlo to Mirsa, and back. "And both you and Carlo support this heretic?"

"Until recently, we three and Bertus were hailed as heroes here, by the prince himself," Mirsa shrugged. "With his help, the four of us defeated an Orclord that could have eventually made his way this far east." She grimaced. "You're welcome."

"You'd think Carlo would have mentioned this," Chelani glared at the Blademaster as she took a swig of ale.

"Would you?" Mirsa asked, raising an eyebrow.

Choking on her drink, Chelani wiped her mouth with her sleeve and shook her head. "Are all Magi this plain-spoken?"

"Just the best ones," Carlo sighed. "Another one of them sits there, about to be condemned for trying too hard to set the world right."

"The hour has arrived!" one of the Warriors called, and the men in the room shifted toward the pit, focused on Kevon. "Stand, and be judged!"

"I thought this was a trial," Kevon responded, leaning forward and taking his feet. "Do I even get to defend myself?"

"You have violated the tenets of the Warrior's Guild, and likely those of the Mage's Guild, as well!" another voice called above the jeers directed at Kevon.

"Can anyone recite the oaths?" Carlo cried out, standing and turning to the crowd. "Do any of you *know* someone who can?"

The Blademaster waited in silence, taking a few steps back toward the sandpit, looking for a response. "No! You don't! The oaths were abandoned before I was a Novice. We don't swear them, we barely talk about them. The 'tenets' based on them are the last remnants of the Guild's origins, that we have been moving away from as we see the world change. In my youth, there were no women Warriors, no Blademistresses, and we might have tried Chelani in much the same manner as Kevon here. Should we punish her?"

Exclamations of surprised threaded through the crowd, and Carlo continued.

"Jonby!" Carlo called. "You took up the bow to hunt for your family, before you began the way of the sword."

"Aye?"

"And you gave it up to become a Novice, didn't you?" Carlo asked. "So you could devote all of your efforts to becoming the best Warrior you could be?"

"I still hunt," Jonby answered. "Have a venison hanging off the kitchen now," he laughed.

"As it should be," Carlo nodded. "Magic was Kevon's archery. He began learning it before I taught him the sword. If he had told me, I wouldn't have trained him. When he did tell me, I tried to kill him. Either of those would have been a grave mistake."

The background noise in the room faded to silence, as the rest of the Warriors in the room began listening to what Carlo had to say.

"In his own words, Alacrit proclaimed this man a hero," Carlo continued. "He has defeated more evil Magi and demons than most of you here, combined. How many of you remember how things were twenty years ago? Ten? How have things changed? Does the future look darker?"

Murmurs of agreement started amongst some of the older Warriors.

"If you know what I'm talking about, know that punishing Kevon strikes a blow for the enemy." Carlo closed his eyes and shook his head. "I won't ask you to believe the things I do, or even the things I've seen."

The Blademaster opened his eyes and gazed out into the crowd. "Can you believe in what you know of me?"

Sporadic cheers broke the silence.

"He's wanted by the crown!" someone called over the noise.

"That's the first place we're headed in the morning, after you release him," Carlo raised his voice in rebuttal. "You're all invited."

"You're not worried about the ones that left?" Kevon asked, rubbing his wrists.

"They won't make it across the district," Blademistress Chelani spoke before Carlo could answer, "Let alone all the way to the Palace, after dusk. The Dark Magi still own the night in Navlia."

"That needs to change," Carlo grumbled.

"No arguing that," Chelani agreed, sloshing her mug. "It's

been tried."

"Those guys might be trouble in the morning, but we'll be moving with five times as many as they are," the Blademistress added. "I'm not worried. Who knew Carlo was such an orator?"

"You should hear him sing," Kevon laughed.

"The Mage's Guild will not be as easy to convince," Mirsa warned. "Magi consider themselves enlightened already. I cannot leverage a Chelani as you did, and they are less likely to believe what we know to be truth. I cannot say I fault them, I would not believe if I had not seen things with my own eyes. Passion does not stir them as it does your people."

"Beyond that, we still need to convince Alacrit himself, and these *Eleri*?" Carlo asked. "Gaining the trust of both Guilds should stop the siege of the Dwarven Hold, but the majority of the army are just soldiers, not Warriors. They may follow directions from Alacrit in defiance of their original mission. I cannot say what Avolentz would do if Alacrit ordered an attack."

"That jackass would do anything Alacrit asked, if he wanted to keep his commission," Chelani snorted. "He wasn't a general three weeks ago."

"Has he changed that much?" Carlo asked. "I knew him to be a loyal soldier, often to a fault. But reckless in the face of destruction? The Dwarves are in far better position than the army can best."

"He's been reckless, since his brother fell on the southern front," Chelani explained. "His face does not betray his madness, but the only thing he has left is his honor in the eyes of the prince."

"Are they in danger?" Mirsa's voice took on an edge of panic. "Did I leave her there to…"

"Don't worry," Kevon reassured the Mage. "Rhysabeth-Dane and the Unbound would rout the army before they had a chance to breach the door. Maisy is safe."

"Safer than you are," Chelani grimaced. "You may have

the support of most of the Guild members here, but the Mage's Guild is another matter."

"We won't be able to stray from our plan to go directly to the palace in the morning," Kevon frowned. "I don't think they would stop Mirsa though."

"Most of the Magi in Navlia have retreated to the palace, because of the nighttime attacks by the Dark Magi." Mirsa explained. "I used to know several, but most of those who have not run to Alacrit for aid have fled the city, or been killed."

"We aren't likely to find sympathy with Magi who are under the prince's protection," Carlo grunted. "Are we?"

"Is there any chance you might be able to find one who is not?" Kevon asked.

"I'll try," Mirsa shrugged. "I'll turn in now, and leave just before dawn."

CHAPTER 47

"**S**he's returned!" One of Carlo's soldiers rushed into the chamber, wheezing. "Bring water!"

Bertus snatched up a waterskin, and followed the soldier back down the passage toward the surface. They met the Huntmistress halfway, collapsed on the dirt-fall, wringing the last drops of water from a Stoneguard's waterskin.

"Here, drink this." Bertus offered the full container, and Anneliese snatched it from his hands. She gulped down the first half of the water before taking a breath.

"Easy," the Warrior cautioned.

"I know," Anneliese snarled, curling a protecting arm around the leather vessel. "I haven't had a drink in two days."

"We expected you back two days ago," Bertus sat down next to her, on the side away from the waterskin. "Another group of Stoneguard has arrived, in your absence. We scouted toward the south the last two days around noon. What happened?"

"The first suitable place, that could be defensible, I found after a day and a half's travel to the southeast," Anneliese began. "I left at midday, to prevent being spotted leaving this place, and walked toward and around any landmark I thought large enough to provide some kind of shelter."

"A day and a half?" Bertus scratched his head. "We won't be able to make it that far with this many."

"We'll make it in half a day," Anneliese took another swig of water and struggled to her feet. "Marching directly. A little longer, depending on what we have to fight. Now that I know where it is."

"What is it?" Bertus asked.

"A small plateau," the Huntmistress answered. "It took me the better part of a day to sneak around it, but there are no caves, and the sides are sloped out. It provides no shade in the afternoon, so most of the creatures out there avoid it."

"We can delve into it, rather than raising walls," Bertus smiled. "That will make it easier on Reko."

"Let's hope," Anneliese finished off the water, and handed the empty skin back to Bertus. "I need another one of these, and a nap, before anything else."

"It's almost time," Marelle glanced upward, lifting her eyepatch as she did so. "The sun is nearing its peak, the gargoyles are no longer flying over."

"We've been preparing for this for a day and a half," Bertus announced. "You know what to do."

Anneliese and the Hunters moved out first, followed by half of the Stoneguard troops. Bertus rounded up Carlo's soldiers and the ancients, all laden with supplies; waterskins, prepared *covaninal*, extra weapons, and bedrolls. The rest of the Stoneguard followed behind, leaving four of their number, one Ancient, and one of Carlo's soldiers behind to guard the entrance to the transit system.

The sun beat down on the broken desert landscape, as the travelers threw squat shadows, excepting Anneliese and her Hunters. The men and dwarves dripped with sweat, bearing their burdens along behind the leaders at a jog.

"If we are not delayed, we should reach the plateau shortly after nightfall," Anneliese announced, dropping back to check on the troops in the center of the formation, as they slowed to a brisk walk. "We've seen several groups of different creatures, sheltering themselves from the sun. All have taken notice of us as we pass, none have dared approach. Our numbers should deter them for a time. I don't know what will happen when darkness falls."

"Keep Yusa protected, and we may not have to find out," Bertus suggested. "Without him, we'll have to sleep in shifts, fight throughout the night, until we can dig in. We've done it before, and I'm not eager to try it again."

"Orcs and gargoyles are the biggest threat along this stretch," Anneliese glanced upward, scanning the sky for the leathery demons. "The few leapers we have seen have not stirred at our passage, and I have yet to spot any reapers. It may be too hot for them here."

"We'll do what we can to keep watch for them," Marelle assured the Huntmistress. "I can see what approaches from any direction, save the south. The darkness is too great, and it grows worse as we move nearer."

"Focus on the skies," Anneliese instructed, starting back toward the front of the column, goading the leaders back to a jog. "Drink some more water, you'll need it soon enough."

The first attack began just before dusk.

Nightmarish forms jangled out of the elongated shadow of a twisted outcropping of rock to the west of the company's path. Stoneguard from the front and rear ranks called out to each other, formed up on their right flank, facing the approaching threat.

"Reapers," Marelle muttered to Bertus. "I was hoping she was right about them."

"Stay here, keep watch, protect Yusa and the Ancients," Bertus suggested, dropping his bags of supplies and moving up through the Dwarven line to the front.

Dwarves moved to one side or the other as Bertus advanced, readying his crossbow while he moved. He paused with the line that stood behind the kneeling axe-wielders that claimed the front, and steadied his aim as he heard the countdown in Dwarven. He loosed his bolt a moment behind the others, and cast his crossbow aside as he joined the Stoneguard that leapt to their feet, charging the monstrous creatures that seemed to blend in and out of the evening shadows with every lurch.

He drew the ancient Dwarven blade, and shouted a battlecry, surging forward to engage the nearest reaper with a blur of age-tempered metal.

Faster than thought, he whirled about the battlefield, lurching to intercept a counter-stroke of a reaper's scythe, or deliver the death-blow to a distracted enemy. He ducked and rolled beneath the axe-swings of his companions, bounding to his feet to sever the limbs or top-set eyes of the darkly gleaming demons.

Brutal minutes passed, the lingering heat of the day combined with the exertion of the run compounded the fatigue building in Bertus's muscles. A final push by the rest of the Dwarven line overwhelmed the remnants of the convocation of reapers. Moments later, the last creature fell to a Stoneguard's axe.

Bertus made his way back through the dimming battlefield, skewering any enemy that dared twitch as he passed by.

"An hour or more, at the rate we've been going," Anneliese observed, looking at the plateau ahead, glowing in rose-hued tones as the sun sank over the horizon. "Other creatures are approaching. We'd best move along before we're attacked again."

The company redoubled their speed. The Elven Hunters paused every so often to shoot down gargoyles that circled too close in the deepening night sky, and the Stoneguard line swept out from the main force to rebuff groups of leapers, orcs, and reapers that ventured too close.

Two Stoneguard and one of Carlo's soldiers fell in the last skirmish before they reached the base of the plateau, as a trio of large bull orc charged the left flank of the formation.

Marelle escorted Yusa to the plateau wall so that Reko

could begin his work. She watched him begin, and dashed back out through the surrounding ring of defenders to join Bertus and Anneliese in what remained of the skirmish.

The larger and smaller beasts had already fallen to the axes and arrows of the Stonguard and Hunter lines, but the remaining bull's blend of speed and strength gave it an edge over its defeated fellows.

Marelle dodged around a knot of dwarves reloading crossbows, and glanced over at the Elven line of Hunters. She could see that Anneliese and all but one of her subordinates had cast aside their bows, and were spreading out to encircle the raging orc.

If I could control the power within me, use it when I needed it, this would be the time, Marelle thought, thinking back to the practice session against Bertus aboard Yusa's ship. She could see Bertus leaping, dodging, and slashing as he maneuvered around the orc on the other side of the circle enclosing it. *He's using at least a portion of his ability. Maybe I can, too.*

Gripping the blade of her short sword, Marelle breathed out, and tried to relax and center herself. Her mind began cataloguing the movements of the orc and its antagonists before her, as well as the others to her sides, and even some behind her as she heard their movements. She hefted the blade, feeling the balance of the light, responsive metal, attuning herself to it. Her senses focused on the battle sharpened, while her others faded into the background.

A volley of crossbow fire slammed into the orc's side, causing little damage, but distracting it. Bertus moved to take advantage of the hiccup in the beast's movement, and Marelle seized her moment.

Summoning up every bit of resolve she could muster, the assassin took three running steps and leapt over the pair of Stoneguard that started to circle around in front of her. She sidestepped to the left as the orc raised its club, turning to wind up for its next attack, and stayed clear of its field of vision. Two short hops and a bounding leap off of the carcass of the larger of the fallen orcs landed her square between the beast's shoulder blades, hanging from the hilt of the sword she'd buried in its back.

The orc lurched forward, bellowing, as Marelle tightened her grip and pulled herself up, still dangling a yard above the ground. She planted her feet in the small of its back, and pushed, pulling and twisting at the stuck hilt. Feeling no give, she drew a dagger and timed a leap upward, grasping a fold of the orc's thick skin in one hand, using the stuck sword as a foothold. She plunged the dagger into the flesh around the orc's neck, the visceral *squish* satisfying and revolting her at the same time.

Marelle wrenched the dagger free, noticing the blade was free of all but a few streaks of blood. She stabbed again and again, but the bunching of the skin and flesh sealed the clean-edged wounds with pressure alone, doing nothing more than aggravating the already enraged bull.

Taking a moment to think, Marelle began to appreciate the work Bertus was doing. The Warrior did his best to taunt their giant enemy, moving in to strike with his Dwarven blade between the slowing strikes of the wounded orc. He carved wedges out of joints, taking two or three swings to inflict serious damage at weak points, as the surrounding Stoneguard danced in an ancient rhythm that resulted in near continuous damage from their large-bladed battle axes.

Feeling a pattern to the staggering of the orc, Marelle tensed to spring, and vaulted the extra few feet up to the creature's head, landing with a foot on either side of the beast's wide neck. She grabbed a handful of insect infested ear-hair with her left hand, and jabbed the dagger she held in her right hand as deep into his right ear as she could manage.

The orc's motions shifted, looser, more random. A giant hand swatted at Marelle, and she back-flipped off of the bull's neck to avoid being crushed. She landed, and drew two more daggers, preparing to rush forward again.

The Stoneguard that she'd landed beside reached out to

hold her arm, prevent her from moving forward.

"*Bham,*" he grunted, moments before the stricken behemoth lost its balance, and fell forward, shaking the ground as it landed, and shuddered into silence.

Marelle nodded to the dwarf, and sheathed her weapons after scanning the surrounding area, and the darkened skies. She looked through the crowd surrounding the entrance to the plateau, and saw the chamber Reko was expanding within it, not yet large enough to hold even a third them yet.

"We need to get these people inside," Marelle called to Bertus, accepting her sword and dagger from the Stoneguard who had retrieved them. "There are two bands of reapers closing from the north and the east, and the imps are starting to come out. A cloud of them is minutes away, maybe less."

CHAPTER 48

"Eat up, lad," Carlo ordered. "We might not have this chance for a while."

"I'm not sure that's the best thing for me to do this morning," Kevon argued, wincing as he sipped on the dark bitter brew that steamed in the mug before him. "I didn't sleep well. Couldn't stop worrying about Marelle and the others. Who knows what they are up against?"

"I don't," Carlo admitted. "None of us can. I know that most things we're apt to face in the next few hours at the palace would be better on a full stomach. Eat."

Chelani nodded in agreement, chewing on a strip of bacon, and sopping up a sloshing of gravy on her plate with a chunk of biscuit.

Kevon tried to eat, but the knot in his stomach twisted tighter. The bacon tasted of ash, and even gravy could not moisten the dry biscuit enough for Kevon to choke down more than a bite of each. He shoved his plate aside, and continued sipping the acrid tea.

"I should be going," Mirsa announced, dropping a finished melon rind onto her plate, and dabbing the corner of her mouth with a cloth napkin. "I have further to go today than the rest of you."

"The first rays of light break over the city walls," a Warrior announced, striding in from the Guildhall's entrance. "It should be somewhat safe."

"Good enough for me," Mirsa pushed her chair back and stood, stretching and yawning. "I'll see you all at the palace in a little while.

Kevon stood and escorted her to the door. The walk did nothing to ease the writhing in his stomach, it gurgled and growled even more as he returned to the common area.

"Try some of this," Chelani suggested, handing Kevon a slice of salted heartmelon. "The Mage enjoyed it."

Kevon smiled, and nibbled at the stringy raw fruit to placate the Blademistress. After a few bites, the jitters from the tea subsided, and his appetite started to return to normal. He finished the portion of melon, and two more slices of bacon. "Better," he admitted.

"We'll need to get moving before long," Carlo muttered over the increasing commotion in the filling Commons. "Take your time getting ready, take your time traveling, to give the Mage a chance to catch up. If we don't at least begin, we'll lose some of the support we gained last night."

"Fair enough," Kevon nodded, wiping the bacon grease off of his lips and fingers, and dropping the napkin on the table. "My sword!" he roared, above the chaos, and the room fell silent. He stood, breathing deep, maintaining a threatening posture. "If I am to present myself as one of you, I can't go before the prince without my sword. Where has it been taken? Return it to me at once!"

Novices scurried to locate the blade, inquiring with the men that had led the gathering the night before.

Carlo nodded his approval, and began his own slow preparations for departure.

"That's better," Kevon nodded, belting on his sword after a Novice returned it. "We'll leave as soon as both of you are ready."

"As presentable as they're going to be," Chelani announced half an hour later, straightening the collar of the last Novice in the line that prepared to follow the group to the palace. "If I catch any of you slouching while you're there..."

"I'm sure they won't," Carlo interrupted. "We'd best be on our way."

Kevon, Carlo, and Chelani led the procession that

streamed out into the early morning light of the city. War- riors followed behind them in two rows, marching more like soldiers than they would when not on active duty within the army. The varied uniforms of the Warriors drew more atten- tion to the parade that wound its way toward the palace than standard military maneuvers would have.

Warriors from the dissenting faction met them halfway to the palace, stepping to the side and falling in behind the others.

"Halt!" the cry came from atop the gates as they neared the palace walls. "You have no business here. Begone!"

"No business?" Kevon shouted in challenge. "Your prince has sent an army against the Dwarven people, in the name of the Warrior's Guild, to capture me. We all have busi- ness here!"

"Kevon?" a voice called from further down the wall.

"Who... Xaever?" Kevon peered up toward the speaker, who jogged toward the gatehouse.

"Blademaster Carlo! Blademaster Chelani!" the War- smith called as he reached the tower that led down inside the gates. "Open the gates!"

"Not one to follow politics, are you?" Carlo asked Xaever as he shook the Warsmith's hand through the opening gate.

"On the contrary," Xaever smiled. "Alacrit can ill afford to anger the Warrior's Guild, with his army so far from home. I'm making sure he addresses your concerns. Send word ahead that the Heroes have returned to Navlia. His Majesty will want to greet them properly."

"Too easy," Chelani cautioned.

"Xaever's a friend," Kevon reassured her. "He'll be fair, at least."

"I don't imagine Alacrit will allow all these weapons in- side the palace," the Warsmith cautioned. "If..."

"We'll gladly give them up," Carlo shrugged, handing off his borrowed sword to a nearby soldier. "I think Kevon should keep his, as a sign of good faith by the prince. The rest of us will leave ours here."

"Can't be any worse than the elf," Xaever mumbled.

"What's that?" Carlo asked.

"Certainly works for myself," the Warsmith grimaced and directed the Warriors off to the side, where a squad of soldiers waited to collect their weapons.

"Thank you, Xaever," Kevon extended a hand in greeting.

Xaever gritted his teeth, and returned the gesture with a slow deliberateness. "Things have changed since we met last. Alacrit has done much for the Guilds in this city, they find themselves beholden to him."

"Something's wrong..." Kevon guessed.

"I want there not to be," Xaever shook his head. "But if things are as they say..."

"These are not ordinary times," Kevon began. "There is much you haven't been told."

"You'll need to stay and keep watch, lad," Carlo grunted at Xaever, "for when the Magi arrive."

"All of the Magi in Navlia are already here," Xaever frowned, "So..."

"They made it here before us?" Carlo asked. "I'll remember not to underestimate the little lady..."

"No," Xaever shook his head. "The Dark Magi have killed all of the other Mages in the city, those not behind these walls. It's been over a season since we had any word..."

"Will she be safe during the day?" Kevon asked, looking from Xaever to Carlo, to Chelani. His hand moved to the sword at his side. "I have to go find her."

"I don't think your leaving is such a good idea," Chelani frowned, stepping back to look at the surrounding sea of Warriors. "Let me round up a few volunteers, we'll find her."

The Blademistress moved out of the gathering crowd and selected five such 'volunteers', and they began retrieving their weapons from the pile in preparation to depart.

"Please hurry," Carlo asked as Chelani and the others turned to leave. "...Anneliese would never forgive me if anything happened to her."

The Blademistress nodded through narrowed eye-slits, and a hint of a smile danced on her lips before she led the other Warriors out of the courtyard gates at a jog.

◆ ◆ ◆

"Stay back!"

"But, I..." Mirsa struggled to peer around the corner as the Mage's hand on her left shoulder held her, for the most part, against the rough stone building. She slipped out of his restraining grasp, and whirled to the right, moving between the building's corner and her former mentor, gaining a full view of the battleground.

The shattered husks of two obsidian reapers smoldered in the alleyway, but the two remaining horrors advanced, not ten yards from where Mirsa and Briltor Magus stood.

"*Bera mot!*" Briltor growled under his breath, clenching his left fist with enough force to pop his knuckles.

Mirsa felt the outflow of Fire and Movement magic, heard and saw the twitching screech of the lead reaper as it spun, slashing at the creature behind it before flames flared out of its leathery joints, and it clattered into a smoking heap of nightmarish refuse.

"*Phes movra!*" she intoned, gathering her fear and rage, funneling it into a cyclone of flame that spun from her hand, crossing the distance to the chittering monster before the last syllable escaped her lips. The twisting inferno wobbled across the demon's upper body, splashing flames into its top-mounted eye, then lurching lower into its screeching maw. The infuriated Mage expended extra effort to intensify the heat and reach of the flames as they funneled into the creature's mouth.

The reaper staggered, and stumbled to the side as a loud

'pop' rocked its frame.

Mirsa released the spell in her mind as their last foe dropped to the ground without as much as a spasm. "After them..." she wheezed, taking two halting steps forward before Briltor grabbed a fold of cloth on the back of her robe.

"They have escaped," he sighed. "The sun rises, and their power wanes. We should find somewhere to recover, ourselves."

"No time for that," Mirsa argued. "I have to gather the Mage's Guild to weigh in on Kevon's trial today at the palace."

"The Guild has been fractured, destroyed here in Navlia," Briltor rubbed at his chin. "My hidden dwelling outside the city walls is the only place outside of the palace I've felt safe in seasons, and I''ve not been to the palace in quite a while. There may be a few Guild members hiding with Alacrit."

"Destroyed..." Mirsa leaned against the wall, and doubled over, her hands resting on her knees. "No more Mage's Guild in Navlia? Magi that are trapped in the palace will not go against Alacrit's wishes. How can we...?"

"If it is important to you, child," Briltor reached down and took one of Mirsa's hands. "I shall accompany you." He startled at the noise from the road behind them.

Mirsa could feel him readying a spell in his mind and hear him beginning to speak the words to ignite the destructive forces he wrestled with.

"Mirsa," Chelani called, lowering her sword. "We've been looking everywhere for you."

"We have heard Kevon and his mentor plead their case," Alacrit said, standing from his throne to address those assembled. "Perhaps a demonstration of what he is capable of is in order."

"Should..." Kevon glanced sidelong at Carlo. "Should I?"

"Something small?" Carlo suggested. "No fire."

Kevon drew his sword, and grasped it by the hilt and the blade, turning so that all could see his blatant contact with the forbidden metal. He sorted through the symbols swimming in his mind, and focused on the Light and Wind runes.

Trickling energy into the Light rune, Kevon directed the magic around himself, causing his skin to glow. He increased the power, and closed his eyes. He amplified the spell until the surrounding crowd began murmuring in discomfort, then backed off until they quieted before reopening his eyes. Kevon shifted his grip on the blade and stepped forward into the open between Carlo and Alacrit. He pinched the grip with just enough force, and let the blade fall from his other hand, rolling the momentum into a figure-eight motion that had served him well in Alacrit's defense, not far from here.

Swish, swish, swish. The blade cut through the air at an unhurried pace, just fast enough to hear. Kevon's concentration deepened, and he let the magic flow into the Wind rune. The air in the room began a slow dance, circling around the point just beyond the reach of Kevon's blade before him. He gathered the wind in front of him, compressing layer upon layer as it spun toward the center.

Swish, swish, swish. The wind around Kevon grew in volume to match the slashes of his blade, and he released the spell, finished with the demonstration.

The compressed sphere of air he'd gathered dissipated with a thunderous *boom*, knocking Kevon back a step, tearing the sword from his hand. The weapon clattered to the floor, skidding to a stop at Carlo's feet.

"I'm..." Kevon blurted, waving his hands in front of him in panic.

A nearby urn performed a slow pirouette, its porous stone base sounding a protesting groan against the smooth surface of the marble pillar before it teetered off the edge, smashing to bits as it hit the floor.

"Sorry," he finished, bowing to Alacrit.

"Damages notwithstanding," the prince remarked,

smoothing his windblown hair, "This appears to be a valuable estimate of your abilities?"

"Those that are fit for indoors," Kevon mumbled.

"It's not natural!" one of the dissenting Warriors called from the back of the assembly. "How can we allow him to train with us, to become even more powerful than he is now?"

"Using magic while shielded from it," one of the Magi beside Alacrit shuddered. "The very idea of it terrifies me, as it should you all."

"Yet you hailed him as a hero when he used his terrifying magic to slay the Orclord that would have ravaged our lands," Briltor Magus raised his voice as he skirted around the Warriors at the back of the assembly. "Where were your fears then?"

"We didn't know it was him, then!" an angry voice called out. "This is different!"

"Would you ask a butcher to ply his trade with a spoon?" the Mage continued, making his way through the room to Kevon's side. "Would you?" he boomed.

Acknowledging the dismissals, Briltor Magus continued. "This young man is powerful. There is no doubt about that. He is dangerous. But to who? Has he turned against the crown?" The Mage waited for a few moments before speaking again. "He has come here from across the Realm, submitting himself for judgement to his prince. Would you slay a loyal hound for snatching a fowl from the air before you could shoot it with an arrow? No! I say this is one and the same."

Murmurs of agreement began building in the crowd behind Kevon, and the assembled Magi surrounding Alacrit exchanged glances with each other and Briltor Magus.

"I say hear him out, and give him what he needs to continue his service to you, my lord." Briltor knelt beside Kevon, and bowed to Alacrit.

"I..." Alacrit glanced at the crowd before him. "I shall take some time to ponder this counsel, and study in the archives. You will all excuse me, and be welcome in these halls."

"How long does he need to study this?" Carlo wondered aloud after Alacrit left the room. "He knew before we told him about Kevon, about Bertus, and I expect a few other things.

"The royal library is larger than one would assume," Briltor shrugged, climbing to his feet. "One could spend a lifetime there and not read through it all."

"And you are?" Kevon asked.

"Briltor Magus," he announced, bowing to Kevon.

"Mirsa's mentor," Kevon nodded. "I remember now. You've been a great help in the past. Thank you for this."

"I don't know that I would be thanking me," Briltor warned, lowering his voice. "We've put Alacrit in a position that may force him to release you, regardless of what he wants. He will not like that. You must be prepared to leave once he allows it, rescue allies who might not be safe here."

"Magi," Mirsa clarified. "We need to recruit more Mages. There are only three of us right now. We'll need more to face any larger threats."

"We can't just bring them with us to the Hold," Kevon frowned. "Too much at stake for unknowns with that much power."

"You argue Alacrit's point with eloquence," the Master Mage chuckled. "Though you have proven yourself, others have not. Quite the dilemma."

"We'll have to train and test them somewhere else," Mirsa whispered. "There is a place…"

"Where are you…" Kevon began, and the color drained from his face as he guessed her intent. "No. I couldn't ask you… I don't want to go there myself."

"It's remote, abandoned, the last place anyone would expect," Mirsa shrugged. "If you helped us repair the outer walls, part of the recruits' training could be the restoration of the compound."

"Are you sure?" Kevon asked. "We could find somewhere else…"

"There is already something wonderful that had its beginnings in that place, waiting for me to return to her in the Hold," Mirsa argued. "With more effort, we can make it what I believed it to be all along, a force for good."

Echoes of dying Magi and roaring flames pressed into Kevon's mind. Memories of Mirsa's screams as the Adept Waine lost his life beneath the ruins reverberated through his soul, and he shook his head to clear it.

"If you can bear it, I'll try," Kevon decided. "We'll need a handful of Magi, at least, to make it worthwhile."

"I can help with their training," Briltor offered. "I did little enough when the darkness festered there."

"Your help just now has been invaluable," Kevon admitted. "Anything more would be most welcome."

CHAPTER 49

"The prince will see you now," the guard at the door announced.

"Being welcome in these halls means something far different than it used to," Carlo growled, marching to the door of the room they'd been held in overnight. "Coming?" he asked, waiting for Kevon and Mirsa.

"Seems we're the last to arrive," Mirsa observed as they entered the audience chamber.

The crowd parted to allow them passage to where Alacrit waited.

"Kevon 'ap Holten, Warsmith Adept," Alacrit began. "It pains me to speak those words. Regardless of your current support by the Guilds, your actions go against generations of tradition."

"They do," Kevon acknowledged, to rumblings of dissent from those gathered behind him.

"There is enough division in the Guilds that I could destroy you, and still retain my throne," Alacrit mused, and laughter peppered the air from some of the Warriors toward the back of the assembly. "I choose otherwise."

"Thank you, my liege," Kevon bowed.

"Your pardon does not come without price," the prince continued. "The Dark Magi must be scoured from my city."

"I cannot stay," Kevon shook his head. "The dwarves move on the source of the darkness, far to the south. We are needed there."

"Give me three weeks with the men we have gathered here," Carlo crossed his arms. "And we'll crush the dark ones that remain here, take back the night."

"Carlo has defeated as many of the demons the Dark Magi use as any man alive," Kevon agreed. "Is this acceptable?"

Alacrit closed his eyes for a moment, and reopened them with a grin. "I am ready to take my city back. Who's with me?"

The chamber shook with the roars of the gathered Warriors.

◆ ◆ ◆

"There are still those that oppose what we are doing," Chelani warned Carlo. "A number of them departed right after Alacrit pardoned Kevon. I'm sure they are not opposed to the destruction of the Dark Magi, but once that threat is gone..."

"We'll deal with that when the time comes," Carlo responded. "I have to meet with Xaever and set up training dummies. The men will be more effective if they know what can and can't kill these demons."

"We need to start training, as well," Mirsa said, looking to Kevon. "Briltor has gotten four other Magi to commit to joining us."

"I doubt we could take more than that without angering Alacrit again," Kevon conceded. He looked at Briltor Magus. "Have them gather their things, and we'll make our way to the Sending chamber."

"You'll have to watch them," Carlo cautioned. "There may be some working in concert with the Dark Magi that will be bolder once they are out from under the roof of the palace."

Mirsa's mentor nodded, and turned to leave.

"I think our time here would be best spent studying their Sending chamber," Kevon told Mirsa. "I'd feel better waiting there, in case Alacrit changes his mind."

"We'll need supplies," Mirsa frowned. "I'll have provisions delivered after I show you the way."

"I hadn't considered..." Kevon admitted. "I'm sure we'll

be able to get additional supplies from the Hold once you're established, to get you started."

They made their way through the hallways to the backside of the palace, and into the garden.

"Very nice," Kevon grinned as they stepped out into the open and the garden unfolded before them. "There is only one other garden in the Realm that even comes close, far to the north." He slowed as they reached the circular cobblestone formation near the outer wall. "Just below us, right?"

Mirsa nodded and led Kevon through the guard-post, and opened the hidden passageway that led down to the Sending room.

"I've never felt an enchantment this strong, outside of the Dark portals we've encountered," Kevon remarked, marveling at the skill and precision it would have required to lay down such powerful magic. "I'm sorry I don't have more time to study it."

"Stay here for a while, I'll return with what supplies I can," Mirsa shrugged, climbing the stone stairway back up to the garden.

Kevon began making his way around the room, sampling the flavors of enchantment that infused each of the runes inscribed in the floor. He took note of which enchantments were focal, and which were layered power sources that could be drawn upon to power the guided spells. He was arranging his thoughts on how the design might be improved when Mirsa returned much later with the others.

"I'll go first," Kevon offered. "We don't know what to expect. The other volunteers could follow every few minutes, Briltor and Mirsa last?"

"Each Mage providing their own power for the spell, guided by Mirsa and myself," Briltor Magus agreed. "No one will arrive defenseless, drained of their magic. You never know what might be waiting."

"Nothing worse than the last time we were there, I hope," Kevon grunted.

Kevon stood in the center of the chamber and reached out with his mind to tap into the Enchanted rune formation below him. The spell-sigils, already wavering in his mind, snapped to vibrant clarity as he made the connection. Stabilizing and strengthening enchantments guided the forming spell, and Kevon pictured the courtyard between the central tower and the outer dining hall. He eased his own power into the spell…

"Trouble?" Mirsa asked, as Kevon stood, frowning.

"Odd," Kevon shrugged. "Guess I'll try outside the drawbridge."

The spell built again in Kevon's mind, and he flooded the symbols with power. The images in his mind flashed dazzling azure as the magic took form, and reality shifted around him.

The breeze blowing from the northwest whispered across Kevon's face, easing the heat from the midmorning sun, but carrying whiffs of mildew from the remnants of the moat surrounding the ruins. Kevon wrinkled his nose, drew his sword, and started across the drawbridge that led back into the heart of the broken tower complex.

That's why, Kevon thought as he spotted the heap of stone from the outer wall that had fallen over the spot he had first chosen to target with his Sending. He turned to survey the area outside the ruin before he stepped into the inner courtyard from the drawbridge. Seeing nothing to cause concern, he turned his attention to the wreckage ahead of him.

The blasted remains of the inner tower were overgrown with weeds, appearing more like natural rock formations than the jumbled fragments of cut stone he knew them to be. A hare poked its nose around the corner of one of the piles, snuffling at the wild grains that grew in tufts under the jagged overhang. It froze as it spotted him.

Probably not any orcs around, if I'm the threat, Kevon thought, sheathing his sword.

Kevon extended his senses beyond himself, using the Earth rune inscribed on his sword to feel along and under the ground. His awareness skimmed over the piles of rubble, and dove down toward the cavern below, where the last remnants of the magical distortion from seasons ago lingered. He waited for the space of a few breaths, feeling the footsteps of rodents, small game, and nothing else for as far as the spell reached.

Twisting the magic to another end, he forced more power into L'drom's rune, and began repairing the damage to the outer walls. The cut stone had different memories of where it belonged, and Kevon had to work more by matching fractures together to complete whole slabs, then fit the slabs in the proper places based on size and shape of the missing pieces. After a few minutes, less than a quarter of the rubble in the inner courtyard had been cleared, and the walls were complete only halfway up the outer frame. Segments of the destroyed mess hall resisted the reorganization, siphoning away more magic than Kevon could spare. *Iron,* he thought, as he slowed the flow of magic, and withdrew from the spell before it could drain him further.

"Don't stop because of me," one of Briltor's recruits said from the end of the drawbridge. "I can't feel what you are doing, because of the sword? It's still something to watch."

"Much more complex than what I am used to," Kevon admitted. "So many small pieces moving at once. Even if I weren't exhausted, I'd need to stop for a while."

"Understood," the Mage nodded. "So, this is where it all happened?"

"The destruction of several Dark Magi," Kevon answered. "The loss of a great friend, and L'mort nearly killing me when he attempted to cross over into our world. If that's what you're asking."

"Where you killed the Orclord?" the Mage asked.

"A few miles to the southeast," Kevon shrugged. "It's probably still there..."

"Garrimor," the Mage introduced himself, dropping his sack of supplies. "I'm sorry. I've been in awe of the four of you since before I knew you were a Mage."

"And since then?" Kevon asked.

"Shocked. Confused. Mostly inspired," Garrimor grinned. "I'd love to know how you do it."

"I don't know that I would share that knowledge if I believed it was safe," Kevon shook his head. "Risking injury or death to attempt it, only to be branded a heretic?"

"I understand," Garrimor conceded. "The trouble it has gotten you in..."

Kevon grimaced at the comment, and looked past Garrimor to where the next recruit appeared with another bulging burlap sack.

The last two recruits and Mirsa appeared in rapid succession.

"Briltor will be along in a few more minutes," Mirsa announced, crossing the drawbridge to join the others, tossing her sack of supplies onto the pile just inside the stone archway. "You've already repaired quite a bit of the outside walls," she observed. "You won't have enough power to get back to the Hold for quite a while, will you?"

"Not on my own," Kevon nodded. "Unless we aim for..." he chuckled. "That might work. How much strength do you have left?"

CHAPTER 50

Mirsa leaned against the pile of rubble, drained from the spell, the lack of immediate access to the Sending enchantments. Targeting the Sending chamber beneath the Hold had helped, but it had still taken most of the magic both she and Kevon had left to complete the spell. They had not wanted to trust any of the new recruits with the knowledge of the chamber, access to the Hold would be made far too easy for potential enemies if that knowledge fell into the wrong hands. Kevon had even taken the lead on the spell, Mirsa had only felt the magic drain away, shielded from her senses by his connection to the sword.

"Ma'am," Garrimor interrupted her thoughts. "Master Briltor has arrived."

"Kevon has already departed?" Briltor asked as soon as Mirsa walked into view.

"He'll return in a few days, with Maisy, and more supplies," she answered. "It'll give us a chance to rebuild as part of our training."

"Excellent," Briltor nodded. "The outer wall seems solid, for now. I would like to begin on the inner tower, if you would start repairs on the moat?"

"Garrimor," Mirsa began, "Select another recruit, and follow me." She nodded to Briltor Magus as she walked past the others to the tower entrance.

"Are you ready to begin?" Mirsa asked the others as they joined her in the center of the lowered drawbridge. Without waiting for an answer, she extended her magical senses down into the murk below, latching onto the thread of latent Water magic, and began her spell.

"Steady your Aid runes, copy my Water and Movement runes the best you can," Mirsa lectured, waiting until the shimmering forms in her mind solidified further before starting the actual work of the spell.

Garrimor gasped as Mirsa took control of the borrowed magic and began pulsing ripples in the cloudy pool of water below.

"Slowly, find the rhythm," she whispered, building the spell up enough that water sloshed over the side of the moat to the outside edge. "Focus deeper, and up. Deeper, and up!"

The runes flared as the spellwork tossed a knotted mass of bleached driftwood and bone free of the clogged channel, freeing up more room for unimpeded water.

"Don't lose it," she cautioned, adjusting the spell to the scattered waves, and reforming them into a more unified motion. "Keep it going. Deeper..."

"And up!" Garrimor laughed, as the next wave ejected a larger pile of debris.

"Good!" Mirsa responded, loosening her grasp on the spell. "Garrimor, you take over, keep working in this direction. I'll work the other way, and we'll see how far we can get. Make sure you don't spend all your energy on this, keep some in reserve in case something happens out here. We're far from any help, and will need to be more careful here than in the palace."

"Yes, Master Mirsa."

She felt Garrimor's concentration deepen, as he overtook control of the spell the three had been collaborating on. She distanced herself mentally from the magic they worked, and began one of her own. She felt the edges of the spell the other Magi controlled waver, and she added a rune of Concealment to her own spell. The magic deepened as she walked off the drawbridge and around the edge of the moat away from the others. She caught a wave's energy slapping back from the other team, and harnessed it with her Art, scooping up a giant mass of garbage, flinging it clear of the polluted channel.

Mirsa paused, reveling in the waves of magic that rolled over her, wondering what the trip to the Plane of Water must have been like. To have been enfolded in it, able to breathe it in without drowning. *To meet the one who filled the oceans,* she thought, sighing. *Perhaps I'll be able to meet her when this is all over.*

Ten minutes later she glanced over her shoulder, and could see the others beginning to move out of sight around the curve of the outer tower. She finished the next section of moat, scouring the trash from a large section with a surge that originated close to where the other Magi stood. The wave crested with a crackle of brown foam and a spray of detritus that scattered over dozens of yards past the edge of the moat. She released the magic, and started back toward the tower's entrance.

Garrimor spotted Mirsa's return, and began his own journey back to the tower's entrance, the other recruit in tow.

"A third of the moat cleared," Mirsa estimated as the other two walked into earshot. "It should be easy to finish tomorrow."

"Hours before nightfall," Garrimor observed, looking over the mountains to the west, where the sun still hung a handsbreadth over the top of the range. "What are we to do until then?"

"We secure the outer tower, help with the work on the inner tower, and take care of these supplies," Mirsa suggested. "Let's start by raising the drawbridge."

"The ropes are long rotted away," the other recruit pointed to the bits of knotted rope that still clung to one side of the bridge, and the scraggly lengths that hung from eyelets on either side of the archway.

"We'll do what we can," Mirsa answered, leading them over the bridge and into the tower courtyard. "Each of you, to one side of the arch. The outside of the arch, on the inside of the wall. See the brass pegs?"

Without waiting, Mirsa began another spell, forming Enhancement and Movement spells. "Help me," she ordered, and wrestled the offered power from her two assistants. She clutched at the far end of the drawbridge with her Art, and it creaked aloft. "*Odio vam...*"

The drawbridge leapt inward as the words Mirsa intoned sharpened the focus of her Movement rune, and she pushed more of the borrowed power into the mental construct. With a final creak, the raised walkway *thudded* into the carved depression against the outside of the tower.

"Now. Push them in now," Mirsa commanded, and the others shoved the neutral metal pegs, three to a side, through their stone channels into the holes cut for them long ago. "There," she breathed, releasing the spell. "Nothing's getting in that way." She looked to the sky, and grimaced.

"Looks like there is a lot left to do on the inner tower," Garrimor commented, looking at the mostly untouched rubble at the center of the courtyard. He tilted his head, and peered to the structure built into the eastern wall of the outer tower. "I can feel them working, over there."

"Easier to fix up for the night than starting on the inner tower right away," Mirsa observed. "Let's see what we can do to help. Grab the supplies."

CHAPTER 51

"**H**old up," Mirsa cautioned, easing out of the spell that she and three of the new recruits had just begun, preparing to restore part of the ground level of the inner tower's stonework. "Do any of you feel that?"

"It feels a little like what the attacks by the Dark Magi were like," Garrimor answered, "but the magic is not there."

"Or it is Concealed," she scowled, and closed her eyes, and tried to locate the source of the disturbance. "West side, in the shade," she reported. "If this is an attack, it may take all of us to repel it. Follow me."

The symbols for Concealment, Water, and Enhancement linked up in Mirsa's mind as she ran for the opened gateway to the drawbridge. She powered them with a trickle of magic to keep them hidden, and felt the potential grow as she neared the moat and the latent magic within.

"Nothing," Mirsa whispered as she stepped out onto the drawbridge, and slowed to look both ways. "I felt it further around to the west, but it's gone now." She jogged across the bridge, and started to cut around the moat's edge.

A faint scream sounded in the direction they were headed.

"Not Briltor," Mirsa muttered under her breath, sure that the tone of the scream was far too high pitched to belong to the older Master Mage. "What does that mean?"

Mirsa ran wide around one of the piles of waterlogged debris from the previous day's cleanup, and stopped as the distance and angle of her approach gave her a clear view of the horror ahead.

Briltor Magus faced one of the recruits, a good fifty yards further than he stood. Between them stood two Obsidian Reapers, advancing.

"No! How could you?" the younger Mage screamed, as the walking nightmares closed in on her.

Mirsa's mind twinged as a bolt of flame leapt from the young Mage's hand, and struck a glancing blow off of one of the reapers' dusky carapaces. As that reaper screeched in frustration, the other leapt the last dozen yards to impale her with a swipe of its scythe-arm.

The years of training spent with the gentle-seeming Mage, the talks that ran into the early morning about magical techniques. All of it came rushing back, slamming like a fist in Mirsa's gut as the man's true loyalties were revealed.

The reapers turned, as if they were one, and the discarded remains of the slain Mage slumped to the ground.

"I'd hoped to do this a little more quietly," Briltor called as he turned to face Mirsa and the others. "We had been struggling with how to divide the loyalists in the palace, weaken their numbers even further. My thanks."

"You helped me after we defeated Gurlin," Mirsa fumed, shaking her fist at the Master Mage. "How could you?"

"How could I keep an eye on a minor enemy with potential to become a larger problem in the future?" Briltor scoffed. "How could I not? Enough talk. This ends now."

"It does," Mirsa whispered, and reached out with a Concealed Control spell. She touched the minds of each of the reapers, and found them gripped by a force beyond her ability to affect at all. Her lips curled into a smile as she shifted the target of her spell to the scythe-arm of the reaper approaching on Briltor's left. She clenched her fist and groaned in wordless exertion, forcing the creature's arm in a wobbly arc that caught the unwary Mage in the side, slashing open his cloak and the flesh below his ribcage.

Released from the spell that held their minds in thrall,

the reapers turned on Briltor. Within moments, the Mage's screams stopped, and the demons squared off in a grotesque tug-of-war over his limp form. One managed to wrangle a lifeless arm into its thorax-mouth, and tear it from Briltor's body.

"We can't fight them," Mirsa conceded. "We can't outrun them. Help me shape the Darkness." She gathered Garrimor's offered power into her own, and started opening a Dark portal between the feasting reapers and the remaining Mages.

Both reapers froze as the gateway opened. One released his hold on the shredded scraps of Briltor's body, and charged for the distortion, disappearing from view as he merged with the foul tear in reality. The remaining reaper clutched its prize close, and stumbled toward the pulsating gate.

"Hurry..." Mirsa hissed, struggling to keep the passageway open as her magical reserves dwindled. The sun warming her skin ate through the energy she fed into the spell maintaining the portal. She trembled for a few more moments, and the churning gateway shrank in lurches, each contraction revealing more of the demon and the surrounding carnage behind the chaotic blemish that separated it from the rest of the Magi.

The portal writhed out of view, and the reaper stopped, shrieking through a mouthful of Briltor-flesh.

"Run," Mirsa croaked, and turned to flee with the others.

Fear provided a much needed burst of speed, and Mirsa closed the gap between herself and the others faster than she thought possible. The clicking of chitin and garbled screeches of the pursuing reaper gave ample inspiration to maintain the pace of her frenzied retreat.

Garrimor reached the drawbridge a mere ten paces before Mirsa, and stumbled.

Over the panic and chaos already blaring through her mind, Mirsa thought she could hear Maisy crying. Her fear redoubled, and mingled with anger at the pursuing demon. *How DARE it threaten her child,* her instincts screamed.

"Get up! Move!" she shouted, missing only a single step

as she clutched the back of Garrimor's robe, lifting the Mage to his feet as she ran by. They reached the stone archway that led into the tower courtyard, and the reaper's chitinous clattering changed pitch as it moved from dirt and stone to the Enchanted wood of the drawbridge.

Knowing there was not enough time to make it to either of the structures across the courtyard, Mirsa stooped and snatched up a stone from the ground. She whirled to face her pursuer. She hurled the rock, and it smashed into the reaper's carapace just above its mouth.

The reaper stopped for a moment, and screeched challenge, waving its arms in menacing circles.

"Nice toss," a voice laced with admiration commented. "Don't throw this."

Mirsa's jaw went slack as Kevon handed her Maisy, and stepped forward to face the reaper.

The Warsmith drew his sword, and small stones from around the courtyard leapt from the ground, floating toward him. "Is this the only one?" he called over his shoulder, slashing the air with the blade. The floating rocks hurtled toward the reaper, and it stumbled back under the barrage of impacting stones.

"Yes!" Mirsa cried, crumpling to the ground, covering Maisy's face, shielding her from the horror on the other side of the gateway.

Kevon stopped, and a moment later a wave from the moat swept over the drawbridge, carrying the reaper down into the moat.

"What happened?" he asked, sheathing his sword as he returned. "Is everyone all right? Where's Briltor? I thought there were two other girls…"

"It was the right move to bring recruits here before moving them to the Hold," Kevon decided, after hearing the whole story about the attack. "The damage Briltor could have done in the depths of the Dwarven Kingdom…"

Mirsa sat, now silent, holding her child on her lap.

"I'm sure that Briltor was the only one that was a danger," Kevon added. "We could move the rest of you now…"

"No," Mirsa shook her head. "There will be more recruits, more possibilities for treachery. I'd prefer they happened here. The Magi here now are more committed to the battle against the darkness, and will do what it takes to stand against it."

"Would you like me to take Maisy back to the Hold with me?" Kevon asked. "If there is going to be danger here…"

"I can't be apart from her," Mirsa sighed. "I know that now. You've brought us more supplies, seed, rope. They should have the drawbridge repaired by now. With the traitors out of our midst, this place is not much more dangerous than another. I doubt anyone else even knows we are here."

"Can I help with anything else?" Kevon pressed. "Finding and training Magi for our cause is one of the most important things we can do now. I don't want this to fail any more than I want to see you or Maisy hurt."

"They will own this tower once the repairs have been completed," Mirsa shook her head. "They'll be proud of it, as I once was, and defend it with their lives. It will take us weeks to do what you could do in days, but it will be worth it."

"I wish I had word of Bertus," Kevon admitted, "But there has been none. I'll journey through the passages to the south as soon as I return to the Hold, and bring him back to you if I can."

"Him if you can, word if you can't," Mirsa smiled. "We'd be on the Glimmering Isle if we weren't needed elsewhere."

"I know." Kevon stood and traced his finger along Maisy's cheek.

"You'd better go," Mirsa scolded. "See to your wife."

Kevon nodded, and arranged the runes in his mind. He focused the magic, concentrating on his destination beneath the Dwarven Hold, and vanished before the moisture in his eyes could form into tears.

CHAPTER 52

"The army has already turned south from Eastport," Rhysabeth-Dane reported as she entered the briefing room. "I can't be sure it's all of them, but the formation looks the same, except for the Magi."

"They're back at the palace, I'd wager," Kevon nodded. "They could return here at any time, but it would take more than a handful of Magi to threaten the Hold."

"Kylgren-Wode and the others have moved further south from the end of the line," the Rider continued. "They are hesitant to send more than a few reinforcements through, without more word than that."

"I'd like you to remain here, watching over the Hold with the Unbound," Kevon requested. "Without any Magi remaining here, the Hold would be more vulnerable than we can afford. I can take any forces we can spare to the south, and reinforce the others."

"I'll speak with our king," Rhysabeth-Dane nodded. "You'll have your reinforcements."

Kevon followed Rhysabeth-Dane out of the chamber, but turned right toward the Sending chamber, instead of following the Rider left toward the main part of the Hold. He navigated the few remaining turns without thought, reaching out with his senses to try and feel the enchantments ahead, slight as they were. He stalked into the room, and knelt near the edge of the circle, placing his hand on the inner ring of the Sending enchantment The runes sharpened in his mind as he made contact, and he waited long minutes, letting his amassed magic slide into the enchantment, brightening its presence in his thoughts. Kevon's stomach turned as his magical reserves emptied, and the still-sharp sigils dimmed and flattened, slipping from his grasp as the magic ran out.

The Mage stood, and looked at the patterns in the stone for a few moments before he turned to leave.

"These are the two transports that have been returned from this line," Rhysabeth-Dane explained as she goaded the Stoneguard and Dwarven Regulars into the sledges, along with the extra supplies that had been arranged for the trip. "There are more that we can use if we need more troops in a hurry," she added.

"I'll bring word if they are needed," Kevon assured her. "We'll send these two back again, so that there won't be any risk of sending transports toward each other. It there is no other word in a week or more, you may want to send someone else."

"Bargthar-Stoun will decide," Rhysabeth-Dane nodded at Kevon's instructions. "I'll let him know." She glanced at the forward sledge. "The first transport looks ready to go. I assume you'll want to be on it?"

"Right," Kevon affirmed. "I'm not spending a minute longer here than I have to. Not when she's..."

"I know," the diminutive Rider whispered, wrapping her tiny fingers around part of Kevon's hand. "Keep Kylgren-Wode out of trouble, for me, will you?"

Kevon thought he could see a sheen of moisture forming over the dwarf's eyes as she turned to leave, but said nothing. He marched down the ramp that led to the forward loading dock on the line, and hopped into the last empty seat. The slight amount of magic in his depleted reserves slipped away as he bumped shoulders with an armored Stoneguard. He smiled at his seatmate, and sat back as the drumming started.

How many hours of this? Kevon wondered as the transport began moving along the spinning conveyor. The frustration of not being able to Send himself to his destination was tempered by his complete lack of magic. Pressed in alongside the snoring Stoneguard to his right, he would not be able to use magic for anything until after they reached the other end of the line. *It didn't use to be this way,* he thought, remembering his first experience helping Send his former Master from his home town of Laston, and the years between then and the time he had begun traveling with the use of the spell. *The journey was often better than the destination.*

Memories of evening campfires, training with Carlo, listening to Waine's stories, and stolen glances with Marelle before her innocence had been lost drifted through Kevon's mind as the deep rhythm of the drums lulled him to sleep.

A change in the tempo of the drumming stirred Kevon from his rest. The beat of the drums had an echo from ahead, and the whine of the stone rollers spread over a wider range as the Dwarven-crafted cylinders spun at different rates because of it.

Leaning away from the yawning Stoneguard beside him, Kevon became aware of the chaotic interplay of the drum-activated Earth magic that reverberated up and down the passageway. The caged energy rippled along in waves like waves in a sunlit pond, combining or cancelling each other out in a confusing dance that only he could see. He straightened up, and the chaos surrounding him faded as his skin came back into contact with the armor of the drowsing dwarf.

The Stoneguard looked up, blinked twice, and jostled Kevon's arm with his elbow.

"I know," Kevon muttered, looking over at the dwarf. "We're almost there."

The ichor-stained blade drew free of the dusky leather

joint as Kevon ducked under the limp scythe-arm, stepping forward and whirling wrist and body to jab the sword's point into the reaper's central mouth. He twisted the blade, and yanked it as he leapt back to avoid the demon's convulsing death throes.

A shout rang out from across the battlefield. The Dwarven line was collapsing, not from casualties, but from the sheer crush of shining black carapaces that pressed in against them. The short steel axes that most of the Stoneguard used were not taking the reapers down as fast as they were piling up against that flank.

Kevon ducked into the center of the formation, and closed his eyes. He took hold of the Earth rune burned into the essence of the blade, shutting out the fractured Dark magic that suffused the area. With a grunt of effort from the expenditure of magic, Kevon directed the power to drive earthen spikes upward into the horde of swarming demons.

Half of the reapers on the far flank dangled, impaled on the earthen skewers. The quarter that faced the dwarves in the front of the skirmish had nowhere to retreat, and fell before the renewed barrage of Dwarven steel. The remaining quarter struggled to extricate themselves from between their lifeless fellows mounted on the magically raised spikes.

Trying to even his breathing, Kevon wiped the gore from his sword as the Stoneguard line advanced to slay the remaining reapers.

"March clear!" he shouted after scanning the carnage for surviving enemies. "We're losing the light! Five minutes rest, and we press on!"

Dwarven translators passed along the message, and the slow shuffle from the battlefield began. Knots of Stoneguard lingered around two of their fallen fellows. Kevon gazed upon them for a long moment before turning to march along with the rest of the company.

Kevon sat in silence as the rest of the dwarves bantered. He knew a few of their names, but had no connections to these following him as he did with Rhysabeth-Dane, Kylgren-Wode, or even Britger, the Dwarven King's nephew.

There's no doubting their commitment, he thought, gazing back at the fallen dwarves on the field they had just left behind. *It's just awkward trying to get to know them when I may have to be halfway across the realm at any moment.*

"Huh?" Kevon startled at the nudge from one of the company's three translators. "Ah. Yes. We should be going. Let's move them out."

Half a dozen steps toward the plateau ahead, and Kevon could see dwarves falling into step with him in his peripheral vision. Another dozen steps further and snatches of a simple Dwarven marching tune were being hummed by several nearby. "Double-time!" he shouted, increasing his speed, trying not to smile as the clumsy tune lurched to keep pace, to a smattering of Stoneguard chuckles. "Watch our flanks! Look to the skies!"

The miles fell away beneath their feet. Smallish bands of orcs got near enough to see what the company was, and ventured off in search of easier prey. Lone reapers approached to within screaming distance, but did nothing more than threaten. Small flights of gargoyles dipped out of the skies, but wheeled away at the first crossbow bolt. Kevon called a halt only when the way ahead was crowded with orcs.

"Small bands, not together, waiting on something..." Kevon whispered to the translator that stood between him and the senior Dwarven officer. "What are they waiting for? What are they looking at? Is it our fellows, cornered?"

"We have the numbers to break through," the translator conveyed the message from his superior. "We will need the wall to our back during the night."

"Agreed," Kevon nodded. "Should we spread out, say three ranks deep? That would make it look like there are more of us to charge, maybe prevent a fight at all."

"You'll lead with a flaming sword, like in the tapestry?" the translator asked.

"Not here, not now," Kevon grimaced. "Too hard with the broken magic all around. I'll use Light."

He drew the blade halfway from its sheath, and fed power into the Light rune. The sword took on a bright yellowish-white glow, and murmurs of approval sounded from all around.

"That settles it," Kevon chuckled. "Form up."

"Blast," Kevon muttered under his breath as the orcs ahead of them shifted formation, their company having been spotted at last. He stepped forward, and raised his voice. "We go now, then. Charge!"

The mostly formed line broke into an uneven advance. Kevon jogged along at the center, a few paces ahead of the line, sword drawn. As they got within earshot of the orcs, Kevon fed power into the blade's Light enchantment, and bent the spell to his will. The sword burst into a dazzling spectacle, light flowing from every inch of its surface. Kevon swung it, two-handed, and light-trails glimmered and faded behind it. Intensifying his concentration on the spell, Kevon lashed out in specific directions, casting glowing arcs ahead of him toward the Orcish line, slices that surged through the air and exploded in glittering flashes before reaching their targets.

Howling with all the rage and frustration he could muster, Kevon slowed, and raised the sword above his head. He roared as he swung the gleaming blade downward, and a tidal wave of churning brilliance splashed down, leaping and cresting in a slow, spreading froth that radiated out toward all of the orcs visible before them.

Within moments, the Orcish line broke, splitting in two and running headlong to either side of the advancing flood of light. Kevon knelt, trembling from the exertion of maintaining the spell as the howls of the fleeing orcs faded with distance. He held the symbol in his mind as long as he could, but as his reserves drained, the image blurred and slipped from his grasp as the light faded away.

"What would that have…?" the Dwarven translator who had stopped next to Kevon asked, awestruck.

"Nothing," Kevon sighed, climbing to his feet. "Orcs are dumb. Let's keep moving."

"Sir, there's…" the translator began, pointing to the two approaching figures in the waning light.

"We're here," Kevon whispered, as he recognized Marelle and Bertus.

"Twenty feet?" Kevon peered into the partially cleared tunnel. "How have you…" He forced himself into silence. "The fracturing of magic here left over from the war. The proximity of the Dark Seat."

"Without a proper focus, Reko can't even show himself here without depleting his magic," Yusa explained. "Whenever he recovers his full strength, we push back as far as we can. Those of us that are left can almost fit in the tunnel comfortably."

"Fighting, day and night, to defend this?" Kevon asked, peering at the carnage strewn around the entrance.

"Mostly night," Bertus grumbled.

"I'm spent from scaring off those orcs," Kevon admitted, "But if you have some magic I can borrow, we can get all of us inside."

"Let me know when you are ready," Yusa nodded. "Reko really needs the sleep."

"Carlo?" Anneliese asked, her stern glance drilling into Kevon's awareness.

"Leading Alacrit's forces against the Dark Magi in Navlia," Kevon answered, frowning. "I wish I had better news than that."

"He's alive," the Huntmistress smiled. "That is better

news than it could have been."

Kevon flinched as Anneliese, glancing up and to the west, drew her bow and loosed an arrow with a quiet nonchalance.

"Clearing the city of those Magi should take a few weeks, then?" she asked, as a gargoyle's corpse crunched to the ground two dozen yards away.

"I didn't even know it was attacking..." Kevon moved his hand to his sword-hilt.

"It wasn't," Anneliese smiled. "The rest of them are moving to a safer distance, though."

"Good thinking," Kevon nodded, relaxing. "If Carlo gets good information, the Dark Magi in Navlia could be dealt with in far less time than that. They have already split their numbers to try and attack us from within."

"Is that so?" Anneliese scanned the sky, looking for another target as a Stoneguard trotted back with the arrow from her previous kill. "They were unsuccessful?"

"Mostly," Kevon answered. "One recruit lost, so far." He looked to where Yusa stood, an expectant look on his face. "Let's get this taken care of."

"Trying again!" Yusa called, and survivors poured from the tunnel, Stoneguard taking the perimeter, other soldiers and elves in the second rank. The Ancients were the only ones still inside the tunnel mouth, sitting to one side without speaking. "Further in, then?"

Kevon led the way down to the far end of the short passage, and placed one hand on the back wall, the other on his sword's hilt. "You've been pushing it all back," he commented. "Each time has been more difficult because of pressure building up behind here. Time to think in other directions."

Shifting his focus from exploration to action, Kevon reached out for the power Reko offered to supplement his flagging reserves. Depressions formed to either side of his position, expanding conical shapes that groaned under the stress of moving earth.

Kevon shook his head, trying to throw off the chaos of the mangled magical residue that surrounded him, and wrapped himself deeper in the sharpness of the Earth rune that flowed into his mind from the sword. Within heartbeats, two tunnels twenty feet long stretched outward from where he stood. A tweak of effort, and the floors in the new tunnels rippled and flattened to match the surface of the established passage.

More, Kevon thought, pressing forward. He stepped slowly, as the earth ahead of him parted to either side in a steady wedge, the already compressed stone vibrating like an off-key lyre-string. Twenty feet further, Kevon paused and repeated the process he'd used on the first two side tunnels. As he finished the floor sections of the latest expansion, he felt the power flowing from Reko start to give out.

"That's it for now," Kevon announced, winding the spell to a close. "We can add on or enlarge rooms later as needed."

"Reko says he's learned a few things that should help him work better on his own," Yusa shrugged.

"Most of it is the sword," Kevon admitted. "The fabric of magic around here is so disturbed, the pure focus of the enchantments is just about the only thing that can get me past it."

"You need to go up," Alanna suggested. "I can't see through the mesa here with any consistency, but I've never seen anything but gargoyles on top. A small fort would give us a good vantage point to scout out the area."

"And let us be spotted from miles around," Yusa argued.

"By what?" Anneliese asked. "Nothing has scaled to the top yet, and gargoyles are easily dealt with."

"Get everyone in here, get it lit up, and post guards at the entrance until we can figure out what to do with it," Kevon commanded. "We're all tired, and will make better decisions in the morning."

◆ ◆ ◆

Kevon yawned and shifted, his neck popping from its lengthy stay in its awkward position. He untangled himself from Marelle's arms, soothing her disgruntled murmurs, and made his way down the clear main hallway to the exit.

"Any trouble last night?" he asked the dwarves flanking the opening.

The Stoneguard troops peered at each other, pointing fingers and muttering.

"None of you speak Common," Kevon shook his head. "Of course. Any..." He smashed a closed fist into his open palm several times, grunting as he did so.

Laughter rang out, and one of the dwarves leaned out and pointed to a group of scattered orc carcasses.

"Nothing you couldn't handle, then. Good. Carry on." Kevon nodded, and turned back down the passageway.

He stopped at the last junction, where he had ended the work last night. Placing his hand on the wall and opening his senses in preparation to begin again, he steeled himself against the dull roar of magical white noise that he'd managed to block out only hours before. He gripped the hilt of the sword, and let the purity of the inscribed Earth rune guide his Art.

A quick mental sweep of the surrounding plateau revealed no nearby tunnels that would cause problems, and nothing but sparse plant and small animal life on the broken plain above. The center of the formation was forward, up, and a touch to the right. Kevon pressed harder against the wall, and began the work in earnest.

The section of wall in front of Kevon slid back as the stone behind it slid up and down, compressing into a stone staircase and smooth ceiling that led up toward his goal. Kevon tried to keep the stairs uniform in size, but had to curve them more than once to avoid large pockets of dirt and sand that would have weakened the walls or crashed through the ceiling. He twisted and narrowed the passage to maneuver it between some areas that rejected his magic, branching fingers of *something* that threatened to nullify his power if he worked too close to them.

The power gave out perhaps a dozen feet from the surface, beneath a slab of solid stone in the center of the mesa. Deprived of the connection to the Earth magic that had replaced his need for sight to work the spell, Kevon felt an instant vulnerability in the complete darkness of the stairwell. He steadied himself against the wall, and turned to sit while his senses readjusted.

"Need some help?" a voice whispered near his ear.

He fought the urge to strike out, realizing it was Marelle after a fraction of a second. "I was too focused on what was ahead of me," Kevon admitted. "I had no idea you were following."

"I had just gotten here," she chuckled, "When you went all... wobbly."

Imagining the grin on her face, Kevon leaned forward for a kiss, to where he'd heard her talking.

I have missed this... Marelle growled in his mind as their lips touched. *And a tunnel crowded with dwarves was... less than inspiring.* She plucked unerringly at the fastenings of his clothing, guiding his hands with thought projections that he followed with varying degrees of accuracy.

In moments, Kevon could feel Marelle pressed against him, her control in the absence of light both frightening and tantalizing. He ignored his body's protest against the sharp, newly formed stone stairs, and did his best to keep up with his wife's mental demands.

A short while later, sore, out of breath, and content, Kevon groaned in mock dismay.

"What?" Marelle asked, stirring against his braced knees.

"They are going to light this whole stairwell up, aren't they?"

"I suppose they will," she teased. "We'll have to find a

better place. Shouldn't be that difficult."

"I'd better join them below," Kevon sighed. "See what else we can do to fortify this place, keep a solid foothold in the region."

"Only the Ancients have stirred this morning, besides those guarding the entrance," Marelle reported. "I doubt they would complain if you didn't wake them, after what they've been through the last few days."

Kevon reached out and pulled Marelle close, burying his face in the hair that draped at her neck. I *would love nothing more than to stay here in the darkness, in this void, that contains nothing but you, for as long as I can,* His thoughts took on a somber tone. *Not even you can see how far the reach of the darkness has spread, how close those who support L'mort are to bringing him here and destroying the balance of the world, forever. I'd rather be certain there was going to be a world left to love you in, than not.*

I know, Marelle thought in return. *Though you must admit, sometimes the not knowing can make it pretty great.*

Kevon sighed, a shallow breath out through his nose, then inhaled a deep draught of Marelle's scent, stopping only when his lungs threatened to burst. He squeezed her tight, nuzzled through her tangled locks of hair, and kissed her neck. "I have to go," he whispered, releasing her so that she could stand. "Let's go together, see what we can do."

He could feel her unfocused aura of disappointment as she slipped through his arms to stand in the darkness, and re-adjust her clothing. He fumbled with his own, clumsier now without her eerie guidance, but managing after a few moments. He stood, stretched out a hand to take hers, and started back down the stairwell.

CHAPTER 53

"**C**oming in," Kevon announced through the sentry slots in the stone door.

Muffled Dwarven affirmations filtered back through, and the catch-bolts rasped free before the door started sliding open over the thin bed of rollers beneath it.

Watching the evening sky as the rest of the group filed through the narrow doorway, Kevon pulled Marelle close. *There was nothing you could have done, nothing any of us could have done.*

Wordless grief and distorted images of the battle earlier flooded back through their shared connection, and Kevon relived parts of the horror from Marelle's perspective.

"There is one less Dark Magi to carry out their plan," Kevon reassured her. "We won't stop until they have all been defeated."

Marelle gripped him tighter as the quartet of Dwarven regulars lumbered past, carrying their two fallen Stoneguard brethren.

Taking a last glance at the sky and surrounding landscape, Kevon turned to guide Marelle through the doorway into the catacombs.

"We've been told many more would have died if not for you," one of the translators who had stayed behind commented as Kevon neared the stairs to the upper levels.

"They would not have been here to die, if it wasn't for me," Kevon answered.

"And the darkness might already be upon us," the dwarf countered. "We all know the price we've been asked to pay. Do not dishonor that."

"I dare not," Kevon agreed. "Your people have been shouldering much of the responsibility. We would be lost without you."

"We are honored to be of service, after ages of isolation."

"We'll have more Magi to support our troops here in a few days," Kevon explained. "I can't promise this won't happen again, but..."

"You're doing your best. We know."

Kevon placed his hand on the dwarf's shoulder, and squeezed as he followed Marelle upstairs.

"Are there any immediate threats?" Kevon asked Marelle, catching up to her as she reached the top of the stairwell that led into the fortress complex.

"A handful of gargoyles, far to the north," she answered. "There are a few more bands of orcs to the south, but nothing organized."

"Heading out to the battlements?" he asked, already certain of the answer. He waited for her nod of affirmation. "I'll be along after a while."

Taking the hallway ahead that led to the center of the stone structure, Kevon lengthened his stride, his purpose clear as he approached the new Sending room. He knelt on the floor next to the focusing sigil, and placed a hand on it. Kevon concentrated, blocking out as much of the chaos that polluted the area's magic as he could, intent on the faint impression tied to the stone symbol he touched. When his thoughts were as uncluttered as he could manage, he guided the power he held in reserve to strengthen the foundation of the enchantment.

When the power gave out, and the chaos resurfaced, Kevon stilled his mind, and felt the enchantment, stronger than before. Satisfied, he made his way back through the fortress halls toward the stairs that led up to the battlements, and Marelle.

◆ ◆ ◆

"Three more..." Marelle's stance shifted as she peered down through the floor and part of the mesa at something Kevon could not sense.

"Three more..." Kevon started to ask, but read the answer in the expression on her face. "Casualties."

"This has to stop," Marelle hissed. "If we had been out there with them, maybe..."

"We had been patrolling the last five days," Kevon argued as Marelle dropped her eyepatch into place to shut out the sight of the procession below. "We can't be out there all of the time. People still die when we are. But you're right. There is more that needs to be done. It's time to bring in more reinforcements."

"It's ready then?" she asked.

"Without knowing where the Sending Chamber is at the Tower, I can't go directly there. It's too difficult to cut through the... cluttered magic in the area. I can't even see the spot I used the last time I went there, let alone push myself through to it. Reko has been helping with the enchantment since it has started to take form, I think it's strong enough to get me to the Dwarven Hold, or Navlia, rune to rune. I've felt the connection to the Hold, but think it would take more power than I have to finish the Sending."

"If Reko helps..."

"I can go from here to the Hold, and from the Hold to the tower," Kevon nodded. "If Mirsa has a Sending chamber prepared..."

"You wouldn't have to be gone long," Marelle breathed. "You could bring others to help, directly from there."

"I'll speak to Yusa, and see if Reko can help me tomorrow morning. I should be at the tower by midafternoon, and know more by tomorrow evening."

"You could be back in less than a day?" Marelle asked.

"Might be longer," Kevon responded with a sidelong glance.

"No need to take chances," Marelle decided, taking him by the hand and leading him down the hallway toward their chamber.

◆ ◆ ◆

"We could use the extra help," Yusa nodded after a brief pause.

"It will shift the patrol schedules," Kevon advised. "It could get more difficult until I return."

"We'll... Yes, I'm telling him..." Yusa shook his head, frowning. "We'll put off further improvements to either the catacombs or the upper fortress until then. That should free me up for an extra patrol rotation."

"Marelle wants to stay out with the patrols more," Kevon offered. "The two of you, Bertus, myself, Anneliese... I feel better when two of us are along. There are still casualties..."

"Fewer, though," Yusa nodded. "I know. We'll keep up."

"I'd like to leave first thing in the morning," Kevon continued. "It could take most of your power to help with the Sending."

"I'll trade patrols with Bertus," Yusa shrugged. "Nothing slows him down."

"This hard living has only tempered him," Kevon agreed. "I'd be a fool to think that was the whole explanation..."

"Yes," Yusa chuckled. "Marelle as well. Reko would love to find out exactly what Mirsa and Anneliese really think about those two." Yusa grinned for a moment before frowning as if he'd been admonished.

"You'll meet me in the Sending chamber in the morning, then?" Kevon asked, turning to leave.

"Aye. We'll be there."

◆ ◆ ◆

"Oof..." Kevon staggered as his feet landed on the sigiled floor of the larger, darker Sending chamber in the Dwarven Hold. He gauged the reserves he had remaining, and concluded they were not enough to travel to the tower, without knowledge of a working Sending chamber on the other end of the spell. There was enough stored power in the outer rune-form to do it, but Kevon was loath to use the layered energy for anything short of an emergency.

I could see how things are going here, in the Hold, Kevon thought, breaking contact with the stony enchantments at his feet. *It would take twice as long to find someone to give a report as it would to recover here and continue on to the tower. I may have to return here to make the trip back, if the Sending chamber at the tower is not as complete.*

Kevon walked over to the wall near the exit, sat, leaned back, and closed his eyes to rest.

"No!"

Trembling, Kevon clutched at his chest, and tried to calm his racing heart and his frantic breathing. "I... there..."

A fleeting memory of a dream that melded his dead friend Waine's face onto a score of lifeless Dwarven Stoneguard evaporated as he regained his composure.

His hand dropped from his chest to the hilt of his sword, and the precise structure of the four symbols that solidified in his mind steadied him further. Kevon checked his magical reserves, and felt confident he could perform the Sending to the tower, and have extra power left over.

He stood and made his way back to the center of the chamber, releasing the sword as he walked. Kevon tapped back into the Sending rune on the floor beneath him, kneeling to make contact with the stone symbol as he pictured the drawbridge before the tower, his destination for the spell. He felt the barriers to the magic fall away as he gathered the required power, and his intended destination blurred and re-formed in his mind. He offered the magic to the glowing constructs in his mind, and reality shifted around him.

Kevon shielded his eyes as he detonated a sphere of Light above the tower compound, minutes after his shouts remained unanswered.

Another minute passed, and Kevon could hear the bolts sliding on the drawbridge, and the ropes creaking as it began to lower.

"I'll have to settle for word, then?" Mirsa asked as Kevon closed the distance to meet her halfway across the drawbridge.

"For now," Kevon nodded. "Our troops are holding in the far south, but not gaining. We need something more."

"Something you can get here?" Mirsa asked, pivoting to return to the interior of the tower. "Come along, then. See what we have built."

"Much different than I remember," Kevon admitted as he stepped inside the walls, and the compound unfolded before him. He stopped and watched as younger Magi dueled with elemental forces, slinging fire from an Enchanted rod, or blasts of wind from a staff. The powered runes flickered in and out of his consciousness as their use ebbed and flowed through the training grounds.

"There are many more than when I was here last," Kevon remarked.

"I've been back to Navlia five times since then, gathering more recruits, testing them, executing more than one," she shrugged. "You know the difficulties we have faced."

"How many are here, now?"

"Twenty three," Mirsa beamed. "All loyal to our cause."

"How many can you spare?" Kevon asked, lowering his voice.

"I..." Mirsa frowned. "There are three that are not suited for anything but instruction. They should remain here with the younger students. That leaves... eight? Yes. Eight Magi at

Journeyman rank or higher that would be of use to us on the battlefield. I would prefer that the two Journeymen had more time to prepare..."

"Let them," Kevon countered. "They may be of more use here with the other students. Is there anyone you trust to take charge of this if you were to leave?"

"She's one of the eight..." Mirsa nodded, "But, yes."

"Five more Magi," Kevon chuckled. "Plus yourself. Easily twice as many as I was counting on, and more in training. When could they be ready to leave?"

"Eirama should be able to take over the leadership of training now that the grounds are nearly restored," Mirsa's brow furrowed in concentration. "More duties would shift to the remaining Journeymen, but I don't see that being a problem. The Novices are eager to help out. I wouldn't feel right leaving before tomorrow."

"If you can wait that long, so can I," Kevon conceded. "How far along is your Sending chamber?"

"It's a start, though I think the chamber in the Dwarven Hold is further along," Kevon announced, standing after breaking the connection to the runes carved in the floor of the chamber. "I barely made it to the Hold Chamber as it was, I'd rather not risk it on the return trip. The chamber in Navlia would work better, but I don't like relying on Alacrit's hospitality."

"He's been fine the last few times Maisy and I have visited," Mirsa offered, "But I understand. If I could have recruited Magi in the Hold, I would have."

"If seven of us are passing through, we may be able to strengthen the enchantments there, too," Kevon added. "I would like to be able to travel there with more ease than a day in the underground passageway, and a day overland between the transit line and the fortress. It would be worth spending an additional day or two there to add to the enchantments."

"You should meet the others," Mirsa suggested, gesturing to the chamber's exit. "We can start making arrangements, and rest up for the trip tomorrow."

Kevon followed Mirsa out of the chamber and through the passageways to the combined dining and kitchen area. Magi of all ages jostled and joked as they prepared the afternoon meal.

Unbuckling his sword belt, Kevon leaned his weapon in the corner near the entrance, and stepped in to help.

"Hand me that bag, will you?" Kevon asked a nearby Novice. He dumped the contents onto the smooth stone counter, and sorted through the pieces of *covaninal*. He split the few remaining halves into smaller sections, and began pinching and tearing the inner lining from the sections.

"What is that?" the Novice asked, pointing to the bowl Kevon had begun filling with the prepared sections.

"Something I brought," Kevon answered. "Just a taste, though. We're not ready to start growing them here, yet."

"Our gardens are doing well," the youth shrugged. Lettuce is up, we'll have corn and potatoes soon. I crafted a stone corral against the north wall. As soon as the grass has recovered there, Master Mirsa said she will bring goats from Navlia."

"Someone will," Mirsa smiled as she touched the young Mage's shoulder on her way past him to the washbasin. "Bringing the chickens was an ordeal. "The bread?" she asked another nearby Mage.

The magic in the room shifted. Kevon could feel the Fire rune the Mage was using fade, and a Movement rune began to glow as the stone doors of the oven creaked open.

"A few more minutes," he responded, closing the doors with his Art, and resuming the Fire spell. "We're almost out of flour."

"Do we have extra potions to barter with?" she asked another nearby Novice.

"We haven't reached the numbers you have requested, but we're closer on healing potions. We should be able to spare four or five of those and stay on schedule."

"Plan on visiting Kron in the next few days," Mirsa bit her lip. "Master Melga will accompany you."

"This looks great," Kevon sat the pile of skins aside, and took a deep breath. "Smells good, too. I think the bread is about… Is that honey?"

"Found a hive in the foothills to the southwest," another Novice beamed. "It took three of us all afternoon, but we managed to convince the bees to let us fill the jug we placed under their hive, and then repair the drain-hole."

"Without getting stung?" Kevon exclaimed. "Brilliant!"

"Well," the Novice grinned. "*I* didn't get stung."

"Nevertheless," Kevon shrugged, "It's impressive. I look forward to trying it." He lifted the bowl of peeled fruit and pointed out the doorway. "To the dining hall, yes?"

Other Magi circulated in with plates and bowls of food, and took their places around the smooth marble table. Mirsa was the last to leave the kitchen, shooing a pair of Novices before her.

"Please, everyone, sit," her voice echoed through the oversized room as she called for attention. "We have an announcement to make."

"We are in dire need of extra Magi to help push further into the darkness to the south," Kevon said as soon as there was a break in the commotion as the Mages settled into their chairs. "In addition to sparing you from the Dark Magi that overtook Navlia, this is why you were brought here."

Low murmurs of agreement wafted through the ranks of Magi.

"I will be returning with Kevon," Mirsa added, and the room fell silent. "I'll be back, of course, but I believe you can manage without me. Only some of us will be leaving, the school will remain intact. Little will change, but the Journeymen and Novices will be asked to take on additional responsibility."

"Maisy's going too?" one of the younger Novices asked, her voice cracking.

"Yes," Mirsa smiled. "But we will visit soon. Remember, this is why we are here. We're training to strike at the darkness, and overturn its grip on our realm."

After a few moments, reluctant affirmations circulated through the assembled Mages, and they began to eat.

Reminded of a more orderly version of the mess hall at the Dwarven Hold, Kevon nibbled at a hunk of bread. He took in the feel of the reserved camaraderie that he could sense woven through the group, in even so short a time. He formed a Movement rune, and used the powered sigil to slide the bowl of prepared *covaninal* in front of the Novice seated to his left. Once the Mage had taken a section, he pushed the bowl further down the table, pausing so the Magi could serve themselves.

Chuckles broke out, and Kevon could feel other Movement runes forming. Plates and bowls screeched along the surface of the stone table in an awkward dance as the attendees took turns concentrating on moving dishes and taking food from them.

Unable to keep from smiling, Mirsa tried to glare at Kevon. "Is this how you squander your talents in the south?" she asked.

"Not in the slightest," Kevon's eyes widened. "Reko is not known for his sense of humor, he is the only other Mage in the fortress."

"Fortress!" one of the Novices across from Kevon exclaimed. "What's it like there?"

"Somewhat like this," Kevon shrugged. "Though high on a flat mountain, and made of thick, sealed stone to keep out the imps and gargoyles. Doorways to the upper walks are guarded by armored soldiers, dwarves, and elves. Food is grown in the catacombs below. Patrols fight orcs and demons every day as we range further from the fortress, seeking out where the darkness gathers."

"We knew but a portion of this," one of the two Journey-men Mages at the table whispered into the sudden stillness.

"It is not something we share without a reason," Kevon replied. "I pray it will do more good than harm, here."

"We're ready," another Mage announced, sitting up straighter in his seat, locking eyes with Kevon. "Just show us the way."

"It's not that simple," Kevon sighed. "Using magic there is... like trying to sprint... through the moat. Underlying chaos constantly interferes with your Art, keeping you unfocused, taxing your strength. It is where the War of the Magi was fought, and the very fabric of magic there is damaged."

"Extra power, extra focus..." a nearby Mage commented. "We have a few rods and staves we've been Enchanting. Would those help?"

"Without a doubt," Kevon answered. "As many as we can bring to bear. Being able to command the elements better could make all the difference."

"Those that remain behind will continue their basic classwork, but shift more focus onto Enchanting and Alchemy," Mirsa explained. "Stockpiling weapons and supplies for use in the coming war."

"I wish I was ready to help more, now," the Novice beside Kevon lamented.

"It is my hope that the evil is beaten back before that time comes," Kevon put an arm around the youth's shoulders. "But should we fail, you and your classmates may be the ones that are left to save the Realm. Do not lose sight of that. Do not question what you have to offer."

"I won't," came the whispered reply.

Gazing around at the Magi focused on him, Kevon forced his clenched jaw into the beginnings of a smile. "And yes, we are here training for the coming conflict, but we mustn't forget what we are fighting to save. The bonds that join us, the experiences we share. You have family, both here, and back home. Our survival does not mean nearly as much without that. The more it means to you, the harder you will fight to protect it. Make sure to always build something worth saving."

"What he means," Mirsa clarified, "is enjoy your food, and run along and play afterward. We've all been far too serious of late. We can be somber again after the evening meal."

The previous level of chaos resumed after Kevon nodded. Dishes slid about the table as if possessed, and the main topic of conversation was the taste of the *covaninal*. The Novices finished their meals first, and took their dishes back to the kitchen area before scurrying outside.

"I'll miss it here," Mirsa admitted. "I never thought to feel that way again, about this place."

"There is something to be said for turning this site into a tool to oppose the darkness," Kevon agreed. "A fitting shift toward balance."

Mirsa stacked the plates nearest to her and picked them up as she stood. "There is much to be done before we depart tomorrow."

CHAPTER 54

"We should go now, before I lose my nerve," Mirsa suggested to Kevon as the last volunteer, Garrimor, made his way into the Sending chamber.

"I know they'll miss you," Kevon admitted, "but they have the framework you set in place to continue in your absence. Everything will be fine here."

Opening his mind to the runes embedded in the floor of the chamber, Kevon closed his eyes and readied the spell. "Mirsa will go first, I will go last. Offer up your magic, and I will perform the Sendings."

Bouncing Maisy to keep her quiet, Mirsa stepped to the center of the rune inscribed chamber.

"Ready?" Kevon began to ask, and he felt Mirsa's Aid rune form. He latched onto the thought-form, and used the power to fill the waiting spell runes Enchanted into the flooring. Targeting the destination in the Dwarven Hold, Kevon felt the power requirement dip as the more refined Sending runes overlaid the ones before him. With a firm mental *push*, Kevon completed the spell, guiding Mirsa and Maisy across the vast distances between the two locations. He drew in a sharp breath as the magic he'd powered the spell with vanished along with the Mage who had been supplying it, but his own magic shifted to compensate.

"Go..." Kevon hissed, maintaining the link between the ends of the spell. He clawed at the magic that radiated from the newly formed Aid rune that Garrimor channeled his strength into. The Mage slid through the spell's inner workings before he reached the center of the chamber, and vanished. Five more iterations, and Kevon was alone in the chamber, the rush of the extended magical strain humming through his entire being. He dipped into his remaining reserves of power, and with a final push, vanished.

"We'll spend the day here," Kevon announced as he struggled to his feet, shaky in the absence of the magic that had been coursing through him. "The next crossing will be more difficult."

"I'm going to find Rhysabeth-Dane," Mirsa announced. "Avoid anything with red cloth ties."

◆ ◆ ◆

"Through. The. Tunnel."

"Yeah. Tamaraith told me," Kevon grinned at Mirsa. "He said that the whole affair was something to see. The passages from the landing above are too narrow, so Brightwing had to walk in the front door. They cleared the halls for the most part..."

"She seems to know what he is thinking, and he trusts her more than you would think was possible." Mirsa nibbled on a handful of roasted seeds, and murmured in approval at the unfamiliar flavor. "What are these?"

"*Covaninal* seeds," Kevon answered. "They can't replant all the seeds from the plants that grow every day, so they've been figuring out other uses for the excess. Brined and smoked, they're delicious. Fermented and pressed, they make a passable torch oil."

"The Ancients were already weaving cloth from the tassels, right?" Mirsa chewed on a few more seeds.

"They've got most of their textile production converted over to handle it now," Kevon confirmed. "There should enough cloth stockpiled by the end of the season to start clothing the entire Hold. They haven't even tested how the fabric works under armor."

"You heard *why* she took the griffin through the tunnel," Mirsa's tone darkened. "Didn't you?"

"To warn us that Alacrit's troops have not withdrawn from Eastport," Kevon frowned. "Bargthar-Stoun said that she estimated half of their troops were camped outside Eastport. The other half could be traveling through the forest to Navlia, or lodging in the port itself. Even the half we know about makes me more than a little nervous about leaving."

"How long would it take to send word to the fortress in the south, without a griffin, if something were to happen here?" Mirsa asked.

"Two days, best guess. If one knew the way to the fortress, and had the forces to make the crossing." Kevon shrugged. "Not quick enough. What do you suggest?"

"Ask for volunteers?" Mirsa asked. "If two Magi remain, they can continue to improve the Sending chamber here. Keep contact with the tower. Bring priority messages. That would still leave seven Magi at the fortress."

"Do it." Kevon stood, and an Ancient scooped up his dishes and threaded her way back to the kitchen area. "You know them better than I do. Try and get the best fit. Get them settled, and bring all of the Magi to the Sending chamber in two hours. I'll explain it to the king."

"You go through first," Kevon suggested, looking to Mirsa. "You're known to many there. You're in charge until I come through."

"That's fine." Mirsa nodded. "Garrimor and Shiah will be staying behind."

"Very well, you're with me." Kevon gestured to the volunteers, and waited until they took up station on either side of him, near the edge of the enchantment. "I'll lead, as before, but the two of you will help with each Sending, to get a better picture of the destination at the fortress. Just enough to see it, because you won't be going through now. We should have enough power between all of us to Send everyone through but me. Half an hour of rest, and then…"

"We Send you last," Garrimor finished. "Got it. Let's get started so I can get back to the library."

"You picked well," Kevon chuckled in Mirsa's direction. "Ready?"

"I hope I didn't keep you…" Kevon stumbled, spent, into the empty chamber.

"You should join them on the battlements," Marelle suggested from behind him, in the doorway of the chamber. "The others cannot fight off the gargoyles and enlarge an entrance for the griffin at the same time."

Kevon sprinted down the hallway to the stairs that led up to the narrow door to the battlements. He twisted to the side to clear the doorframe, bursting out into the fading evening light to aerial chaos.

Anneliese held her bow at half draw, tracking the action above, and calling out targets for her Hunters.

"Where is…" Kevon's words faded as his neck craned in response to Brightwing's shrieking, and he spotted Rhysabeth-Dane, a streaking arc of Dwarven steel and fury atop the feathered fury of her mount.

"She's slowing," Marelle announced. "We need to get them inside before she's overwhelmed."

"I can widen this doorway," Kevon stepped back and placed one hand on the stone, the other on the hilt of his sword. "Not on my own. Where is Yusa?"

"Out on patrol," Marelle answered. "Not due back for hours. Shall I fetch Mirsa?"

Opening his senses, Kevon glanced further down the battlement to where the Magi clustered between blended groups of soldiers and Elven Hunters. Wind magic flared in time with Mirsa's gestures with a short rod. Torrents of flame poured from a pair of long staves wielded by the two other Magi near her. "Not Mirsa. One of them."

Marelle darted down the walkway, sliding around her allies with effortless grace, until she reached Mirsa and the others. She gestured, and Mirsa took a few steps further away, toward the other group of Magi. The two other Mages followed Marelle's slower retreat toward the doorway where Kevon waited.

"Or both of them," Kevon muttered under his breath, hoping that at least one of them had saved their own magic, opting to draw most of their power from the Fire staves they carried.

Another flight of gargoyles winged down from above, headed on an intercept course for Rhysabeth-Dane and Bright-wing. As Mirsa and her new grouping of Magi began working spells to deflect and delay them, one of the staff-wielders paused to unleash another torrent of flames in their direction.

The cascade of fire burst into the empty space between the Dwarven Rider and the attacking demons, and the leading gargoyles flew headlong into the conflagration. The next ranks banked, half pulling clear of the magical flames, while more of their number could not respond in time, and tumbled from the sky on singed or burning wings.

The rear of the formation split, winging around the shrinking flare of heat and light, reforming on the other side.

Roaring challenge, Rhysabeth-Dane slashed at wing and limb as Brightwing turned his dive upward through the re-mains of the attacking swarm. The griffin maneuvered with back-swept wings, twitching wingtips to pitch and swerve through the chaos, lashing out kicks with its leonine hind claws if pursuers drew too close.

Stunned, in awe of the minute librarian's airborne prow-ess, Kevon broke from his paralysis as he felt strange, faint magic working from a distance. A strangled cry erupted from his throat as the remaining gargoyles dropped and banked in unison.

The arrow Anneliese had held at half-draw since Kevon reached the battlements whispered the secrets of death to one of the lead gargoyles, and two more shafts cleared her bow before the end of Kevon's next breath. Hunters fired at will as Rhysabeth-Dane and Brightwing climbed higher above the swooping demons.

In two heartbeats, half of the remaining attackers plummeted to the smooth stone roof below the upper walk, felled by arrows and bolts or attacks by Mirsa and her Magi. Another two heartbeats, and the winged terrors were upon them, striking with enough force to topple the fortress's defenders from their feet.

The Mage closest to Kevon dove forward, twisting in the air to land on her back, unleashing a wave of fire upward from her staff as the gargoyles swept over the wall. The Mage that had hesitated moments before summoned up another flood of Fire magic from the Enchanted staff. The instant a tongue of flame began to sprout from the end of the weapon, a gargoyle swerved from its path toward one of the soldiers, shifting to intersect with him.

The Mage's cry of surprise as the gargoyle seized his staff in one claw and his free arm in the other was cut short as it tore and squeezed his windpipe with its hind claws. Two powerful wingbeats, and the gargoyle had lifted the Mage up and over the battlement wall to cast him to the ground three stories below.

Devastated equally by the loss of one of the new recruits, and the guilt he felt about not even learning the Mage's name, Kevon gripped the hilt of his sword tighter, and began working magic of his own. Sudden updrafts caused the demons to tangle into one another, downdrafts forcing their flight paths to an abrupt end against the walls below the walkway. Within moments, the attacking force was reduced to a handful of fleeing demons, and Kevon collapsed in the doorway that led back inside, drained of the little magic he'd regained since his arrival.

"You'll be all right, just sit up," Marelle lifted him to a seated position as the remaining Magi snuck past, escorted by soldiers and Elven Hunters.

"These tiny doors aren't very welcoming," Rhysabeth-Dane critiqued as Brightwing landed nearby.

"We're working on that," Kevon replied as he retook his feet. "If they will slide the door closed, and lend me their magic, we'll get you inside." He walked over to the doorway, and placed his hand on the door as soon as it rumbled to a close. He connected the stone to the Earth rune on the sword he held in his other hand, and sparked the transformation with power floating about, shared from the other side of the wall.

The door melted back into the frame, ripples of stone smoothing as the door and frame became whole again. Kevon shifted the intent of the spell, and a larger door, half the width of the walkway, began to separate out from the wall. The door portion thinned as stone flowed to the other side, thickening and splitting to receive the door when it opened. The stone rollers previously formed shifted under the wider base, groaning under the strain of the stressed granite. They moved only so far before the magic gave out.

"A cloud of imps approaches," Marelle whispered. "We should get inside."

"Everyone, push!" Kevon groaned, leaning up against the newly formed door. "Get it open, now!"

The door held fast in place, as more Dwarves and soldiers pushed in to try and take hold of the smooth surface from the outside. Marelle crouched, and braced herself to push. "Now!" she croaked.

The door rumbled and screeched as it slid into the recessed space crafted for it. Shouts of encouragement turned to dismay as the enthusiastic mob slid the door open, gaining speed as they pushed. The door clanked to a halt with little more than an inch of surface poking out beyond the threshold.

"Ahh..." Kevon groaned, snatching at the lip of the door. "Never mind! Let's get inside, now!"

Clucking softly, Rhysabeth-Dane led Brightwing through the open door behind the others, into the stairwell that led down into the fortress.

Less than a minute before they arrive, Marelle thought to Kevon through her hand on his. *This opening is far too large to defend.*

The Magi, excepting Mirsa, stood slumped against the wall of the stairwell, eyeing the griffin opposite them in the passage.

Kevon knew the loss of their friend weighed on them, but there was no time to spare. "Rhysabeth-Dane, take Brightwing down into the fortress, clear the hallway. Marksmen, shift to cover the open door. Magi, form up behind me."

Soldiers and Hunters stepped to, the armored soldiers keeping to the left, on the side of the wall furthest from the Magi. Kevon turned to address the gathered magic-users.

"You're tired. You're spent. I know. So am I." Kevon frowned. We were barely able to open the door, when most of us could lay hands on it." He gestured to the exposed nub that was all that could be seen of the heavy stone door. "An hour, Stoneguard with ladders, maybe. We have seconds. In a moment, I'll ask for your magic again. I know there won't be much to take, but I will take it, and it might hurt. We can't let the imps into the fortress, there are far too many to fight." He turned and leaned against the wall, and linked up with the Earth rune that floated in his mind, sharp and dim. "Prepare yourselves."

When the fifth Aid rune bubbled into his awareness, Kevon lit the rune with the spark of power he had recovered, and sent his awareness back into the stone. He focused on the door, nestled between the slabs of wall, its hastily prepared track setting the balance of the door off by a minute amount. As soon as Kevon knew how he needed to spend the little power he would harvest from the others, he reached out for it, drawing it forth through the assisting runes with near desperation. He felt all of the Aid runes go dark, and funneled the nugget of power he'd accumulated from them at the Earth rune.

He willed the stone to obey, to conform to his desires. The first burst of intent balanced the inner slab on the first roller, and the rest of the energy went into the violent *shove* that should have wrenched the door closed.

Nothing.

The door squeaked and fell back into its unaligned position.

Kevon shouted in frustration, and pounded his fist on the wall before him.

You did your best, Marelle thought, wrapping her hand around the fist that clenched the sword. *We should be able to hold them off for...*

The iron ring Marelle wore on her left hand sang out in Kevon's mind as it touched him, still filled with some Earth magic from seasons ago. The power unraveled from the trinket at Kevon's bidding, and flowed through the focus engraved on the sword.

The door shrieked over the rollers and slammed closed. Kevon leapt to the side, and pressed hands up against the stone to keep it from bouncing, but it rebounded from the shock, stopping when it had reopened two inches.

"Just in time," Marelle sighed, and the shrieking and scrabbling of the arriving imps began. Poison tipped claws extended through the gap, and the nearest soldier jumped back.

"I don't think they will be able to move it," Kevon said, "But if enough gargoyles return..."

"We'll keep it from happening," Anneliese announced, stabbing her drawn shortsword through the gap into the mess of clutching claws. "Just make sure you fix this tomorrow."

CHAPTER 55

"We'll miss him," Mirsa huddled with two of the other Magi, mourning the loss of their comrade. "He was one of the first to join our cause, and he supported all of us, to the end."

"Another thing we learned last night," Kevon stepped as the conversation stalled. "One Griffin Rider is not enough to have on hand, not here. Rhysabeth-Dane will have to return to the Dwarven Hold."

"And how is she to do that?" Mirsa asked. "Brightwing is uncomfortable enough in these wide halls, he will not go back into the tunnels. I learned that much from my time with Rhysabeth-Dane last night. I doubt we have the strength to Send him to the Hold."

"We might have the strength, but it would not be enough to Send them both." Kevon clenched his jaw. "We couldn't risk the delay, it wouldn't be safe having them separated. Can you imagine?" He shook off images of the griffin half-galloping, half-flying through the lower levels of the Hold, eluding the grasp of panicked Stoneguard.

"How will she…?"

"I'll let you know when I figure it out," Kevon shrugged. "Maybe she has some idea."

"How much can the griffin carry?" one of the Magi standing near Mirsa asked, looking up at Kevon.

"He's carried me along with Rhysabeth-Dane, for short distances," Kevon answered. "I would not want to test his strength across the distances they need to travel."

"But someone smaller…"

"Nalsi, what are you getting at?" Kevon failed to mask his impatience with the young Mage.

"You don't want her to be on her own, unprotected, with so many of those gargoyles about," Nalsi shrugged. "What if I went with her?"

"She'd travel slower, be less maneuverable. Unable to use her sword, if you were with her." Kevon shook his head. "Try again."

"She wouldn't have to fight if I was there," Nalsi argued. "I can keep the creatures at bay, if you'd let me try."

"Magic is nearly unusable," Kevon countered. "Let it go."

"*Here*." Nalsi's voice rose as she squared off against Kevon. "But a day's flight from here?"

"That..." Kevon began.

"Might work..." Mirsa added. "If you left midmorning. Enchanted focal rods could help cut through the distortion long enough to get you clear..."

"Talk to Rhysabeth-Dane." Kevon grimaced. "If she wants to attempt it, you'll need practice."

"...She always did like hearing stories of our travels," Mirsa chuckled as soon as the eager Mage was out of earshot, off to find the Dwarven Rider.

"When you are ready, we can discuss patrol rotations." Kevon turned to leave. "The faster we find the source of the darkness..."

"You'll have to be faster than that before we can leave," Rhysabeth-Dane chastised Nalsi as she helped the Mage dismount from her seat on the modified saddle. "Anneliese will not be around to shoot the gargoyles you cannot handle once we leave the fortress."

"I won't need her to," Nalsi retorted, "as soon as I get used to the way Brightwing moves, the way the gargoyles attack, the way magic here is warped by the darkness... It's not as simple as just riding a griffin."

"Riding a griffin is not such a simple task," the dwarf huffed.

"My point, exactly," Nalsi winked at Rhysabeth-Dane. "I'm doing that, along with making the other adjustments. You should understand that as well as anyone."

"Just..." the tiny Rider struggled to retain her demeanor of frustration. "Do better tomorrow."

"I will, I promise." Nalsi bent at the knees to hug her riding partner. "Thank you for working with me."

Brightwing squawked as the Mage trotted into the entrance.

"Yes, yes," Rhysabeth-Dane scowled as she turned to ruffle the griffin's feathers. "I'm growing fond of her too." She watched the skies for a while as Brightwing stretched and flapped his wings, cooling himself before being led into the stifling upper halls of the fortress.

Rhysabeth-Dane rolled her eyes at Anneliese's smile as she approached the door.

"She's good," the Huntmistress commented as the Dwarven Rider began walking past.

"Good enough to replace the speed we won't have, and the steel I can't use?" Rhysabeth-Dane wondered aloud. "We'll see."

"Has the second team reported back in?" Kevon asked Yusa. "We just came in the west entrance, and had not seen them. I'd prefer it if Marelle could stay here and coordinate, but we're shorthanded since we started running an extra scouting mission every day."

"I've heard nothing," Yusa reported. "Neither has Reko. You'll just have to wait."

"Which section were they going to cover today? Our team went *here*." Kevon pointed to a spot on the crude map laid out on the table between them.

"Further, and heading a more southerly direction," Yusa waved a hand over a general area, and shrugged. "I would suggest sending Rhysabeth-Dane back out, but it is rather late for that."

"I'll head up to the south wall, and take a look. If they are too close, I wouldn't be able to see them, so I could head down to the south entrance to the catacombs." Kevon turned and left Yusa to study his charts and lists.

"Gather the Magi!" Kevon shouted, ducking into the doorway that led back into the fortress. Two steps down the stairway from the landing, the door slammed closed, and the stone bolt mechanism dropped into place. Kevon released the magic, and the hilt of his sword, and started running faster. "Rouse the Stoneguard! Bring everyone!"

"What's happening?" Mirsa asked, poking her head through a doorway in the first level of the catacombs.

"The last search party is headed back in," Kevon gasped, bracing against the doorframe to deflect the tide of armored dwarves. "They're not alone."

The Mage peered through the space between Kevon and the doorway, looking for a break in the flow of deadly metal. She edged out into the hallway as she spotted Anneliese and a group of Hunters in formation around two other Magi.

Anneliese stepped aside to allow Mirsa into the center of the sheltered grouping. Kevon moved to the front left of the arrangement, picking up the pace to match the double-time of the flow of foot traffic.

Too fast, not fast enough, Kevon's anticipation rose as they were swept along down through the widened hallways of the catacombs below the fortress. The other Magi, used to the danger of being surrounded by armored allies, moved with a cautious confidence tempered by a lifetime of practice. *Will the others be able to make it back before the darkness overtakes them?* He wondered. *Will our combined forces be enough to repel it? Are our defenses adequate?*

The questions melted away as the stream of allied forces spilled out into the deepening evening, through the narrow opening of the south passage.

Stoneguard, Dwarven Regulars, and Navlian soldiers milled around the expanding arc of the outer perimeter, clustering into preferred fighting formations. The Elven Hunters that surrounded the Magi stayed close, directing the flow of combatants around the vulnerable spellcasters with little more than their stances and stern glares.

Anneliese called out, and more Hunters shifted in to cover the flanks of the Magi. Nodding his thanks, Kevon slipped ahead, threading his way through the hazardous defenses to the front of the formation.

As he stepped forward, clear of the press of armored soldiers and dwarves, Kevon allowed himself to glance back up at the sky. The dark forms that streaked the dimming sky strained forward, intensifying their pursuit.

"I need five volunteers!" Kevon called as he strained to focus on the group surging homeward, and he could see the struggles of those bearing wounded. Without waiting, he charged ahead toward the flagging group of fighters.

"How goes the battle?" Rhysabeth-Dane asked Kevon as he entered the chamber where she and Brightwing kept residence.

"Marelle is resting, her injuries will heal." Kevon shook his head. "It took nearly an hour to find the Magi influencing the creatures, and slay them. Four in all. With nothing but their natural urges driving them, the creatures of darkness are less of a threat."

"If the skies are clear at dawn, Nalsi and I will leave for

the Hold. Imps will be sheltered for the day, and gargoyles should be exhausted from night patrols." Rhysabeth-Dane grimaced. "The Mage is as ready as can be expected, and we need the Unbound here as soon as we can get them. Any further delay would be costly."

"Agreed," Kevon nodded. "I'll lead a force out to the south before first light, see if we can draw some attention that direction."

"Almost a week's journey back to the Hold, pushing Brightwing as hard as he will go," the Rider mused. "Gathering the Unbound could take a few days, but the return trip should be much quicker."

"Nalsi should be able to return on her own, and won't slow you down," Kevon agreed. "Two weeks, then."

"If there was any way it could be done faster," Rhysabeth-Dane sighed. "Brightwing is terrified of the transit-line. It's tough enough keeping him confined to the fortress most of the day."

"I don't know how much more focused the attacks will get, now that they are certain where we're gathered," Kevon shrugged. "It may take most of the strength we have here to hold them off until you return."

Kevon rolled forward, and leapt up to strike with his sword. The blade wobbled as it sliced through the leathery joint, and the reaper's scythe-arm separated from its body. Powering through the spray of hot ichor, the Warsmith spun, leveled out his swing, and took the creature's top eye with his next motion. Kevon paused to catch his breath, and two Stoneguard with pikes charged, finishing off the wounded demon.

A distant mote over the plateau behind them caught Kevon's eye. The bright speck climbed with impressive speed, and faded as it fled toward the north. "Good luck," he whispered, unsure if it was to the griffin and its riders, or to himself. He flicked the gore from his blade, and marched back into the battle ahead of him.

CHAPTER 56

"**W**e can't continue like this," Mirsa announced to the leaders gathered in the strategy room.

"She's right," Bertus nodded, stepping up alongside the Mage. "Our losses are mounting faster than we can reinforce ourselves. This last wave of Dwarven Stoneguard from the Hold will help a great deal, but..." He sighed. "At this rate, it might be as if they had never come, by the time Rhysabeth-Dane returns with the Unbound."

"We send more archers, they counter with reapers," Kevon growled. "More infantry, they aren't equipped to deal with the gargoyles. And the Magi aren't able to stop the orcs, their weapons and armor protect them against the weakened magic we can raise against them. We'd have to commit a third of our forces to each patrol to have an answer for whatever was thrown against us."

"We're not going to find our target if we slow our patrols down that much," Reko volunteered. "We could not muster two patrols that size each day."

"I wouldn't leave our fortress that lightly defended," Kevon agreed, stepping closer to the map. "We've explored this whole area *here*, and should have *this* area swept in the next two days. Any further scouting will have to be out past the limit of our previous trips. *We have nothing.*"

"Our teams will have to travel further, retrace old steps to push ahead for new information," Marelle frowned. "We need something more..."

"We need Carlo." Kevon decided. "If anyone can improve

mixed unit tactics, it's him. He may also be able to…"

"He's doing the Prince's bidding, as a condition of our release," Mirsa reminded Kevon. "We may not be able to get him."

"I'm going to get him," Kevon shrugged. "We need him."

"What should we…?" Yusa asked.

"Dig in here," Kevon suggested. "Focus on fortifications, repairs, rest. Fight if they come to us, but take care when choosing who does the fighting."

"We could Send half of our remaining Magi to the end of the transit line," Mirsa added, "to escort additional forces."

"That's good," Kevon agreed. "That corridor is fairly clear. Low risk, to speed a sizeable advantage in forces. Do it."

"Who will you take with you?" Marelle asked, following Kevon out of the room.

"No one," he shook his head. "I can't risk anyone else. If they decide to move against me, I can defend myself. I should have enough magic to Send Carlo and myself either one at a time, or both through the paired Sending rooms here and in Navlia."

"I'll gather some Magi to aid with the Sending," Marelle turned back toward the hallway that led to the wing of the catacombs where the Magic-users stayed. "It will delay their departure for a few hours, if that. You will want to be rested when you arrive."

"Easy!" Kevon shouted as he felt runes forming in the minds of the two Magi guarding the Sending chamber under the palace gardens in Navlia. "I'm an ally, remember?" He lifted his hand from its habitual resting place on the hilt of his sword, and felt an eerie vulnerability as the pristine runes etched into the blade faded from his mind.

"What business do you have here?" the elder Mage asked, releasing the Fire rune he'd begun to feed with power.

"An audience with Alacrit, or Blademaster Carlo," Kevon smiled, and lowered his hands. "Whichever is easier."

"Escort the *heretic* to the barracks," the elder Mage ordered his subordinate. "He can find his way from there."

"Thank you, I think," Kevon frowned and followed the younger Mage out of the chamber. His escort led him up and around through the gardens and the back entrance that led into the palace proper.

"You know your way from here?" the Mage asked in a shaky voice.

"Very well," Kevon confirmed. "Thank you for bringing me this far."

After the Mage disappeared around the corner back down the hallway, Kevon poked his head around the corner. "Blademaster Carlo?"

"Leading a patrol through the city," a soldier called from the barracks beyond Carlo's office. "He's due back within the hour."

"He's on a schedule, then," Kevon made his way through the office to the barracks door. "The city has been retaken, for the most part?"

"You'll have to..." the soldier squinted as Kevon approached. "Ah. Warsmith. It has been a week since the dark ones have shown their faces. Longer still since they offered any real resistance. The Commander insists on scouring the city for them, daily."

"I'm afraid I know where they went," Kevon shook his head. "If you see him before I do, let him know I am here?"

"Of course, sir."

"We have gotten rather used to his leadership," Alacrit sighed. "He's brought the military and the Warrior's Guild into close cooperation. Nothing, no one, has been able to do that since anyone remembers."

"He's needed at the front," Kevon held his stance, and crossed his arms. "We're getting more reinforcements, but it's not enough. The Dwarves are fearsome in battle, but it's been so long since they fought a war…"

"You need a strategist."

"I'm doing the best I can, and Anneliese has been invaluable…"

"He has done much here," Alacrit's expression clouded, as he stood from his throne. "I hate to lose him, but I wish I could do more."

"We would be grateful for reinforcements, but I still need to work out the best way to move them."

"You finally ask for troops," Alacrit chuckled. "In a roundabout manner. I shall do my best to be ready when you need them."

"You have forces in and around Eastport?" Kevon asked.

"Three companies more than usual," Alacrit admitted.

"Send them back to the Dwarven Hold, if you can," Kevon suggested. "I can have them deployed from there."

"Supplies? I can arrange…"

"No need, sire," Kevon waved off Alacrit's offer. "The dwarves have everything well in hand. I'll figure out the best way to proceed once Carlo and I have the chance to discuss it."

"I'll send word right away," the prince shrugged. "You'll make sure they are expected?"

"Of course."

"I've been ready to join you for weeks," Carlo rumbled. "I have personally selected a mixed battalion of soldiers and Warriors willing to accompany me on a march across the frontier into whatever awaits us beyond the wastelands."

"And competent lieutenants to lead them, no doubt?" Kevon mused.

"Of course. I'd be a fool not to…" The Blademaster tilted

his head and glared at Kevon. "Just what are you on about?"

"Send them north," Kevon suggested, "To the Dwarven Hold. There will be three additional companies waiting there, less if we can work out how best to move them."

Carlo scowled, scratching at the skin under the collar of his chain gorget. "I'm going to have to change my armor, aren't I?"

"There's not enough time to wait for you to ride for a season or more to join us in the south," Kevon offered. "So, yes."

"How is Anneliese?" Carlo asked, standing and fumbling at the fastenings of his layered chain and ring-mail, before calling out to a page for assistance.

"She's doing well," Kevon answered, wincing at the complexity of the operation before him. "More irritable, lately. I assume it's because she misses you."

"That lovely creature was wise in the ways of war before my parents were born," Carlo snorted, shrugging an arm out of his armor. "She'll be around long after I'm gone, I have no doubt."

"Doesn't change the fact," Kevon smirked. "She sees something in you, different than the rest of us. She may be addled."

"Mind your tongue, pup," Carlo cautioned, "That's my elf you're maligning."

Kevon helped one of Carlo's soldiers fetch a suitable set of padded leather while the Blademaster struggled out of his metallic trappings.

"I just got used to coffee again," Carlo grumbled, rotating his shoulder to smooth a crease in the armor he'd shrugged into. "Now it's back to the frontier."

"It's more like the Dwarven Hold," Kevon grimaced. "With monsters. I can... see about getting coffee."

"I'm not eager to participate in this... magic again," Carlo protested, his steps carrying him out in front of Kevon as they made their way back toward the gardens. "But I know how important it is that we return there with all haste."

"Your reluctance is... noted?" Kevon chuckled. "I'll see you there in a few days, I'm sure. You should have a better grasp of the situation by then, and I'll help implement whatever plan you have when I return."

"A few days?" Carlo paused, the wrought-iron grate that led to the gardens halfway open in his hands. "You're staying here? What business do you still have..."

"Not here," Kevon clarified, shaking his head. "I've got to figure a way to move troops to the south, faster than we can now, if we're to survive the press of the darkness."

"Back to the Hold, then?" Carlo asked, resuming the journey to the Sending chamber.

"I've got an idea, but I need to make sure it will work before..." Kevon sighed. "Juggling our needs, and the security of the Hold..."

"No need to explain," Carlo shrugged. "Let me know what we have to work with, and I'll plan for that."

"So much..." Kevon rubbed at his temples, glancing to the side at the colorful flowers as they walked through the garden. "Sometimes I wonder if we are fighting for... if it is too late to make a difference. There is so much darkness..."

"There is," Carlo agreed, opening the secret passage that led down to the Sending chamber. "Too much. Too much for anyone else to do anything about. That's why we have to keep going. And unless you can find someone else to handle that pig-sticker of yours..."

"I know." Kevon paused before the stairwell leading down. "I'm not going to quit. That's not..." He gripped the hilt of his sword, and the runes lit up in his mind. The familiar distraction washed over him. The mix of absolute certainty and overwhelming responsibility washed over him, an electric chill dancing across his skin. "It's not something you need to worry about."

"I wouldn't let you magic me all over creation and back if I was worried about that," Carlo scowled. "Let's get this over with."

CHAPTER 57

"**W**hoa!" Kevon tumbled backward, sprawling on the cold stone floor after appearing face to face with a kneeling Garrimor.

"Kevon!" the Mage laughed. "I was just strengthening the extra reserve enchantment before I headed to dinner. What are you doing here?"

"Ahh. Yes, just a moment." Kevon knelt with his hand on a different part of the same rune structure the other Mage had just been working on. He let the full weight of his magical reserves uncoil from within him, and begin to flow into the construct. As the power transferred, he had to expend some effort to force the last third of his energy into the rune. "Might need this, sooner than we thought."

Garrimor gazed at Kevon as the Warsmith stood and took a deep breath. "Is everything all right?"

"I'll explain while we eat," Kevon answered, starting for the door. "Things are moving faster than we anticipated."

"You've found something, then," Garrimor asked Kevon as they moved along the rearranged chow line in the Dwarven mess hall. He stabbed a hunk of roasted meat with a bronze serving fork, and transferred it to his plate before moving down the line. "How bad is it?"

"It's getting worse," Kevon admitted. "And we haven't found what we're looking for yet."

"Losses?" Garrimor asked, pausing with a serving spoon half in a tub of seasoned *covaninal*.

"Substantial," Kevon took a hunk of crusted bread and

a few slices of a different marinated meat. "Some of your fellows among them. I'm sorry."

"We knew what we were volunteering for," Garrimor sighed, and headed for an open table. He shook his head as he sat down. "We'd all have been dead if not for you and Mirsa. I'm with you, no matter the cost. I think the others are, too."

"Heartening, considering the turmoil we've been experiencing in the south."

"You need us to join you there?" Garrimor asked, leaning forward in his seat.

"Not yet," Kevon shook his head. "Troops are headed here from Eastport, and potentially from Navlia. Several Companies. They need Sent to the front lines."

"That's an awful lot of folks to be parading down through the Hold," Garrimor's face contorted into a scowl. "I don't see the dwarves allowing that."

"Agreed," Kevon nodded. "That's why we'll have you moving them from the front entrance to the Sending chamber."

"Armored troops," Garrimor chuckled. "Aren't going to work."

"Their armor and weapons can be loaded onto the transit line, and sent through to them," Kevon explained. "Soldiers with supplies can go through the Sending chamber, and their equipment can be brought to them via caravan from the other end of the line."

"I'd hate to be the one that has to talk them into it," Garrimor admitted.

"I know," Kevon sighed. "It's difficult enough getting someone who trusts me to go through with it. They'll have their orders, which will help. Beyond that..."

"They won't trust you," Garrimor said, "Why can't you convince someone that they do trust?"

"Carlo might do the job, but he's needed in the south," Kevon chewed on one of the strips of meat. "Well, they'll be bringing someone they trust. I'll just take some of their senior officers down and show them, bring them back, and they will convince the others."

"It's just as well," Garrimor offered. "The delay could help the Dwarven tailors get a jump on the extra garments needed, if these soldiers are going to relinquish their armor."

"That's right," Kevon pushed his plate away. "We'll have to... We'll have to move quickly. This will take more preparation than I thought. Have some tailors meet me up near the entrance in an hour. There is one more thing I want to check on."

Kevon entered the meeting hall, followed by one of the elder blacksmiths. He made his way over to where Garrimor stood with the small knot of Dwarven tailors.

"Thanks for meeting with us," Kevon began as soon as he recognized one of the translators. "I know that things have been difficult recently, and that is not about to change. I have more to ask of you."

"What can they help with?" the translator asked after a round of shrugs and some mumbling.

"I expect some of Alacrit's army to return in the coming weeks," he began. "To help us, this time. They'll be forced to abandon their weapons and armor here, and have it brought to them later. I'd like to make sure that they are comfortable with the idea."

"New garments for an army?" one of the tailors asked, through the translator. "We've re-clothed most of the Hold since the Ancients returned to us, and have been stockpiling fabric from the overabundance of *covaninal* silk. If we start now, we should be able to turn out more than enough clothing for as many soldiers as you can march through that door."

"What about armor?" Kevon asked. "With this new material, can you fashion padded cloth armor that can fit under their outer coverings? Something durable enough to be worn on its own?"

"That would take three times the fabric, at least," the tailor answered. "Many of the Ancients have been restless. We can set them to spinning and weaving to prepare for this need."

"I'd like to get work areas set up here, so that the soldiers won't have to venture further into the Hold than they need to," Kevon pointed to the north end of the chamber. "Perhaps only fittings and alterations will need done here. I'd also like to be able to repair and improve the armor we're taking from them. The vast majority of the work could be done below, in the Smithing district, but fitting will need to be done here. We can start moving a few forges up now, to have ready for when the real work starts."

Garrimor nodded. "Shiny new armor might help ease their minds," he shrugged. "We should start with the soldiers that Carlo left here."

"Have them set up," Kevon instructed the translator. "Find me if they have any questions. Garrimor, return to the Tower, and bring back anyone they can spare to prepare for and help with the Sendings once the troops arrive."

"I'll return shortly," Garrimor nodded to Kevon, and started down the hallway to the Sending chamber.

"I should clear this with Bargthar-Stoun," Kevon chuckled.

"Dwarves are a lot tougher to Send," Garrimor wiped the sweat from his brow. "I don't know how much longer I can keep helping."

"We're almost done with this group," Kevon answered. "If you need to, you can rotate out while one of the others gets some more practice. As long as we don't dip into the room's reserves for this, we'll be fine."

"I think…" Garrimor looked over at the handful of

Stoneguard that milled around near the room's entrance. "I should be fine." He gestured for the next dwarf to step into the center of the circle of runes.

"Great," Kevon stood and started for the door. "I'll send in two replacements. You'll need practice leading the spell."

The Warsmith worked his way down to the throne room. Finding it empty, he made his way past it into the transit hub.

"Need some help with that?" he asked, pointing toward the pieces of wagon that two Dwarven Regulars were loading into a transport bound for the Fortress. He grabbed an end and between the three of them, finished loading the sledge in a matter of minutes.

"I thought they had already taken a wagon earlier," Kevon wondered aloud as the drumming of the transport subsided.

"Yah. Two," the remaining dwarf nodded, as he began working a winch to hoist another sledge onto the cleared runway. "Two wagon."

"It was going to be a chore to crew one wagon," Kevon shook his head. "How are we going to... oh."

Kevon nodded as he watched the quartet of harnessed riding-voles being led down the staircase from the throne room. "I should have thought of that. How are they going to keep them calm for the entire ride?"

As if to answer the question, one of the handlers produced a bowl, which he filled with water from a waiting pitcher. He crumbled some kind of chunky powder into the water, and placed it on the floor in front of one of the voles. When it had finished drinking, another handler led it into the front row of the troop sledge, and cajoled it into laying down.

"I see," Kevon chuckled as he watched the scene repeat itself. "And two voles should be more than enough to pull one of those wagons, even fully loaded down with armor. I'll send word to have an escort sent tomorrow. They can haul the first load soon after they arrive."

◆ ◆ ◆

"I can't ask you to send more troops than you already have," Kevon cautioned Bargthar-Stoun. "With Alacrit's troops arriving, you need to show strength. I don't believe that they will do anything, but would advise being prepared just in case."

"More Stoneguard training, below," the king answered. "Best half Regulars, train more. Busy making new armor."

"I thought I'd seen some new faces," Kevon nodded. "I wish Bertus, Carlo, or I could spare the time to help, to train with them. As it is, I am needed on the front soon. Has there been word from Rhysabeth-Dane?"

"Watch skies," the king shook his head. "No news. Soldiers enter canyon."

"They've made good time," Kevon sighed. "Two full days before we expected them. They'll strike camp near the gates tonight, I'll greet them in the morning."

"Very good," Bargthar-Stoun nodded, followed with a sheepish smile. "You do the...?"

"Again?" Kevon asked. "You've already..."

"*The thing...*" Bargthar-Stoun growled.

"All right." Kevon took a few steps back, and drew his sword.

The surrounding Stoneguard turned to look, but did not react further.

Readying his magical reserves, Kevon channeled the power through a Fire rune, and the sword he held aloft blazed bright, a living image that mirrored the tapestry hanging on the wall to his right.

"Dwarves you need, we send." The king nodded as Kevon extinguished the flame and returned the sword to its scabbard.

"We could not do this without you, and your people." Kevon bowed, and turned to leave.

◆ ◆ ◆

"Something is happening near the Spire," Garrimor exclaimed, bursting into the war room. "I was in the upper halls when I felt it!"

"Magic?" Kevon asked, furrowing his brow. "From above..." He glanced back to the map on the table before him, and moved the carved wooden griffin to the top of the Hold. "Rhysabeth-Dane is here."

"Should I..."

"I'm heading up to meet her," Kevon decided aloud, rushing around the Mage to the doorway.

Kevon sprinted through the hall to the chamber where the forges and tailoring stations were nearly ready for use. He dodged around two other Magi, muttering as he ran. He made it up two stairwells to the top level of the service tunnels before the fatigue of the last few days crushed down on him. He slowed, wobbling, as he entered the long stairwell that led up toward the central spire. He put a hand on the wall of the narrow corridor and stopped to catch his breath, regain his composure.

"There you are," Rhysabeth-Dane called from the bend in the stairwell above.

"I'd heard you had arrived," Kevon answered. "Where is Nalsi?"

"Saying goodbye to Brightwing," she laughed, bounding down the steps. "They've bonded."

"Have you seen any of the Unbound?" Kevon asked, catching the dwarf's hug as she crashed into him.

"A few on the way in. Brightwing will round some up this evening before he returns to roost," She flung herself back from the embrace and peered up at him. "Have they seen the army marching in?"

"They're here at our request," Kevon explained. "Reinforcements we are sending back to the south."

"I didn't want to have to fight them," the tiny Rider scowled. "But I would."

"They're fortunate," Kevon decided.

"How is Tamaraith?" she asked.

"I have not been to see him yet," Kevon admitted. "Nor have I seen the Elven Ambassador. We've not had time for games."

"Let's go see the skergiz, at least," Rhysabeth-Dane suggested. "Then I need to visit my library."

"After you."

CHAPTER 58

"General Avolentz," Kevon greeted the soldier as he approached the meeting place, hand extended in friendship. "Be welcome. We are honored that you have returned."

"As ordered," Avolentz hesitated, then extended his own hand in greeting, and clasped arms with Kevon. "You have need of us?"

"I wish it were not so," Kevon grimaced. We should speak inside. Bring guards as you wish. I... see no Magi with you."

"They were recalled as soon as we got the orders."

"Just as well," Kevon grinned. "I might have sent them away myself. If you will follow me..."

"I must have something to tell my lieutenants," Avolentz protested, holding his ground.

"I'm going to show you the front lines of this war," Kevon said, turning back toward the Hold. "You will convince the others to join us."

"I would see the front, as well," the Warrior Vellamic called from the cluster of guards that hung back from the gathering.

"Of course," Kevon answered. "Carlo will be pleased to see you again."

"The craftsmanship is beyond dispute," Avolentz commented, inspecting the armor of one of Carlo's remaining troops. "The weapons have been reworked, as well?"

"Keen Dwarven edges," the soldier answered, drawing his blade and handing it to the general. "The crossbows are the most improved, accurate at twice the distance they were before."

"And all this in the name of friendship, after we laid siege to this place." Avolentz returned the sword to the soldier and paced over to the forges, where the veteran Dwarven smiths worked the finishing touches on a ringmail shirt, and a saber.

"If you would head over to the fitting area, the tailors can measure you and finish up your new garments," Kevon gestured over to the right side of the chamber. "They can begin on your weapons immediately, and your armor once they finish the replacements."

Avolentz hesitated, but Vellamic undid his sword-belt and refastened it, hanging it on the horn of one of the unused anvils between the two working smiths.

"The faster we do this, the sooner we get to the front," the older Warrior chortled, marching over to the waiting tailors.

"My guards will stay here, armed, while the Warrior and I visit the front, as you say..." Avolentz's glare focused on Kevon. "If this is a trick..."

"You don't know me that well," Kevon answered. "And this alliance is important, so I'll ignore that last comment."

"Very well," Avolentz shrugged. He unbuckled his weapons and handed them to one of his guards. "We shall begin."

"I wouldn't want to get in a serious fight in these," Vellamic snorted, stretching in his new padded armor. "But it will wear better under my mail than anything I've had before."

"We'll have to see about getting the rest of the army outfitted in this," Avolentz agreed. "It would be worth whatever price they asked."

"They're preparing to outfit the whole army," Kevon sighed. "As one of their contributions to the alliance. In addition to taking most of the losses thus far on the front. You just make sure to do your part. Follow me to the Sending Chamber."

Garrimor and Kevon led the group down the hallway past the stables and into the Enchanted room.

"Who's first?" asked one of the waiting Magi that encircled the chamber's embedded sigil. "Step into the center."

"I'll go." Vellamic offered, moving forward. "Can't let the youngsters have all the fun."

"Then we'll begin," Garrimor took his place at the rune, kneeling to make contact and increase the spell's efficiency.

Kevon felt the magic build, and Vellamic disappeared. "After you," he motioned to Avolentz.

The general walked to where Vellamic had been, and waited.

The magic built, and faltered. It rose again, and dissipated once more.

"Lose the blade," Kevon warned, glaring at Avolentz.

The general smirked, and removed a sheathed knife from underneath his *covaninal* silk padding. "I had to try." He tossed the weapon to one of his guards, and nodded to Kevon.

"Wait..." Kevon cautioned the Magi that began their spell anew. "Let me."

He walked in closer to Avolentz, and drew his sword. "You need to trust us? Is that it?"

"I don't know how to answer that, with your drawn steel before me."

"Take it." Kevon shrugged, flipping the blade around and extending it hilt-first. "Return it to me when we have your trust."

Avolentz accepted the sword, and held it in a calm stance as Kevon tapped into the magic of the other Magi. Two breaths, a moment of focus, and the general, along with the sword, vanished.

"Was that wise?" Garrimor asked.

"I hope so," Kevon answered, strolling into the center

of the ensorcelled floor. He concentrated again, and shifted to the Sending chamber in the wastes.

"Follow me," Kevon ordered, leading the way out of the dim chamber, through the more confining hallways of the fortress. "Vellamic, you should join Carlo if he is in the war room, down that hallway to the left. Avolentz, we're heading up to the parapets to see what we can while the sun is at its strongest. If Marelle is about, let her know I've returned."

"I shall," Vellamic nodded as he turned down the hall Kevon had indicated.

"Is there really much to see of the creatures of darkness at noontime?" Avolentz asked.

"It varies," Kevon chuckled. "If we're lucky, it will just be orcs."

"*Kevon!*" one of the Stoneguard at the upper doorway called as they rounded the stairwell leading up to the exit.

"We need to go out," Kevon explained as they approached. "Can he borrow your sword?"

"You want this one back, eh?" Avolentz sneered.

"If something were to happen, yes." Kevon admitted. "We'd be much better off if *I* had that sword."

Avolentz passed Kevon's sword back, and took the replacement the Stoneguard offered as the other dwarf worked the catch on the door and began sliding it open. He hefted the dull silver-iron blade. "I like this one better anyway."

"Good. Keep it ready."

"How far below ground were we...?" Avolentz asked, and then stilled as he saw the expanse of sky through the opening doorway. "What would make it up here during the day?" he asked as Kevon ventured out into the light.

"Gargoyles," Kevon answered, searching the skies for sign of the vile winged beasts. "Great imps that can bear the light. Some of the most dangerous creatures here."

"Worse than the obsidian reapers?" Avolentz scanned the skies, his eyes darting about as he craned his neck to and fro.

"The elves excel at bringing down gargoyles," Kevon explained. "The dwarves are quite accomplished at slaying reapers. Our Magi are hindered here, but can be tasked to handle either, or the leapers when they happen to attack. Orcs are the ones that challenge them the most."

"We've been fighting orcs on the frontier for generations," Avolentz argued.

"Our soldiers are as adept as the elves and dwarves at slaying orcs," Kevon agreed. "The ones that remain here have gotten better at fighting all manner of creatures from the shadows. The difference has been the level of organization since the Dark Magi have left Navlia and come here. The different creatures, moving in concert, have become more deadly."

"There!" Avolentz pointed to shapes moving in the distance. "Orcs?"

"They're larger here than you're used to," Kevon answered, peering in the direction Avolentz indicated. "One part of the reason we need so much help."

"You patrol out in this, regularly?" the general asked. "If there is spare armor, I would like to go out and see for myself."

"Let's speak with Carlo before we make that decision." Kevon turned to go back into the fortress.

"Accounts of attacks have clustered more orcs here, here, and here. Leapers here and here." Carlo pointed to markers on the map. "Reapers have clustered mainly in these areas, heavier here. Where have the gargoyle attacks been reported?"

"All along here," Kevon stepped up alongside the Commander and pointed to several locations. "They only thin out *this* far back toward..."

"I see." Carlo interrupted, placing small winged markers on the map. "How frequent are the attacks in this area?"

"At least as many," Marelle confirmed. "We lost a handful of soldiers there yesterday to them."

"Judging from the intensity of the different types of attacks..." Carlo moved to the far side of the map and pulled a length of twine from his pocket. "Reapers could be centered here." He trapped one point on the twine under his thumb, and swung the end across the map, the arc encompassing all of the reaper-markers. He placed a small stone where his thumb had been.

"Orcs could be *there*," Kevon pointed to another spot on the map.

"Let's see..." Carlo duplicated the twine measurement with the orc markers. "Yes, they could be," he nodded, putting down another stone.

"Leapers," Avolentz offered, pointing to a different location.

"Of course," Carlo smiled at the general, placing a stone without measuring.

"Gargoyles have a much larger range," Marelle commented. "The attack patterns, the directions I have seen them flying to and from attacks, point to somewhere over *there*."

"Off the map," Carlo grunted. "Only just. We'll put the marker here on the edge."

"Now you have an idea of where to stop the attacks, at their source," Avolentz nodded.

"I'm not as concerned about that," Carlo chuckled, working his twine on the map again, near the center of the placed stones. He dropped a larger stone, near the marker at the estimated center of the orc attacks. "I'm curious as to what is going on *here*."

"The Magi organizing the attacks," Avolentz breathed. "Of course. A central location, removed from most of the danger."

"The patrol you accompany can be sent out in that direction," Kevon offered.

"Someone else will have to take my place," Avolentz shook his head. "I need to return to the Hold and speed the transfer of my men to this outpost."

CHAPTER 59

"I'm glad you got to familiarize yourself with the workings of the fortress," Kevon sighed as he walked into the Hold's war room and spotted the general. "But we missed Rhysabeth-Dane and the Unbound by a few hours. Nalsi went with them. We could have used another Mage."

"The second batch of soldiers have been measured and fitted, turned in their armor and weapons," Avolentz turned to address Kevon. "Some have gone deeper into the Hold to train with the Stoneguard."

"Brave men," Kevon nodded. "Even when the Stoneguard fool around, it's serious."

"You should have your Mage back in a matter of days," Avolentz mused. "The last leg into the deep wastes will be less dangerous with the number of griffin accompanying them."

"I hope so," Kevon answered, moving up to look at the documents the general stood over. "Have you estimated the time it will take to get them all transferred?"

"Four weeks, if things go better than expected," Avolentz pointed to the scrawled schedule notes. "We'll have to slow down toward the end, start sending extra water with them. One of your Magi explained the water situation there, how it was much harder to come by there than anywhere else. They had improved the situation, but not much else could be done."

"I hadn't heard that those resources were stretched so thin," Kevon scratched his head. "*Covaninal* helps, but I suppose with this many extra…"

"We'll handle it," Avolentz smiled. "You should finish up what you need to here before you have to leave."

"I'm glad you're with us on this," Kevon reached out to clasp arms with the general.

"You're certain the armor and weapons will be delivered... quickly?"

"It's important enough that I will see to it personally," Kevon answered, releasing Avolentz's arm. "I'll see if they will Send a replacement for me here, but the crew is able to keep up with the rate we're sending troops through."

"I don't see any need to move them faster," Avolentz shrugged. "You haven't been helping with every group going through. I would hate to pull another Mage off the front lines just for this."

"Noted," Kevon nodded. "The work should go quicker as they practice, anyway. I'll just finish up here and go check on the equipment."

"Hey!" You guys haven't finished putting that together yet?"

"It's the second wagon," the Mage overseeing the project grumbled after lowering the staff he'd trained on Kevon. "The first wagon is taking its second trip to the fortress now. We need this one to keep up with the loads coming through."

"The faster we can move it, the better," Kevon looked at the pile of armor and the bundles of swords stacked nearby, then to the pile of wagon parts. "What can I help with?"

One of the Stoneguard working on the wagon dropped his end of an axle, and scratched his head. He lifted the wooden mallet he had in his hand, and mumbled something in Dwarven.

"How about I help with the wagon? Is there a picture?" Kevon laughed.

◆ ◆ ◆

"Tighten that," the soldier pointed to one of the body cleats as he shook the top buckboard. "I'll get the brake put together right. They're almost done loading the other wagon. Let's get going so we can take both back at once."

"That's the plan," Kevon grunted, leaning on the lever that tightened the cleat into the top plank. "If *someone* had listened…"

"*Bah.*" the Stoneguard kicked at one of the suits of armor left in the pile as he glared Kevon's direction.

"Almost done," Kevon pulled the lever free of the crude bolt's notch and tossed it onto the front bench. "Can we load this while you fix the brake?"

"Please do," the soldier answered from beneath the rear axle. "And hand me that mallet?"

Kevon goaded the Stoneguard into a competition, finishing loading his half of the pile moments after the laughing dwarf. They took another minute to handle each end of the bundled swords, and strapped the load down as the soldier crawled out from under the wagon.

"All right. We should be ready to go," he said, tugging on the brake assembly. "This seems to be working now. I'll head out and grab our voles. The other team is getting them harnessed for us."

"We'll wait here," Kevon leaned against the loaded wagon and wiped the sheen of sweat off his forehead.

"Will you be riding in the wagon, or should we saddle up another vole for you?" the soldier paused by the exit and waited for Kevon's response.

"I'll…" Kevon looked at the Mage that huddled in the corner. "I'll be okay in the wagon this time."

"We'll be hauling two or three behind each wagon this trip," the soldier shrugged as he slipped out of the chamber.

"I knew they sent enough to haul two wagons," Kevon

muttered. "When did they bring the others over?"

The remaining Stoneguard grimaced, and pointed to Kevon, then the center of the front bench. He pointed to the Mage, and to one side of the bench. He climbed up on the other side, and grunted.

"Yeah. Okay," Kevon frowned, and walked over to where the Mage sat. "It's time to go."

"Right!" the Journeyman said, startling awake. "I'm… ready. It'll be good to be trapped inside that other stone prison for a change."

"I'd suggest rotating you back out to the Hold, but that's not much better," Kevon placed a hand on the young Mage's shoulder. "Perhaps when more troops have arrived, and Carlo has rearranged things, they will need more support back at the Tower. In a few weeks, you could be training new recruits."

"I'm not sure I'll make it a few more weeks," he whispered. "We almost didn't make it here. I volunteered to stay behind with the second wagon so I wouldn't have to go back out so soon."

"I think there are plenty of us to fend off any attackers that may show themselves," Kevon reassured the trembling lad. "Focus, do your part. That's all we can ask of you. Let's get you up into the wagon."

After a moment, color seemed to return to the youth's face. "Okay."

The Stoneguard already had one crossbow readied, and tinkered with another.

"Good idea," Kevon chuckled as he helped the Mage up onto the bench.

The soldier returned with two harnessed voles and help. They attached the beasts to the front of the wagon, and tossed Kevon the reins. "It shouldn't be difficult," he called up. "Our team knows the way, these guys should follow just fine."

The Stoneguard mimed pulling the brake lever, and grinned.

"Lead the way," Kevon sighed, shaking his head at the

cantankerous dwarf.

The wagon rolled out of the chamber into the widened passage beyond. A magically carved stable with a few remaining voles and attending soldiers and Ancients was a new addition to the right. Hold-style iron lighting-stone baskets lined the ceiling down past where the sand-fall had been.

"That's it," one of the soldiers called from behind, stepping away from the tethered voles he'd secured to the back of the wagon.

They continued on, and spotted a ramp up to a pair of open wooden doors just around the corner.

"Hurry!" a voice called from outside. "Gargoyles on the horizon!"

Kevon clicked his tongue at the voles, which did nothing. They picked up speed as they hit the ramp, and the wagon jostled out into the brilliant daylight.

"Quick, away from the entrance!"

Kevon looked to where the soldiers pointed as they closed the doors behind, and hopped onto their saddled voles. He flicked the reins, and the wagon lurched ahead. He sensed the magic forming nearby, and he could feel the sand shifting and smoothing behind them as they rode away from the scrub camouflaged entrance.

The vole team sprinted after the wagon ahead, darting through the miniature canyons standing between them and the open wastes beyond. The Stoneguard leaned on the brake twice before corners, and Kevon breathed a sigh of relief.

Out in the open, the magic shifted from Earth to Fire as the Mage prepared for the danger from above.

"You handle the first wave," Kevon shouted over the grinding of the wagon's wheels over the broken landscape. "After that, you take the reins, and I'll worry about the rest!"

The Mage nodded, his knuckles whitening as he gripped his staff tighter.

Crossbows thrummed and bowstrings sung as the swooping nightmares drew near. Keening wails mingled with the terrible battle-shrieks of the diving gargoyles as bolts and arrows connected and tore through dark ashen flesh.

Kevon's skin crawled as he felt the malevolence from the stored magic in the Mage's staff flood into the sky. Fire magic tore through the latent twisted Darkness that permeated the area, even this far from the more intense distortion of magic near the fortress.

Smoldering heaps of gargoyle carcass hurtled to the ground, slamming to the earth in all directions. The harnessed voles on Kevon's wagon shied away from an impact ahead of them, veering around the convulsing mass of charred, twisted carcass.

The Mage beside Kevon faltered a moment, but resumed his attack with renewed ferocity. After a handful of breaths, Kevon could feel the power lessening as the enchantments layered into the Mage's staff unraveled into a final burst of flame.

"My turn," Kevon shouted, handing the reins to the right, and resting his hand on the sword at his left hip as he turned his attention to the sky.

Wind magic bloomed in Kevon's mind as he connected with the rune engraved within the sword. He clenched his outstretched fist as he focused on the swarm of gargoyles descending, and his focus branched out to half of the careening demons. He spoke, the word drowned out by the screeching, but it served its purpose, solidifying his effort with the extra focus. His knuckles cracked as he closed his fist tighter, and the magic responded.

Bonds of wind tightened around a great many of the gargoyles, wrapping themselves in their own wings. Smooth descents turned to chaotic freefall, tumbling into their allies. A chain reaction of tangled earthbound demons rained down all around them. Kevon leapt from his place between the Stoneguard and the Mage, and swung his sword to lop off the head of a nearby gargoyle before it could regain its senses.

Kevon swept across the rear half of the battlefield,

slashing and stabbing, finishing off the wounded gargoyles as he reached them. The soldiers from the lead wagon cleared the front side, while the Magi and Stoneguard from both wagons kept the remaining swarm at bay with fire from crossbows and staves.

"They're changing tactics," Kevon cried as the swarm shifted and looked to begin regrouping toward the south, directly in their path.

"Dark Mage," one of the soldiers pointed to a figure in the distance. "Looks like he's summoning reinforcements."

"We're headed that way," Kevon shrugged. "Might as well get some work done. Let's regroup and run him down."

"We were worried about you," Marelle met Kevon and the others a few dozen yards from the north entrance to the underside of the fortress. "We expected you a day or more sooner, from the reports coming from the Hold."

"There were issues," Kevon laughed, sliding out of the saddle of his riding vole. "We've got enough Stoneguard armor here to outfit two dozen more, though. If half of those start accompanying the wagons, there shouldn't be nearly as many problems getting through from now on."

"We'll need that equipment sooner than later," Marelle cautioned, stepping into Kevon's embrace. "There is a wave of attackers sweeping in from the southeast."

"Move it in!" Kevon hollered to the wagon drivers, motioning toward the opened entrance. "Looks like we're not getting that rest!"

The wagons rolled into the open door, and down the wide hallway to the stable. Single vole-riders followed the wagons, and Kevon dropped the reins of his mount, allowing it to follow the others inside.

"You'll want to speak with Carlo, and Rhysabeth-Dane," Marelle steered Kevon toward the entrance. "There have been some… changes."

Kevon hiked through the lower reaches of the fortress, dodging around the increased levels of frantic activity that coursed through the enlarged arteries of the complex. He took the stairs to the upper level two at a time, and turned down the hallway toward the war room once he reached the fortress's more structured passageways.

"Have you found them yet?" Kevon asked, marching into the war room.

"We haven't sent anyone out the last few days," Carlo grumbled. "Our first patrol came back half destroyed. The creatures of darkness are massing, they avoided our men until they had superior strength. If both Bertus and Marelle had not been along with that patrol…"

"And this group that's approaching?" Kevon asked.

"Hundreds strong," Carlo answered. He pointed to where the circles on the map converged. "From this direction. They're perhaps an hour out, if Rhysabeth-Dane's estimates are correct."

"A group this large will either have the strength or the magic to breach our defenses," Kevon sighed. "We can't wait this out."

"Take Kevon up to the aviary," Carlo told Marelle. "Rhysabeth-Dane and most of the Unbound are resting from their flight back from scouting. I want the alarm raised ten minutes before they arrive, and those cat-birds in the air five minutes after that. We'll need half the Magi up top, the other half on the ground, split between the south and west gates. You'll have to spot them, and give the warning."

"Right away," Marelle answered, and led Kevon back out of the room.

CHAPTER 60

"Kevon!" Rhysabeth-Dane charged into the Blademage, her hug rocking him back on his heels. "We didn't have much time to talk when we saw each other last. There's a lot you need to know."

"I thought Nalsi was up here," Kevon squinted, peering around.

"She'll be joining us in later," the dwarf assured him. "Yusa said he'd to head up here soon, too. Nalsi's one of the things I wanted to talk to you about."

"She rode with you on the return trip," Kevon nodded. "Is she getting too attached to you and Brightwing to be effective anywhere else?"

"Not exactly the issue," the tiny Rider's lip twitched as she peered past Kevon to one of the aviary's two entrances.

A griffin screeched behind him, and Kevon startled at the voice that spoke over it.

"Easy, Slatebeak. He didn't mean anything by it."

Kevon turned to see Nalsi slipping down from the saddle atop the still-hissing griffin. She stroked the beast's neck feathers with her gloved hand as she ducked underneath his head to join the others.

"So... you're riding on your own now," Kevon scratched his head.

"Slatebeak chose her on the trip back, two days before we reached the fortress," Rhysabeth-Dane explained. "She'd been riding with me for long enough that she knew how everything worked. I think Slatebeak had a Rider before, he took the saddle with no complaints when we got here."

"The feeling of being joined to your griffin," Nalsi sighed. "It's something words can't capture. Not magic, but similar. No images, just emotions. I don't know what I'd do if I had to choose between... but I don't!"

"Report," Rhysabeth-Dane scowled at the Mage's exuberant outburst.

"The gargoyles are maintaining above the troops moving on the ground," Nalsi shrugged. "None of them would break off to attack us, and we got closer than we should have. It took us half an hour to get back, but they're moving slower than we were. It should be at least another hour or two before they get here."

"So they've slowed since we checked last," Marelle removed her eyepatch and gazed at the stone wall. "You should get as many of the Unbound inside to rest as you can. I'll check their distance in another half hour."

"How many other Riders are there?" Kevon asked, still shocked by Nalsi's entrance.

"There are two Unbound that have been courting some soldiers," Rhysabeth-Dane chuckled. "They're not having any of it."

"I don't know that I blame them," Kevon shuddered. "I know I've ridden with you on Brightwing, but the experience is not something I would like to make a habit of."

"It's different when you are riding on your own," Nalsi smiled. "I don't know if I could go back to somewhere Slatebeak would not be welcome. He's... part of me now."

"I would have no time to practice the sword," Kevon laughed. "As attractive as you make it sound, I will avoid that particular pleasure."

"They steer clear of me," Marelle shrugged. "They sense something different, perhaps? Bertus has been trying to get any griffin's attention since he heard Nalsi was a new Rider. He's had no luck. It rather upsets him."

"The approaching army, could you tell what kind of

ground forces they are bringing?" Kevon asked Nalsi as Rhysa-beth-Dane headed outside with Brightwing in tow.

"Colors and shapes," Nalsi shrugged. "Large shapes I assumed were bull orc. Mixtures of dark and light that could be reapers and leapers. A glimpse of tan on the trailing end. Slate-beak thinks they are chimaera."

"I'll have to take a look when they get closer," Kevon nodded to Nalsi and followed Rhysabeth-Dane down the hall-way that led outside. He smiled at the Stoneguard that worked the doorway, and walked out onto the upper court-yard.

"This was the best they could do without you here," Marelle explained. "The griffin don't really like landing this low, but it works."

"There would be a lot involved in bringing more stone up from the lower levels for this," Kevon shrugged. "All of the chambers below that are in use complicate things further. I don't know what I would have done differently."

"A central pillar of stone that you can use to move ma-terial from one floor to another," Yusa suggested from behind Kevon. "At least, that's what Reko would do."

"I'll keep that in mind," Kevon turned to clasp arms with the ship captain. "This may work for the Riders and the Unbound, but we'll have to move to the battlements to be of any use, to be able to see any of the battle below at all."

"That's if we engage them out in the open," Marelle said. "I don't know that I want enemy Magi getting too close to our defenses in such large numbers."

"Agreed," Kevon glanced up at the swirling formations of Unbound circling above. "We'll have to go tell Carlo..."

"Reko is having another Mage deliver the message," Yusa shrugged. "Should we move to the battlements for a better view?"

"Let's," Kevon nodded, and headed back inside the fort-ress.

"Nothing," Marelle leaned forward and peered to the

southeast. "They're too far away on the ground and in the air for me to see."

"Let me try something," Kevon said, thinking back to the battle between the gargoyles and the Unbound he'd watched through magical means. He let his focus drift to center on the Light and Wind runes he felt through his contact with the sword. He summoned up a morsel of energy, and crafted a lens of magic. He peered through the wavy oval that appeared between him and the region to the southeast he was targeting.

"Nothing..." he whispered as he shifted position to look at different spots in the distance. "Wait, there's something. Gargoyles."

Kevon concentrated, and moved the magical lens downward, losing sight of the tiny flying specks in the distance. He stopped as he saw the blurred mass of creatures beneath their airborne allies. "Wow, that's a lot of them. Hold on."

Pushing harder, weaving extra power into the construct hanging out in midair before him, Kevon forced the image closer, clearer, though still wavering and blurring as the interference of the region shifted.

"They've stopped," Kevon announced as the image stilled long enough to verify his suspicion. "I imagine they'll try to attack sometime after nightfall, when their power is greater."

"Hours to wait, then," Yusa chuckled. "And just when things were getting exciting again."

"Well," Kevon shuddered, releasing the spell. "I wouldn't say there is no excitement. It looks like the Dark Magi are riding the chimaera."

"We'll be needed down below," Carlo pounded his fist on the map table. "None of these troops have experience fighting

Chimaera. There's maybe a dozen of us? Did you see how many there were?"

"I just got a glimpse," Kevon shook his head. "Nalsi mentioned a tan fringe on the approaching horde. That does not sound like just a few."

"Damnation. There's not enough time to train anyone else to fight them. Stoneguard have a knack for it, or surviving it, anyway." Carlo paced back and forth. "They're going to hang back and control the battle from the rear, aren't they?"

"Seems likely," Kevon answered. "It won't be easy to get to them, if they do what we think they will."

Carlo grabbed a fresh sheet of parchment and a quill. He inked out a large 'V', and shifted the parchment so that the point aimed toward where the approaching army lay on the map. "Stoneguard, in this formation," he began, pointing to the sweeping lines. He drew a circle near the apex of the figure, and a wide oval that stretched from one end of the back to the other. "We're up here, to the front. We have the experience fighting both Magi and Chimaera. The Stoneguard can drive through the center. If we can keep up the momentum, and break through, we can burst out on the other side to deal with the leaders."

"Who is back here?" Kevon asked, pointing at the oval.

"Everyone else," Carlo shrugged. "I won't know how to deploy them until we get into the thick of it and see which creatures break which direction."

"I can relay instructions to Yusa," Kevon offered. "Everyone here trusts him. He can deploy different troops as needed."

"Are there any men from his crew left here?" Carlo asked. "If they can relay commands by flag, or lantern, it would free you up for the battle."

"There is one sailor here," Marelle answered, glancing down through the floor. "I'll have one of the Magi Send him back to the Hold to get the others."

Carlo nodded, and began to brood over the map once

again.

"I think it will work," Kevon began. "We should…"

"Spread the word we will move at dusk," Carlo commanded. "Everyone rests, in their armor. Units in the lower catacombs, unit commanders in the rooms nearby, ready for commands."

"Yes, Sir!" Kevon nodded to Carlo and turned to leave.

"If you see Anneliese, would you send her up?"

"Of course," Kevon grinned, and marched out into the hallway.

"Better," Carlo grumbled, looking at the formation. "It should not have taken ten minutes to get this right."

"They're used to just rolling through enemies based on superior strength and equipment," Kevon shrugged. "I think they know how much we depend on them to hold the line. They should be fine."

Carlo sighed, and looked back to where the other units were forming up. "Now for this mess."

Kevon held his tongue, and watched the Blademaster as he marched up and down the length of the assembly, shouting orders that echoed through the unit commanders and against the rock face behind them.

"Crossbow squad! Keep spread out! Focus on the skies! Don't hit the griffin!" Carlo hollered. "…Cavalry… Keep those beasts in check. Be ready to move to support as ordered, but stay clear of the signal corps! Infantry! Protect your Magi! They will save your life!"

Kevon turned and slipped through the Stoneguard at the front of the wedge formation. He made his way along the crumbling, darkened landscape, up to the edge of the slope that led down into the blasted terrain below. He glanced up at the cloud-streaked night sky, and thought he saw the clouds shifting. It was not until a winged figure crossed in front of the full moon that Kevon could see how close the enemy had come. Light magic flared to life, an instinct dredged up from his earliest childhood... to banish the darkness. The blade of his sword blazed with perfect brilliance even through its scabbard, one facet of M'lani's gift.

"Carlo!" Kevon cried, turning back to raise the alarm. "We'd better get them moving! They're closer than we thought!"

◆ ◆ ◆

"I can't keep this up all night, and neither can Nalsi," Kevon commented, following close behind the Blademaster. "I know I can do more." With a flick of his mind, he bound the wings of a low-flying gargoyle with threads of Wind magic. The horned beast tumbled into the chaos that roiled before the advancing formation of Stoneguard and their supporting units with an eerie shriek.

"Tell me that wasn't you," Carlo shot back, turning to scowl at Kevon. "We'll need the light for as long as you can keep it up."

"We need to drive ahead, faster!" Kevon sidestepped and slashed at the leaper knight that landed within the formation. Earth magic flowed through him without thought, strengthening his swing. The sword sliced through the creature's thick armored hide as if it were spoiled fruit.

Entrails spilled out of the beast. It screeched, fell into the pile of its own innards, and shuddered twice before falling still.

Kevon stepped around the fresh obstacle, retaking his spot behind Carlo without hurrying.

"Wait," Carlo said, slowing further. "The fighting has slowed. They're shifting their forces."

"Our moment is now," Anneliese said, loosing another arrow from her bow. "Can we regroup to counter them?"

"I need a better picture of their deployment," Carlo

growled. "Marelle!"

"Orcs shifting to our left, leapers too." Marelle scanned the other side of the battlefield. "Gargoyles are moving to support the increased numbers of reapers on our right. There is a portal ahead that is bringing more of them across."

"Let them know it's time," Carlo shouted to Yusa's signalmen. "Cavalry to the left, bring the Magi up!"

The sailors stopped, and flipped flags in cryptic motions, to be answered in kind by their two shipmates flanking Yusa at the leading edge of the infantry squad that closed the rear of the marching wedge.

Yusa shouted commands, and their forces responded with an almost sluggish adequacy.

The leading edge of the infantry began marching in double-time, the sheltered Magi scampering along behind as the line expanded to encircle them. The remaining half of the infantry drifted to the right, positioning themselves between the reapers that tried to outflank the wedge on their side.

The vole-cavalry swung wide to the left, followed by a handful of Elven Hunters that took turns threading deadly-accurate shots through the fray, bringing down both leapers and orcs.

"Kevon..." Carlo stretched out his hand as he watched his units shift. "Now."

Finally, Kevon thought, redoubling the energy flowing through the Light enchantment on his sword. The hemisphere of daylight that centered on Kevon expanded further, revealing more gargoyles swarming above.

Shrieks of demonic surprise at the widened scope of the light turned to screams of terror as Rhysabeth-Dane and the Unbound plummeted from above, Nalsi's concealing illusion discarded as the battle was joined.

Brightwing led the flight of griffin downward, tearing a swath of destruction through the ranks of the gargoyles, clearing the way for Nalsi and Slatebeak.

As the Mage guided her winged steed lower and started

to bank for her turn, Kevon felt the Aid runes form behind him. He resisted the urge to contribute, but could feel the exhilaration as Nalsi focused all of the extra magic through her staff.

In the space of three heartbeats, half of the reapers on the right flank were dead. The wash of flame that rivaled the diffuse light emanating from Kevon's sword was a faint afterimage in his mind, as was the memory of the short-lived Aid runes. He blinked both away as the Stoneguard doubled their speed.

The Dwarves laughed and called to each other in jest and encouragement as they cut down disoriented reapers and stunned orcs. Unladen griffin clawed and tore at the still confused gargoyles, quick, killing strikes that rained winged corpses down on the smoldering battlefield.

Up, up, up! Kevon thought, watching Nalsi turn and find Rhysabeth-Dane. The Riders banked and twisted, climbing back into the relative darkness outside of the daylit bubble.

"Get moving," Marelle shouted in his ear, her free hand pressing into the middle of his back.

"Wait..." Kevon cautioned, as Kylgren-Wode shouted a command in the Dwarven tongue.

On cue, every third Stoneguard on the right flank shifted inside and moved across the wedge to reinforce the left side of the formation. The remaining dwarves spread out to cover the gaps, seeming more at ease with room to swing their war-axes.

Kevon thought he caught a friendly insult as one Stoneguard trapped a reaper's scythe-arm with a twist of his axe, and his neighbor severed the extended limb. "Okay, now."

With the way ahead to the apex of the formation clear of shifting dwarves, Kevon sprinted up to rejoin Carlo and the rest of the command squad.

The signalmen were flagging again, and as Kevon and Marelle arrived they turned to keep step with the formation.

"Shifting bow support to our ground forces since the

Unbound have arrived," Carlo shouted as Kevon jogged up alongside him. "Which direction is your portal?"

"One on the ground ahead and to the right," Kevon panted. "Another in the air above and to the left."

"Let's get to the one on the ground and shut it down."

"It's not like the fixed portals," Kevon shook his head. "It will close on its own, if we deal with the Mage sustaining it."

"Well?" Carlo gruffed.

"Give me a minute." Kevon brightened the aura of light coming from the sword, shifting it forward as much as his focus would allow.

A dozen or more chimaera, most mounted by dark robed figures, appeared at the far edge of the light. Kevon could feel the portal ahead wavering as the Light magic infused the area around it. Gargoyles circling above the far end of the battlefield banked and dove toward the front of the wedge formation.

"The griffin will...?" Carlo began asking.

"Not likely, after what I just showed them," Kevon answered. "I hope Nalsi sticks with them."

The sky ahead darkened again with leathery gray wings, and Kevon split his concentration. He tapped back into the clarity of the Wind rune on the sword. With spellwork too quick to counter even if it were not shielded by his connection to the blade, he struck the gargoyles with converging gusts of wind. Groups of the demons slammed together, entangling into falling masses of wings and claws that were easy marks for griffin and archer alike.

"*Forward!*" Carlo roared, and the formation of armored dwarves surged ahead through the roiling press of the creatures of darkness.

"They're retreating," Kevon called, as he felt the nearest Dark portal collapse, and another form further ahead. "They're not giving up." He scurried along behind Carlo, hopping over fallen orc and leaper carcasses, mindful of the distance between all of the armored allies around him. The drain of the Light spell pulsed at the back of his mind, wavering at the intrusion of so many creatures of darkness. The ever-present underlying chaos of fractured Dark magic grated at his concentration, even through the stabilizing support of the Light rune he used as a focus.

"Which way now?" Carlo shouted, stepping into a gap left by a fallen Stoneguard on the right.

"Keep going!" Kevon answered, refocusing the magic forward again. He stepped up onto the still form of a large orc that lay fallen in his path, and the increased height gave him a better vantage point for an instant. Black cloth robes flowed atop lurching chimaera at the edge of the influence of the light.

"They're just ahead! Now!" Kevon called to Carlo.

At Carlo's shout in broken Dwarven, the Stoneguard for-mation changed tactics, easing up on offense to focus on de-fense and speed. The line bunched and writhed as they pushed ahead at breakneck speed, dodging and shoving stunned en-emies aside to gain ground on the fleeing Magi. The tip of the formation split as it pushed through the last wave of demons, slowing enough to resume their killing tactics while staying ahead of the broken retreat.

Elven Hunters released a flurry of arrows, and drew blades to engage the overflow of monsters that circled around the backside of the open wedge. Vole-riders disengaged from their skirmishes on the outer edge to circle around and join the troops sprinting after the leaders of the dark army.

"They're getting away!" Carlo shouted, glancing side-long at Kevon.

The Blademage snarled, leaping over a fissure in the broken landscape, stumbling and recovering as the light slipped further back, and the chimaera riders neared the edge of the magical illumination.

"No, they're not," Marelle cried, pointing to the dark-ened sky above their quarry.

A torrent of flames poured from an arcing point in the

blackness beyond the limit of Kevon's magic, and the Unbound following Nalsi and Rhysabeth-Dane glowed crimson in its violent radiance. The flames played over two of the five visible Dark Magi and their chimaera mounts before the spell was countered by the survivors.

Nalsi and Slatebeak dove and twisted out of the path of gargoyles that streaked to intercept them. Rhysabeth-Dane and Brightwing blazed a trail through the winged demons, a blur of steel and talons that wove back and forth between the light and shadows.

Bursts of flame started from Nalsi's staff a handful of times, but the magic was severed, winking out before it could travel far enough to do any damage.

Kevon focused, and reached out, pulling shards of Earth up in front of the retreating Magi, and only one chimaera made the leap over them, and into the darkness beyond.

Two portals began to open, and one of the Dark Magi lurched forward toward them, tumbling to the ground with an arrow in his chest. The portal nearest to him blurred and dissolved in the light of the sword.

"You'll never make it!" Kevon called to the Mage hiding behind the stone formations his chimaera had slammed into. "One step toward it, and Anneliese will end you. Surrender."

"You can't stop Him," the Dark Mage screamed in reply.

Kevon felt a different flavor of magic at work, but as he sensed it, the wounded chimaera sprang into action, stumbling toward them. Kevon reached deep for the power to respond to the beast's distraction, but his reserves were already on the brink of giving out. He watched with detached resignation as Anneliese put two arrows in the chimaera, while the Dark Mage dove through the portal and vanished.

Free from direction of the Magi, the remainder of the dark army fled from the light, the few that stayed were dispatched within moments.

"Guys?" Kevon wobbled as the rush of battle drained away. "You might want to light some torches."

The light faded as Kevon slumped to the ground.

CHAPTER 61

"**I**s she back yet?" Kevon asked Nalsi. "We have fresh bread from the Hold. I know she has been getting tired of *covaninal.*"

"She hasn't slept in three days," the Mage shook her head, and wrapped her arms around her griffin's neck. "Since she heard."

"We knew she would take it hardest," Kevon nodded, "Though Mirsa and Bertus are grieving nearly as much as the other Dwarves he was close to. We'll all miss him."

Kevon closed his eyes, remembering back four nights ago to the battle in the lowlands to the southwest. By the time he had recovered from the exertion of the march and the accompanying magic, the wounded and dead had already been secured for the return trip. Piles of enemy demons had been set ablaze, reducing the food available for their scavenging brethren. The journey back through the smoke and haze in the darkness was surreal, at best. It was not until they were almost back to the lower entrances of the fortress that Kevon had realized Kylgren-Wode numbered among the dead.

Unable to find Rhysabeth-Dane with the griffin, or in her quarters, Kevon had enlisted Marelle's enhanced sight to seek the Dwarven Rider out. When they discovered she was waiting in Kylgren-Wode's chambers, asleep, they couldn't bear to wake her with the awful news. She arose the next day, confused, and Kevon took upon himself the unenviable task of breaking her heart.

Rhysabeth-Dane attended the brief ceremony they held for the fallen. A dozen Stoneguard had perished, along with

Kylgren-Wode, seven of Carlo's soldiers, and five Unbound. Hundreds of demons had been slain, and hundreds more routed, but that made little difference to those gathered in mourning. Without shedding a single tear, the Dwarven Rider left the assembly, and took Brightwing and half of the Unbound scouting in the wastes toward the southwest, and the center of Carlo's target area on the map. She'd returned numerous times to eat and replenish supplies, but would leave less than an hour after landing, taking different groups of Unbound along. By the end of the second day, neither she nor Brightwing looked fit to fly, but they stopped only long enough for water and food before taking back to the skies.

"Are the new soldiers settling in?" Nalsi asked. "They've been pouring in since all the other Magi returned to the Hold."

"We've been running wagons nonstop to pick up shipments of armor and weapons," Kevon answered, "As you know, there has been no resistance. I think they are gathering strength at their center, either to protect the focus of their power, or to amass enough strength to crush us in one attack. It's what I would do, it is what we're trying to do."

The Stoneguard at the doorway that led to the roof outside started cursing and hauling on the door, trying to open it as fast as he could by himself.

Rhysabeth-Dane stormed past him as soon as the door was open wide enough to admit her. Wobbling as she entered the Griffin stables, she reached out a hand to Kevon. "I... found..."

Kevon rushed to her side as she teetered and fell. He scooped her up, hefted her limp form over his shoulder. He watched Brightwing's response as the griffin pushed his way in through the doorway, but the exhausted beast only squawked and threw himself down on the nearest empty pile of straw.

"What did she...?" Nalsi asked, approaching, but keeping her distance from the weapons both Rhysabeth-Dane and Kevon carried.

"Mean?" Kevon sighed. "I hope she will remember what

she found when she wakes up. I'll take her to her quarters. Have someone bring food and water. Check and see if there is a healing potion that can be spared. Maybe some blackthorn tea."

"I'll have some water brought up and heat it," Nalsi added. "She needs cleaned up and put into fresh clothes. I'll handle it."

"Let us know as soon as she is awake," Kevon added, following the Mage into the hallway that led to the living area deeper in the fortress.

◆ ◆ ◆

"Just who I was looking for," Carlo grunted as Kevon slipped into the war room. "The barracks need expanded, again."

"I'll see to it," Kevon nodded. "I just thought you should know, Rhysabeth-Dane just returned. She found something, but passed out before she could tell us. Nalsi is attending to her now."

"It had best be the location we seek," Carlo wrinkled his nose. "This Keep smells like codpiece. The Vole and Griffin stables were bad enough, but the dwarves have started slicing and frying that damn fruit. It *almost* smells like bacon. Nearly all of our water has to be used for drinking, they're bathing on a rotation, or not at all."

"I added another hallway to the barracks yesterday," Kevon frowned, "How many men do we have now?"

"All told?" Carlo asked. "We should have well over a thousand fighters by this time tomorrow, not to mention the non-combatants."

"The equipment?" Kevon asked.

"They've stepped up the deliveries through the tunnels, sending more voles and Ancients along with the gear. They have been packing more equipment into each sledge, along with the extra cavalry mounts and support staff. I wouldn't normally attempt to manage a force this size without at least two more experienced lieutenants, but it's working so far."

"I'll fix the water problem first, then add on to the barracks. Nalsi will let us know when Rhysabeth-Dane wakes." Kevon waited for the Commander's nod before ducking back out into the hallway and heading down into the lower reaches of the fortress, to the catacombs below near ground level at the bottom of the mesa.

Kevon reached the water station, an enclosed stone cistern fused with the wall behind it, where he and the others had used Earth and Water magic to reroute an underground stream upward to spill into the prepared container. A lever-operated hatch controlled the flow out of the stone tank, down a small sluice to the collection area, but the pressure leading into the vessel was weak, at times little more than a trickle. They had done what they could over the last few weeks to stabilize and improve it, to little effect.

"Something different," Kevon muttered, drumming his fingers on the edge of the stone lid, his mind searching for possibilities. He rested his hand on the hilt of his sword, and connected to the Earth rune right away. A trickle of power, and the cistern lid was malleable, ready to bend to his whim. He sculpted a small opening near the center, a plain hexagon no wider than his thumb, the symbol for Magic. The sound of trickling water increased. Kevon shifted his will to etch out a ring of interlinked runes skirting around the opening, six more hexagonal forms with on edge connected to the gap.

"Water," he whispered, retaining his hold on the Earth rune for sculpting, but activating the Water rune on the sword to pattern his etching after. He sketched imprint after imprint around the gap, keeping the center of the formation as the bottom. The linked runes seemed to flow into one another, the seams between them disappearing without Kevon's direction. He stopped when there was only one empty Magic rune left. "Have to power it," he scowled. He released the Earth rune, and routed all of his will through the Water rune, focusing his magic on the linked runes, building their potency. The energy rushed out of him, and the symbols dulled in his mind.

"I'll have to surround it with an Enchantment rune, and put a decent amount of power into the Magic rune," Kevon grimaced. "But it should work."

"What should?" Marelle asked, glancing at the work he'd completed.

"Oh," Kevon startled at her sudden arrival. "I think this should be enough power, once it's fully charged, to open a small portal to the Plane of Water."

"That's a long way to go for a drink," Marelle frowned.

"If there were another way..." Kevon began. "I think this is our best option. I wouldn't try making it any larger though, even if the magic around here was not disrupted."

"Avolentz has returned," Marelle shook her head as she changed the subject. "They have halted sending Alacrit's troops, and have resumed sending Stoneguard and Dwarven Regulars."

"Carlo wanted more leadership," Kevon grinned, stepping away from his project. "That'll teach him."

"Things are getting crowded again," she added. "With the added Magi Sending from the Hold, they're pushing through dwarves faster than they used to move soldiers."

"That amount of magic use will be useful once we bring them through to help us here," Kevon mused, taking Marelle's hand and walking back up toward the center of the fortress. "The constant strain improves and expands magical reserves, as well as skill. We'll need every advantage we can get once we pinpoint their stronghold."

"There you are!" Avolentz began, clanking down the connecting stairs.

"You've found your armor already," Kevon commented. "We don't usually wear it unless we're preparing to march. Easier to deal with soldiers and Magi both in the hallways."

"Yes, yes, right," Avolentz shook his head. "You're the one I need to see about quarters?"

"I'm exhausted from trying to deal with our water shortage," Kevon sighed. "Give me about an hour, and I'll begin renovations."

"Excellent." Avolentz leaned against the wall so Kevon and Marelle could pass. "The other Mage, the redhead. She paraded the recent arrivals through the upper end of the fortress...?"

"Seeing if any of the Unbound would accept them," Kevon gritted his teeth. "I'm not so sure we have the time to spend training new Riders, letting them bond with the griffin."

"The changes to the command structure alone..."

"They would report to Rhysabeth-Dane," Kevon snapped, turning to look back down the stairwell over his shoulder. "Unequivocally. If they are allowed to train with the griffin at all. We may need to march within hours. *I will let you know.*"

Pity you're exhausted, Marelle thought at Kevon as they rounded the corner toward the main residences, the words slid into his mind, laced with inappropriate images.

Mentally, Kevon answered, gripping her hand tighter and increasing his pace. *I told him an hour.*

"There," Kevon sighed, and released the magic. "It's not fancy. Eight to a room."

"You just made a new hallway and... twenty... rooms on each side of it?" Avolentz's eyes widened in the torch-light. "Five more and..."

"Not today." Kevon leaned against the end of the hallway and took a series of deep breaths. "Coordinate with the Ancients to get these rooms lit and furnished. You might want to round up the soldiers that are quartered in the old residences and move them here, the dwarves will not be able to use these quarters comfortably. We'll need to shift things around, with more of them coming through than we expected."

"Excellent idea," Avolentz admitted. "I'll form details and have it done before nightfall."

"I'm going to go rest a while," Kevon straightened and began walking back down the newly fashioned hallway, motioning for Avolentz to move the same direction.

"I thought you rested before this," the soldier tilted his head in confusion.

"I made no such claim."

"Ah. Well then," Avolentz smiled. "You should..."

"Kevon!" Nalsi scurried down the hallway, darting to the side to slip past Avolentz. "Rhysabeth-Dane is awake! You're both needed in the war room!"

"So much for resting," Kevon grimaced. "Thank you, Nalsi." He clapped Avolentz on the shoulder. "You know the way. Let's go."

"They're growing stronger, bringing more and more demons into our realm," Rhysabeth-Dane cautioned as Kevon and Avolentz entered the war room. "There is no shortage of them either. I saw a portal in midair, dumping a stream of leapers into a broken pile on the ground. I think that's what they are *feeding* their army."

"Yes," Carlo nodded. "It's disturbing. But *where* is it?"

"They were gathered in a caldera, one carved out of the mountain range, *here*," Rhysabeth-Dane pointed to a spot at the far edge of the circle they had guessed the enemy would be gathering. "There are places it will be difficult to move quickly through, here, and here, but once we make it to these flats, you can spread out and prepare for the attack however you want."

"What kind of obstacles?" Carlo pressed. "We have no reports from beyond *here*. I need to know what to expect."

"Broken landscape, deep, dry riverbeds," Rhysabeth-Dane shrugged. "I didn't get low enough to see it all up close."

"I want patrols flying this route at all times. *Now*." Carlo's voice deepened. "Clear or not, we'll start the march tomorrow morning. I want voles loaded up with supplies to start riding out and caching them within the hour. Anything they can deliver beforehand is that much less we have to carry with us." He turned to Kevon. "Return to the Hold. Rally the Magi. They can keep sending troops, but they need to be here themselves by nightfall."

"Sir." Kevon nodded, and stepped back into the hallway. He jogged down the corridor and up the stairs to the junction that led to the Sending chamber, and stepped inside. He waited until the next dwarf popped into existence in the middle of the giant rune, and dashed into the center of the sigil. He knelt, touching both layers of the inscribed runes. He drew guidance from the inner figure, and strength from the outer, borrowing the layered power he and the other Magi had concentrated there. Without a word, he vanished.

CHAPTER 62

K evon sat at the edge of the bunk, and straightened his tunic, adjusted his boots. He closed his eyes, and tried not to think of the march ahead. Nightmares about their last encounter with the dark army had riddled his sleep, and he'd startled awake to be soothed by Marelle's comforting thoughts more than once.

The troops are starting to gather in formation outside, Marelle thought, brushing his hand.

Reko just alerted all of the Magi to be ready, Kevon replied mentally. *Nalsi and her patrol report the path clear for as far as she can tell.*

The hallway outside their room seemed emptier, but more frantic, those remaining in the fortress and catacombs below it looked to be scurrying to leave or in preparation for some other support function. Kevon considered making his way further up to the Sending chamber and expending his magic to recharge the power he had consumed the day before, but thought better of it. He wanted every advantage once he stepped out of these sheltering walls.

"Breakfast and travel packs staged near the entrance below," Marelle commented, as she slipped her eyepatch on, and yawned. "That's all I need to know right now."

Kevon shouldered his pack full of supplies. He accepted the flat bread that was filled with fried fruit and scrambled eggs, and kept pace with the others around him, moving out into the open. "I'm glad the vole-riders are hauling extra supplies," he commented as they made their way out into the open.

Robed Magi stood in a cluster to the left, conversing amongst themselves. Elven Hunters attired in tans and reds clustered around Anneliese, already seeming to blend into their surroundings. A line of vole cavalry waited against the cliff-side to the right for supplies to be loaded as they fed and watered their mounts.

"Water..." Kevon muttered. Relieved he had not spent his reserves on the portal, he finished off his breakfast and slid along the wall of the corridor back into the catacombs. Ducking into the chamber with the cistern, he focused his will into the Magic rune joining the circle of Water runes around the opening in the lid.

The magic flowed into the construct, filling it to the same glowing intensity in his mind. He poured more power into the Water runes, stabilized by the contact with his sword. With the last bit of power, he gave the focused runes *direction*. He pressed with his mind toward the *elsewhere* that he and his friends had ventured beneath the sea, and the miniature portal took shape. One final *push* and the magic solidified, becoming self-sustaining.

"There," Kevon sighed, letting go of the forces that still danced in his mind. He heard the gurgling noises from inside the cistern increase, and shut himself off from the rest of the magic. "Hopefully, we won't need it much longer." He turned to see Marelle waiting in the doorway for him.

"The elves have already left, scouting ahead," she reported. Carlo is ready to leave, but the dwarves won't leave without you."

"Of course not," Kevon groaned. "Appearances. The mural. This... is why they're here."

"I'd hate to disappoint them."

"As would I. Let's get back out there."

Kevon spotted the last of the vole cavalry disappearing down into the lowlands to the southeast as he ventured back out into the open. He could not see the elves anywhere, but decided against asking if they had already left or not. He made his way alongside the glinting mass of dwarves, their raucous banter hushing as he passed by. An eerie silence settled over the field as he stepped up next to Carlo.

"I'd say they're ready to be done with this," Carlo grunted. "I can't say I blame them. We've all paid far too great a price for this foolishness."

"Our last battle was just a down-payment on the bill we are due," Marelle agreed. "I, for one, am eager to collect."

"There's the Merchant I remember," The corner of Carlo's mouth turned up in a smile. "I'm sure your father is proud."

"Is he?" Marelle asked, shaking her head. "Is he even my father? I've been wondering about that since before we left the ship. Rhysabeth-Dane and the *Eleri* have all but told me he could not have been, or worse, he was something beyond fathoming."

Carlo grimaced, and said nothing.

"Something to think about while we march, if nothing else," she shrugged, turning to follow the lingering dust cloud left by the departing cavalry.

Kevon blinked, watching her walk away.

"Move out?" Carlo suggested in a questioning tone.

Shouts from his gathered officers rang out, shattering the awkward silence.

"Moving out, Sir!" Kevon responded as he saw the Commander's eyes glance at him, then lurch toward Marelle.

"Two hours march, ten minutes rest," a nearby soldier complained. "It's nearly dark. How long do they expect us to keep this up?"

"Be glad you are in the front of the formation," Avolentz chastised the speaker. "Those at the rear will be marching an hour longer than you. You'll already have eaten and be asleep before they catch up. The vole-riders have made most of this trek three times in the last day and a half, and will be riding most of the night to make it back to the fortress. Perhaps saving your breath is the best use of your remaining five minutes."

"S-sir!" the soldier mumbled a hasty affirmative, and ate the rest of his *covaninal* in silence, to glares from the rest of his squad.

"They're in good spirits, so far," the general chuckled, returning to the impromptu command center. "For the most part."

"They've been training hard, but this is pushing them farther than we have yet," Kevon sighed. "I'm glad we haven't encountered any resistance, but at the same time..."

"It's eerie," Carlo agreed. "I don't like it."

"Should we stop here?" Kevon asked. "The next supplies cache is another two hours away, maybe three in the dark."

"If we marched hard from here at daybreak, it would put us at the edge of the caldera at noon," Carlo estimated, measuring distances by torchlight on the small map he'd brought along. "I'd rather push on, get an hour or two less sleep, and approach slower, in formation, from further away. We could still be there just before noon, when they're weakest."

"I'll make another pass before returning to the fortress," Nalsi nodded, turning to look at her griffin. "It's clear enough, there's plenty of moon, and it's just rising. If anything is amiss, I'll warn you on my way back. If not, you'll just see us flying over."

"Safe travels," Kevon nodded to the Rider as she strolled past him. "We'll see you on the battlefield tomorrow."

"That you will."

A flicker of torchlight caught her smile, illuminating her flame colored locks. Her face, beginning to show wrinkles of world-weariness, was an anchor in Kevon's thoughts that he appreciated more than he had realized until now. Since the loss of Kylgren-Wode, the new Rider had been the main line of communication between them and Rhysabeth-Dane.

She'll be fine, Marelle thought through their clasped

hands. *Focus on tomorrow.*

"Give the men another five minutes to adjust to the moonlight, and we'll move out again," Carlo ordered. "Spread the word."

"The gargoyles are staying above the caldera," Anneliese frowned, looking along the line of the formation that spread out into the distance. "You should be able to march for an hour or more before they spot you."

"Stay close, then," Carlo cautioned. "I don't want you stranded out ahead where you would be unable to reveal yourselves, and rendered useless for the battle. Perhaps it's time you split up and joined your assigned units."

Anneliese nodded and began the hike back out to her clustered Hunters.

"Send word to the cavalry to move up on our flanks," Carlo continued. "The Magi and their escorts should already be in position, but I want to be sure before we start moving."

"We'll have to stay here at the front to keep the dwarves in check," Kevon chuckled. "Once the fighting starts, I can't imagine anything holding them back."

"With the signal corps, we should be fine where we are," Carlo craned his neck to glance down the formation. "Avolentz, we'll move you down toward the left flank. Take two flaggers, and Yusa. Anneliese is assigned to that area. That should give you enough support to hold against most anything."

"Right flank?" Bertus asked.

"Marelle should go with you," Carlo nodded. "We don't have an extra Mage to spare, I can't send Kevon. We might try and see if Nalsi can cover the right."

"I understand," Marelle squeezed Kevon's hand and slid her fingers out of his. "We'll see each other after the battle."

"Take two of the signal crew," Carlo reminded her as she

and Bertus began the trek toward the right side of the front.

The signal crew started waving flags, and relayed messages to Carlo.

"Most of the others are in place," the Commander announced, stepping further ahead of the front line. "We can start moving as soon as our front line is deployed."

"I'm surprised that all of the Unbound have walked this long since their arrival this morning," Kevon scratched his head. "I hope they can stay on the ground until we begin the attack."

◆ ◆ ◆

"Signal the griffin," Carlo ordered, as the cloud of gargoyles shifted formation.

All four of the remaining signal crew leapt into action, waving their flags over the heads of the Dwarven army that followed close behind.

"This is it, be ready. We want to take the fight to them. Double-time!" the Commander roared.

Kevon drew his sword and held it aloft for a moment as he increased his marching speed.

Grunts of excitement ran through the ranks of the dwarves following. The sound took on more ominous tones as weapons whispered free of their sheaths, clanking and scraping against armor and shields as the formation sped up.

"If they hadn't seen us, they'll hear that," Kevon laughed as Carlo fixed his shield and limbered his sword, walking backward to survey the livening army behind them.

"This is without question the most fearsome force I have had the honor of commanding," he told Kevon, stepping around to resume his advance. "What lies ahead is beyond doubt the most deadly opposition in our Realm, but we've already proven what we can accomplish against them, on their terms. I'm eager to see how they fare against us in the light, when we don't have to focus a good deal of our efforts on overcoming the night."

"Should have said that at breakfast," Kevon joked.

"It would have been lost on many," Carlo shrugged. "The rest already feel it. They will give it their all. No one is here against their will. They know if we don't turn back the tide of darkness, there will be none that can."

"To victory," Kevon nodded to Carlo, and brandished the sword once more, wrapping himself in the weapon's guiding power, and extending his senses through the vile chaos that permeated the battlefield that lay ahead.

The flight of griffin overhead tickled the back of Kevon's mind, as the leathery wings and claws of the approaching flight of gargoyles raked through his consciousness. He flicked a bead of power at one of the lead gargoyles, but at this distance the barrier of Wind he erected did little more than slow the grotesque beast.

Stay back, keep together. Kevon's mind wandered back to the briefing Carlo had held with Rhysabeth-Dane and Nalsi. *Don't let them draw you away from us too far. Break up their formations, but leave plenty of open area that the Magi and archers can use to their advantage.*

The Unbound, led by the pair of Riders, circled in the sky above, climbing high above the marching troops, higher already than the approaching demons.

"Shame they couldn't attack from cover like last time," Carlo clicked his tongue.

"Rhysabeth-Dane says it shouldn't make too much of a difference, attacking from above, out of the sun. They'll have the advantage for certain."

"Good, because it looks like they're outnumbered."

Kevon shielded his eyes to watch the approaching gargoyles, and even against the rising din of the Dwarven war machine grinding behind him, heard the approaching wave of leapers.

"Steady now!" Carlo barked, slowing and gesturing for the flag crew to step back behind the first few ranks of

Dwarves.

Kevon kept more distance between himself and the front line than Carlo, who had settled into an opening that the signal crew had slipped through.

"Careful, boy," the Commander shouted as the wave of sickly-white demons lurched toward them.

Kevon reached out with his mind, through the sword's Earth rune, and felt the patterns of the lead leapers as they bounded along.

Hop, hop, hop... NOW! He thought, and a small earthen barrier slid up. Arm-thick, waist high, less than ten paces across, it snaked in a squiggle pattern not twenty paces from Kevon.

Five leapers smashed into the sudden wall, shattering it under the crashing impacts. Their lifeless bodies pitched forward through the rubble, tripping up others who had anticipated cleaner landings.

A Dwarven crossbow volley resulted in similar pile-ups along the visible front, and then the battle was joined.

Leaps that carried the pasty demons deep into the third and fourth ranks did not inspire the fear that might have broken a lesser force. Casual overhead swings of war-axes dispatched most of the overeager leapers before they hit the ground. The ripples in the march were dictated more by fallen enemies than actual fighting.

The front line wavered and slowed as the shape of the attack changed, leapers stopping short of the advancing line to spring forward into the front ranks like demented battering rams.

Kevon sidestepped one leaper after another, cutting down those he could reach in time, depending on the strength of the line behind him to deal with anything that slipped past the small sphere of his influence.

Darker shades of evil cropped up in the gaps between the bounding leapers. Reapers and orcs skittered and marched behind the wave of leapers, advancing with inexorable purpose.

This must be taking an incredible amount of control, Kevon thought, hopping to the side to avoid one leaper's charge, and slashing at another that landed too close. *Can we break it?*

The wave of leapers thinned, and the battlefield before them started to open up between the advancing fronts. Kevon used a gust of Wind magic to sweep the feet out from under the last leaper ahead of him before it landed, and hurried the few paces forward to dispatch the keening beast. He stepped on the creature's back, and used the extra leverage to pull his sword free of its still quivering corpse. A flick of the blade and Water magic, and the gore coating the weapon's surface flew free. Kevon took a few steps forward and sheathed the blade. He knelt, and pressed outward with his senses.

In his mind's eye, Kevon could see the fragile tethers that stretched from the unseen Magi behind the enemy forces to each individual demon that marched toward them. *That's their weakness,* he thought. *They need to keep them all focused so they don't fight each other.*

Testing his theory, he formed the Counter and Control runes, and slashed the connections of several reapers near the back edge of the march, those nearest the orcs that marched behind.

The orc line flexed as freed reapers struck out at orcs that remained held in check by their controlling Magi. One of the larger bulls toppled, before the Control spells resumed and the interruption disappeared behind the advancing line of gleaming black chitin.

"It's not enough," Kevon groaned, retaking his feet. "It's too much effort for too little result. We have to take out the enemy Magi, and then their army will destroy itself."

"I would rather that than destroy them ourselves," Carlo responded as he caught up to Kevon. "How do you propose we do that?"

"We have to get to them," Kevon answered. "The Riders and the Unbound are our best chance."

Carlo looked to the chaos that filled the skies. "They're busy right now," he grunted. "Have any other ideas?"

"Hold on," Kevon sighed, reaching for the sword's hilt and kneeling to touch the ground. He refocused his attention forward as Carlo barked orders to his signal crew to halt their advance.

Kevon read the lines of force that led from part of the army before him, through the fragmented Dark magic that suffused the area. His senses spinning from the sustained effort, he aligned the focal point with a working of Earth magic focused through the sword. When he was confident that the magic was positioned, he shoved his will into the spell. He shouted, a wordless scream that accompanied the swift upward clawing motion of his outstretched free hand.

A full third of the reapers in the center of the advancing line stopped.

Ignoring the chaos his action had just created, Kevon traced another set of lines, and readied another spike of Earth magic.

He released the coiled magic, but it slipped away as soon as he moved to strike. He tried again, only to be stopped before he was even halfway through preparing the energy required to attack the next Mage.

"They've figured it out," Kevon shook his head as he stood. "They can't sense my magic, but they're countering it blindly. I can't do it again unless they're distracted."

"Help the Riders," Carlo ordered, pointing a thumb at the sky. "They'll be your distraction. Fall back through the front lines while we buy you time."

Kevon nodded, and began jogging toward the front of the Dwarven army, motioning for a clear path. He trotted a dozen ranks deep, and stopped, communicating with hand signals for the surrounding Dwarves to stand well clear of him as the path he'd come through closed up behind him. He retook the hilt of the sword, and turned his gaze skyward.

CHAPTER 63

"**Y**ou might want to do something about the weakness forming in the line to our left," Anneliese commented to Avolentz as she sidestepped a charge from an armored leaper and loosed a pair of deadly arrows at two large orcs charging toward the area she'd just mentioned.

"And leave you with nothing to do?" the general laughed, and motioned to the line behind him to shift and cover the gaps.

"I only have so many arrows," the Huntmistress retorted, sliding the bow under the leather strap that angled down from her shoulder quiver to her swordbelt. She released the weapon and drew her short bladed sword, dancing into the oncoming surge of demons. She ducked, slashing the arm free from a reaper at the shoulder joint. She took two quick steps and leapt past the screaming beast, high into the air. She landed hard on the back of a leaper, her boot heel crunching through layers of thick skin to bone buried deep within. The pasty creature keened and fell to the side as she leaped off to attack her next target.

She shrugged off an ineffective strike from the young bull orc she'd just disemboweled, and slid around behind the fading beast to hamstring one of its larger brethren before fighting her way back toward Yusa and Avolentz.

"Miss us?" Avolentz panted, leaning on his blood-smeared greatsword, his face and armor spattered in a rainbow of different colors of blood and ichor from the enemies that lay in heaps around them.

"Stow the yammering," Yusa hollered, smashing his cudgel into the skull of a charging orc. "All three of you. What the hell is a 'fiss moovra'?"

Yusa staggered as flames erupted in front of a diving gargoyle, and the creature plummeted into a pile of corpses, smoking and twitching for a moment after impact.

"Oh no," the sailor growled, shaking his fist in front of his own face. "Don't drag me into that. Magic is *your* job!"

"If it's helping," Avolentz huffed, standing tall and raising his blade, "I think it's your job too. Forward, men!"

Avolentz charged over the heap of bodies, and his sweeping parries tore the scythe-arms from three reapers as he rushed through to strike at an advancing chimaera.

The line shifted forward to aid the general, dispatching the wounded demons Avolentz left in his wake.

Darting forward to get a better angle, Anneliese drew her bow and buried three arrows in the chimaera's flank as it turned to ready a strike with its poison-spiked tail. She laughed at the beast's pained screams, and switched weapons again to engage a trio of armored leapers.

"*Phes... movra!*" Yusa yelled, sounding more confident than his last attempt, and a brilliant globe of fire streaked from his outstretched hand to strike the snarling chimaera in the opposite flank as it swiveled to face the circling Avolentz. The magical orb detonated, creating a gaping crater of charred flesh. The beast turned to claw at its damaged side, and fell, flapping its working wing in erratic lurches.

"More of that!" Avolentz roared, leaping atop the fallen chimaera. He plunged the first two feet of his sword into the twisted creature's ribcage and tore it free with a flourish, bounding on toward his next target.

Marelle slid through the chaos, sword and dagger glinting in the afternoon sun. She slashed and jabbed at one enemy after another. The blade carved large, crippling wounds, while the knife struck killing blows when weaknesses showed themselves.

The battlefield writhed in her vision, similar but distinct images overlapping and recombining in a haze of shifting translucent demons. The vision in her altered eye pulsed and lurched, but she compensated with her normal vision, and continued her ferocious trek through the thick of the enemy forces.

"Hold!" Bertus cried from somewhere behind her, at the steady, unmoving line where Stoneguard hacked away at the oncoming horde.

Plenty of killing to be done there, but it's tedious, lacks artistry, Marelle thought as she glanced in his direction. *I'd better go help anyway.*

She sprinted through a chance opening that led back toward the others. Vaulting over a crouching leaper, Marelle sprang up over the fray. She changed direction by dragging her sword around the neck of a convenient bull orc, and stabbed a reaper square in the top of its eyeball as she slid past and landed in front of it. She swore as the knife stuck, and tore from her grasp.

I'll be back for that, she thought as she rolled under the reflexive swipes of the creature's scythe-arms, drew a replacement knife, and began fighting her way back to her friends.

The twisted energy of further distorted Darkness tugged at Marelle's vision, from beyond her peripheral range. A shadowy figure wreathed in chaos stood beside an expanding portal that loomed over the battlefield. Reapers skittered in from the sides of the massive doorway, but the ground trembled as a leg taller than a man, a wickedly curving onyx-hued blade, stabbed into the ground a hundred yards from the front lines.

Marelle turned, leaping, dodging, cutting her way through the next few seconds it took her to reach the front, and Bertus. "That," she shouted, pointing at the monstrosity lumbering through the portal, "Cannot happen."

Bertus shouted orders, and the line shifted, closing up as he stepped free of it, lighter armored dwarves stepping up from the ranks behind. He dashed forward kicking a bull orc in the chest, stunning the beast before cleaving its weapon arm and head from its body. Taking a few quick breaths, he stepped over the fallen orc, and turned back to Marelle.

"Lead the way."

Marelle nodded, and sprinted for the portal. She wove in and out of the crush of advancing demons, diving under, leaping over, killing only when it would not slow her down. Her heart pounded in her chest, and she could feel Bertus close on her heels, hear his rapid footfalls and the shrieks of his victims as he kept pace. She ran harder.

Three steps off of two orcs and a reaper turned into a diving somersault, severing one of the hind legs from an armored leaper as she landed. She dodged around the toppling demon, parrying a reaper's attack and hamstringed an orc as she rolled to her feet and resumed her wild run.

Bertus's bellows as he struck down more foes close behind her faded as she saw more of the behemoth emerging from the portal. She missed a step, and stumbled, her sword clattering to the ground beneath a reaper that turned to face her. She stood, not needing to look at her palms. The stinging of torn flesh seared at the forefront of her heightened senses, and her anger flared white hot.

"Mind if I run ahead?" Bertus called as he bounded past, shuffling a step and incapacitating the reaper with two swipes of his ancient Dwarven blade.

Marelle surged forward, recovering her sword and slicing off a strip of her tunic as she leapt over the flailing demon. *Step. Step. Dodge. Leap. Duck.* Her hands were wrapped and she had almost caught up to Bertus within the space of ten breaths.

The Warrior's unnatural strength and superior weapon cleared the path ahead in a wider swath than she had for him, albeit at a slower pace.

Marelle tested her weapons against demons that straggled into Bertus's wake, wincing at the pain that screamed through her senses with every sword-stroke, every dagger swipe.

Already struggling with the pain, Marelle steeled her nerves as more of the gigantic demon emerged from the portal.

Darkly gleaming chitin scimitars slid out of the putrid abyss, stretching twice as long as a man's height before the elbow joints emerged. Two more legs swiveled into view, and tensed as a portion of the creature's body lurched into view.

The beast's roar resounded over the battlefield, its slavering jaws dripping with saliva and other things that Marelle was loathe to speculate about. The arms that had preceded the body connected at the corner of the mouth, and set to work stabbing and shoveling orcs and leapers from below into its gnashing maw.

Another lurching step forward, and the creature shrieked, fanning the empty blades on each arm into wedges three wide. It held the fanned fingers to the sides of what passed for its chin, throwing deeper shadows on the faceted bulb that hung underneath, just in front of the first set of legs.

The demon's movement slowed to a halt, and its legs bent, its body crouching low. A swollen, low-hanging sac writhed, and the bottom end dilated. An Obsidian Reaper slipped free, dropping onto the battlefield below. The newborn tore free of the remnants of its birth, and began its march toward the Dwarven line.

"My weapons won't be able to..." Marelle began as she overtook Bertus.

"Mine either." he panted, cutting down an orc and leaping over it. "I think we may just need to deal with *that*."

Marelle followed Bertus's gaze to the Dark-shrouded figure standing at the edge of the portal. The raw Dark energy stabbed into her vision, and she shook her head to clear the sensation. She glanced back up at the towering Queen Reaper, and shuddered. "Let's get to it."

The two charged ahead, blazing a path of destruction through their scattered enemies.

Bertus swerved to the left as the shadowy figure began its retreat. He plowed through a knot of leapers, leaving pieces of each twitching on the battlefield behind him.

A leg from the overhanging queen stabbed downward, and Marelle slid to the right, kicking an orc in the head to help correct her trajectory back toward where Bertus began engaging the dark figure.

Their enemy leapt and whirled, his movements mostly concealed behind the veil of Dark magic. Wicked blades curved outward to strike at Bertus, slicing and nicking here and there, never intersecting steel.

The ancient Dwarven blade swung with increasing speed. Bertus advanced, his sword-strokes claiming demons to either side that ventured too close, but never connecting with the foe that danced before him.

"Watch out!" Marelle shouted, diving past a freshly dropped reaper's attack.

"*Oof,*" Bertus grunted, leaping back as the Reaper Queen's mandible-scimitar sliced into the ground between the Dark Mage and himself.

"Now!" she cried, sprinting forward as the sword-fingers wrenched strips of earth free and dropped them on the upward motion, to rain back down in a shower of dust and clods.

The shrouded figure slowed as Bertus and Marelle angled in from different directions. The surrounding demons rushed clear, throwing themselves against the advancing Dwarven army.

"He can't face us both," Bertus hissed, and began his attacks anew.

Marelle whirled in, blocking the Dark One's retreat with a blur of flashing steel.

Bertus pressed the attack, sliding around one attack

after another, swinging his sword at a frantic pace.

The Dark shrouded figure whirled back toward Marelle.

She leaned backward, avoiding the reaper-blades aimed at her neck, but her shortsword tangled in the Dark One's cloak as he spun. The blade slipped free of her bandaged hand, flung aside to the ground.

Bertus chopped through the space his enemy had just occupied, the haze of the Dark One's passage lingering as he cartwheeled away.

"No!" Marelle screamed as another Dark portal opened in front of the fleeing Mage. She drew and flung daggers one after the other. *Boot, boot, wrist, wrist... damn!* she thought as she released her last thrown knife, reaching for the last blade she'd left stuck in a reaper minutes earlier.

The Dark One grunted and stumbled as a thrown knife struck him. The whorling Darkness that surrounded him evaporated as the portal in front of him collapsed.

Marelle caught up her sword as she sprinted after the stricken Mage, who still writhed in pain.

With a strangled cry, the Dark One wrenched the knife free and cast it aside. The swirling Darkness reformed as the Mage turned, pointing upward as he did so.

Without thinking, Marelle slowed and followed his gesture, to where the Reaper Queen flailed and shrieked under the crush of the portal closing around her. She turned back in time to see the remnants of another collapsing portal where the Dark One had been.

"Run," Bertus took hold of Marelle's hand and began pulling as fat droplets of steaming ichor started to rain down upon them.

CHAPTER 64

*T*he line is breaking.

Kevon startled at Reko's thought-forms whispering across his mind, and chanced a glance back down to the front of the battlefield.

Hold just a little longer, he replied, furious at the slight expenditure of magic required. *We've almost taken control of the upper battlefield.*

Focusing on the Wind rune inscribed on the sword, Kevon slammed three gargoyles with stunning blasts of air, and the Unbound made quick work of them. He dazed two more before the counter-magic started to interfere again.

"There's either a lot more of them than we thought, or they are far better prepared than we are," Kevon grumbled, switching tactics, targeting different quadrants of the sky above at random, getting a strike in once in a while, as the griffin and Riders above continued to tear through the dwindling numbers of the gargoyles.

The lines of Control that filled the sky faded, and the remaining gargoyles screeched and broke off their attack, attempting to flee. The Unbound made short work of the disorganized remainder of the demons, while Rhysabeth-Dane and Nalsi led some of their Unbound followers higher over the battlefield toward the source of the Control magic.

Find the Magi, Kevon reminded Nalsi with an illusion-enhanced whisper. *Break them, and we win the day.*

Kevon released the magic. He closed his eyes and rubbed his temples for a moment before looking to the battle ahead for visible signs of interruption of the controlling spells that kept the demon army in check. He gauged his reserves were down to about a third, and wondered how long they would hold.

Nalsi dove, unleashing the flames she had withheld the entire battle.

Without trying, Kevon felt the rising of several counter-magic runes. Two of them ended with a *sploosh* of power, the others slicing through Nalsi's staff's inferno, ending the blazing swath that poured down behind enemy lines.

Now, he thought, expending half of the magic he had left to strike upward at the places he felt the counter-magic coming from with Earth power. Two of the spikes struck true, but his second attempt met redirected counter-runes.

The enemy line shrank back in confusion without the direction of the driving Magi. Dwarven war-cries rose as the Stoneguard rallied and began to press forward.

"No!" Kevon cried as the sky above the enemy Magi opened and more gargoyles poured out from the hovering Dark portals. He grasped the sword and flung power into Earth spells, managing to get two or three to connect before the magic ran out. He drew the blade and charged through the ranks of dwarves to the front. As he began moving, he saw the portals collapse into nothingness, and the flow of gargoyles ended.

Kevon reached the front, and sliced into three orcs and a reaper before the enemy army turned to flee.

"Bring up the cavalry, and the Magi!" Carlo shouted to the signal-crew. "They're on the run. Finish it!"

Nalsi strafed the far end of the battlefield again with flame, and Kevon felt all the other magic in the broken caldera wink out. The gargoyles flew in confused, random patterns while the more focused Unbound descended on them, scouring the newly arrived demons from the sky.

"We've broken the Magi," Kevon wheezed, looking to Carlo for instruction.

"Rest a moment while the others move into position,"

Carlo ordered. "Without their Magi, we should tear through the rest of these without many more casualties."

"Let's hope," Kevon answered, rocking back on his heels. He cleared his throat and spat battlefield dust, then started taking deep, calming breaths. His apprehension and the knotted pit in his stomach twisted deeper, and he cried out as the taste of the Dark rune caressed his mind.

"There!" Kevon cried out, pointing the tip of his sword to the portal and the Dark Mage standing in front of it atop the upper ridge on the far side of the caldera.

The Dark magic waned as the portal closed, and Kevon could feel a different spell building. He sensed the Earth rune, distant, imperfect in the chaos, but strong, powered by a Mage with deep reserves of magical energy. Unable to bring even a weak counter-rune to the battle with the scraps of energy he'd regenerated, Kevon stood and watched as the distant Magi completed his spell, and the side of the mountain shuddered and collapsed.

"Oh... no..." one of the signal-crew moaned at the sight of the horrors emerging from the dust and rubble.

"Recall the cavalry," Carlo ordered. "Gather the Magi here. We may have to retreat."

Kevon wiped the sweat from his eyes and gazed toward the open side of the mountain. "I was not counting on that," he sighed. "One, we've handled before. Two or three, with this army, sure."

"Five... six." Carlo swore under his breath, and turned to Kevon. "How on Ærth are we going to kill six Orclords?"

CHAPTER 65

"Lead the Magi back through the lines," Carlo ordered as soon as they converged near the command area. "Figure out what you can manage, and be ready to aid our retreat if it comes to that. I don't see the lesser creatures being much of a threat, but I'm not looking forward to running all the way back to the fortress with those pursuing us."

"Follow me," Kevon whispered to the nearby Magi, and the sea of Dwarves parted as he approached.

"How much strength have you left?" Kevon asked as they reached the back edge of the formation.

"Some," Yusa shrugged. "Not much?"

"Eat. Drink. Rest," Kevon took a few measured breaths before he continued. "Defend yourselves if you need to, but watch for my signal, a flash of light. Be ready to aid."

"What are you going to do?" Yusa followed Kevon back toward the front, stopping as the Blademage began threading his way back between the parting dwarves.

"I have no idea," Kevon admitted, then shouted ahead to alert the forward ranks to his passage.

"What're you...?" Carlo asked as Kevon rejoined him.

"They're holding in reserve, and will help me if I need it," Kevon answered. "It didn't feel right waiting at the back. I'm sure the dwarves prefer to have me up here, too."

"I'll take every advantage we can get," Carlo chuckled. "What in the blazes is happening over there?"

"They're hungry," Kevon shuddered as the Orclords set upon the pile of carcasses in the center of the caldera that the rest of the dark army had been feasting on before the battle.

One of the beasts stood, and turned toward the waiting army. It pounded its head with its great fists, and roared at the sky before gazing downward and beginning a steady march toward Kevon and his allies.

"It's a lot tougher to control than they're used to," Kevon guessed. "They expected to have more Magi when they resorted to this."

"They can only send one at a time?" Carlo asked. "Can we handle one at a time?"

"The first one, sure," Kevon answered. "The sword and the Magi behind us about make up for the sympathetic magic I can't draw from the ground here. I can whip up a spike that will run him through. Then it will depend on what the others have left, and how fast that Mage can send another one after us."

"So we should kill the Mage, and run away." Carlo decided.

"Please, can we?" Kevon asked, with a half-hearted chuckle. "We've slain a lot of their Magi, and dispatched a good deal of their army here."

"I can't imagine they would show these Orclords they've been holding in reserve if they weren't desperate," Carlo agreed. "So how do we kill him?"

"They're already working on it," Kevon pointed to the Unbound diving toward the distant Mage. "Look!"

Portals flashed in and out of existence. Gargoyles popped into being in front of diving griffin, and half a dozen collisions resulted in demons and griffin plummeting to the caldera floor below. More portals winked open and closed, and other Unbound vanished, swallowed up.

"Whatever you're going to do," Carlo shouted, "Do it now!"

With a whisper of Wind magic, Kevon peered through a distortion and saw the foe they faced. "Keldra," he spat.

"From the tower on..." Carlo grimaced. "*Damnation.*"

Rhysabeth-Dane and Nalsi banked in different directions and spun around to converge toward Keldra's position.

Have to try something, Kevon thought, channeling a trickle of power through the Light rune on the sword. A burst of radiance shone in the sky over the Dwarven army, and Kevon felt the strings of offered power from the Magi behind him.

Gathering the magical threads, Kevon wove them into his own reserves and began forming a handful of different spells.

Keldra staggered as the ground beneath him buckled, but he countered the weak spell an instant after it took shape.

Smiling, Kevon shifted to the Wind spell he'd held in reserve, and bashed the staff the Dark Mage held aloft out of his hands to fall the hundreds of feet down the steep wall of the caldera to the rocks below.

The approaching Orclord roared, glancing over its shoulder to the brawl starting over the remnants of the food pile.

"Not so tough without your magic stick, are you?" Kevon chuckled. He jabbed and feinted at the Mage with Wind and Earth spells for a few seconds until Nalsi dove in close.

Keldra countered the blast of flame, but his control over the Orclord slipped away as the Dark Mage seemed to shift to focus on defense.

And... there! Kevon thought as he wove Earth and Wind spells together into a many-pronged attack that blasted the enemy Mage off the side of the cliff.

"Yes!" Carlo shouted, and the army behind them roared.

No, Kevon thought as his insides twisted up once more. Below the falling Mage, Kevon could feel a Dark portal opening.

Using most of the power left at his disposal, Kevon unleashed a dazzling burst of Light magic between Keldra and the portal. Overpowered, the Dark magic dissolved, and Keldra fell to the rocks below.

"Is that it, lad?" Carlo asked, blinking and rubbing his eyes. "Is he done for?"

"He is," Kevon gulped, exploring the depths of the reserves the other Magi still offered. "I don't know if we have enough magic left for even this Orclord."

Carlo looked to where the Orclord strolled through the remnants of the dark army, stooping to snatch up reapers to crush and swallow whole. Half of the orcs rallied to their giant brother, the other half fleeing with the rest of the reapers.

"I think this one's going to be a problem," Carlo shook his head. "If we can retreat, the others may be slowed by the battlefield remains for long enough that we can make it back to the fortress. We can hold there."

Kevon released the magic. "A few minutes, and we'll have enough power to kill it."

"We'll buy you those minutes," Carlo nodded, and began barking orders to the remaining member of the signal-crew.

"Wait," Kevon groaned, as his senses wrenched again. "Something's not right."

The portal that opened near the Orclord closed in seconds, but darkness continued to swirl around the figure that emerged from it. Reaper-screeches sounded, and some of the scattered demons rushed to the newcomer's side.

"I don't see this working in our favor," Carlo murmured.

"No," Kevon agreed, and opened his senses to gather any information he could from the mysterious interloper.

The Darkness was a strong, vile force that flowed around the newcomer, but it was not being used for anything. No magic that Kevon could feel kept the distortion around the shrieking figure maintained, *it just WAS.*

"I'd rather not talk with this... whoever it is," Kevon stammered. "I'm good with killing the Orclord and running away. We did not need *this!*"

"Is it a Mage?" Carlo asked, taking a step forward.

"It would have to be, to go through one of those Dark portals," Kevon's voice cracked, uncertainty he'd not felt in a long while showing in his voice. "But I think this is something different."

"Ahh!" Kevon cried out as his guts twisted with the spike of Dark power that formed a portal that the newcomer and a handful of his reaper followers dashed into.

Another portal opened a few yards away, and they reappeared, screeching, and on the offensive.

In the moments before the newcomer clashed with Carlo's Stoneguard escorts, Kevon got a better look at him.

It was a man, and an old one, at that. A frazzled shock of pure white hair atop its head and a trimmed gray beard showed through the distortion waves as the man danced toward the advancing dwarves. Kevon could see the man wore armor crafted from reaper carapace, fitted and worn with age and use, but light enough it did not hamper his movement. High arcing leaps with closely held blades that absorbed light rather than reflecting it flowed into savage slashes of the midnight-hued weapons, and a fallen Stoneguard.

Carlo blocked the attacker's rush with his shield, and kicked out to unbalance him for a follow-up slash.

The man hissed, ducking back to avoid the kick, and found the weakness in another Stoneguard's defenses. More dwarves rushed forward to avenge their fallen brothers, but the portal reopened, and the mysterious figure back-flipped into it and vanished, leaving the reapers behind to engage.

Kevon whirled and slashed as the portal opened behind him. The distorted fellow dropped to the ground and rolled even as Kevon's sword intersected and disrupted the Dark portal.

Dark portals began forming on all sides of Kevon. He lashed out at them instinctively, slicing through the magic before anything could venture forth from the Plane of Darkness.

The distorted stranger shrieked again, brandishing his blades, and gazed to the sky where Rhysabeth-Dane and Brightwing swooped down at him.

With a wave of one of his wickedly curved blades, the

feral Dark Mage opened up a Dark portal between himself and Rhysabeth-Dane, and closed it a second later when the Rider and her griffin disappeared through it.

"No!" Kevon shouted, leaping toward the gnarled beast of a man. The Rider and her steed were gone, and Kevon did not have the strength to open a portal of his own to attempt a rescue. He howled in anguish, forcing a thread of power through an improvised Movement rune to speed his attack.

The man blocked with one of his reaper-scythe blades, and Kevon's vision blurred as the area exploded with raw Dark magic.

Kevon snatched the power before it could be absorbed into the depths of the sword, pushing down the urge to vomit. He crafted a portal in the same area as the one they'd disappeared into, and held it open as he burned through the Dark magic that coursed through his soul like venom. He kicked the man full in his chestplate, but his wiry adversary grinned, meeting Kevon's glare with shiny black orbs for eyes. He flipped back through a newly opened portal, and vanished.

"*Graaaaah!*" Kevon screamed, shaking as the last of the Dark magic left him. The portal began to close, and Rhysabeth-Dane and Brightwing flew out just before it became too narrow. "Oh!" he cried, dropping the sword and falling to the ground, propping himself up to vomit.

"Where'd he go?" Carlo asked, pulling his sword free from the last reaper the feral Mage had brought with him. "What... what's wrong?"

"We need..." Kevon wheezed between gasps for breath. "To get... away from... here... now."

"The Orclord..." Carlo argued.

Kevon reached out for his fallen sword and the threads of power that the Magi in the back of the formation still offered. He pulled in all that he could take from them, and focused it through the blade and the ground.

A single stone shaft erupted from the ground in front of the advancing Orclord, and speared through the center of its chest and out through the base of its neck. It roared, gurgled, and fell, snapping the stone lance that was the instrument of its demise.

The remainder of the dark army broke and fled, splitting into groups that followed the mountain range to either side of the caldera where the remaining Orclords still fed.

"Kevon. Kevon!" Carlo shouted, running to his friend as he slumped back down on the ground.

"Mar..." Kevon whispered, his eyes threatening to roll back in his head. "Martin..." he coughed, as a gentler darkness enfolded him.

CHAPTER 66

"Finally awake," Carlo rumbled, handing Kevon a waterskin. "Drink. It's been hours since we began the march back to the fortress."

"My mouth feels like it's stuffed full of *covaninal* silk," Kevon groaned, and sat up in the makeshift litter attached to the riding-vole. "The Orclords?"

"Still feasting on the battlefield," Carlo shrugged, looking to the southeastern sky. "The last time Nalsi reported."

"Rhysabeth-Dane?" Kevon asked, between draughts from the skin.

"There," Carlo pointed across the temporary encampment to another litter, where Brightwing curled up, sleeping, near the Dwarven Rider's feet. "She's sleeping, finally. By the time we got to her, all the healing potions we brought along had been used."

"What's being done for..." Kevon struggled to his feet and took a few halting steps toward the still form of the dwarf. His muscles ached from the exertion of the past few days, and he still tasted the evil of the Dark rune he'd had to wrestle with to get her back. Flashes of the battle spun through his head, and he staggered. "Martin!"

"You called out his name before you collapsed," Carlo reached out to steady Kevon. "Why is that?"

"It was..." Kevon whispered. "Somehow, it was him. I saw it in his face when we clashed. His eyes were all wrong, but it was Martin, I'm sure of it. He looked older than you..."

"We already know time passes strangely in those

places," Carlo shrugged. "He's spent decades in the darkness, and learned a few things?"

"He wasn't a Mage when I knew him, or even when we last saw him," Kevon shook his head. "Holten would have groomed him for more if there had been any capacity for what he just showed he could do. I'm sure of it. The only..."

"What?"

"The blades..." Kevon groaned. "When we crossed swords, the magic in his blade unraveled, and I took control of it. Those blades could be the source of his power, he has just practiced long enough to control the release of the magic from them. With enough time, that should be possible if you had any aptitude at all."

"A Mage who's not a Mage," Carlo let out a low whistle. "One who has been nursing a grudge and training in impossible conditions for maybe as long as either of us has been alive."

"I deprived him of half of his magic," Kevon shrugged. "That's something."

"It may have already been years where he is at," Carlo countered.

"And if the source of his power is L'mort himself it wouldn't take years to replace that single lost resource." Kevon scowled. "I was hoping for better news."

"She's awake."

"Oh!" Kevon staggered the rest of the way to Rhysabeth-Dane, slowing as Brightwing raised his head to glare in Kevon's direction. "How do you feel?"

"Lucky to... be alive," the Rider whispered. "Over an hour... lost, fighting, fleeing. I'd almost... given up hope."

"It was less than a minute here," Kevon lowered his gaze. "I didn't have the strength to open another portal. It was lucky I could steal the power to do so that soon."

The tiny dwarf startled as she took a breath, and a wound on her arm reopened.

"I'm sorry that you had to go though that," Kevon sniffed, reaching to readjust the bandage. "No one should ever have to go through that. All of that darkness. You should..."

Brilliance washed through Kevon's mind as his right hand touched the wound, his left brushing against his sword's hilt. Streamers of light bent and flowed into the jagged cut, visible even behind the bandage now. The warmth emanating from Kevon's hand felt familiar, something that he thought he should be able to remember, but could not quite grasp.

Rhysabeth-Dane winced, drawing in a slow breath, but held still as the skin around the wound pulsated, and knit together.

Letting the magic take control, Kevon did his best to keep from interfering with it. He let the power flow from him, and the Light rune brightened in his mind. Ethereal whispers drifted through his thoughts, ghostly fingers caressing the inside of his skull, an icy warmth that calmed as it excited.

"Something forgotten," Kevon murmured, letting go of both Rhysabeth-Dane and the sword as the Light rune began to glow in deeper intensity.

"I've seen something like this before," Anneliese interjected from nearby. "I watched from above, in the trees. You were the one at the center, surrounded by my people. Brought back from the edge of death, over the course of several weeks."

"It's all Light..." Kevon breathed. "Light, life, creation, healing. It's all light it's all Her."

"You've got a special connection to her, there," Carlo nodded. "That's... I don't rightly know what to make of it."

"I don't either," Kevon admitted. "Are you all right?"

"Thirsty," Rhysabeth-Dane sighed. "Better."

"I think you're going to be fine," Kevon stood and handed her a waterskin that Carlo passed to him. "There must be other wounded. Take me to them."

"Not the triumphant return we planned," Carlo sat his pack down on the stone desk in the fortress's war-room, and glanced at the others filtering into the room behind him. "Just when we defeat one enemy, new ones rise to take their places."

"The loss of even one Orclord here will serve to weaken L'mort's hold on this realm, I hope." Kevon looked into Carlo's eyes. "We need more strength to truly defeat the forces we know are aligning against us."

"We could try and recruit more Elves," the Commander suggested. "Anneliese should be able to convince the Elders to aid us in some way."

"I would have liked easier access to fire," Kevon admitted. "I should finish the quest given to me by M'lani, and seek out the Seat of Fire."

"The book!" Rhysabeth-Dane interjected. "I'm so close to finishing the translation, I'm sure of it. If I could only..."

"Go with Anneliese," Kevon suggested. "If you pass through Eastport, and leave word with the myrnar at the embassy to have scholars meet you on the Glimmering Isle..."

"We'll have Elven, Myrnar, and Dwarven scholars all in one place. Brightwing has been able to communicate much of what the symbols of Wind mean, and he'll be with me."

"Someone will have to stay behind and defend this place," Bertus shrugged. "Mirsa and I can coordinate things here, with Avolentz's support."

"If I hadn't witnessed your fighting prowess myself, I might have been offended by that suggestion," the general chuckled. "As things stand now, my men and I would be honored to assist you."

"Many of my people have lost their lives in the last few days," Britger-Stoun began. "There may be more that we can do, given the strength of the foes we face. I will ask my uncle to open the Deep Vaults. There may be help within them that we can bring to this fight."

"I'd like to make sure we have enough Magi to adequately defend our interests," Kevon added. 'Three, minimum, everywhere. I'd like nine, or a dozen here, if possible."

"Nalsi, with the majority of the Unbound, is one that

should remain here," Carlo nodded. "We'll draw up assignments before we decide who leaves tomorrow."

"Britger-Stoun is already on his way to speak to the king," Carlo announced as Kevon blinked into view in the middle of the Sending chamber.

"Rhysabeth-Dane should reach Eastport within the week," Kevon reminded the Blademaster. "You'll want to be there when she arrives."

"She said to send the skergiz her regards," Carlo countered, turning to exit the chamber. "I have travel arrangements to make, and they don't include voles."

Kevon watched as Carlo left, then waited for Yusa and Mirsa to arrive before setting out to find Tamaraith.

"Alright. Let me see if I'm understanding this. You think the Fire seat could be at the base of the volcano in Malcaea, near the center of Skergiz territory." Kevon waited for the faint hissing that passed for a nod from Tamaraith. "You think you could get us there, as long as the right factions are still in power?"

"You say we need this, and it was kind of already on our list of things to do," Yusa shrugged. "Everyone else is ready to do their part so that we can return to the south and finish what we started."

"We can't be the one thing that holds up the war effort," Marelle raised an eyebrow as she looked at Kevon. "You really want to get shown up by an old man and a dwarf on a boat?"

"We need to survive it," Kevon answered. "The safest place I can recall near the volcano is the smithy. We can't just appear inside an inn with our friend here."

The skergiz rasped in laughter.

"Just go first and make sure the way is clear," Marelle suggested.

"I have to go last, to make sure you all get there," Kevon

explained. "No one else can Send me, either, because of the sword."

"All right," Yusa squinted. "Marelle and I first, then Tamaraith. You follow as soon as you can."

"That may work," Kevon admitted. "Let's prepare what we need tonight, and leave first thing in the morning."

"That can wait," Yusa laughed. "I smelled griddle-cakes as we passed by the mess hall. Have you tried them yet, Tamaraith?"

The skergiz followed Yusa out of the room, rattling a negative, his tail lashing invisible figure-eights as he stalked out behind the Captain.

Griddle cakes? Marelle thought at Kevon as she leaned into his arms.

They can wait, he answered in kind. He held her close without thinking anything for a few moments before stepping back and sliding his hand into hers.

EPILOGUE

"It's strange," Mirsa chuckled, as Anneliese stepped up alongside her at the stone railing. "Not a single griffin. Rhysabeth-Dane told me that there were quite a few Unbound that chose to stay behind when she led them south to the fortress."

"I saw a handful of them yesterday," the Huntmistress offered. "Perhaps they hunt this afternoon."

"I've been here since dawn," the Mage sighed. "I hoped to see *something*. Not even a hawk has graced the western sky. It's better than watching for gargoyles, though."

"I'm here," Anneliese squeezed Mirsa's hand. "You should get something to eat, sleep for a watch before I have to leave for Eastport, and you rotate back to the fortress. We can't be on high alert every waking moment. It warps the spirit."

"Makes you see things..." Mirsa whispered, her eyelids fluttering as she turned her attention back toward the passageway leading down to the lower Hold.

"That's..." Anneliese's hand gripped Mirsa's tighter. "I see it too," she breathed, pointing to the winged figure in the distance to the north as it climbed into the clouds, angling back toward the east.

"That was no griffin," the Mage commented, leaning over the stone railing to get a better look at the patch of sky where they'd noticed the creature.

Dread gripped Mirsa as she caught another flash of the winged beast as it slipped from one concealing cloud to another. The massive wingspan, and elongated neck and tail pointed to one distinct possibility. "Dragon," she sighed. "Just what we need."

Mirsa took a step back when the winged azure lizard plummeted from the clouds, banking to soar above the valley that ran below them from the north to the southwest. "There's someone..." She caught flashes of red, brown, and gold as the brilliant blue dragon and its rider streaked past. "Is that...?"

"It seems the Claw of the Griffinsworn has become something more than when we last knew her," Anneliese answered, moving toward the upper stairwell. "Do you think the Griffin roost above is sturdy enough to bear them?"

"I'll gather the Magi, in case it is not." Mirsa dashed down the stairs, dodging around a Hunter who was headed up to the lookout. *Maybe we do stand a chance against the Darkness,* she thought, allowing herself a glimmer of hope. She burst out into the upper service tunnels, and began sprinting toward the center of the Hold.

Maybe.

ABOUT THE AUTHOR

Chris Hollaway lives in a small town in rural Idaho with his wife, two daughters, a pack of wild dogs, and a herd of guinea pigs. He is a Small Business Development Center advisor by day, and a were-cyborg by night.

Chris is currently working on the fifth and final volume of *The Blademage Saga.* He is contemplating a sister trilogy, and working on a Sci-Fi/Fantasy crossover, among other things.

He's got a board game to the alpha-test stage, if anyone is interested.

See what he's working on at sleepingdrake.com.

Made in the USA
Columbia, SC
01 July 2019